SOLOMON'S
WHISPER

FIFTH IN THE LIV BERGEN MYSTERY SERIES

SANDRA
BRANNAN

RIVER GROVE
BOOKS

Published by River Grove Books
Austin, TX
www.rivergrovebooks.com

Distributed by River Grove Books

For ordering information or special discounts for bulk purchases, please contact River Grove Books at PO Box 91869, Austin, TX 78709, 512.891.6100.

Design, cover design, and composition by Greenleaf Book Group
Cover image: ©iStockphoto.com/Nastco

Publisher's Cataloging Publication Data is available.

ISBN: 978-1-63299-022-8

First Edition

Other Edition(s):
eBook ISBN: 978-1-62634-119-7

For Recie and her family
and everyone like them
who have served in the military.

Thank you for protecting my freedom of speech
and so many other freedoms
I enjoy as an American.

CHAPTER 1

I SUCKED IN A breath, enjoying the odors unique to newly constructed buildings: tile glue, fresh paint, potent PVC adhesive, and the freshly fried coatings of wiring elements. It had taken weeks to move our equipment and furniture out of the office in downtown Denver, out toward old Stapleton International Airport, and I was glad when Calvin Lemley, our special agent in charge, announced Friday that we would report to the new FBI Denver Division offices after the weekend.

But what a long weekend it had been without Jack Linwood, Evidence Response Team supervisor for the FBI.

I loved Mondays. Lonely weekend over and excited about walking into this gorgeous, state-of-the-art federal building, I was more exhilarated about coming to work than ever. My eyes scanned the expansive lobby, the steel and glass capturing the early light of another Rocky Mountain sunrise. And I thought to myself how much had changed in the past five months, since Christmas. New career, new apartment, new office building. Oh, and a new love.

Unfortunately, I'd realized this only after Jack left for his annual fishing trip last Friday. And with his ridiculous rule of remaining completely incommunicado for two weeks, that meant I wouldn't get a chance to tell him for a long time. We'd been dating for months and I always enjoyed our companionship, but it wasn't until I spent this weekend alone that I realized I might just be falling into more than "like" with my coworker.

I smiled at the two security guards as I passed through the high-tech screening device just inside the entrance. "Good morning, Paul. Hi, Tanner."

"Morning, Liv," said the aging guard with gray hair. He waved his thick fingers to greet me. "Smart girl, coming in early. Did you get yourself a close parking spot?"

Same Paul, different location.

"Came in early to find my way to the office. What do you guys think of this place?"

I didn't let on that I knew Paul was a retired FBI special agent, who I assumed had taken this security guard job to earn a few extra bucks. I'd seen his name on some case files. And I figured he didn't want to advertise his past, since he hadn't mentioned it when I first met him.

Born and raised in the Black Hills of South Dakota, I'd been a limestone miner most of my life—family business in the mountain states of the West—but my inclination to problem solve led me here as a special agent. And after what happened to my nephew this past Christmas right after I'd gotten back from Quantico, I wasn't so sure I'd made the right choice.

"It's great," said the younger security guard with the shaved head, who was acting cooler than usual.

"Will take some getting used to, with all the fancy monitors and gizmos and all," Paul added.

"Post-nine-eleven world," I said, collecting my belongings off the belt and continuing through the lobby. "See ya."

As I walked to the elevators, I could see the guards' reflection in the metal framing around the bank of elevators and could feel their eyes scanning my backside. I wondered what they could possibly find interesting about the formless dark pantsuit I was wearing. Ever since Christmas, when I'd worked the high-profile Williams abduction case and had been caught off guard wearing nothing but jeans and a sweatshirt—and at one point had worn Special Agent Phil Kelleher's custom-fit Italian suit pants—I vowed never to be caught dead wearing anything but a bureau-approved, genderless pantsuit. Dark, conservative, professional, and unfashionable garb that was sure to please Special Agent Streeter Pierce—the guy who convinced me to become an agent—and my SAC, Calvin Lemley. But as far as appearances went, might as well sew "vanity-free" labels on these off-the-rack suits of mine. Maybe even "man-repellant." Or "100 percent guaranteed effective birth control."

Since the ensembles cost only a hundred bucks each, I bought enough to have spares: one wadded up in the bottom drawer of my desk and one tucked under the backseat of my SUV. Prepared. Streeter had warned me to do that my first day at work, suggesting that eventually I'd work a crime scene with rotting carcasses and would need a change of clothes, but I'd figured I would have plenty of time to buy some over the holidays.

Now I finally had the suits, but I refuse to give up my steel-toed boots. Something about taking the girl out of the mine but not the mine out of the girl came to mind.

So here I was, wearing one of the half-dozen identical suits hanging in my closet and nevertheless attracting the ogling stares of these guys. All I could figure is that they must have the most uneventful job in the universe if staring at behinds in shapeless pants is what they do for excitement.

As I walked toward the bay of elevators, I apparently wasn't as far from the guards as they thought. I heard the younger one mumble, "Those eyes. So green."

"Ask her out," Paul said.

I could see the men's reflections in the shiny silver facing near the bay of elevators, and I resisted a smile as I watched Paul reach for a donut. I lifted my head to watch the lights of the elevators and assess which would arrive first.

"Like I'd have a chance. Look at her," Tanner answered as he jerked his head in my direction. I continued to pretend not to hear or see them.

Paul chuckled and took a bite out of the jelly-filled donut, crumbs cascading off his rotund belly. From my perspective, it would seem that anyone standing at the elevators was out of earshot of the screening station. But as I scanned the structure, examined the carefully crafted bomb-resistant, bulletproof steel and glass construction, I spotted the flaw in the "green" design—it captured energy, but it also captured and rebounded sound in every direction.

I made a mental note of this.

"Nothing ventured," Paul said, motioning for another employee to move through the screening device and down one of the maze of halls on floor one.

"What do you know about her?"

Before Paul could answer, another federal employee arrived and passed through the screening station, holding up the identification badge that hung around his neck. The man mumbled greetings and the guards mumbled back.

Once the man was making his way toward me, Paul said, "Twenty-nine. Maybe twenty-eight."

Thirty, I thought. Turned the big three-o on April Fools' Day. What a birthday! Thoughts of my wicked celebration with Jack, who was determined to make me forget I was aging, were interrupted when I heard the elevator arriving and the man next to me clearing his throat.

"Morning," I said to the man, who nodded. I hoped the guards had heard me and realized we could hear them.

Apparently not. "Never been married," Paul continued. "Workaholic. A real looker. What more do you need to know?"

I saw the young, fit guard shrug his well-toned shoulders and spread his fingers across his shiny black head. I practiced a quick response to use in case Tanner did ask me out.

"Listen," Paul said as he lowered his belt slightly below his belly. "I'd be all over her in a minute if I were your age."

"You're married."

Both guards quieted down as yet another early arrival passed through the fancy screener. I felt grateful as the elevator doors opened and I stepped quickly inside, the other federal employee following me.

Before the doors closed, I heard the younger guard ask, "Maybe she's not married because she spends so much time working."

Awkward, hearing speculation about my love life. To make things worse, for some reason the elevator doors weren't closing. Nothing was blocking them, and the third employee had taken the stairs. I pushed the button for my floor several times. The other man hit the third-floor button a few more times. Nothing.

I could still hear Paul's voice. "Never know 'til you try. No guts, no glory."

The man beside me sighed, looking quite irritated as he continued to press the elevator buttons in vain.

"Stop with the stupid clichés," Tanner said. "Why Liv? Her badge says Genevieve Bergen."

I sighed and stepped out of the elevator to wait for one of the other cars. I noticed Paul greet another employee who was making her way through the glass entrance doors. Again, their eyes immediately fell to her backside as she moved through the scanning device. Consistent, I'll give them that. Once the woman was standing at the elevators with us, Paul answered, "Her real name is Genevieve. Liv's a nickname. An Irish-Norwegian thing."

I deeply regretted not piping up earlier when I had the chance.

"Genevieve. Beautiful."

The man standing next to me glanced down at my security badge for the first time, which caused the other woman to do the same. "Do they not know we can hear them?" she said.

"Apparently not," the man going to floor three answered.

I wanted to bolt for the stairs.

Paul shrugged. "Seventh-born of nine kids. You know how older siblings can be. Your brother's an ass, right?"

"God forbid they know this much about all of us," the woman mumbled, staring up at the lights of one elevator ticking its way to ground floor.

I was going to the top, fourth floor. Could easily walk, even though the floors were abnormally spacious and it would be more like taking eight flights of stairs. The problem was that I'd have to walk by the guards again to get to the stairwell.

"I shouldn't say those things. Can't call your brother an ass. Can't say Liv's got a nice ass. Have you been to those sexual harassment classes yet? A guy pays a beautiful lady a compliment and look what it gets him? Makes you nervous to say anything anymore. Times have changed," Paul commiserated before taking the last bite of his donut.

I wondered if he'd been pushed into early retirement because of his firm hold on beliefs like this. I watched his reflection as he dusted the powder from his fingers by gently slapping his hands together, and then as he wiped his palms clean on the seat of his uniform pants.

With white lips and a mouthful of half-chewed donut, the older guard added, "But Liv's not like that. When I first met her, I told her she was a looker and asked about her name. She just thanked me and said, 'My Irish Catholic mother gave me that name, but I prefer to be called Liv. What's your name?' That girl's a combination of classy girl-next-door and someone to drink beers with, you know?"

The two federal employees standing on either side of me chuckled. I hung my head and buried my face in my hand. Thankfully, the elevator arrived.

As he swallowed the last of his coffee, tossing the Styrofoam cup in the waste receptacle and wiping away the remnants of his breakfast from his mouth, Paul added, "She's one of the few who take the time to get to know you. Most of the employees around here are stuffy. Some are downright rude. They treat us security guards like we're scum or something. Never say good morning, never even look us in the face."

The man headed to three said, "Make it stop."

The woman hummed an agreement. I was the first to step into the elevator, doing so before the doors opened completely. I pressed the button for my floor.

Just as the doors began to close, I heard Paul say, "On second thought, Tanner, maybe you shouldn't ask her out. I think she has her eye on the big dog, Pierce."

I shoved my arm out to reverse the closing doors, marched out of the elevator, and stomped back over to the security area.

A faint call came from behind me: "Go get 'em."

A bell sounded as the elevator began its ascent.

CHAPTER 2

HOMICIDE INVESTIGATOR NICK SEWELL lifted the gate from the stubborn hold of the last hinge. "Dear God, what is this?"

He hadn't meant for the four uniformed police officers to hear him, let alone to make an entrance that warranted all their stares. He had just been taken aback at the scene of them standing on the edge of the small, shallow grave. A fifth man, someone Sewell did not recognize, stood several feet back from the hole, away from the officers, over by the fence to Sewell's right on the opposite side of the yard Sewell had just entered. The man's trembling fingers were pinching a lit cigarette as he paced near a corner of the backyard, just below the porch of a small brown house.

The youngest of the four officers stepped aside to allow her boss a better view of the small skeleton that lay exposed in the rich, black soil of the unearthed grave. Although the air was cool and crisp without heat from the low, rising sun, the tension and anger around the morbid scene in the backyard was heavy. Most days Sewell would consider his hometown—Kansas City, Missouri—rather quaint. But at the moment he was feeling nothing but edgy and uncomfortable, the untold story of the little bones unnerving him.

The muscles of Sewell's jaw tensed and flexed as he stared at the remains of what used to be a young child lying on his or her side with the hands and arms dangling behind the back, a half-inch hole piercing the skull.

In an even tone, Sewell asked, "What's the story?"

The officer standing next to him answered by jerking a thumb at the nervous man by the porch. "That guy there, Jim Lytle, placed a call to emergency services about forty-five minutes ago." He pointed at the youngest officer and said, "Rosemary and I answered the call and found the place looking like this. She called for backup and I called you."

"Helluva way to start a Monday morning," the policewoman said.

Sewell studied the man and then looked at Rosemary, who lifted her black eyes to him almost apologetically. She showed no other emotion, no trembling in her hands, which he would have expected to find from an officer at her first crime scene. Looking back at the grave, he frowned. Without another word, Sewell turned away and walked over to the twitchy man.

"You Jim Lytle? The guy who called this in?" Twitchy man sucked hard on his cigarette and grabbed Sewell's extended hand and nodded. "My name's Nicholas Sewell. I'm a homicide investigator for the Kansas City Police Department." Sewell firmly gripped Lytle's quivering hand and pumped. The frumpy, disheveled man, who had trampled a path edged with dozens of spent cigarettes in the lumpy, patchy lawn, appeared exhausted by the action, his complexion growing pale.

"Are you a neighbor?" Sewell asked.

The man's darting eyes seemed to periodically land on the roof of the house on the other side of the fence, near where he paced. The neighbor nodded and said nothing.

"Is that your house?" Sewell asked, jerking his chin to the house over the fence.

The man nodded again.

Sewell studied the man's craggy, deep-lined face and bloodshot eyes, heavy bags sagging with age. Sewell guessed Lytle to be in his late sixties, to have lived through numerous and hard knocks in life, and to favor an occasional drink or two, considering the bright ruddy nose compared to his gray complexion—becoming grayer with every word—and compared to the otherwise pallid skin of his neck, arms, and hands. By the unkempt appearance, Sewell also guessed that Lytle was either not married or had a wife who was a terrible housekeeper.

As if he had known him all his life, Sewell asked, "What's this about, Jim?"

Bleary-eyed, the man sighed and rubbed his bare arm with one hand, revealing the old naval tattoo beneath the short sleeve of his plaid shirt. In a tobacco-altered voice, Lytle answered, "Don't know. I . . . I just woke up. Hadn't seen Carl in a few days, so I . . ."

As the neighbor stammered, Sewell asked, "Who's Carl?"

"Carl Halbrook. The guy who lives here. I come over for coffee," Lytle answered.

Sewell scanned the brown house that was long past needing several coats of paint and well into the early rot of structural decay. "And?"

Jerking a thumb toward the house behind him, over the fence, Lytle added, "I've lived in this neighborhood for all my grown life. Carl moved in about twenty or thirty years ago. Can't say for sure. My memory's never been very good."

Sewell watched Lytle rub his callused hand down the full length of his left arm, over the scaly skin, over the faded tattoo, over thousands of goose bumps. The methodical rubbing sounded like a carpenter at work diligently sanding a table leg.

"Guess it's been about a couple days since I seen him," Lytle explained. "Got worried. His newspapers are piling up and his car's out front. So, I helped myself inside to take a look. Suppose I'm in trouble for doing that, aren't I? Did I break some law or something? I mean, I was just worried about Carl and all. I didn't touch nothing. You going to arrest me?"

Lytle had a pathetic expression plastered on his face.

Sewell sighed and answered, "Just tell me what you found and how you ended up coming out here."

"I didn't find nothing, except the television was on. Carl wasn't anywhere to be found in there, so I came out back. I saw the open beer on the table by his TV chair and figured something happened. I mean, Carl drinks a lot of beer, but not in the morning. We drink coffee in the morning. I looked around the house real quick. Didn't see him. I wondered if maybe he came out back to barbecue Friday night and had a heart attack or something. He done that from time to time, you know. Barbecue, I mean. So I came out back and found this." Lytle waved his arm toward the unearthed grave beneath the uniformed officers' feet.

As he studied Lytle's expression and demeanor, Sewell sensed that the neighbor was telling the truth. But as a detective, he knew he had to be cautious not to dismiss anyone from the suspect list too soon. He asked, "What time did all this happen?"

Lytle had difficulty tearing his eyes away from the grave. When he did, his expression appeared repentant, like a child about to be scolded, his eyes, drawn back as if magnetized to the shallow grave. Lytle had begun rubbing his arm again. "About an hour ago. I come over just as our morning show comes on. Have coffee and watch. Carl and I do that every weekday. Talk politics and stuff. He's so smart and all."

"Where's Carl now?" Sewell asked, anticipating the neighbor's answer.

"Don't know." Lytle shrugged his sagging shoulders, which accentuated his sunken chest and potbelly. "If I knew, I'd ask him what's going on and maybe this whole thing wouldn't be creeping me out so much."

Sewell watched as Lytle's eyes were drawn slowly back to the bones.

With narrowing eyes, Sewell asked, "Who is that?"

Lytle twitched. "I don't know who that is. I don't know nothing. That's why I called you people." Lytle's rubbing intensified.

"If you don't know who this is, do you have any idea why this child is buried here in your friend's backyard?" Sewell questioned.

"Child?" Lytle's eyes grew wide. "Don't know. Seems pretty strange to me."

"Does Carl know?"

"Ask him. Don't ask me!"

Nick Sewell could almost smell Jim Lytle's fear.

Officer Haskell called from a corner of the yard, "Nick, check this out."

Sewell frowned. Directing one of the officers, he said, "Why don't you escort Mr. Lytle back to his house so he can warm up, relax before we ask him a few more questions. Have him make some coffee. Stay with him."

As the tall, middle-aged officer walked toward them, Sewell saw relief wash over Lytle's face. When he saw the neighbor disappear beyond the side gate of the backyard, Sewell walked quickly back to the corner of the yard where Haskell was standing. The light from the rising sun was barely touching the cold, black shade, but it was bright enough for Sewell to clearly see into the shadowy area beneath the thick bushes by Haskell's feet.

Where a fresh mound of dirt had been piled.

Another grave, Sewell thought.

"What do we have, Doug?" Sewell said, rubbing his small hand across his wrinkled brow.

"Looks like something else is buried back here."

Sewell grimaced. "Let's find out what it is. Take your time. We have all day. And be careful on this one. Evidence."

CHAPTER 3

I CAME FACE TO face with Paul, waggled my finger, indicating for him to follow me, walked over to a private corner, and whispered, "We could hear every word over there. Even when you were mumbling, whispering. Every stinking word."

Paul Hyatt's cheeks turned rosy, his eyes dragging reluctantly toward the elevators, then back to Tanner.

"Yes, even you saying you'd be all over me if you were younger. And the reflection in the shiny façade of the elevator banks lets us watch your every move, too. And I'm not looking to get you guys in trouble. I just want to know some things."

I moved our conversation outside, into the cool morning air. Paul followed, saying, "I didn't mean anything by that—"

I turned to meet his eyes only when we were far enough from the entrance. "You used to be an agent."

His eyes widened, and then narrowed.

"I don't know why you don't want Tanner to know or the newer federal employees. But I know. I saw your name in the files. I'd guess HR made you take an early retirement for some reason. Am I right?" I paused for a minute and looked over his shoulder at the entrance. Through the glass, I could see Tanner, who looked as if he was teetering between a decision to ignore me or sound an alarm. Luckily, he grew too busy screening the wave of employees coming to work. "I won't breathe a word to anyone. If you'll tell me one thing."

Paul licked his lips and said, "I thought what I was saying about you was a compliment."

"Doesn't matter to the HR folks, does it? Compliment or not, you're not supposed to be talking like that about women or looking at their ass as they walk away, right?"

He shook his head. "I didn't. Tanner was—"

"Don't care. And don't lie. What I want to know is something I can't get from Pierce."

His eyes widened as he stole glances over his shoulder in Tanner's direction. "I can't tell you anything. Even if I knew. Especially about Pierce."

"But you can tell me if I'm right. A yes or no answer is all I need." I held his stare, remembering the article I'd found about Paula Pierce's murder, how stunned I was to learn she'd looked so similar to me. "Was Streeter Pierce's wife killed because he was working a case? Because he was with the FBI?"

Paul Hyatt's features softened. "Does it matter? Because if it does, I misjudged you."

I shook my head. "It won't affect how I feel about Streeter one way or the other."

"Then why are you asking?"

"For me," I said, feeling a lump rise in my throat.

Before I could continue, Paul's face collapsed, the hardness around his eyes softening. "Yes and yes. To both questions. And he won't let this happen to you, Liv, if that's what's holding you back from hanging out with him."

I realized Paul was confused. Instead of explaining that I was concerned about my family's well-being, given my selfish decision to leave the family business to pursue a career with the FBI—and that I was concerned I was possibly endangering them more by being a special agent—I decided to let it drop.

"Thanks, Paul. And I won't breathe a word that I know you used to be an agent." I turned and walked back inside. As I maneuvered through the scanning device, I turned and said, "I'd say yes, Tanner, but I'm already in a serious relationship."

Without looking back, I headed toward the elevators.

I was finally alone for the ascent to the fourth floor, thinking how I'd take the four flights of stairs in the future. I stepped off the elevator in my sensible boots—also "man-repellant"—and walked across the tiled waiting area of the Federal Bureau of Investigation to the heavy metal door leading to the bureau offices. As I punched my security number into the door's keypad, I peered into the bulletproof reception area, which was still dark.

The motherly FBI receptionist could always be found in her protected area during business hours, which were from eight fifteen in the morning until five at night. Regardless of when I came or left the office, I habitually looked for her wide, generous smile and jolly laugh that erupted like a volcano, especially when Streeter Pierce was around. The woman loved Streeter. Who didn't, I thought.

No one was at the desk on the other side of the bulletproof glass. I pulled the heavy door open and went inside the well-lit foyer. Walking down the corridor to my office—a huge step up from the Stout Street cubicles—I could smell the freshly brewed coffee in the break room and saw the morning sun spill through the windows, highlighting the fine dust particles of new office construction that danced in the enclosed energy-efficient space.

I understood that controlled air systems only worked if windows and doors remained shut at all times, but I had never grown accustomed to them. Call me country, but I preferred a wide-open window allowing fresh air to fill my lungs, even if it meant uncontrolled temperatures and elevated expense to this state-of-the-art sustainable building structure.

I was walking past the unoccupied offices as I headed toward the break room when I heard his gravelly tone behind me. "Got a minute?"

Before I turned to face him, I knew that the voice belonged to Special Agent Streeter Pierce. That just-swallowed-rusty-daggers-for-breakfast vocal melody was as unique as the man himself.

"Absolutely," I said and followed him obediently to his corner office, as if my morning coffee addiction didn't have a death grip on my gray matter.

I knew I was in trouble when he closed the glass door behind me, something he rarely ever did.

"What do you think of your new digs?" I said, trying not to sound worried as I lowered myself into a chair across from his desk, studying his unreadable expression.

I seemed to have caught him off guard, given the glance he exchanged with me as he rounded the corner. He scanned his office as if he hadn't even noticed. "I'll get used to it."

His eyes were clear and bright, crow's feet emphasizing his frequent smiles. The white shock of short hair was like a bright halo above his tanned, rugged face as it reflected the early light of sunrise on his face.

"Pretty fancy," I said. "The old space was a bit cramped, not to mention the lights kept turning off at five."

"Along with the air conditioning. And of course, hopefully the basement doesn't flood every spring."

I grinned, fixating on Streeter's expression as he sunk into his chair. "Didn't know about the A/C or the flooding. Haven't been here long enough. But I think I can get used to this place. This isn't about the Williams case again, is it?"

"I'd say it has everything to do with the Williams case," Streeter answered, his expression wary and his thick fingers drumming a beat on the edge of his wooden desk. He held up a single sheet of paper, which I recognized.

I'd written that letter four months ago.

"I haven't changed my mind, Streeter," I said.

"It hasn't been six months. You agreed on six months."

"I did. I promised. And I won't break that promise to you, but . . ." I lost my words. Or my nerve. Or something. He stared at me with those piercing eyes of his, a blue that I could only describe as Capri. Not a real word for describing the color, but more of a feeling.

"But you don't think six months will make a difference. You still want to quit the bureau, go back to limestone mining?" Streeter asked.

"It's not about mining. Or that I want to quit the bureau. Like I told you before, I just don't want to put my family in danger anymore."

Streeter pinned me with a stare. "Liv, you didn't endanger your nephew.

His neighbor Fletcher did. If anything, you saved Noah *because* you were with the FBI."

"I didn't save Noah," I stated matter-of-factly. "Noah saved the little boy that Fletcher kidnapped. And if I hadn't been working so hard on the child's abduction case, maybe I would have taken the time to listen to Noah and found the boy earlier. Before the kidnapper got his hands on my nephew."

I searched his face, his eyes, for understanding.

Streeter shook his head and dropped his stare to his hands, to the fingers no longer drumming. "It doesn't work that way. How can I convince you?"

"And how can I convince you?" From the puzzled look on Streeter's face, I could tell I had thrown him a curveball. "That I seem to be endangering my family as an agent. First, my brother Jens. Then my sister Elizabeth—"

"Wait," Streeter interrupted. "You weren't an FBI agent during those two incidents. You were a miner."

I closed my eyes. "Okay, but then there was my sister Frances's family. Noah in particular. He was left to die, Streeter."

"But he didn't. And you found him. *Because* you were a special agent."

"I wasn't around to listen to him because I was too busy working as a special agent," I argued.

"And what makes you think you wouldn't have been too busy working as a miner?"

That pulled me up short. He was right. I could definitely see that happening, me getting too wrapped up in my work. "I know I promised you six months before I formally sent my resignation to Calvin, but every day for the last four months all I have been able to think about is who's next."

Streeter looked up at me again and simply said, "Don't quit. Just . . . just give me a chance to show you that working with the bureau does not mean you're endangering your family."

I leveled my gaze at him and asked, "Okay. If you can tell me one thing." From his stillness, I could see I had his full attention. "Can you look me in the eye and tell me that you being a special agent had nothing to do with your wife's death?"

I recognized the flash of emotion—anger or hurt—in his eyes. Then, his shoulders sagged, as did his expression. The corners of his brows, eyes, and mouth drooped like melting wax. I wished I'd never asked. After a long moment, I was about to apologize to him when he said, "Give yourself time to think about your decision. Until June. Like you promised me."

"Streeter, I—"

But he didn't let me finish. With a forced smile, he said, "Now get out of here and get to work."

I left his glass office feeling as if I'd just thrown a fistful of boulders.

CHAPTER 4

WHEN SEWELL APPEARED IN the door of her office, Police Chief Jean Tilton said, "Close the door, Nick, and have a seat."

He did as he was told, sitting in the stiff chair in front of her desk. Sewell, along with everyone else in the department, always did exactly as his no-nonsense boss asked. Tilton had been the Kansas City police chief for over sixteen years and had earned her reputation for being tough but fair, and for running a very efficient and professional department.

"What was so important it couldn't wait, Chief?"

Tilton peered at him over the small reading glasses she wore near the bottom of the bridge of her nose, clipped just above its round tip. Her short black hair, which was unflatteringly styled, made her plump face look even larger.

She lifted the report in her hand and said, "I have a personal request by the mayor to answer questions about the skeletal remains found in Halbrook's backyard."

"That was quick."

"We haven't issued a statement since we found the remains three hours ago. I have to answer the public's concern tomorrow at a news conference scheduled by the mayor for ten o'clock. I know you've been working all morning. What do you have?"

Out of sheer exhaustion from hours of investigating, Sewell rolled his eyes to the ceiling and blew out a long breath. "Chief, this is an odd one. First, let me tell you what we found. The ME's initial conclusions are that the bones were the remains of a white girl, approximately eleven years old, seventy to eighty pounds, and medium build. Her hands had been bound behind her back and she had suffered a blow to her mouth, which had broken out three front teeth. A gunshot had grazed her skull, and a second mortal wound was inflicted to the back of her head from a .38 pistol at point-blank range. Of course, we'll have to wait for the formal report and wouldn't want to share this initial assessment with the mayor or the public."

"What else?"

"From the remains, it appears she had been buried in the same spot for decades."

"Decades?" Tilton asked skeptically. "Can you be more specific?"

"I think I can," Sewell answered confidently as he leaned forward and rested his arms on his knees. "I would say she has been there in that shallow grave for exactly twenty-six years, two months, and fourteen days."

"What?" Tilton scoffed, then scowled when she saw only seriousness on Sewell's face. "Oh, come on, Nick. How can they know that? The ME's good, but not that good. Our forensics can't conclude something that specific, even if they had years to analyze the remains, let alone three hours."

"Not the ME. This is my belief," Sewell continued. "She had kinky brown hair, light skin, and light blue eyes. She was probably still wearing the uniform skirt and white blouse she had on the day she disappeared from St. Margaret's School."

Tilton's beady gray eyes widened and her mouth fell open involuntarily as she suddenly understood what Sewell had been trying to tell her. Removing her glasses, she sat back in her chair and said, "The Greenwood girl."

Sewell nodded.

When the significance of his findings finally sunk in, she exclaimed slowly, "Oh my God. That unsolved kidnapping has been haunting this department for over twenty-five years. That's how I came into this job, Nick. The former police chief resigned in shame, thinking he had failed the community for not making an arrest and for not having any strong leads. Frederick Greenwood spent over a quarter of a million dollars before he died just to find his daughter, not counting the six hundred thousand he lost to the kidnapper."

"That's right," Sewell said as he marveled at his boss's memory of the forgotten case. Even though he remembered the Greenwood case well. Lived it. Felt the horrible impact the case had on the morale of the entire police department for years. Nick had forgotten some of the details until he started flipping through the old files and newspaper clippings just before his meeting with the chief. But he'd remembered most.

"Frederick was old, at the time," she said.

"Seventy-one when his daughter was kidnapped," Sewell said. "He dedicated the last six years of his life trying to find out what had happened to her. Her name was Vanessa. She had two other siblings, one younger brother, Larry, who would be in his early thirties now, and an older brother, Mark."

"I think Mark was my age," she said. "Must have been a stepbrother based on the news articles at the time. He was just graduating from college. Same as me."

"About mid- to late forties now." Sewell added, "Vanessa's mother, Bella Greenwood, was only thirty-six at the time of her daughter's disappearance and still lives here in Kansas City."

Sewell noticed Tilton's eyes wander toward the window. "She's still involved in everything."

"The Greenwood name has been attached to benefits, fundraising galas, and community projects for decades."

"Big difference in their ages. Like decades. She was the May bride to his December, as one tabloid put it," Tilton added. "Greenwood was one of Kansas City's wealthiest back then. I suppose that's what made his daughter so vulnerable. She got kidnapped right out of the classroom. What did you say earlier? St. Margaret's? I remember a controversy of some sort over the school's responsibility."

Sewell nodded and leaned back in the chair. He rubbed his hands through his thinning hair. "A woman had picked Vanessa up from school just before dismissal, saying that the girl's mother, Bella, had suffered a stroke. The woman told the school official that she was Vanessa's aunt. When the school official brought Vanessa out of class, the woman grabbed her hand and led her out of the school. Even though one of Vanessa's classmates begged her not to go with the woman, pleaded with the teacher to let her go with Vanessa. The school official, who later made a positive identification of the woman, had said that Vanessa did not seem to be alarmed by the woman."

"Yet the woman who claimed to be the aunt ended up being a complete stranger, according to the papers."

"We didn't know that for sure at the time," Sewell continued. "A kidnapper called within hours and told the Greenwoods that if they called the police, they would never see their daughter alive again. They had known before the kidnapper's call that Vanessa had been abducted and had time to get their thoughts together, thanks to the classmate of Vanessa's who was insistent about the school following up with Bella Greenwood. Someone from the school had called their home shortly after the girl's disappearance to see how Bella was doing since the stroke. Bella had answered the phone."

"Oh, that's right. Now I remember," Tilton said as she stood quickly and began to pace. "There were so many odd things about that case. One of them was that the Greenwoods had millions of dollars, yet the kidnappers only asked for six hundred thousand, all in tens and twenties. Demanded it be shrink-wrapped. Right?"

"Which told us the kidnappers were smart. Wanted to bury the money or store it somewhere it might get wet."

Tilton shifted her eyes from the window to Sewell. "Carl Halbrook's backyard. You're digging it up as we speak, aren't you? You think the money's still there," she said.

"Not all of it. But we'll find it," he said. "The former police chief had speculated that the kidnapper asked for such a small amount because any more than that would weigh too much to carry. Each of the two suitcases they asked for weighed something like eighty pounds."

"Or take too long to shrink-wrap. They asked for it immediately, even though they didn't actually get the money for a week."

He nodded. "Greenwood later told police that the kidnappers got lost on the first attempt to exchange the ransom for the girl. Greenwood didn't want to involve the police. I suppose it was because not only had they threatened to kill his daughter, but also because Kansas City has always been known as one of the crime capitals of America."

"Maybe he knew the criminals in this city meant business, who knows."

Sewell pondered the idea before adding sincerely, "I don't know what I would have done if it were my daughter, considering the outlaws in history who had made this city their home. Jesse James, the Younger brothers, the Dalton brothers, Pretty Boy Floyd, Harvey Bailey, not to mention the Union Station Massacre. I'm sure Greenwood had lived during the years when Kansas City was the home of the most powerful Mafia in the country. What could he do?"

"He made a terrible mistake by not involving the police," Tilton concluded.

"That's easy for us to think, in hindsight," Sewell countered. When he realized his insubordination, he added quickly, "Years ago, we found the woman who matched the description of the kidnapper given by the school officials. Her name was Marcia Henderson, a forty-one-year-old con artist who had been in and out of prison and frequently worked as a prostitute. We found her dead of an overdose two months after the kidnapping in a seedy hotel in Saint Louis. She was no relation to the Greenwoods, and they had never seen her before in their lives."

"But the money was never found," the chief recalled, rising and walking toward the window. "And the police were sure a man was involved, right?"

"Yes," Sewell sighed. "The kidnapper who had demanded money from Greenwood was a man. They never figured out who he was, but some speculated Marcia Henderson's death wasn't accidental, or a suicide. The rumor was that the unidentified man and the Henderson woman got into an argument over the money. The guy killed Henderson, made it look like an overdose. Then took off with the money, never to be found."

"And neither was Vanessa Greenwood," she added.

"Right." He watched the chief plop her plump frame back into the chair, the cushions groaning as she did.

"How does this tie in to the Halbrook case?" Tilton asked, putting her glasses back on the end of her nose.

"This is where it gets a bit strange," he hesitated. "I did some digging in the records. Some of the people, who were interrogated over twenty-five years ago, mentioned several men's names that hung around Henderson from time to time. They were all seedy characters and could all be considered suspects. Interestingly enough, what I dug up was that one of those characters, Clyde Hall, lived with Henderson on and off several times in the years preceding Vanessa's disappearance. Apparently, he had once been a very rich man in his youth, but spent all of his inheritance. Having become accustomed to the good life, he turned to cons and burglaries to fund his habits and eventually ended up in prison for a few years. It was rumored that's where Henderson and Hall first met."

"We must have checked him out," Tilton remarked incredulously at the implication that the police had missed something so obvious.

"Oh, of course," Sewell said. "His alibi was that he was in Saint Louis on the day of the kidnapping and he spent several weeks there visiting friends. With some further checking, friends had seen him on the morning of the kidnapping and two days later. They confirmed he was in Saint Louis during those weeks, but they admitted to having only seen him a few times during his stay. Saint Louis is only a few hours' driving distance from Kansas City. He could have easily made it back and forth as many times as he chose, and no one would have even missed him."

"And what a coincidence that Marcia Henderson was found dead in Saint Louis," the chief concluded sarcastically.

"Right," he confirmed.

Frowning, Tilton asked, "Where is Clyde Hall now?"

"He sort of disappeared off the face of the earth a few months after the kidnapping," he answered.

"How convenient," she said with disdain. "This just keeps getting worse."

"Yes and no. Hall, who was the primary suspect in the Greenwood kidnapping, managed to elude the police for the past twenty-six years, but we think we finally found him." Jean Tilton's puzzled expression encouraged him to continue. "After her death, Marcia Henderson's home went up for sale, but did not sell for a couple of years. The market was depressed and the house had not been taken care of by Henderson. It was in bad repair. Then, a handyman who had just moved to town, Carl Halbrook, bought the house, paid cash, and has lived there ever since." Sewell raised his eyebrows, hoping she would understand the connection, but seeing her expression, he realized she hadn't. "Clyde Hall dropped off the face of the earth and reemerged with a new identity, Chief. That's what I think."

"Carl Halbrook," she said, closing her eyes in complete understanding. "Once the heat is finally off him, Clyde Hall comes back to town, sees that no one has bought his dead girlfriend's house yet, and purchases the property as Carl Halbrook with some of the ransom money. You suppose he knew the little girl was buried in the backyard? He does it so no one ever finds her and somehow ties him to the kidnapping and murder?"

"Or to retrieve the rest of the money. Whatever remained with Henderson. That's what I think," Sewell said. "I'm trying to locate Carl Halbrook's dentist as we speak. Then I can confirm my suspicions."

"How did you manage to figure that out, Nick?" she asked, sincerely.

"Instinct. And from the ME's initial autopsy report in the field. We don't have too many children of that age go missing, Chief. Especially back then. Once I had a chance to review the records just before I came in here, I recalled what the detective suspected twenty-six years ago. About Marcia Henderson. So, I asked our lab to check old dental records of Clyde Hall against Carl Halbrook's teeth. To expedite this, they involved the FBI, just so you have a heads-up. But first we have to find Halbrook's dentist. Then we can see if we have a match, Chief." Sewell smiled for the first time in days.

"So the case might finally be solved. After all these years. We just might finally know what happened to Vanessa."

"Not to mention, her mother can finally lay Vanessa to rest in a proper burial."

"And once we get those dental records, we can prove who assisted Marcia Henderson in the kidnapping and brutal murder of that little, defenseless angel," Tilton summarized, folding her pudgy arms across her ample breasts. "Case closed."

"Not quite," Nick Sewell said. "What I haven't told you yet is that we found a second body buried in the backyard near Vanessa's grave."

Tilton dragged her eyes to Sewell's. "Two murders? How could that have been missed?"

"Not a murder from twenty-six years ago. Recently. The neighbor already identified him. This is far from being case closed until I find out who killed Carl Halbrook."

CHAPTER 5

THE THOUGHT OF THE freshly decaying corpse lying so close to the skeletal remains of the little girl buried decades earlier was more than unsettling to Nick Sewell. The image chilled him.

He'd known who was buried beneath the fresh mound before the investigative team of police started digging. He knew they'd find the missing homeowner Carl Halbrook buried near the unearthed grave of little Vanessa.

What he didn't know was why.

"Once we unearthed Halbrook from his shallow grave in his own backyard, I could tell from the skin slippage that he'd been dead about three days or so, which correlated with the neighbor's story about when he was last seen," Sewell told Tilton.

"And you have a positive ID?"

He nodded. "The neighbor who called in the dug-up grave of the little girl positively identified Carl Halbrook for me. The ME will confirm it. She thinks Halbrook was probably killed—wounded with a shot to the back of the head and buried alive, with suffocation as the actual cause of death based on the dirt found in his nostrils and mouth—sometime Friday night, Saturday morning. Examination of his lungs will confirm that. She said to wait for her official report, but she sounded confident.

"Thought you might want to read through the cold case files yourself," Sewell said, laying the thick file, filled with aged paper worn from years of handling, on her desk.

"I'll read through this immediately."

"Someone had bound Halbrook's hands behind his back, knocked him in the mouth, probably with the butt of a pistol, and shot him in the head with a .38. Whoever did that first unearthed Vanessa's grave for us to find. Probably even made Halbrook dig his own grave, if I had to guess. He wanted us to know that Carl Halbrook was responsible for Vanessa Greenwood's kidnapping and murder."

"Clever, whoever he or she is," she replied. "Do you think the killer was the guy who called this in? The neighbor?"

Sewell leaned forward again, bracing the weight of his torso through his arms on his knees. "I don't think it was Jim Lytle who did this. I studied and grilled him pretty hard and he seems sincere, but I'll bring him in a few more times for questioning. But what I really think we should do is bring in the one most likely to have a motive for seeing Carl Halbrook dead."

Tilton didn't seem to notice what Sewell had said. Instead, she seemed preoccupied. She rose to her pudgy feet and padded around her desk toward the window again. He noticed her stare out the glass, across the highway that bisected Kansas City. He followed her gaze and saw the sign above the new oncology addition to Regional Hospital. Then he realized Tilton knew exactly what he was getting at.

She said, "Greenwood Oncology Treatment. Right next to the Greenwood Children's Hospital. A lot has come of the evil that ravaged this community a quarter century ago."

Kansas City police chief Jean Tilton stared a long time out at the sign and he imagined she was wondering how to approach this matter and whether it could be approached delicately, just as he had wondered. The words unspoken by Sewell were haunting his boss, he could tell. They both knew he should bring Bella Greenwood in for questioning, because she would have the strongest motive of anyone for finding Clyde Hall, a.k.a.

Carl Halbrook, and seeing him pay for the brutal and senseless murder of her kidnapped daughter decades earlier.

"Has anyone on your team called her yet?"

"No ma'am," Sewell said. "I figured we need to walk softly on this one. Thought we'd let you handle it."

If the Kansas City Police Department brought Bella Greenwood in for questioning, the press would be all over the story. The brutal murder of a nearly seventy-year-old man was headline news alone. That the man killed was the primary suspect in Vanessa Greenwood's kidnapping would catapult the story onto a national platform.

Questioning such a prominent figure in the community for such a heinous murder would easily lead to the assumption that the mother was the leading suspect in this poor girl's brutal murder. And the community loved Bella Greenwood.

Both Jean Tilton's and Bella's reputations would be jeopardized, tainted at best, no matter which way Sewell decided to go with this investigation.

"We should at least find out the latest PI she's hired," Tilton said.

Even though it was reasonable for Sewell to assume that Bella had continued to pay private investigators to hunt down Clyde Hall, Nick could not believe that the gentle, well-mannered lady would be ruthless enough to hire a hit man to murder the man in the same manner as he had her daughter, and she certainly wouldn't do it herself. Regardless, Nick Sewell suspected that Police Chief Jean Tilton certainly wasn't willing to stake her career on any suspicions or rumors. She wanted the facts. So did he.

"If I had been Vanessa's mother, regardless of my oath to the law, I know I would have no trouble putting a bullet in Clyde Hall's head," Tilton said. Then she mumbled, "Vengeance."

Sewell understood. He struggled between doing what he knew to be right, which would mean bringing Bella Greenwood in for questioning, and doing the right thing, which was to turn a blind eye to Bella Greenwood as a suspect, at least for the time being and until further proof was produced that would indicate she could indeed be a suspect. After all, Sewell reasoned, they had no evidence that would implicate Bella other than motive, which was clearly not enough to consider her a suspect. Yet.

Sewell offered, "It's all circumstantial. We need more evidence."

As she sighed and nodded, Jean Tilton faced him. Her eyes were sad. "Thank you for that."

He couldn't help but wonder if his intentions were entirely pure. After all, he had briefly taken into consideration how this story of a murdered suspect found near the remains of his alleged victim would reflect on the police department. On him. As a detective.

Although it was nothing short of fantastic that the twenty-six-year-old crime had finally been solved with the killer being brought to justice, albeit in a morbid fashion, the public would start questioning how a primary suspect in one of the most infamous kidnapping cases in this country's history could simply reemerge in the same city, owning the same house of the overdosed cohort identified as the woman who took Vanessa from her school and living there peacefully for decades without any consequences for his horrific actions.

The story could make the entire department look incapable and result in people reasoning that it was this type of incompetence that made Kansas City the crime capital of the country and that put the "misery" in Missouri. He had heard all of the criticisms countless times before and did not look forward to hearing them again.

After several moments, Jean Tilton surprised Sewell by suggesting, "You should interrogate Jim Lytle again. Why don't you let me contact Bella Greenwood before the press conference tomorrow? Then she's not totally taken by surprise along with the rest of the community. She has the right to know. So does the mayor. I will brief them both tonight."

Nick furrowed his brow. He understood the unspoken decision his boss had just made, but he wondered just how far she would bend the law to protect the community benefactor.

He was becoming very uncomfortable with the thought until she added, "And until we produce formal autopsy reports, dental records of comparison, any solid evidence indicating who may have killed Carl Halbrook, we probably need to keep details of the murder under wraps for now. Understood?"

Nick understood. His boss wasn't saying ignore Bella Greenwood as a possible suspect. She was just saying not to press the issue unless and until they found evidence suggesting they should. That seemed reasonable and Nick was relieved. Standing to go, he replied, "Yes, ma'am. Good luck in the morning."

CHAPTER 6

I'D FINALLY MADE IT to the break room for that much-needed cup of coffee. Sounds counterintuitive, but my body required that caffeine more than ever to calm my nerves.

The bulky back hunched over the counter obviously belonged to my coworker and office neighbor, Special Agent Steve Knapp. He was wiping up the coffee he had just spilled.

"Morning, Steve."

The massive figure turned quickly on his heels, knocking over his empty coffee mug, which clanged and bounced against the veneer countertop.

Startled, he gasped, "Liv, don't sneak up on me like that."

I grinned. I guess my nerves weren't as tightly wound as Steve's were, for whatever reason. "I wasn't sneaking up on you. I just came in for a cup of that coffee you're so well known for."

"Geez, I already feel like a bull in a China shop in this place."

"Great offices, eh? Did you leave some for the rest of us?" I asked, jerking my chin toward the coffee pot.

"Actually," he confessed, rubbing the top of his light brown, buzzed hair with his beefy hand, "I don't even know how to turn this thing on yet.

And even if I did, I didn't make the coffee this morning. Streeter beat me to it."

Steve nodded toward the break room door and across the open area to the corner office enclosed in glass. Behind the desk, piled high with stacks of reports, books, and paperwork, Streeter sat sipping on a cup of coffee. Just where I left him. Reading a report. Hopefully, not the letter I wrote on New Year's Day again. He had already loosened his tie and unbuttoned the top button of his clean, white dress shirt, as if it were the end of a long and tiring day rather than the beginning of a new one. For him, it probably had begun hours ago, I thought. And my question about his line of work affecting his family probably didn't help alleviate the stress of his already busy day.

I asked Steve, "How long has he been here?"

He shrugged. "Your guess is as good as mine. He's always here long before you or me and we're usually the first two here."

"True," I agreed.

I typically arrived at work an hour before I needed to and had yet to arrive before Streeter Pierce. On occasion, when I couldn't sleep or was particularly consumed in thought by a case, I would come to work as early as five thirty or six o'clock. But not before Streeter.

Streeter was the senior field agent not because of the length of time he'd been there but because of his long list of accomplishments. He had been with the bureau for something like fifteen or sixteen years and was nearly legendary, considering the cases he had been assigned and solved during his career. He was the most qualified case agent in the Denver bureau—arguably throughout the entire country—and had mentored many of the bureau's finest agents on how to conduct an investigation, particularly those involving violent crimes. I was happy to boast being one of those lucky agents who he had chosen to mentor.

He was nearly forty, had skin that looked as if he had spent hours on the beach or on a boat—that sun and sea-sprayed look unique to sailors— was ruggedly handsome, and had a shock of short white hair cut in a military style. His blue eyes were captivating, particularly when they turned light shades of green at times he was impassioned about a topic or case. He was not particularly tall, but had a commanding presence that made him appear slightly larger than life.

I'd heard several women describe his deep, gravelly voice as sexy. He had a reputation for being a very private man, a loner, who divulged very little—if anything—about his personal life outside of the bureau.

Before my arrival at the Denver bureau, I had heard the rumors about the death of Streeter's wife. She died several years earlier and he had never remarried. From the photos in the newspapers, I had come to learn how much I resembled his deceased wife.

I had wondered if maybe that's why Streeter was insistent on making me wait six months before finalizing my resignation from the bureau and ending my short-lived career as a field agent. Maybe I reminded him enough of his wife that he wanted me to stick around.

I was regretting even mentioning anything about Streeter's wife to Paul and, even more so, to Streeter himself.

As I stirred some fat-free milk into my coffee, my daydreaming was interrupted by the noisy arrival of two more coworkers, Manny Juarez and Tim Gregory. Manny slapped Tim on the arm as they entered the break room.

"I'm telling you, man," Manny said. "Somebody posted bond and she ditched."

"No way," Tim countered. "That would be so stupid, because she must know they'll find her. And when they do, they'll electrocute that witch without hesitation."

"What are you saying?" asked the short agent with bright, black eyes. "Are you saying she wouldn't have been electrocuted if she had stuck around for the trial? Dream on, buddy."

"Electrocute who?" Steve Knapp asked in a deep voice, the inflection like an excluded child on the playground.

"And why would you call someone a witch? That's not like you, Tim," I scolded, sipping on my coffee that tasted like liquid heaven.

"That Shelly Jones woman."

"Oh, her," I said. "She is a witch and a half. My bad. What about her?"

"Didn't you read the newspaper this morning?" Manny asked. Elbowing his friend, he added, "Gregory thinks the courts forced Shelly into hiding until the trial and led the press to believe they know nothing about it."

The tall, thin agent defended himself. "Well, it stands to reason, Manny. If they had simply let her go free after the arraignment while she was awaiting trial, what do you think the good people of South Carolina would have done to her?"

Without waiting for an answer, Tim Gregory explained his reasoning, "Maybe someone did. Maybe that's what happened. Someone posted the bond and lynched her to a high branch somewhere. Look, Jones had worked the whole community into a frenzy making them believe that some fictitious black man wearing a knit stocking cap stole her car with her two sons strapped in the backseat."

Manny Juarez said, "Blamed the crime on a minority. Witch."

Tim ignored Manny. "Everyone spent all their time looking for this guy, distributing posters, and making appeals on every television and radio station in the state. The car, the kids, the guy was never found, right? Until they dredged the car out of the lake."

Manny made exaggerated motions with his arms. "There was no guy."

Tim paused a moment to study Manny, then nodded. "First, blaming an atrocious kidnapping on a fictitious black man. Then, reveling in the attention and sympathy. Disgusting."

Manny added, "And the worst part is that witch was the one who stood outside her sedan and released the parking brake and then watched it plunge down the ramp into the lake. Just stood there and watched. After she strapped her sons helplessly into their car seats. How in God's name could anyone do that?"

Particularly a mother, I thought.

Steve shuddered. "I hate hearing that story. It's too gruesome to believe there are people like Shelly Jones out there in this world."

Tim fumed. "What's worse is that her kids were only three years old and fourteen months. They couldn't even defend themselves. And she killed them because she thought her boyfriend was going to dump her if he found out she had children."

Manny turned to me. "What kind of woman could do that?"

I shrugged. I was glad to know that my coworkers felt so strongly about people who killed children, but me being a woman didn't mean I had a clue what made someone evil like Shelly Jones tick.

"A witch," Tim answered, pouring himself a cup of coffee. "The ultimate betrayal. For that matter, the entire country felt betrayed. As she stared directly into the cameras for days, weeks, and tearfully said, 'My children wanted me. They needed me. And now I can't help them.' Then she convincingly recounted her story, blaming a man for stealing her car from her own driveway."

"A tall black man," Manny corrected.

"And everyone believed her," Tim said.

Manny said, "My money is betting that the entire community would reinstate good old-fashioned town lynchings if law would allow. And I think that's exactly what happened. That's why she's missing."

"She's missing? That's what you meant earlier?" I asked, finally realizing what the two men had been talking about when they first arrived in the break room.

"Yeah, someone posted a half-million-dollar bond Friday night and the rumors hit the papers this morning that the police don't know where she is now."

"Rumors," I said, realizing this was merely speculation.

Agents George Nichols and Phil Kelleher joined us in the break room and stood quietly listening to the assessment of current events. The buzz in my suit coat pocket had me reaching for my cell in an instant. The morning text message was from Jack. I allowed myself to entertain the idea of hearing, rather than reading, the words he'd texted. And imagined waking up beside him in his big, comfy bed, rather than off fishing. Away from me.

I could see myself being called to the feet of the omniscient Sister Delilah for having such a wicked thought and having to explain that there was nothing more than sleep going on, if that's what she thought.

I missed Jack already. And was glad that going "off the grid" didn't prevent him from sending a daily text affirming his feelings for and connection with me.

His annual fishing trip, his May pilgrimage of renewed manhood— my words, not his—was a much-needed break from his intense work, which involved crazy hours and exhausting days of research and recovery of evidence, his brilliant mind never quieting for a second. I resisted the urge to call him and instead thumb-typed a quick text message telling him how much I wanted to plant kisses all over his beautiful face.

For some reason, just the act of texting such a personal message amid all my coworkers made me blush. Most of them probably already knew I was seeing Jack. If they did, no one mentioned it. For sure, Streeter knew. But Jack and I chose to be discreet about our relationship.

Apparently our discretion had succeeded in fooling even Paul, the all-knowing security guard, who thought I was dating Streeter. God help me if Tanner asked me out on a date. I'd have to be honest and tell him more about my relationship than I already had, and security guard Paul would learn yet another thing about my private life. I think I preferred leaving everything as it was, with Paul thinking there was something going on between me and Streeter. Let them talk.

The tall, refined Phil Kelleher asked, "Are you talking about the Shelly Jones article in this morning's paper?"

"Yeah," Manny answered, making himself a glass of ice water.

Jack's second-in-charge, Mitch Dodson, walked into the crowded break room. I was surprised, considering his office was on the floor below us.

Tim Gregory teased Mitch, "What brings you up to the top floor? Just up to see us beautiful people?"

The agents chuckled.

Dodson, who described himself as "curmudgeonly" (and, from my experiences with the man, seemed to have solid introspective skills), had been with the FBI for two decades, far longer than Jack. I would guess Dodson to be ancient, based on his attitude. But his sharp wit and tireless work ethic would suggest I'd be wrong.

Dodson had walked up from third floor. The Evidence Response Team was on the floor beneath us, just like in the old building. Formal roles were as confusing at ERT as they were for us field agents on this floor. As for all us agents, Howard Magnussen, who reported to Calvin Lemley, the bureau's SAC, was technically the supervisor. Yet we all considered Streeter our department supervisor. Everyone—even Howard—took direction from Streeter, the real leader in our office.

Jack Linwood was the leader on the floor below. What used to be Investigative Control Operations when I started had been recently renamed Evidence Response Team, responsible for recovery and processing of evidence. Jack had earned the promotion rather rapidly, from what other people tell me.

Jack doesn't talk to me about himself. Not his style.

From what I'd heard of office gossip, although Jack had only been with the FBI for a relatively short time compared to other agents his age, he was extremely capable and proficient at his job in the information unit. More importantly to me, he was extremely proficient in the romance department, an exotic lover who possessed amazing skills, which I'd never experienced before and imagined came from somewhere in his mysterious Eastern-hemisphere heritage. *Existential*, the only word I can think of to describe Jack.

Answering gruffly, Dodson explained, "I don't know how to work our coffee pot. It's like you have to be a rocket scientist to even start the thing. Thought I could help myself to a cup up here."

Tim added, "And to think you're the guy in charge of the most technical equipment in this place, Dodson."

"Linwood's in charge. Not me. I'm just temporary."

Jack may have supervised the ERT, but Dodson played a key role in the department, just as Streeter did with the field agents.

"Help yourself, Mitch," I said, smiling at him to make him feel more comfortable amid my antagonistic coworkers. "And just ignore these guys, because none of us know how to run our coffee pot yet, either. Streeter figured it out."

"Figures."

Unlike Jack, whose tall, dark, and handsome features were easy on the eyes, Dodson was a short, frumpy man, a shiny head dotted with wispy strands of white. His face was as round and white as the moon, holding no secrets, his eyes small and constantly in motion. It made me yearn to see Jack's large, dark brown eyes again—so intense, haunting—and to run my fingers through his thick, shaggy black hair.

No one knew Jack like I did. Everyone knew Mitch Dodson.

He was a fixture on the seventeenth floor at the Stout office just as

Howard Magnussen was a fixture on the eighteenth. No one in the Denver bureau knew much about Jack—just as it seemed that no one knew much about Streeter—but for certain, teasing was out of the question. Dodson, on the other hand, was teased frequently.

Manny added, "Well the first order of business, boss—temporary or not—is that you learn how to make coffee for the troops."

Dodson scowled. "Since I'm in charge while Linwood's gone, my first decision was to salvage the old coffee pot from the Stout offices when I couldn't figure out the new one. So Saturday afternoon on my way home from work, I tried to retrieve it. My key didn't work. This morning when I called the general superintendent, his office girl tells me anything we left behind on Friday is already gone. Damn it anyway."

"Your key didn't work? So we're no longer welcome back at the Stout offices?" Steve asked.

"Apparently not," Dodson added. "My new plan is that I come up here for coffee every morning and will defer learning rocket science until Linwood gets back in two weeks. He can show me how the fancy expresso thingy works down there"

"Espresso," I corrected, and regretted it the instant I did.

He glowered at me. "I figure whoever is willing to make me a fresh pot this week gets priority on their cases in the lab."

My heart sunk. Not about the system for prioritizing lab work. I knew Dodson wasn't serious. But that it would be so long until Jack came back. Two weeks. Being without Jack for two weeks was akin to tanning in Everett, Washington. A long wait for just a drop of sunshine.

"Two weeks of you, Dodson? I've never wanted to see Linwood more than I do at this very moment," Tim teased.

Manny batted his hand toward Tim and said, "Well, if we have to put up with you up here, then let's hear your thoughts about the Shelly Jones case, genius."

Dodson harrumphed. "She jumped bail. Took off."

"Or dead," Manny said.

Dodson said, "Forget about Jones. Have you heard what they found in Kansas City this morning? The Greenwood case?" As he scanned our blank faces, Dodson sighed with exasperation. "Didn't Linwood tell any of you up here or am I supposed to forward all his emails on to you, too, while he's gone?"

I wanted to answer, *Does Jack tell us anything?*

If ever I'd met a more tight-lipped individual than Jack Linwood, I certainly couldn't recall. He would be caught dead rather than talk shop over a cup of coffee in the break room. I suspected I was going to learn a lot more about the inner workings of ERT from Dodson siphoning our coffee over the next two weeks than I ever learned in pillow talk with Jack.

"Rookies. The Greenwood case was years ago, where some bimbo and jackass kidnapped the little Greenwood girl from her school. Like, over twenty or thirty years ago. The Kansas City Police Department finally found the girl's skeletal remains. And the killer. At least that's what they suspect. I just got sent a request from them wanting to confirm IDs. The KCPD are on their way to tell her mother as we speak. Goes public tomorrow."

"They asked you?" I asked.

Dodson grinned.

In the silence that followed, Steve shifted his weight and finally asked, "Dodson, what does that have to do with Shelly Jones?"

Dodson eyed Knapp for a long moment, circling the rim of his coffee cup with a heavy fingertip. "Because eventually, we'll catch up with her, too."

Tim added, "Who's this 'we'? Got a mouse in your pocket or something? And what do you mean 'catch up with her'? If you mean justice will prevail, South Carolina still has the death penalty. Electrocution."

Steve said, "Let's hope they aren't afraid to use it."

Tim said, "I still think her disappearance is a cover. The system is hiding her until trial so she doesn't get killed or, more likely, so she doesn't take the easy way out and commit suicide, whether she's locked up or out on bond. I think those guys in South Carolina are just messing with the press's minds on this one."

Manny argued, "Don't think so, pal. When have you ever heard of the police doing something like that? I'm not so optimistic. I think she took off and has skipped the country. What other choice does she have?"

Surprisingly to the rest of the group, ever-proper Phil Kelleher, the agent most likely to never weigh in on current events with speculative input, commented, "One thing is for certain. That woman deserves nothing less than a painful, frightening end to her pitiful life, full of excruciating suffering, just like she delivered to those two young, defenseless boys."

"Phil!" I said, shocked at his voiced brutality. So unlike the consummate professional, so unlike what I'd observed of him since last summer, when we first met.

Streeter walked into the crowded break room, which suddenly became quiet. In his rumbling tone, he asked, "Why'd you stop? What was all the commotion about?"

Dodson smiled slightly. "Daydreaming. About justice. About the sword of Solomon."

CHAPTER 7

WITH A SIGH, STREETER strode through Calvin's plush office, nodded to the unoccupied administrative assistant's desk just outside, and asked, "Where's Jill today?"

Jill Brannock, a tall, thin unmarried woman in her mid-thirties with long, naturally blonde hair that she always wore swept back into a seductively loose twist, was like a permanent fixture beside Calvin Lemley. Jill was likened to the prize found on the top shelf at the carnival games, never to be won, never to be touched, but providing enough alluring appeal to motivate all of the male bureau employees to keep trying. Trying too hard had cost one agent his job.

"She had a family emergency to attend to this weekend and doesn't arrive back until tomorrow morning," Calvin answered. Misperceiving Streeter's interest in his administrative assistant, Calvin quickly added, "Would you like me to tell Jill you were inquiring about her when she comes back?"

"No," Streeter emphatically answered, eyes widening in horror at the thought.

Calvin laughed. "I understand. My mistake. I just thought maybe you were ready. To move on."

From Paula, his wife. Streeter knew what he meant. He took a breath and explained, "I wouldn't want to encourage anything to get started that I have no intention of finishing."

"She's very interested in you, Streeter. There's no formal office policy prohibiting fraternization with fellow employees, you know," Calvin added in a fatherly tone, turning to eye Streeter. "That is, as long as you two are discreet."

Streeter flashed a boyish grin in response. "No chemistry."

Calvin returned a kind smile and offered, "I understand. Chemistry is important." Then, for the first time in years, Calvin broached the off-limits subject when he added in a quiet, compassionate voice, "What happened to Paula was unspeakable, Streeter. If I were you and that had happened to Lelani, I don't know if I could have overcome the challenges you have." His voice quivered with the comparison to his own beloved wife, and he cleared his throat. "But you must move on. You have lived alone for too long and Paula would not have wanted that, I'm sure. Isn't there anyone with whom you feel . . . chemistry?"

Streeter's cheeks flushed and he looked down at his busy hands, which were nervously wringing one another in his lap. His expression was answer enough for his longtime mentor and friend. "Well then, what are you waiting for? Go after her, Streeter. What's stopping you?"

Ten cavernous years in age difference and a man named Linwood, Streeter thought. When Streeter opened his mouth, making not a sound and still staring at his fidgeting hands, Calvin asked more confidently, "What's stopping you from living your life?"

With a wounded expression, Streeter looked up at Calvin and said nothing. Calvin smiled kindly again and said, "I won't pursue the topic any further. Ever again. Just think about what I've said."

Streeter realized Calvin had waited a long time to share his thoughts and had decided this was the time. Seeing that his words had unearthed painful memories of Streeter's buried past, Calvin must have realized that nothing good could come of any further advice.

Calvin sighed and clasped his hands together, abruptly changing the subject. "But asking you about your love life or the level of your interest in my administrative assistant wasn't why I invited you in here, Streeter."

"Why did you ask me in here? Without Magnussen?"

Calvin's lips pursed. "I wanted to talk with you about a transfer. To another bureau."

Streeter worked hard to swallow, his throat becoming suddenly dry with the idea of being uprooted and transferred to a new location. His words sounded more like a cough when he asked, "A transfer?"

"A promotion. To SAC. Formal offer from DC."

Streeter worked at remaining calm, to control his breathing. Reeling from the tender advice from his admired friend about learning how to live, how to love again, he had been taken completely off guard by the sharp detour of their conversation. He stared blankly up at Calvin with total confusion. His hands went limp in his lap as he instantly pushed aside the painful memories of Paula's death, as suddenly as they had been resurrected. And now all he could think about was moving away from Liv.

"Where?"

"Rapid City."

Liv's hometown, Streeter thought.

"It's official. After Shank's heart attack last summer, the bureau waited patiently for a prognosis on his recovery. He's retiring. They're making you a formal offer as SAC to replace him."

Streeter blinked, licked his parched lips.

"Before you say anything, there's more," Calvin said. He had turned from the window and was now settling into his chair at the large mahogany desk. "There's Howard Magnussen, too."

"What about him?" Streeter asked, furrowing his brow.

"He's retiring. Are you interested in a promotion to assistant SAC? Here in Denver? Supervising all of the field agents? Formally?"

Streeter said, "I hadn't figured on you asking me to consider Magnussen's job. But I had imagined you were going to try again to convince me to take a job in some other field office. I keep telling you. I'm fine living here. Staying in Denver. But Rapid City? I know you don't understand this, but I'm closer to the past there than I am here. I told you, Calvin, I don't want—"

"Streeter," Calvin interrupted, holding his hands skyward, palms up in surrender. "I know. I got the hint the fortieth time you declined my offers for promotions elsewhere. Besides, I would never encourage you to go back to the Rapid City field office. Too many memories and I care too much about you as a friend. I just had to make the formal request."

For the first time since he had entered Calvin's office, Streeter smiled easily, which seemed to please Calvin. "You had me worried there for a second."

"I won't push the transfer, but I do think you need to consider a promotion here," Calvin replied. "Howard is retiring in July. I'd like you take on his responsibilities as assistant SAC. You can still do some field investigations from time to time, but more importantly, you can help really mold and shape the younger agents, such as Manny Juarez and Liv Bergen. Even Tim Gregory shows some promise."

Dumbfounded, Streeter sat motionless and listened. He was surprised and pleased to hear Liv's name amongst the candidates for consideration as potential talents to develop, especially since she was so new to the bureau. Maybe that would be the key to keeping her from resigning.

Calvin continued, "They look up to you now anyway, Streeter. Most of the agents in your unit see you as their supervisor, regardless of the formal structure. Most of them probably don't even know that Howard is their supervisor. It's not like he's a commanding leader, you know."

Streeter lowered his eyes. "Magnussen is a good man."

Calvin explained candidly, "Look, Howard only has a few weeks left, less than two months. He's retiring on his twenty-fifth anniversary with the bureau. He's excited about reaching such a milestone, but we all know he would have jumped ship years ago if he had been eligible. He just doesn't enjoy this line of work anymore. It's time for him to go and we need to allow him the dignity he deserves by throwing him one heck of a retirement party."

Streeter sighed. "Calvin, you know how much I enjoy my work. I just don't want to be stuck behind a desk."

"That's what I'm offering you. You don't have to sit behind a desk the whole time. You can help train and develop your squad by participating with them in the field as often as you choose. You have excellent agents. We need to elevate them to the next level. Quite frankly, Streeter, I see that their growth is a bit stunted in your shadow as a coworker."

The comment had come out of left field. And stung. Streeter would have preferred that Calvin kept that observation to himself, though he knew there was truth in what the SAC said.

"Think about it, Streeter. Your fellow squad members are working with a living legend. You can't help it. You're damn good at what you do and have earned your hero status. But that can be very intimidating for those young agents who are supposedly your peers. If you were their supervisor, they may not feel so intimidated. Instead, they will try to emulate your skills, and I suspect they will try desperately to please you."

Until now, Streeter had never considered that the agents he was trying to develop might be inhibited because of him. That's what he admired most about Calvin. His straightforwardness.

"You would do a good job at mentoring those agents. The downside is that we'll probably lose a few to headquarters or other field offices as they progress under your tutelage, especially Bergen."

Streeter tensed. He couldn't imagine life without Liv, even if what they had was nothing more than a platonic working relationship. Her attitude and hunger to learn was his motivation to come to work every day. The threat of her leaving the Denver field office for some other promotion alone would make it easy for Streeter to decline the assistant SAC promotion, but he also knew that if he remained as Liv's peer, it would not assure him she would stay. She was too talented.

Either way, she would eventually be whisked from the Denver office, and the more he helped her develop, the more likely it was she'd be promoted elsewhere. Maybe he should do everything he could to encourage her to resign in June. Then once he saw where she landed in the mining industry, he could angle for a transfer nearby.

What was he thinking? He'd never made decisions based on a woman before, not even with his wife. Why was he considering Liv now?

Calvin added, "Listen, Streeter. I'll tell DC you declined the Rapid City transfer but I need you to think about your decision on Howard's job."

"Wait, don't do that," Streeter said. "How long do I have?"

"What do you mean? Before you have to decide? Howard's retiring in July. But you should know, whoever takes that position will likely be taking my job. Eventually. I'll be retiring in a year and a half, but I do not want anyone to know that yet. I'll be a lame duck if that gets out. I've already told the AD with CID that you're my choice to replace me."

The silence that followed was heavy. Streeter felt honored but not excited about the demands of the position as SAC, overseeing the entire Denver field office.

Take it easy, Streeter reminded himself. One step at a time.

"They want you to take on the assistant SAC before they select you for my position. They want to see more clearly your managerial style. They want me to make it official. You as supervisor of the field agents. They want me to convince you to take on the SAC role. I told them we'd scare you off completely if we did that, so they conceded with this assistant SAC position I'm offering you. That's understandable and reasonable for them to want," Calvin explained.

Streeter could tell that his mentor was studying his pensive expression.

"They're sending someone up to start interviewing. To bridge the transition. For Howard's job."

"When?" Streeter asked, dreading "the who" more than "the when."

"Today or tomorrow," Calvin said. "Look, I already know your management style, Streeter. It's obvious to me how you handle the squad now. You'll be tough, but fair. You won't allow horseplay, and yet you'll be compassionate. You will uphold the utmost professionalism, yet remain flexible to accommodate the agents' personal lives. You will not play favorites. You will speak your mind honestly with your people. And you will provide an excellent role model for them as you have for years."

"I appreciate the compliments," Streeter said. His mind was still dragging from Calvin's announcement that corporate headquarters had decided on an extended assignment to Denver for the transition. Added stress and more eyes. But as his mind caught up with Calvin's praises, his spirits lifted.

"I'm not blowing sunshine up your dress, Streeter. I mean this. Why do you think I've submitted your name so many times for promotions? It certainly isn't because I wanted you to leave here. I just didn't want to hold you back."

The words hung in the air and danced through Streeter's brain. He was experiencing what he imaged to be euphoria, listening to his mentor's kind exposition. Streeter absorbed the moment as one of the highlights of his career.

This was worth every hour, every painstaking crime scene he had investigated over the past sixteen years. He had always hoped his dedication and hard work would someday earn him reward or recognition by someone like Lemley, someone he respected and admired, and this was his payout, his moment.

Streeter humbly said, "Calvin, I am honored that you would think so highly of me and believe so firmly in my abilities. I will consider your offer and I want you to know how appreciative I am that you even considered me."

"Easy for me to do," Calvin answered honestly.

"But I need to know. How soon do you need an answer from me?"

"Get back with me in two weeks, if you would. We're under the gun on this," Calvin responded.

"That's on my decision about taking Magnussen's job," Streeter said. He stood up, intending to go home early for the day to his cozy log home in Conifer, a sleepy little mountain town west of Denver. He planned to celebrate by watching the sunset and replaying over and over in his mind the compliments Calvin had paid him. He would avoid dissecting and analyzing his mentor's words as anything other than positive as the early evening thunderstorms of May rolled in, the hail pounding on the cabin's roof just as he poured himself a whiskey.

He had a lot to think about and even more to do.

And just as he anticipated, Calvin Lemley's jaw dropped when Streeter asked, "But how long before I have to give you an answer on the SAC position at the Rapid City field office?"

CHAPTER 8

MY KNEES WENT ALL wobbly on me when I saw the expression on Streeter's face as I walked through his door. Though his glass-encased office was warm from a long day of sunshine pouring in and the mountains in the distance were framed in a brilliant pink and purple hue as the sun set behind them, his mood was icy, direct. Reminded me of the time in third grade when I was caught in the playground selling bubble gum—the worst kind of contraband at my Catholic grade school—and was doomed to face Sister Maria in the principal's office.

"Please, sit down," Streeter said.

The way he said those words made me even more nervous. I wondered if I had screwed up somehow and this was the tone he used for verbal reprimands. A soothing rumble that was as enticing as an old-fashioned ice cream maker churning on the ice and salt.

"Am I in some kind of trouble? Do I need my lawyer present?"

His grin was crooked and belied the sadness in his eyes.

I wondered if he'd received bad news. I wondered if someone close to him—or me—was sick, hurt, dead. I hoped for something less tragic. Maybe Streeter was still smarting from my question earlier today about the connection between his wife's death and Streeter being an FBI agent. About personal casualties being my biggest fear in chasing this dream job.

And as quickly as I thought it, Streeter answered, "You asked me a question earlier. About Paula's death. My wife. You asked if her death was somehow related to me being an FBI agent."

"I had no right." My admission was simple, yet powerful and true.

"No, you didn't." His response was simple as well. "But you have your reasons for asking. And for worrying. What you need to understand is that your worries are normal for a special agent. Just like they are for any law enforcement or military personnel. We're all trained to fight and protect, aren't we?"

I nodded, wondering if this was a trick question. Like when Sister Maria asked if all kids loved bubble gum, if I thought Satan loved bubble gum.

"Let me ask you this," Streeter said, leaning forward in his high-backed leather chair, the soft hide whispering beneath his movements like a well-worn saddle beneath a cowboy. "Think back. When you first started mining. Mining is dangerous, isn't it?"

I found myself cocking my head, studying his face. I actually distinctly remembered the feeling of when I first started mining. Not counting all my school years working for the company in reclamation, planting and watering trees, mending fences, and filing paperwork at the office, I remembered when I was old enough to first climb into a haul truck, into a crusher shack, behind the wheel of a loader, and onto a drill.

And I distinctly remember wondering if I was ready to die doing a job I loved.

"Yes, mining can be a dangerous business," I answered quietly. "If one is not careful."

I was concerned I might screw up somehow, would cause damage to the expensive mining equipment or to myself. The idea of hurting others is what I found absolutely petrifying. And it wasn't until I was working on clearing out the trap of a jaw crusher when I realized how quickly my life could end with a single mistake by me or by a coworker. I first imagined my family encircling my casket when I started clearing out the rock from the discharge belt beneath the crusher one handful at a time, praying the lodged rock above me wouldn't shower down on my head before I wriggled my way back out. Another time, when I was hurrying to finish loading a shot as an unexpected lightning storm rolled in, I had a second vision of my family watching as my casket was lowered into the ground.

"And you never worried that by being a miner you may somehow endanger your family?" Streeter asked.

I thought about the time when, during a permit hearing process, one irate neighbor to a future quarry had actually brandished a knife and threatened that if I went forward with the permitting process, he would be forced to do something drastic to my mother. I knew he didn't know my mother. And I knew that everyone's Achilles' heel was a threat to his or her mother. Logic would suggest I should have ignored the nut job. But the primal instinct in me to protect my mother had me wanting to reach up and pinch the jugular vein until his head turned blue and popped off.

"I did," I answered. "Many times."

I could see Streeter's method in patiently pointing out the inconsistency of my fear. But getting me to recognize the irrationality and eliminating the fear are not necessarily congruous. The fear remained in the pit of my gut as sure as it had been there when I sat in Sister Delilah's third-grade class, day after day, willing her not to call on me.

"Okay, so what made you stay? In the mining business?" Streeter was as still and serious as I'd ever seen him.

His eyes were bluish green now, but his demeanor incredibly calm and unflappable. I stared into those eyes for what seemed like an eternity, wondering where I'd seen that color before. Then I realized they were the color of sage.

"Well, I've loved the industry ever since I was a kid. Family business. So I was exposed to rocks early in life. Also, I am fascinated with the concept of creating new value in this world, extracting reserves for use in modern living, being in a basic industry." I had to think about where this conversation was leading me. And then it dawned on me. "I suppose I thrive on danger, if I were honest with myself."

A grin tugged at the corner of his mouth.

"But in mining, as opposed to me being in the FBI, I'm helping my family rather than putting them in any danger."

I thought about our tradition each spring. We'd have a picnic lunch at the original quarry my great-grandfather opened eighty years ago. We'd wait for a loaded shot to be detonated on the same day at the same time each year to commemorate my great-grandfather's first blast. And then we'd eat our picnic lunch. Like a blessing before a meal, only it was an explosion. My great-grandfather had been dead a long time, but it was our way to honor him and the family business he started nearly a century ago. Every minute I worked in the mines I knew someone in the community was benefiting from my efforts.

Especially my family.

The hint of a grin was replaced with an arched eyebrow. "Is that so? You aren't at risk of having a deadly accident? Destroying a nearby building? Blowing up the office? Or running the company into financial ruin? Wouldn't all of that be considered a risk of doing your job as a miner?"

I thought about the time my grandfather and great-grandfather nearly went bankrupt and again how I'd lost an aunt when I was only nine. She was my father's younger sister—only thirty-two at the time—and her crew found her the next morning frozen to death two feet from her truck after a sudden blizzard hit the plains of South Dakota. She was the supervisor at a remote site and was making sure everyone else made it home to their families before the storm hit. But no one had checked on her.

"It's not the same. Many of my family members are miners, too. We live, eat, pray, and work together."

He held my gaze much longer than I thought he would. Eventually, he drew in a long breath. "Well, this is partially my fault."

"How's that?"

"When I first asked you to join the bureau, you asked if you could work part-time."

I remembered that discussion well. We were on our way to find my sister Elizabeth at the Hanson cabin near Rochford in the Black Hills of South Dakota during the Crooked Man case. I'd thought Streeter was about to ask me out on a date. I had been wrong. But as a concession, I suppose I was still flattered that he had asked me to come to work with him. I flicked my eyes toward the windows, away from his green-blue eyes that kept drawing me in like the waters around the island of Capri.

I sighed, studying the dark clouds as they rolled in over the sinking sun. "I was so excited about becoming a special agent, I abandoned the idea of splitting attentions between two careers and instead committed to you—I mean, to working for you, of course."

I cut my eyes toward him, hoping he hadn't noticed my poor choice of words. He seemed not to, his eyes drawn to the same beautifully dark skies above the Rocky Mountains.

"After six months, when you decide whether or not you're staying or going, I hope you consider working here part-time. As another option. As Beulah's handler only." His eyes swung toward me as he leaned back comfortably, his chin resting on his steepled fingers, his elbows on the arms of his chair.

He appeared tired.

"How long have you been here?" I asked.

Suddenly alert, he asked cautiously, "In Denver? Or with the FBI?"

"No, I mean today. When did you arrive?"

It was his turn to cock his head slightly, offering me a puzzled expression.

"Simple question. When did you come to work this morning?"

He reached his arms to the sky, resting his head on the palms of his hands, and yawned. I'd never seen him yawn. Covering his mouth with one hand, he said, "Excuse me."

"Lack of oxygen," I said. "Yawning. Your body's way of drawing in a healthy dose of oxygen when tired."

"Just thinking about the hour I arrived triggered the yawn. Which was four thirty, by the way," Streeter finally answered.

"And is that healthy for a family? Working all hours of the day and night?" I grinned.

"The only family I've got works right here on the top floor," he answered.

"There's always hope," I said.

"Yes," he answered. After an uncomfortable beat, he continued, "If you decide to leave the bureau, will you be going back to mining in Fort Collins or to corporate headquarters in Rapid City?"

Streeter was still leaning far back in his chair, his head resting against his hands, his elbows spread wide and high. The relaxed, vulnerable pose of an overworked man. I noticed he was sprouting whiskers that gave his face even more character than it already had. I felt a familiar stirring and thought of Jack, how much I missed him.

"I don't know. I hadn't really thought of that. Why do you ask?"

He shrugged, keeping his hands folded behind his head.

I closed my eyes and imagined what I'd do. "I suppose I'll go wherever there's an opening. No one will be displaced just because I want to come back. My brother has already chosen my replacement at Fort Collins and it might be awkward for the new manager to have me report to him."

I opened my eyes and stopped babbling long enough to see if I'd answered his question appropriately. He seemed to be hanging on my every word, so I added, "Probably Rapid City, if I had to guess. Why, Streeter?"

"Are you interested in a transfer? To the Rapid City bureau? It might be more to your liking in regards to your low tolerance for risk to your family."

I leaned back in the stiff chair and let out a long breath. "You're saying that reservation work and the motorcycle rally hold less danger than the issues around here?"

He shook his head. "I'm saying they are issues you've grown up with all your life. You might feel more comfortable in familiar surroundings. I'm saying there is the potential for a promotion that—"

"Let me stop you right there," I said, holding up my hands like a traffic cop. "I did not take this job to earn promotions. Wait, do you think I deserve a promotion?"

The softening around his eyes told me how amused he was by my question. Or by my scattered thoughts. His low, gravelly voice cut the silence that followed. "I do."

A grin spread so quickly across my face, I didn't even try to hide it. "So you think I'm doing okay?"

This time, Streeter narrowed his eyes, confused. "More than okay. Why would you think you weren't?"

"You haven't said anything," I said, embarrassed that I'd even brought up the subject. Sounded too much to my own ears like I was fishing for compliments. "Like a thirty-day performance evaluation. Or ninety-day. Anything."

"You want a raise?" he asked.

I put my cop hands up again, only this time they were waving around like slow-motion jazz hands. "No, no. Nothing like that. I meant I thought you might be . . . disappointed in my performance. Starting with the Williams case."

"Why in heaven's name would you think that?" he asked. "You've done a great job, Liv. Calvin was telling me earlier today that you are probably not going to be with us for long—"

"You told him? I asked you to keep that between you and me," I whined.

He raised an eyebrow. "And I did. What I was saying before you interrupted me was that Calvin has heard more rumblings of offers coming your way from Quantico as well as being a candidate for promotions with other bureaus besides this one."

I was shocked. I had no idea. I didn't even know anyone had noticed me. I didn't know how long I stared at Streeter and I could almost hear my loving mother say, *Close your mouth, dear*, so I snapped my gaping mouth shut. But eventually I managed to say, "I'm flattered. But I'm not looking for promotions or to move on. I only came to work with the bureau to work under you, Streeter."

Under him? Did I actually just choose those words?

Streeter lowered his big hands and rested them on the arms of his chair, watching his own fingers splay wide over the ends. I couldn't read his expression, since he'd lowered his face, too, the setting sun at his back.

"Streeter? Why haven't you taken any promotions? Surely you've been asked hundreds of times. Or are you? Is that what this is about?" I asked, suddenly worried that even if I'd turned down opportunities to work with Streeter, maybe he wasn't about to turn down opportunities for himself regardless of what that meant for me. I mean, what did I expect? Streeter was just a coworker and that's all I was to him.

"I am and that's why I . . ." His words trailed off and he sat still for quite some time before adding, "I've never been all that interested in promotions."

I waited for more. But nothing came.

He sat up suddenly, drew in a deep breath, and said, "So if I can prove to you that you can actually help your family as a special agent, would you seriously reconsider your decision to resign?"

Before I could adjust to the sudden turn in conversation or answer his question, Streeter sat forward in his chair, plucked a file from a pile, and slid it across the oak desk. I stared at the file that sat in front of me as if it were a coiled snake about to strike, worried about where this new conversation was going. Does he want me to stay? Or go? Then my eyes landed on the familiar name, the unforgettable date, typed on the jacket of the file.

Brianna Keller.

"Her cold case file. You want to work it?" Streeter asked.

Of course I did. I almost snatched the file from his desk and ran out of his office so I could get started.

I couldn't wait to find the asshole who killed my sister Barbara's little girl seven years ago.

CHAPTER 9

AS I PUFFED IN rhythm with each pounding step, I looked at my waterproof wristwatch and calculated my pace to be a seven-minute, forty-second mile. I was on mile four of my daily five-mile run. I'd found an apartment I could sublet for six months and enjoyed my quiet, suburban neighborhood off Yale Drive on the south side of Denver. I missed bunking in with my niece at my sister Frances's house in Wheat Ridge, but moving out was a small price to pay to assure that my nephew Noah's life reached some level of normalcy, along with the rest of Frances's family.

Darkness was beginning to creep into the cloud-covered sky, so I picked up my pace to cover the last mile, images of Brianna filling my head with every step along with a jody my sister Barbara taught me:

> *The best-looking guy I ever saw*
>
> *Was drinking his bourbon through a straw.*
>
> *I walked up to that guy I found*
>
> *And gave that man the run around.*
>
> *He said, "Pretty lady can I buy you a drink?"*

I smiled at him and then I winked.

That good-looking guy is now my spouse.

I'm in the Army and he cleans house.

My feet pounded against the pavement in perfect cadence. I had been slightly off my normal eight-minute-mile pace tonight—faster, actually—but I attributed that to the adrenaline that had coursed through me since Streeter assigned me Brianna's cold case. I pushed a little harder in the final stretch of my run, eager to get started reading the file.

As I stretched my stride across the final mile of grass and asphalt that led to my neighborhood, I thought about my sister Barbara, the second-oldest of us nine Bergen kids. Barbara Bera Bergen. I know. Cruel of my parents, right? But they had their reasons. Our parents were nothing but a mixture of kindness and love and they invested a great deal of thought into our names.

Our first names were selected by my mother, who chose to name us alphabetically after the saints. B for Barbara, since she is second-born. My first name is Genevieve, G being the seventh letter of the alphabet. Seventh-born. My dad says Genevieve must be the patron saint of piss and vinegar. He's close. Disasters and fever.

Barbara is the patron saint of miners and, coincidentally, of the army and marines. Coincidentally because my sister Barbara is a colonel in the army. She's also a divorced mother of two living children and is a boatload of dynamite packed into a tiny package. She's a lot like my sister Elizabeth, only Barbara's demeanor isn't as imposing. Most people describe Barbara as someone they'd want beside them in a battlefield, whereas Elizabeth was someone they wouldn't want to meet in a lighted alley.

Barbara had married Shorty Keller right out of high school, and Brianna was the youngest of their three children. Shorty lost it after Brianna's death and crumbled under the weight of his grief. He told my sister he could no longer handle being a househusband, seeing the ghost of Brianna in every empty corner of their home. And he ditched. Barbara was left to pick up the pieces on her own with the other two older children, a boy and a girl.

After seven years, Shorty Jr. followed his mom's passion and joined the army right out of high school. Sidney was in her second year at college. Thanks to their mother's spirited can-do nature, both kids were doing great, despite the tragedies they had to endure at such a young age—losing a sister, their parents divorcing, their dad flaking out.

That reminds me. Bera, Barbara's middle name, means "spirited" in Norwegian. My dad chose our middle names and, because of his heritage, used Norwegian names, often alphabetical to match mom's saint name, except for the two boys. And me. Liv means life. I'm glad he broke tradition with me.

On my dresser, I've collected unique rocks from our family's various quarries. There's one rock for each sibling, chosen because of its similarity to the person it represents. Where my rocks are lined up like soldiers, I have a small piece of mica in the second position for Colonel Bergen. Bright, shiny, and packed with layers. Many layers. Layers that give strength. Mica is comprised of delicate and fragile scales that the eye can easily see through when peeled away. But as those flakes are packed tightly together in its natural form, mica is strong and shiny, the inherent composition so durable that it's used as composites for dental work, joint cement, rubber, and welding rods, and so shiny that it's used in paints and toothpaste.

Strong, tough, and spirited, just like Barbara.

I always wondered if it's a natural gift that parents have in predicting their children's personalities or if kids grow into their names. Either way, Barbara Bera is a name that fits Colonel Bergen like a glove.

Thinking of the jody Barbara wrote, my pace hastened. And my heart ached.

My sweet little niece Brianna Keller's life had been reduced to a file.

Streeter knew me better than I thought. I was motivated now more than ever to be a special agent, to muster all the talents I had, to gather enough intelligence, so that I could help bring Brianna's murderer to justice. It was as if God's hand had led me to this moment all along. And I had to think back seven years ago. To the beginning of the end for Brianna.

My sister was stationed at the army ammunition depot in Hawthorne, Nevada. Shorty had found an affordable house near Walker Lake so the kids could experience the great outdoors. Shorty Jr. was finishing up his junior year in high school, excited about the upcoming season of baseball as a first baseman. Sidney had just cut her hair from long to shoulder length, very traumatic for a tween. And Brianna was in her second year in gymnastics, tumbling and floor routine her favorites. She was ten.

On one beautiful spring night seven years ago, Brianna Keller had invited two of her friends over for a slumber party to celebrate the end of the school year. During the late evening hours, Brianna was kidnapped at knifepoint from her bedroom. Her two school friends had been bound, gagged, and blindfolded, but were otherwise left unharmed by the kidnapper.

Shorty was sleeping in an adjoining room but heard nothing of the commotion. Barbara had been called out of town to testify on the benefits of keeping Hawthorne off the official base-closure list to the Base Realignment and Closure Commission that had convened at White Sands Missile Range in New Mexico.

While Colonel Bergen quickly made her way north to Hawthorne to be with her distraught husband and kids and await news of their abducted daughter, Shorty Keller crawled into a bottle to find answers and never climbed back out.

Although the crime scene was processed, examined, and analyzed as thoroughly and professionally as could possibly be expected, evidence collected was sparse. Investigations of all leads led to dead ends, including the detective's initial suspicion of Brianna's father. Mr. Keller was cleared almost immediately because of the passionate accounts given by the two friends who spent the night, explaining how they were bound and gagged by the abductor, who was most certainly not Mr. Keller.

Her body was found two weeks later a few yards off US Highway 95, halfway between Hawthorne and Las Vegas. The autopsy indicated cause of death as multiple blunt force traumas to the right side, abdomen, and skull, wounds consistent with the detective's belief that Brianna was somehow ejected from a fast-moving vehicle.

After a year of leads to nowhere, the detective requested assistance from the Nevada FBI in Las Vegas. That was six years ago. The perpetrator was never apprehended.

Brianna had become a cold case.

And Streeter had convinced the Las Vegas bureau to turn over the investigation to him. So he could turn it over to me. I wondered how many favors he had to promise people to get this accomplished, how much trouble he'd be in if DC ever found out a relative was researching a cold case. I had to make Streeter's willingness to take a risk for me worth it.

And I had a chance to help my family. To help Barbara find peace.

As I sprinted into a runner's euphoria, I wondered what I would be like as a parent. Would I be as strong as my parents had been with us nine kids? Would I be as happy as my siblings were to have children, even those two sisters who'd each lost a child? Would I be able to handle the challenges of extra care needed for children like my nephew Noah, born with severe cerebral palsy, or the grieving Keller kids who'd lost their baby sister Brianna to a heinous crime? Would I keep my maiden name like Barbara did, knowing that my kids would have a different last name? Shorty Jr. and Sidney were Kellers, kids of Colonel Bergen. Confusing at best.

Streeter and Jack popped into my mind—random and pure—the visions coming to my exhausted runner's mind at once surreal and tangible. I missed Jack and wondered whether our relationship was moving into something more serious. Into love. And whether I was actually ready for that. And if so, I wondered why it was so important to me that Streeter remain in my life, a constant consideration in my decisions ever since I met him.

But mostly, I wondered if I was keeping both men in my life to avoid commitment.

A crack of lightning sparked the dark sky, jolting me from my deep thoughts. As I slowed my pace to cool down, I sorted through my thoughts and reversed the actions of my day.

I thought about how fast I'd just run those five miles.

I thought about the power of the file Streeter had slid my way, energizing me beyond any high I had ever experienced.

I thought about our conversation about promotions and changes, recounting every muscular twitch and morphing line in Streeter's face, hoping to understand his purpose and meaning, the hidden message I wasn't quite grasping. And I wondered if my goal to work with Special

Agent Streeter Pierce had been short-lived, regardless of my pending decision to leave the bureau, considering he might be promoted elsewhere.

I thought about how much effort Streeter had gone to in giving me this cold case and how clever he was to shamelessly manipulate my fears, knowing that Brianna's case would reenergize me, moving me beyond my fear of compromising my family's health and well-being.

I thought about my growing love for Jack, the uncertainty of my future with him, and my certainty that no future was worth having without Streeter.

Slowing from a jog, I walked the last half block before my apartment complex. I began stretching my arms. When I got to the steps of my apartment building, the rain began to pour from the skies. It was well past dark and I'd barely noticed that I was running under street lamps the last two miles. I stood under the awning and stretched my Achilles tendons, my calves and shins, my hamstrings, my glutes and back.

While I held my stretches, I thought of little Maximillian Bennett Williams III, the little boy kidnapped on Christmas Eve. Maybe he popped into my mind because of Brianna. Although the case had a relatively good outcome, as kidnappings go, the thought of the emotional stress and anguish that little Max must have suffered bothered me. Imagining what my nephew Noah must have suffered through the ordeal haunted my thoughts frequently.

That, coupled with the disturbing images my coworkers had painted for me today in the break room—of Shelly Jones standing on the banks of Longs Lake, watching her car sink into the deadly abyss, knowing she had strapped her two boys securely in their car seats—had erased all the positive energy I had just gained from my run and would earn me several nights of restless sleep. The images of the atrocities suffered by little children—Brianna, Noah, little Max, the Jones boys—had made me unusually tense.

Sister Delilah's nasally voice rang in my ears, "Beware the sword of Solomon!" Of course she'd use that phrase when she anticipated us making terrible decisions, warning us to rethink the consequences of our actions. But all I could think of was the king's decision to cut the baby in half to reveal the true mother of the child. As a frightened third grader listening to such a horrible story, I couldn't help but wonder if that's really what the king intended or if he had simply grown tired of the two mothers' squabble over the child. Was Solomon wise or wicked, using a baby's life as a test? Hard for me to grasp, even now.

Weird, how my mind works.

I really needed a good, healthy night of adult entertainment with Jack. I made a mental note to check my texts or messages in case he called while I was out running. Forgot to bring my cell phone again.

I stretched my arms behind my back and bent at the waist, feeling the soreness in my left forearm even though it had been three months since the cast was removed.

Although I was repulsed by men like the monster who kidnapped little Max and Noah at Christmas, I knew his monstrosity paled in comparison to the likes of Shelly Jones, who torturously murdered her own flesh and blood for the sake of retaining a boyfriend. What would King Solomon have done with her?

Was it wrong for me to hope that the sword of Solomon would have come down heavy on Shelly Jones and all the wicked people out there for what they'd done? That whoever killed Brianna would also suffer Solomon's sword?

Seven years was long enough.

Like Dodson said. Justice. Sword of Solomon.

Yes, that's it. I wanted wrath to pour down on the wicked. A King Solomon. I wanted a hero. A superhero. Someone faster than the speeding moral decay. Stronger than a powerfully evil motive. Able to leap building animosities in a single bound. Someone wise enough to find a way to separate good from evil with one swift swipe of a sword.

The sword of Solomon.

Or at least a whisper from Solomon to someone who could do his dirty work for him, even if he had to keep up the appearance of being just.

Take that, Sister Delilah. And I ain't saying a single Hail Mary as penance after confessing that evil thought.

Rain had turned to a curtain of hail, making it difficult for me to see, so I decided to finish up my stretching. And my thinking. I stepped inside the apartment entrance and turned back to watch the inclement weather through the glass door. I checked my wristwatch. I'd completed the run in exactly thirty-seven minutes, which meant an average mile of seven minutes and twenty-five seconds. I grinned with pleasure, excited to tell Jack, and breathed deeply to relax my muscles and lungs as I lifted my knees, marching in place.

With sweat dripping from my forehead, I wiped my face with the tails of my T-shirt, exposing my bare waist. Even though I was breathing hard and hail was pounding against concrete, I thought I had heard a faint clicking noise somewhere in the lobby behind me, maybe by the bank of mailboxes on the left. I glanced over my shoulder. Seeing nothing, I stretched my legs and arms in various positions, listening to hail and the rumbling of distant thunderclouds.

I was startled by a recurrence of the clicking noise and spun around, my heart leaping into my throat.

In a smooth, almost childish voice, the man who stepped from the shadows near the mailboxes said, "Good evening, Miss Bergen."

CHAPTER 10

"GEEZ, YOU SCARED THE living shit out of me."

I turned to see the neighbor I'd met at the apartment complex barbecue two months ago, just after I moved in. Camera Casey, as everyone around here called him, was instantly recognizable because he always had three cameras dangling from straps around his neck, one of which was still in his long bony fingers.

Had he just taken a picture of me? Again?

He giggled. "You said *shit.*"

I remembered how he had followed me around at the Barbecue Winter Bonanza party in late February taking what seemed to be an excessive amount of pictures. Of me. I had left the party early because of it, but later told myself that I was simply exaggerating his attentions toward me and that the man had been taking excessive amounts of pictures of everyone. I assumed I would eventually see the pictures show up in a neighborhood newsletter or directory. Or on some social network.

Muscles instantly tightened in my back and shoulders. I wrapped my hand around the base of my neck. "I meant *crap.* I shouldn't swear. Sorry."

I was standing inches from him, could smell him. Not his breath. Something else, but I wasn't sure what. Acrid. His smile was so wide, his mouth disproportionately large and cartoonish, I thought it might spill beyond the margins of his long, narrow face.

"I didn't mean to startle you. Did you hurt something?" the man asked, his smirk waning as he watched me work my fingers on the muscles in the lower back area of my left side.

"No, I'm fine," I answered. "Your name is . . . Stewart, right?" I asked, trying to recall his real name from the deep recesses of my memory.

A smile spread across his face again. I thought his face would be swallowed by it.

With a melodic hiss not unlike that of a tempter snake, the neighbor answered, "Yes. Stewart Casey. How sweet of you to remember."

Had he just blushed? I tried to put my finger on why his voice was so unnerving. Was it because it sounded childish, odd coming from a man who must be well into his forties, maybe even fifties? I focused on how the man exaggerated the *s* in *yes*, *Stewart*, and *sweet* and wondered if he had sought counseling at an early age for some speech impediment, such as a lisp, which might have resulted in his overcompensating hiss. I told myself to keep smiling at him even though he had closed the distance between us to an uncomfortable proximity. I shoved my hand toward him for a handshake as I stepped back.

"I'm Liv Bergen. I met you and your mother at the barbecue a couple months ago. Nice to meet you again," I offered cordially, waiting for him to shake my hand.

He nervously dropped his camera from his long bony fingers and wiped his hands on his dark, olive green pants before tenderly laying his hand in mine. I gripped his limp hand firmly, and then quickly released it. I resisted the urge to wipe off the clamminess that had lingered on my palm.

"Yes, indeed. Nice," Stewart responded nervously, hissing on *yes* and then again on *nice*, the second hiss being particularly lengthy.

Something tickled my spine, like a cool breeze, only we were standing inside the apartment lobby. Subconsciously, something about this man disturbed me.

"You need to stop running in this chilly weather. It's not safe for you to run in the rain and hail and lightening. You might get hurt," Stewart scolded, as if he were a concerned parent, as he stared at the strands of damp hair that had fallen loose from my ponytail and were now stuck to my forehead and neck from perspiration and rain.

I also noticed how his pale blue eyes scanned the length of my body, as if studying every inch in the process. His blatant assessment of me made me want to slug him, but something told me not to. I decided to end this friendly neighborhood discussion, opting to retreat instead to the safety and confines of my apartment.

Before turning toward the elevator, I nodded and said, "Stewart, thank you for the warning. See you later."

He said nothing and did nothing as he stood watching me push the button for the elevator and then step through its yawning doors once they opened. I was grateful not to have to wait like I had earlier at the new bureau office. As the doors closed, I could have sworn I heard another click from his camera. For some reason, something told me I had just made a terrible mistake. The same feeling I got after asking Streeter the question about his job and its relationship to his wife's death. Couldn't put my finger on why, but I knew I'd done or said something I'd regret.

As I got off the elevator and walked down the hall, I thought about it for a moment. Then I understood what I had done wrong. I had removed the key to my apartment from my pocket. My apartment number was on the tag.

Stewart Casey knew where I lived.

"Well," I said aloud as I walked into my apartment. "I'll just have to be more careful."

Beulah barely lifted her eyelids as she lay sprawled on the couch waiting for me to return from my daily run. I quickly locked and bolted my door and peered through the peephole. Just as I suspected, Stewart Casey had followed me. He just stood there in the hall and stared at my door with one camera in his hands, the other two dangling from the straps around his neck.

Stewart was tall and thin, and had wavy black hair covering the top of his elongated head. His pale blue eyes were almost translucent. He wore a neatly pressed short-sleeved button-down shirt that was olive green and various shades of brown. His matching olive green khaki pants were also neatly pressed, but were gathered in the front by a tightly cinched belt that was hiked too high up on his thin waist. He was laying his head back, still grinning and staring at the door. His lips were moving ever so slightly, as if he was talking to himself.

For the first time, I realized that the man may be mentally challenged somehow and I desperately tried to recall everything his mother and he had said to me at the neighborhood barbecue. The white-haired woman who introduced herself as Stewart's mother had said very little, in fact. Almost nothing but introductory pleasantries. She hadn't even told me her name. I recalled seeing a slight, white-haired man nearby, only he was sitting down by himself. I wondered if that might be Stewart's father.

I also wondered whether they came with Stewart to the party as guests or whether he still lived with them in the building. I couldn't recall ever seeing the strange photographer with the elderly couple since, but that didn't mean much. I was hardly ever around. Beulah and I were constantly at work these days.

I watched the strange man lift one of his cameras to his eye and depress the button with his elongated index finger. At the precise moment he took the picture of my apartment door—I assume to capture the apartment number—I could imagine the sound of the camera's click, just as I had heard it when I'd lifted my shirt earlier to wipe my face. Before I knew he was standing in the shadows.

A shiver skipped a chilly jig down my spine.

Stewart Casey lowered his camera, revealing an even wider smile on his horsey face. Throwing his head back in what appeared to be a laugh, I watched him turn and walk briskly down the hall toward the elevators.

He must be developmentally disabled, I thought.

My cell phone buzzed a tune and I stepped away from the door, let out a long sigh, releasing the tension in my chest that had unknowingly taken hold of me, and hurried to my phone.

"Hello?" I answered.

"Where've you been? Running?"

"Jack! Finally. I've been missing you all day."

"What are you doing running in the rain and hail?" His voice sounded like warm milk on a chilly night.

"How did you know it's raining and hailing?"

"Weather app."

A man of few words, Jack was. "And how did you know I was running in it?"

He laughed.

I didn't let up. "Stalking me?"

"I miss you. Want to cut my fishing trip short already."

"Is it raining there? Where are you?" I asked, knowing he wasn't about to tell me. He never did until he came back.

But he surprised me by saying, "East."

"Are you feeling rejuvenated yet? Ready to come home?"

He laughed again, that soft purr that I'd heard a hundred times if not more and felt against my ear as I rested my head on his bare chest. "I just left, dear."

"Three days ago, actually. Seems like forever. Plus you were gone most of last weekend, too." My heart fluttered, hoping he'd tell me he missed me, too.

He said nothing.

"Jack?"

"I'm here. This just isn't the same as it used to be."

"Your annual fishing trips? Or our budding relationship?"

"Both," he said, only this time he wasn't laughing. I wanted to tell him I was at the early stages of falling in love, but the words lodged in my throat. Sounding sad, he added, "Maybe my sabbaticals from work to find peace aren't as necessary for me as they used to be. Now that I've found you."

My throat clenched; my stomach fluttered. The words of love lodged in my dry throat. Instead, a question that had niggled the back of my mind since Christmas popped onto my tongue. "Jack, on the DIA abduction case at Christmas, did you . . . do something . . . did you . . . protect me from that creep?"

"Are you asking if I hanged the pedophile while he was in our holding cell?" he chuckled.

"You were the last one to see him, talk with him," I said, realizing what a mistake I'd made in asking, yet feeling every second drag on as I waited for his answer.

"No. I did not hang Fletcher in his cell." And before I could ask the follow-up question—if he'd given Fletcher the rope to hang himself—Jack asked, "Would you think less of me if I said I would have done whatever it took to protect you from that filth? If I thought you were in danger?"

"No," I answered honestly. "I would expect that out of someone who loved me." And instantly, my cheeks burned with embarrassment. Why had I said that? Beyond fishing for a compliment, I had laid the trap and set the bait, all but forcing him into being the first to tell me he loved me. Before I told him.

"Well, I'm glad you're home. And safe. I'll sleep better knowing you're back from running. You forgot your phone again when you went out, didn't you?"

"Yep. Come home, Jack."

Silence.

"Well, round yourself up a couple of coolers full of fish and peace and make this your last trip without me. Sound good?"

"Actually, it does. Goodnight, Liv. Love ya."

And he was gone.

CHAPTER 11

HAD JACK SAID HE loved me?

We were in this together.

For the longest time, I sat on the couch beside Beulah, stroking her knobby head and behind her long ears. She let out a groan of satisfaction and fell quickly back into a deep sleep. I was filled with peace at this moment. Although I could kinda see the brilliance in Jack's point about seeking peace elsewhere sometimes. But I don't think we had the same mission for the same reason.

I dropped to the floor to finish my stretching, grabbing the back of my ankles and pulling my chin to the knees of my stiff legs. By now my muscles had cooled and stiffened.

As I stretched, I talked to my dog, "How's my Beulah? Did you have a good day at your new playground? The canine facility at the new office is fabulous, isn't it?"

Without opening her eyes or lifting her head, Beulah drew in a deep breath and let out a low grumbling noise as if to complain that I had interrupted her slumber.

"I'll take that as a yes."

When I finished stretching, I grabbed a bottle of stout beer from the refrigerator and twisted off the top. Sitting on the couch beside Beulah, I opened the file that Streeter had given me and spread the papers across my coffee table. I suddenly realized I had forgotten to tell Jack about the case. Then, as suddenly, I wondered if I shouldn't. I didn't want to get Streeter in hot water. Surely he was breaking bureau protocol in assigning me this case.

As I read through the file, I stroked Beulah's velvety soft coat of short red hair. She let out another low grumbling noise, this time in approval of my attention.

I read through the entire autopsy—cover to cover—instead of skipping to the summary like I'd done before I went running. I was relieved to learn that what they had told my sister seven years ago was true. Brianna had not been sexually molested. And after reading through all of the information, I would guess that the reason why she wasn't molested was that there wasn't time. The medical examiner suggested that the time of death was likely only hours after Brianna was abducted from her home. I read and reread the detective's report he crafted before turning the case over to the Las Vegas bureau for assistance.

His conclusions stunned me. Something he never shared with my sister. Or she had never shared with me. Brianna's damaged, crumpled body—still wearing the nightgown she'd been described as wearing that night—was found in a shallow ditch in the desert sands a few yards from US Highway 95, just short of the 267 turnoff, a state highway that traversed the desert twenty miles into California and across the Sylvania and Sequoia mountain ranges. The Hawthorne detective believed that ten-year-old Brianna, barefoot and wearing nothing but a nightgown, was either thrown from or fell out of the abductor's car at speeds estimated to be in excess of sixty-five miles per hour.

My stomach twisted again with the thought and I wondered if I'd ever shake the feeling of nausea knowing what might have happened to my niece on that stretch of road.

What could have caused someone to throw Brianna from a speeding car on a desolate desert highway in the dark of night? How could she have fallen out? Did the ME really think a child could fall out of a speeding car? Where was the son of a bitch taking her? What would he have done? Had he told her what was going to happen and Brianna decided to get out of the car? What child would do something so brave, so courageous?

Barbara's daughter.

The Las Vegas bureau files did little else than verify the thorough detective's findings after following similar trails that led nowhere. They found no match in the AFIS for the partial print lifted from the remains of her nylon gown, but they did lift a boot print from the back of my niece's gown.

A boot print.

As soon as my mind wondered if the abductor had kicked Brianna from the speeding getaway car, the FBI investigator agreed with the Hawthorne detective's conclusion that the print came postmortem—no bruising to her skin from what appeared to be a significant shove.

The FBI investigator believed that the child's body was moved farther from the road where she had been ejected alive from the car so as not to be detected immediately. He concluded that based on the crime scene photos, Brianna's abductor likely stopped the car, went back to where she had fallen or jumped, discovered she had already died, and rolled her broken body away from the road. With his foot.

Bastard.

I rubbed my eyes with my fingertips to erase the images from my mind, unwilling to look at the envelope of crime scene photos. The horror was easy enough for me to imagine and I didn't want to see the end result of what had been my lovely niece. I had decided to run after reading the summary because reading even that had disturbed me to the core. But my desire to know, to help, far outweighed my desire not to know the details of my niece's last minutes in this world.

I drained the last of my beer, gave Beulah a pat on my way off the couch, and headed to the bathroom to take a shower. Until a shiver of intuition returned to my spine. I tiptoed to the front door, checking the bolt again to make sure it was locked, the chain refastened, and stole a glance through the peephole. Empty hall. I breathed a sigh of relief and headed toward the bathroom for the hot, relaxing shower I had been awaiting, discarding my clothes in the hallway, hoping to wash away my fears and hatred, leaving me only with clarity to help Brianna.

After my shower, I turned on my music and listened to Rod Stewart belting out a touching rendition of "Broken Arrow," an oldie but one of the best songs he ever sang. I slid the royal blue silk chemise slip over my head and let it fall softly down my body, where it stopped mid-thigh. After adjusting the spaghetti straps, I threw my head forward and twisted the towel around my long, wet hair.

I went back for a second bottle of beer and grabbed a pack of crackers and some tuna fish and returned to my place on the couch by Beulah. She didn't stir, even as I ate my canned tuna, what must be a potent smell for a tracking dog.

I read everything in the file again, this time as an investigator, not an aunt. Avoiding the packet of crime scene photos as long as I could, I absorbed every detail in the file, making notes and jotting down names and phone numbers of people I would start calling first thing in the morning. I took a long draw on my beer and decided to open the packet of photos.

At first, I was repulsed, sick to my stomach. I wanted to cast the photos away. Burn them. But then my training kicked in and I looked beyond the fact that I was staring at my dead niece and instead focused on the details. The body was tiny, like a small fawn, much smaller dead than I'd remembered her being alive.

My fear that coyotes and buzzards and other predators had gnawed on her rotting corpse over the two weeks had been allayed. Her carcass was largely untouched, although clearly autolysis and putrefaction had been sped up greatly as the corpse cooked under the desert sun. I studied the stages of the two processes by which the body's enzymes and bacteria, escaping from the intestines, cause tissue and bones and organs to decay, as if the body were a reactor under a nuclear meltdown from within, confirming my belief in the detective's report and the ME's conclusions.

Luckily for me, Brianna was found facedown.

The nightgown was ragged and sun bleached.

I was shocked to see how close her body was to the highway, yet no one had noticed her for two weeks. Apparently the sparse yucca and cacti had been enough to conceal her from passersby.

The detective believed there was one abductor and that he either pushed her from the car or caused her to jump. To jump. From a speed-ing car.

From a photo of the surrounding area, I could see the markers in the desert sands, starting near where her body lay and placed in areas head-ing due north to the road, less than thirty feet away. The line of crime markers was at about a ten- or twenty-degree angle to the road, meaning that when my niece was ejected from the speeding car, which was headed south and slightly east, her motion was likely in a southwesterly direction, her momentum causing her to hit the ground due south of where she left the car, her body rolling due south from where she landed. From the crushing and bruising wounds in the autopsy report, it appeared she'd been hurled from the passenger seat or from the backseat, right door, Brianna's momentum toppling head over heels, her right leg shattered—likely from the initial impact—as well as her right wrist, followed by a mortal fracture to the right side of her skull. Her forehead.

Her abductor—probably stunned that the ten-year-old was not cowed by him or compliant to his demands, which, knowing Brianna, she wouldn't have been—must have snapped, pushed her out. Or made a sudden move that would have caused Brianna to jump.

Even if that detail was not determined, the abductor had stopped his car, gotten out to see if Brianna was alive, and when she wasn't, rolled her with a swift kick or two a few more feet from where she landed to where her body lay for two weeks behind a clump of desert foliage, shielding her from anyone's view from the highway.

In the report, the only item of interest they found along the road between where Brianna jumped or fell and where she was found was a stuffed bunny, gray and ratty with a quirky face and long floppy ears. A photo indicated that the bunny lay almost exactly where Brianna had first landed, the detective's speculation being that the stuffed animal was likely jolted from her clutched hand.

I smiled, thinking how much it reminded me of a bunny my little brother Jens carried around when he was a toddler. I remembered the image so vividly because it was the only time I recall seeing Jens cry as a child—when mom would wash his bunny.

I wondered if my sister Barbara had bought the bunny for Brianna because it reminded her so much of when all of us were kids. When Jens was a toddler, Barbara must have been about twelve or so. I thought about whether I should tell her what I was doing and decided not to get her hopes up. I'd wait to tell her after I found something.

But it wouldn't hurt to call her. To check in. Tell her how much I loved her.

I looked at the clock. Nearly eleven. It was only ten where my sister lived. After Hawthorne, the army moved my sister to Fort Irwin, California, to the National Training Center for her expertise in ammunition storage. She'd still be up watching the late-night news.

I punched in her number.

After filling me in on my niece Sidney's latest college courses and her escapades over spring break and on my nephew Shorty Jr.'s harrowing life as a bomb tech dismantling IEDs, we talked for twenty minutes, catching each other up on what we had heard was going on back home in Rapid City. I finally asked, "Barbara, how's Shorty? Do you ever hear from him?"

There was a long pause, and I'm pretty sure she was deciding how much to tell me.

"It's none of my business, of course. I was just wondering," I added, giving her an out if she needed one.

"I was trying to figure out how to answer your question. I hear *about* him but not from him. Shorty Jr. won't have anything to do with his dad, but Sidney still visits him. He lives in Santa Barbara, about two hundred forty miles from here. With Sidney at UC Irvine, she's as close to him as she is to me, about a hundred fifty miles to either one of us. Funny how life works out that way."

"Is he still . . . drinking?" I asked.

Her laugh sounded sad. "Still drinking. His preferred method for staying medicated."

"Never has gotten over Brianna?" I asked.

"Never will. Can't say that I blame him. Some days, I envy him."

"I'm so sorry," I said.

"Don't feel sorry for me. Feel sorry for the kids. They lost their sister and their dad that night. And Shorty Jr. just can't take it."

"Poor kid. Must be tough, losing his dad to the addiction. Did Shorty ever remarry?"

"Nope."

"How are you doing, sis?"

"Well I'm not looking to get married again, if that's what you mean. And I never was one for drinking," she said.

"I meant about Brianna. How are you coping?"

Barbara sighed. "I have my good days and bad. I miss her, wonder what she'd be like today. But I know she wouldn't like us putting our lives on hold like Shorty has done. She wouldn't like that one bit."

"And wouldn't hesitate to tell her dad that," I said, thinking of her spunkiness.

"No truer words were spoken. She'd tell Shorty a thing or two about getting over her death, I'm sure." My sister sounded happy, even though the topic was tragic.

So I decided to press my luck. "Did they ever give you back any of Brianna's belongings after the initial investigation?"

"Like what? You mean her hairbrush they took for DNA sampling? The photo we gave them of her?" Barbara asked.

"No, I mean any of her belongings she had with her when . . . when she was taken from her room," I asked, worried I had pushed too far already.

"She didn't have anything, except for the nightgown she had on. That's it," Barbara said. "And they kept that for evidence. Said we wouldn't be getting that back and I told them I didn't mind one bit as long as they nailed the son of a bitch who did this to my baby."

I heard a hitch in Barbara's voice. She wasn't about to cry, but she was still passionate about finding her daughter's murderer.

The detective had interviewed the other two girls left behind in Brianna's bedroom, bound and gagged—no prints, no fibers, no nothing—and determined that although the abductor was fully clothed in black, wore a mask, they had enough to believe he was a man. The feel of the hands, the sound of the grunt, the muscular chest—no breasts—when he grabbed one of the girls who tried to run.

"What about her bunny?" I asked.

"What bunny?"

"You know, the gray one with the squished-up face, the super-long ears."

There was a long pause before Barbara answered, "That was Jens. You're confusing Brianna with Jens when he was kid. He had a bunny with a squished-up face."

"Well, didn't Brianna have one, too?" I was looking right at the picture. A gray bunny with extra-long ears and a paunchy stomach. "Gray, ears as long as its body? Beer gut? I thought I remembered her carrying it around by the ears."

"Boots, you're thinking of Jens. He carried his bunny that way when he was a kid. Brianna didn't have a bunny."

"You sure? I could have sworn she—"

"You're wrong!" Barbara shouted, anger exploding that I had never experienced before.

I waited, listening to her breathe. "Look, Barbara, I'm sorry. I just thought . . ."

"No, I'm sorry, Boots." I heard her sniffle. "One time Shorty rented *Watership Down* for the kids. It was a cartoon, but apparently something horrible happened to the rabbits in that story. Brianna had nightmares for weeks. She hated bunnies. They scared her to death."

Alarms sounded in my head. I'd forgotten that. Brianna was fixated on fashion Barbies. Any kind or type. Never on soft, fluffy bunnies, like the one in the photo I was staring at. She'd even clasped her hands over her ears at the mention of the Easter bunny.

Not Brianna's bunny. Then whose?

CHAPTER 12

I WOKE UP REFRESHED after a perfect night of sleep in my queen-size bed under the cool, crisp sheets that I washed two days ago. My trusty red bloodhound was lying beside me, still snoozing. My door was locked. I couldn't feel safer from the evils of the world.

I flung open the window next to my bed and the chilly spring morning spilled into my room. I turned off my alarm clock, which had not yet sounded, and moved toward the bathroom. I let the muscles in my body relax as I enjoyed the aches after a great run last night and looked forward to another long, productive day.

As I prepared for the day, I thought about the bunny found near Brianna's body. I wondered if Barbara might somehow be wrong about the bunny not being Brianna's. Maybe she grabbed one of her friend's sleepover animals? Out of desperation. I imagined how easily it could have been mistaken by the investigators as belonging to my niece. And I hoped that if it truly wasn't her bunny, it could somehow lead me to its owner.

I imagined the sequence—the sound—of the events as one spunky little ten-year-old and one tiny little stuffed bunny landed on the roadside seven years ago along the desert near Death Valley outside of Vegas. The soft thump of a stuffed bunny landing in the dry sand filled my mind with hope.

I heard a noise, something different from the sounds of my normal mornings.

I stood still in my bedroom, already dressed in my drab pantsuit and bending over to tie my boots, hovering to finish only after I strained to hear more noises at the front door.

Had I heard something? Or had my imagination run away with me?

I held my breath, held still, and listened for any unusual sound.

After waiting at least five minutes, I heard what sounded like faint footsteps in the hall. They were soft, but brisk. I heard the neighbor's yappy dog barking at whoever was in the hall, like a good watchdog would do. Beulah had not sounded an alarm about whoever had been lurking outside my door, but I was not surprised. If Beulah had smelled the pedestrian, she too would be howling a warning like the rest of the neighborhood watchdogs, but as for hearing the person, Beulah was nearly deaf.

I stood by the door and listened for more noises in the early morning, but they never came. I assumed what I'd heard was likely the sound of a neighbor in the hall, leaving early for work. Or coming home from a late night. I moved toward my kitchen counter and checked my cell phone and saw that I had a text message.

From Jack.

PHONE OFF. KEEP TEXTING ME ABOUT YOUR CASES. IT'S MY ONLY CONNECTION TO YOU. CALL YOU IN A FEW DAYS WHEN I'M BACK IN RANGE FROM FISHING.

I tossed the phone aside and covered my face with my arm.

"Stupid fish."

After a couple of minutes, I got up, grabbed Beulah's collar, and walked her to the front door to retrieve my daily paper. When I opened the door, I stopped suddenly.

Lying outside my apartment door was a loaf of what appeared to be homemade bread wrapped in clear plastic and a blue ribbon. I stared at the bread as if by doing so, I could convince it to share the secret of who had brought it to me. Suspicion overtook my surprise as I scanned the hall for any signs of life that may indicate who had brought the gift.

Slowly, I crouched down and touched the soft bread with the tips of my fingers—nearly coming out of my skin when Beulah started growling, something I rarely heard her do—and then picked it up. There was no note and I could smell that the freshly baked bread was banana.

As I stood in my doorway regarding the gift, I wondered if it might have come from Stewart Casey. I looked both ways down the hall, listened for any familiar clicks from his camera, grabbed my newspaper, and went back inside. I set the banana bread on my kitchen table, kept Beulah close beside me, and left for work.

My annoyance over the loaf grew on my drive to work. By the time I pulled into the new parking structure and flashed my employee badge at the parking attendant, I had made a decision to throw it away the instant I got home that night.

Just to be safe.

I settled Beulah into the canine club—what Claudia the groomer and caretaker called "day care for doggies"—located in an environmentally controlled kenneling system for the various bomb-sniffing, cadaver-recovery, and tracking dogs trained by the bureau. Most of the "guests" were German shepherds. Beulah was the only bloodhound. But she seemed happy all the same. She'd slept from the moment we got home last night until we left this morning, moving only once to go from the couch to the bed when I turned in for the night.

The feeding, exercising, and care Claudia must be giving these dogs was certainly making Beulah happy. And tired. Claudia wasn't in yet, considering it was only six, but I had a passkey to bring Beulah in anytime I needed. Many of the dogs stayed here full-time, but Beulah was more to me than just a coworker. She was my bud.

I hurried from the canine club back through the parking structure and into the new office building through screening. Tanner barely acknowledged my existence, probably still embarrassed from yesterday. I made my way up to the fourth floor by stairs, dropped off my files, stopped by the break room to grab two cups of coffee, and headed down to the third floor, to the ERT lab. Dodson was hunched over a scope, studying some slides.

"Hi Mitch!" I said from the door to alert him I was behind him.

He didn't move a muscle, just mumbled, "Agent Bergen."

I weaved my way through the various stations and rows of testing equipment to where Mitch was working. He must have smelled the coffee I had brought him because he lifted his head from his work as I neared. "What brings you here?"

"Coffee," I said, lifting his cup and handing it to him.

We both drank in silence until our cups were nearly empty.

Dodson asked, "And?"

"A question."

He looked at me, inquisitively.

"What are you working on?"

"Trying to tie up some loose ends on KCPD's Greenwood case. Apparently, the mother had hired a private investigator—one of us—to collect evidence all these years. A real treasure trove of data compiled on Carl Halbrook. He would have fried if he'd lived long enough."

"So they'll be able to close that case? After decades of not knowing what ever happened to that little girl?"

He nodded. "Thanks to the work of one dedicated PI. So is that why you brought me coffee? To get an update on the Greenwood case?"

I was about to ask my question about Brianna's case when something he'd said struck me. "Wait, what? One of us? You said the PI was one of us."

"An FBI special agent," he said.

"Who?" I asked, thinking back to Jack's connection with a college friend who lived in Kansas City, his occasional weekend trips away, with no explanation, no warning.

Dodson shrugged. "A big secret. Anonymous, according to the KCPD chief. Doesn't matter."

And I remembered Jack stepping off a Kansas City flight at Christmas during the DIA child abduction case. When he begged me not to tell Streeter. Later, he told me he didn't want Streeter to know that he'd been doing a little side work, informally working on a case. Had Jack been working as a PI for Greenwood? Was that the "little side work" he'd been talking about?

I decided I would ask him when he got back. "If a partial fingerprint was run through AFIS seven years ago and again six years ago, is there any chance we'd get a hit today?"

"Depends. If there wasn't a hit because the perp wasn't in the system and he is now, yes. If there wasn't a hit because the print is too distorted or doesn't have enough points to compare, then the answer would be no." Dodson drained his cup and looked up at me. "Unless."

"Unless?" I also drained my cup and eyed the aging man.

"Unless the print could be examined by a human instead of by the computer so that the subtleties of point identification were clarified."

"Can you do that?" My heart raced.

"Send it and I'll see."

I threw my arms around his neck and said, "Thanks, Mitch."

The expression on his face was a mix of disgust and alarm. "Thanks for the coffee."

I ran up the flight of stairs two at a time, excited that maybe Mitch Dodson could help with the fingerprint in Brianna's case file. I scanned in the print and sent it to him. I glanced at my watch. Too early to call the Vegas bureau or the detective in Hawthorne. They were on Pacific Time and I was on Mountain.

For a moment, I assumed that the bunny was not Brianna's and didn't belong to one of her two friends who had spent the night. That left the bunny belonging to a family member of the abductor. Or more likely, to a child previously abducted by the same man.

I logged onto the NCIC system and searched for cold cases with a similar MO, abductions in the area of Hawthorne, and missing persons similar in age to Brianna. I had been searching the data for nearly two hours when I realized I was about to be late for our weekly squad meeting.

At the old office on Stout, the smaller of the two conference rooms always felt stuffy, no matter what time of day any meetings were held and no matter how many people were crammed into the space that was meant to accommodate up to twelve. The new conference room was not only fresh, cool, and roomy, accommodating up to thirty, but was fully loaded with all the latest videoconferencing and presentation equipment.

Assistant SAC Howard Magnussen convened meetings sporadically, whenever the need arose to touch base with the entire squad on any given day, but normally he held weekly meetings only. The new conference room offered a spectacular westerly view of the Rocky Mountains. The squad meeting on this Tuesday was no different, except that we were in the new building. Streeter was still overseeing Howard's meeting, at Howard's request.

Everyone had gathered in the conference room by the time I scooted to the nearest empty chair. I noticed a few people glancing at their watches. One agent asked, "Has anyone seen Streeter this morning?"

Heads shook, people mumbled.

I realized for the first time that I hadn't noticed whether Streeter was at work when I arrived. I was so absorbed with my questions of Dodson and my research on the Brianna Keller cold case that I hadn't thought to say good morning to Streeter. New office space required establishing new routines and I just wasn't there yet.

Another agent asked, "Doesn't that strike any of you as odd? He's usually here before all of us and I haven't seen him yet. Have any of you?"

I was the first to answer. "I haven't."

Streeter's winded voice came from the doorway, "Sorry I'm late. The plane was delayed."

The plane? What plane? Standing next to Streeter, nearly cowering against the white sleeve of his right arm, was the beautiful, petite woman with huge brown eyes, even bigger breasts, and bleached blonde hair, wild with long ringlets. Jenna Tate. From Quantico. Beautiful and smart.

The room grew silent. All eyes were fixed on the gorgeous blonde with Streeter. I was momentarily stunned, not able to comprehend this paired image. The only thing I knew for sure after having Tate as one of my instructors at Quantico was that this woman was called drop-dead, tongue-wagging, centerfold-worthy, irresistibly gorgeous. And she was huddled against Streeter's side like a nervous kitten.

I couldn't tell who, but one of the men let out a long, quiet whistle of approval.

Streeter had difficulty restraining his boyish grin on this morning. "Good morning, everyone. Most of you know Special Agent Jenna Tate from Quantico, but for those of you who don't know her, she's here to work with us on a special case."

The spunky blonde raised and wiggled her perfectly manicured fingers and in a thick Southern drawl said, "Hi y'all. Nice to see you again. Oh, and there's our precious little Agent Bergen."

My throat was dry but I managed to say, "Good morning, Agent Tate."

The agent sitting next to me leaned into my ear, saying under his breath, "I've died and gone to heaven. Fresh donuts. New office. Working with Tate."

A serious expression fell on Streeter's face. When the commotion from all of us field agents subsided, Streeter continued with his introduction. "Tate is the newest member of our squad. Temporarily. She's shadowing Magnussen, who will be retiring in a few short weeks. Tate will be taking his place as acting assistant SAC until headquarters chooses a permanent replacement."

Howard raised his hand. "Calvin asked my opinion about this and I agreed that Agent Tate would provide the continuity we need to make the proper selection of my replacement after I retire in July."

I did not expect this announcement. Streeter never mentioned a word of this to me yesterday.

When I met Jenna Tate last summer on the Crooked Man case, I thought then that she looked nothing like an agent. But I learned how wrong I was to instantly dismiss her ability because she was beautiful, blonde, busty, and voguish. Ergo, a lousy field agent. Instead, I learned that Tate had graduated top of her class from the FBI Academy, over the other thirty-five in her class, and quickly climbed the ranks as a top recruiter for the bureau and as a renowned teacher at Quantico. She had a skill for pointing out good talent, from what I'd heard.

I had learned Tate was born in Mobile, Alabama, raised somewhere in the Midwest, got her bachelor of science in economics at Harvard and her juris doctor at Georgetown. She was a lawyer with Whiting, Jefferson, and Holloway in Cambridge, Massachusetts, as a criminal defense attorney for only six years before being asked to become a partner. She decided to give up all that private practice success to "wrestle down criminals" with the rest of us. Those were her words, not mine. And she had more money than God, according to the rumors at Quantico. Which I suppose I should have guessed, considering her taste in high fashion.

Streeter grabbed Jenna's hand and gave it a squeeze, saying, "Do you want to say anything before I introduce you to the rest of the squad?"

"Why certainly," Tate said. Her pouting lips, frosted expertly in soft pink, reminded me of a centerfold. "I want y'all to know, I'm as happy as a clam that y'all picked me to take the place of the great Howard Magnussen, at least on a temporary basis. I'll have to work extra hard to keep up with you talented people. I feel honored to be working with Howard until July, and of course with Street, the legend." Tate turned to Streeter as if they were the only two in the room and said, "The faculty just can't stop talking about you at the Academy, Street, and it's great to finally work with you again."

Jenna laid both of her dainty, feminine hands on Streeter's upper arm and made a kind of curtsy. Streeter dropped his gaze to the carpet. I rolled my eyes. I wondered why this brilliant woman irritated me. Maybe it was the way she played dumb, pretended to be defenseless, helpless, when she was none of those things. But men seemed to eat it up.

Jenna concluded, "I sure do hope you're patient with little old me, being new and all. Any volunteer who will show me the ropes around here?"

All of the agents raised their hands and murmured their willingness to volunteer. I think I threw up a little bit in my mouth. I'd seen this before. And it was a most effective tool with men who were tools.

"Thank you," Jenna said in response to her welcome, actually blushing from the exuberant attention.

Streeter quieted the group and showed Jenna to an empty chair beside him. "Let me introduce you to the squad."

I zoned out as "Street" introduced us all again to Jenna, trying to place a name on the emotion that roiled in my gut knowing she had been selected to take Howard's place.

Uneasy.

That was all I could come up with.

"Finally, last but never least," Streeter said. "This is Steve Knapp."

"Affectionately known as Hewey," one of the other agents teased.

Jenna in her endearing twang asked, "Like in Baby Hewey? The giant, comic-book baby character? Oh, how cute."

Steve nodded and blushed. His massive frame was shrinking right before my eyes, as if he was crawling inside of himself out of embarrassment. Like a turtle into its shell.

Jenna, coming to the rescue, added, "Would you mind, Agent Knapp, if I call you Hewey, too?"

Steve smiled and sat tall in his chair. With all the sincerity of a child, he replied, "You can call me anything you'd like."

Streeter announced, "Now that introductions are over, I would like to ask for your support and assistance of Tate in her first few days here. Let's try and go easy on her, at least until she's had a chance to unpack her things and get acquainted with you as she and Magnussen begin their work together, okay?"

Mumbles rippled through the room and Jenna smiled appreciatively. "As I said, thank you for supporting me, but I also want to ask that you support Street. I'll be coming and going often in the next few weeks. I'm asking him to continue to direct your work and conduct these weekly squad meetings just like he's done for years. Can you do that for me?"

Everyone clapped.

"I don't plan on making sweeping changes," Streeter said.

My grip on unease loosened a bit.

Until Streeter added, "But I do plan on making a few. First, Liv, I would ask that you give up your office."

CHAPTER 13

HAD I JUST BEEN fired?

I wasn't sure how to respond. For the third time today, I was surprised. And not unlike seeing Jenna cling to Streeter's side as they walked in today, it was not pleasant. Why should I give up my desk to her? I just moved in yesterday. Why is Streeter punishing me?

Streeter explained, "Your office is right next to Magnussen's office. Tate will need to be close to him."

I was able to breathe again. Sensing all eyes on me, I made sure I kept my expression void of any emotion.

"If you don't mind, I would like you in the office next to mine. I would like you to move as soon as you have time. That is, unless you would prefer I offer the office to someone else."

"I'll be moved within the hour," I answered, not only surprised, but shocked. Pleasantly this time. I was moving next to Streeter.

"I want all of you to meet me here this time each Tuesday to give a debrief of the previous week and a briefing on what's ahead for the coming week so we can give Tate plenty of time and space to work with Magnussen. Write up your reports ahead of time and come to these meetings prepared, because I am not intending that they last more than forty-five minutes."

No change. Same Streeter. Breathe.

"Liv, please take Tate and show her your office. Knapp, you make sure you help Tate with anything she might need for the first few days. Make sure she's well stocked with any office supplies she might want. Juarez, I want a debrief on the Velasquez sting when you have ten minutes sometime this morning. Does anybody have anything else they need to say? Good. Same time, same place next Tuesday."

The chairs rolling across the industrial carpet made a smooth sound as everyone crowded out of the conference room. The agents shook Jenna's hand as they left, welcoming her to Denver, her new temporary assignment. I was one of the last ones out of the room. When I approached Jenna, I was reminded how petite the woman actually was. The top of her wild blonde curls met the bottom of my chin. I shook Jenna's hand, desperately trying to ignore how awkwardly large and Amazon-like I felt compared to this wisp of a woman. And trying not to notice her expansive cleavage.

"Nice to have you here, Agent Tate," I offered. "Follow me, and I'll show you where your new office will be."

"I'd prefer to be next to Street. Want to wrestle for it?"

"No thanks," I chuckled, not sure if she was serious or not.

As we made our way through the maze of hallways between the offices and conference rooms, I could see Steve Knapp standing guard by my office door. What used to be my office, soon to be Jenna's. His massive frame was planted tall and unmoving next to the doorway like a guard at Buckingham Palace.

I slapped his arm playfully and said, "Steve, at ease. Agent Tate will let you know if she needs anything."

Jenna flashed him a smile and batted her eyelashes. Steve responded by standing even taller, his chest puffing like a swollen turkey. In her sweet, Southern tone, she cooed, "I will need help unpacking my boxes when they arrive."

"Be happy to help, ma'am," Steve offered with a grin.

"Jenna. Call me Jenna, Hewey," she drawled.

I turned away from the two and had cleared out my desk within a couple of minutes, everything fitting easily into two boxes. While Jenna and Steve talked, I stacked the two newly packed boxes on top of the ten I had yet to unpack and returned to the hall.

I waited for a lull in their conversation, folded my arms and tapped my toe, as I said to Steve, "The sooner I move out, the sooner Jenna can call this office her home."

"I'll help you move," he eagerly volunteered.

I grinned at Jenna and she winked at me.

Steve ducked into my office and grabbed four of the boxes from the stack, carrying them out of sight down the hall.

Jenna's smile widened, revealing perfectly white teeth, as she chuckled, "Oh, you're good, girl. I better keep my eye on you. I see there's a reason Street calls you his best."

His best?

"What I can't figure out is why he calls you by your first name."

My grin faltered. The expression in Jenna's eyes showed a flash of anger. Streeter called everyone except Calvin by their last names. Yet he'd never called me Bergen.

Steve had returned empty-handed and said to me, "Well, let's get moving."

After two trips, we had all my belongings out and into the empty office. My new office had an adjoining wall with Streeter's and with the conference room in which we had all just met. Although I now had a spectacular view of the Rocky Mountains to the west, as did Streeter, my office was nearly half the size of his, but still twice the size of the one I'd just abandoned. What was going on here?

No one ever questioned why Streeter had one of the corner offices with the best views and the most room, offices generally reserved for the SAC or assistant SACs. He had earned it by being one of the best agents in the country, and his seniority with the bureau helped.

When a visitor once asked Howard Magnussen why one of his squad members had a bigger office than he did down on Stout, Howard put it best when he replied, "Because he usually has the biggest problems to solve and he deserves it."

I put my hands on my hips and looked around my new office. I smacked Steve's arm and asked, "What do you think?"

My massive friend looked around the bare office. "It's great. I'm happy for you. But not as happy as I am for me. Jenna is right next to my office. Right next to me. She's new here, which means she'll be asking me for everything she needs, if you know what I mean."

I rolled my eyes. "Knock it off, Hewey. You're dreaming. She may be new, but she's not stupid." I jerked my thumb toward the conference room and added, "Besides, you shouldn't get so cocky, considering all the competition you have."

"Then I better get back to helping Agent Tate and quit wasting my time with you."

"I bet she hasn't had time for a tour of our new building. Or had time to see the new firing range, yet. Go get 'em, Hewey."

"Don't call me that. You know I don't like that nickname," Steve whined.

"I know," I said. "But Agent Tate thinks it's cute. You better tell Jenna that the guys were just teasing when they said everyone calls you Hewey or you'll have to get used to the name."

"For her, it would be worth it." And off he went.

I stood looking around my office, not quite believing yet that it was mine. My desk faced the door, the wall and door to the hallway completely glass. Behind my desk was a wall with windows. To my right, a wall of shelves and filing cabinets. The only wall needing some attention was the north wall, to my left, which was the wall that adjoined Streeter's office. I stood staring at the blank wall for a moment, trying to imagine which picture I'd like to hang.

"Trying to decide what shade of beige this is?" Streeter asked. He was leaning against the doorframe with only his head and one shoulder stuck through the doorway, as if trying to avoid intruding on my new territory.

"I was thinking of painting this wall purple," I said with a serious expression. "Maybe my entire office. What do you think of midnight purple?"

"Classy," Streeter mocked.

I frowned. "So, not purple. Why don't you come in?"

"You haven't invited me," Streeter answered.

"Oh, so that's how it is now? Please, do come in, kind sir. You're welcome in here any time. You don't need to knock. Please don't knock. It's going to be hard enough getting used to being in an office, let alone one next to yours."

Streeter lowered his chin, hiding his smirk.

"By the way, thank you for the office," I offered sincerely. "And the vote of confidence in me, boss."

When he lifted his eyes to meet mine, he was no longer smirking. With all seriousness, he said, "I need you to meet with me on a case right away, if you have time. It's a big one. I just got the call."

"Of course," I said, embarrassed I'd wasted so much of his time on small talk. "Why didn't you say something?"

I quickly followed him back into his office, where he shut the glass door behind me, saying in a low, serious voice, "The new chief of police from Fort Collins, Theresa Fiero, just called me. They've asked for our assistance on the Douglass murder."

"The little reality show star who was murdered a few months ago? The one where no suspects have even been named yet?" I asked.

"Officially, yes." Streeter scowled. "It seems it's become very complicated. Fiero was just hired to replace the former chief of police, who resigned under the pressure of public scrutiny. The mayor is crossways with city council, who wanted to fire the former police chief. On top of the local battle that's surrounding her on this one, the whole country's fixated on this child's murder and everyone has an opinion on who killed that little six-year-old, on who's to blame for the whole ugly mess, and on who's at fault for not arresting a suspect yet. It's a mess, Liv, and Fiero's asking for our help."

I was scowling as well, rubbing my chin as I thought about the well-publicized case. Unaware of his habit when he was deep in thought, Streeter was rubbing his big hands through his shortly cropped, stark white hair.

He added, "I'd like you to run with this one, Liv. I'm making you case agent."

I blinked. "But the Douglass case is one of the most publicized murder cases in the country. You can't make me case agent. I don't have enough experience. Streeter, this is right up your alley. Why don't you keep this one?"

Streeter grinned. "I'll assist you. You'll do fine."

"Surely Lemley won't approve this decision. Not with Tate here from Quantico."

"Especially with Tate here from Quantico. And they both agree with me. This one's yours."

I shook my head, not understanding. "This case will be in the nation's fishbowl and like you said, it's very complicated. Fiero needs you, Streeter. Not me. I'm still too green."

What I was saying was true, not some drivel born of humility. I wasn't skilled enough yet to take on a case like this.

"How are you coming on the Keller case, by the way?"

"Dodson's rerunning a partial print. And I think I might have a lead that may have been overlooked, but I need to talk to the Vegas bureau and the detective in Hawthorne."

Streeter grinned. "See? I gave that cold case to you last night after quitting time and you have already made more progress on it than there's been in years. You will do fine on the Douglass case, Liv. You're ready for this. More than ready. And this case is ready for you. It's a mess and you're the perfect candidate to straighten it out."

I was wide-eyed and grew still. I blinked, and then smiled. But just a little.

"You know you have a dimple?" His comment came out of the blue and, until then, I hadn't known how close I'd been standing to him.

I stepped back and lowered my head. "Why do you call everyone else by their last name? But not me?"

He cleared his throat. "I promised to train you. In less than a month, you may decide to resign. So I don't have much time left. And I always make good on my promises."

I wanted to say something. Something meaningful. "Then when should I start?"

Streeter grinned, picked up a file from his desk, and handed it to me, saying, "How about right now?"

CHAPTER 14

AS THE MORNING RAYS spilled through the tiny windows of her kitchen, Irma Casey shuffled busily about, making breakfast for her husband and son.

She had picked through her white hair, erasing any signs of bedhead, and had carefully applied her foundation, powder, and eye shadow before penciling in brown eyebrows over her nearly invisible white ones. She had filled in her narrow, light pink lips with a light mocha shade of lipstick and outlined them in a darker shade. She had buttoned up a beautifully patterned dress of various shades of brown flowers, accented by a large, lacy white lapel, collar, and cuffs. Sliding on a new pair of pantyhose and slipping into her comfortable brown flat leather shoes, Irma had quietly made her way to the kitchen and slipped on her neatly folded clean white apron. A handsome woman in her late seventies, she had always been particular about looking her best, regardless of the day and regardless of the activities. Today was no different.

Martin sidled up behind her as she was scrambling the eggs and wrapped his arms around her expansive waist. "Morning, sweetheart."

"Good morning," Irma answered, turning to face him and kissing him on the cheek. "Can I pour you some orange juice?"

"Maybe after I drink my roughage," Martin answered, pointing to the jar of orange-flavored soluble fiber his doctor had recommended he drink daily.

Irma offered him a tight smile and asked, "Would you make me one too, please, dear?"

"Certainly," Martin replied. After completing the task, he handed her one of the glasses and toasted her. "To your health."

They both drank their orange drink, wrinkling their noses when they finished.

Irma said, "It never gets any better tasting, does it?"

Taking the emptied glass from her, he shook his head and asked, "Can I help you with something, my dear?"

Martin was a tall, thin man in his early eighties with thick white hair and pale skin. His shoulders had become slightly stooped in his older age and his small potbelly had become more pronounced. Martin stood at least a head taller than his bride of sixty years, but her high hairdo made up a bit of the difference. Because of Irma's influence, Martin also always looked his best. His light gray linen pants had been neatly pressed, with a stiff crease down the middle of each leg. His short-sleeved white button-down shirt, which he had carefully tucked into his belted pants, had been generously starched and pressed. The black wing-tip shoes had been polished and shined just this morning, and the lenses of his silver wire-rimmed glasses had been immaculately cleaned. Although it was Tuesday morning, the retired couple, as always, appeared to be donning their Sunday best.

Irma answered her husband's offer to help, "Thank you, sweetheart. Would you please set the table and turn the bacon?"

"Be happy to," he answered with a smile, followed by a delightful humming.

As Martin carefully laid the dishes on the lace place mats and creatively folded the matching white linen napkins into a shape that looked like a budding lily, he asked his wife, "Is Stewart awake?"

"I don't know. Did you hear him go out last night? I thought I heard him go out around ten thirty or so," she replied, stirring the scrambled eggs in the frying pan and adding a sprinkle of freshly grated Parmesan cheese for flavor.

"You know I don't hear a thing without my hearing aids," Martin answered. After turning the strips of bacon in the frying pan, he gently set the dishes below the ornate napkins and perfectly situated each place setting, fork on the left and spoon and knife on the right.

"What are we going to do about all of his disappearances and his refusal to let us know where he's going?" Irma demanded with concern in her motherly tone.

Martin sighed heavily, distributing three glasses for juice above each place setting. "He's forty-two, Irma. He's a grown man. We aren't going to be around forever to babysit him. He needs to learn to spread his wings and fly on his own."

Irma turned off the burner under the eggs and wiped her hands on the dish towel beside the sink. "He may be forty-two, but he's hardly a grown man in many ways. You heard what the doctors said at his appointment on his fortieth birthday." She peeked around her husband into the hall outside the kitchen, watching to see if her son was within earshot, and leaned toward Martin, whispering, "Stewart has the mentality of a twelve- or thirteen-year-old, and I very much doubt if he will ever grow much beyond that. He may be forty-two, he may know how to drive, and he may insist on being on his own, but Martin, he is a long way from being a grown man."

Irma stared up into her husband's face intently. After a few moments, she added quietly, "Did I tell you what he did at the grocery store last week? He lifted a woman's skirt for no reason. I was so embarrassed and all he did was answer with that smile of his."

Martin chuckled, which earned him a slap to his forearm.

Irma scolded, "It's not funny, Martin. We could be sued. I took the young lady aside and explained that our boy has fragile X syndrome. She reminded me that we had met last year at the neighborhood barbecue. She's the young lady who lives three doors down and across the hall. The door that had the blue flower arrangement and tan ribbons. You know the girl. The redhead who drives the yellow Saturn? She looked a little shook up, but took it very well. What if she hadn't?"

"Irma, I know he's our only child, but you must remember he's just going through puberty. He's interested in what makes girls tick and he's starting to discover they make him tick, if you know what I mean. I'm glad he did that now, so we can teach him the difference between right and wrong. Especially in his behavior with women. Look at it as an opportunity," Martin replied patiently.

After a moment, she sighed. "You're probably right. But it is so frightening to think what he will do next. Especially if we're not around to help him out of his trouble."

Martin patted her arm tenderly and replied, "We can't always be there for him. We won't be around forever. You know that, don't you?"

A tear had filled her eye and she nodded.

Changing the subject as he always did before he became too emotionally invested in the conversation, Martin asked, "What can I do next for you, dear?"

"You can cut the banana bread while I go wake up Stewart," Irma answered.

As she removed her apron, folded it neatly, and placed it on the kitchen counter, Martin scanned the kitchen.

"What banana bread?" he asked.

"It's right over—"

Irma did not finish her sentence when she saw that the place on the counter where she had set her freshly baked banana bread to cool the previous evening was now bare.

Down the hall, Stewart stretched in the morning light as it touched his face through the half-open curtains of his bedroom window. His boxer shorts stretched tight and the sheets rubbed against him. How he loved mornings, Stewart thought as he touched himself. He giggled when he remembered what the teenage boys had said in the booth behind him at the burger joint last week. They talked about how one of the boy's mothers had seen him playing with his "morning missile" and how embarrassed he was.

It wasn't the fact that these boys understood the secret he'd discovered about how much fun he could have playing with his own penis, but that they had so appropriately named it a "morning missile." Long and stiff and ready to fire. Stewart giggled again at the thought.

He was enjoying himself more this morning than he ever had, considering he had experienced one of the best times of his life last night. He had met Liv Bergen again, face to face, and she remembered who he was, had smiled at him, and even shook his hand. No girl had ever done that before, and that automatically meant she was his new girlfriend.

In February, when he first met her at the neighborhood barbecue, Stewart immediately liked her and took lots of pictures of her. That night he also saw Cassandra, the redhead girl, who lived in the apartment down the hall. But he had known her for a long time.

Neither girl knew he had taken so many pictures of them at the party. He was careful, like always, not to let them or his parents know that he had taken any picture of girls, deleting all the digital files he had of Liv and Cassandra. That was his secret. He kept the paper images of them under his mattress.

He always wore three cameras around his neck so people would think he was an important photographer with the local newspaper. That's what important photographers did. They had lots of cameras around their necks. Stewart saw several photographers at a Denver Nuggets game one night and noticed how close to the basketball hoops and players they could get without anyone noticing, just because they had cameras around their necks.

After he asked his parents for a camera three birthdays in a row, Stewart tried his reporter trick at the local junior high school by wrapping all three cameras around his neck and walking out on the basketball floor beside the boys on the bench. Although he wasn't the best photographer in the world, he used up his entire memory card during the game, taking lots of action shots.

Some of the boys even posed for him after the game on their way to the locker room, which made him feel important. He had used up all his memory, but he pretended to take pictures of them anyway to make sure they let him stay close to the game.

His mom was mad at him when she took the memory card in to be processed and saw that he had taken a hundred and eight pictures of one junior high basketball game. When he apologized to her that he would get better with practice, she explained to him that she wasn't upset because of the quality of pictures he had taken. Instead she was upset because of the quantity.

She explained that although the memory card was not very expensive, the pictures were very expensive to develop. She also explained that his dad was retired, which meant he no longer made money, meaning they would have to make sure their savings lasted as long as it could and that they couldn't just fritter it away on developing pictures.

When Stewart cried, upset about losing a new hobby that made him someone important, his mother agreed to let him get six of his favorite images made into photos each month; plus, she agreed to buy him a used color printer and allowed him twelve sheets of clean paper a month to print his next-favorite images.

Stewart loaded his one memory card into his favorite camera yet strapped all three cameras around his neck. When he wanted to stay close to someone or when he wanted to pretend to be an important reporter, he would use one of the two cameras with no memory. When he wanted to capture an image he really liked, he would use the camera with memory. At the end of the month, he'd spend hours studying the hundreds of shots he'd taken to find the six he wanted to make into photos, then his twelve favorites for printing on paper.

No one had ever learned his trick about his important camera. Not even his parents.

After that, he never left the house without his three cameras draped around his neck. It was who he had become. His public image. He was important. He had become so important that the kids in the neighborhood had given him a new name. They called him Camera Casey. It described who he was and he liked it. When he left the house, he was no longer Stewart Casey. Instead, he was Camera Casey. He didn't even like his parents tagging along with him when he was Camera Casey, because he was more important than that. Parents who called him Stewart couldn't hold him back when he was Camera Casey.

The night of the neighborhood barbecue, Stewart had used paper for March and April to print images of Liv and Cassandra from that night. He mostly used the unloaded cameras, saving the one with the memory card for pretty girls. When his mother took his favorite six images to be developed at the grocery store at the end of the month, Stewart begged her to let him pick them up and pay for them so he could feel independent.

The real reason he wanted to pick up the developed pictures was that he thought she would take the pictures from him if she found out what he had shot. He had convinced her and he taped the girls' photos all over the walls in his room. His parents were not allowed in his room. It was his private area and he liked it that way. The only bad part was he had to clean his room himself and do his own laundry. That was what his parents made him do if his room was to remain his private area.

Stewart had taken some other pictures of Liv Bergen since the barbecue, like when she would run and stretch or go for long walks with her dog in the neighborhood. Last night, he took a picture of Liv in the lobby, lifting her shirt to show him her jog bra. She liked him. She'd make a good girlfriend. She was much friendlier than Cassandra.

But Liv would have to let him keep his favorite picture, the picture he most enjoyed when he touched his "morning missile," which was one he secretively took of Cassandra sunning herself by the pool. She was lying on her stomach, wearing only the bottoms of her pink swimming suit, having untied the top. She had fallen asleep, her long red hair spilling over the edge of the lawn chair, and she had shifted her weight slightly, allowing just a bit of her round, white breast to be seen underneath her bare back and side. Stewart had difficulty deciding whether he should take pictures or if he should touch himself that hot August day, but he was happy to have at least taken a few pictures of her first.

He hid the picture of Cassandra lying on her stomach underneath his mattress, just in case his mother ever did come into his private area and demand he take the pictures down from his walls. He looked at that picture of Cassandra often.

And now he'd have one of Liv, too.

Last week at the grocery store, he saw Cassandra in her yellow sundress and took some pictures of her. She was standing in the fruit section and she seemed like she was enjoying Stewart's attentions, until he got too close to her and tried to take a picture underneath her dress.

She pulled away from him and screamed, "What are you doing?"

That embarrassed Stewart, but not as much as when his mother scolded him in public for what he had done. He didn't like Cassandra anymore. He took all of her pictures down from his wall and put them in the back of his dresser drawer, leaving only those of Liv taped all over his room.

Although he had left the picture of Cassandra with the half-exposed breast under his mattress since it was his best picture. Because he didn't like her anymore and she was no longer his girlfriend, he just imagined that it was Liv sunning herself in the pink bikini.

Even before last week's embarrassing moment with Cassandra at the grocery store, Stewart had been thinking about making Liv his girlfriend instead of Cassandra. He had seen her on television in March with some kid in a wheelchair, who was getting some silly medal from the governor of Colorado. He didn't know why Liv was with them. She looked beautiful. Her smile was dazzling and she looked like a beauty pageant queen when she waved to the crowd. At one point when the Channel Nine News camera zoomed in on the kid and on Liv, she had looked directly into the camera's lens and smiled. That smile was for him, Stewart was sure of it.

Yesterday, Stewart decided to get some better pictures of Liv and waited for her outside in the bushes until she returned from her run. But then it rained. So he came inside and waited. He had taken some pictures of her stretching in her gray FBI T-shirt and black shorts before she had left for her run and took some more of her when she came back. He couldn't wait until his mother took the pictures down to the grocery store to have them developed. Besides when she lifted her shirt and he saw her jog bra, there was one other picture of Liv in particular that he thought would turn out good enough to replace the one under his mattress.

When Liv was warming up for her run, she had spread her legs shoulder-width apart and had stretched her arms behind her back, clasping her hands together. It made her breasts stick out in her gray T-shirt. He thought he could see her nipples through her T-shirt and almost dropped his camera. He managed to keep his cool just long enough to take a shot, maybe even clearly enough to see her nipples.

He would replace the picture under his mattress.

The knock on his door startled him. His mother called, "Stewart? Are you awake?"

Stewart rolled his eyes and lay spread-eagle on the bed. "Yes, mother."

"Breakfast is ready. Would you like to join us?" the muffled voice behind the door asked sweetly.

"I'll be right down, mother," Stewart called.

As he pulled on his dark blue pants and white cotton shirt, Stewart thought about Liv and how different she was from Cassandra. Cassandra didn't remember his name and never spoke to him when she passed him in the halls or lobby. He wondered why he ever let her be his girlfriend in the first place. Maybe she should pay for embarrassing him at the grocery store. Stewart slipped his leather loafers over each elongated foot. He should just forget about Cassandra. Besides, he had Liv now and that's all that mattered. She was his new girlfriend and she was prettier than Cassandra anyway.

As he tightened his belt and combed his wavy black hair into place, he smiled at himself in the mirror, realizing how easy it must have been for Liv to fall in love with him. She must feel like the luckiest girl in the world this morning, he thought. As he drew in a deep breath, Stewart could smell the scrambled eggs and bacon that his mother had just cooked. He licked his lips. As he made his way out of his private area and down to the kitchen, he could picture Liv sitting at her kitchen table this morning, drinking her coffee and eating a slice of the banana bread.

And he imagined she'd be thinking of him.

CHAPTER 15

"SPECIAL AGENT MARSHALL, PLEASE," I said.

I heard a series of clicks as the receptionist transferred my call. I glanced at the clock on my desktop. Streeter had asked me to be ready to go with him up to Fort Collins in thirty minutes on the Douglass case. Plenty of time to make some calls on Brianna's case.

The man's voice was low and unemotional. "Marshall."

"This is Special Agent Liv Bergen with the Denver bureau," I said, hoping that was all he'd need to know, imagining that somehow he already knew I was the poor schmuck who ended up with his cold case. But I got no response. "I was given your cold case file on the Keller abduction and wondered if you had time to answer some questions for me."

I heard nothing but slow breathing on the other end of the phone. Then the man asked, "The Brianna Keller case? What'd you say your name was?"

"Liv Bergen. I'm an agent at the Denver bureau." Another long pause. For a second I thought I had the wrong name and I quickly flipped through the file. "Agent Bo Marshall?"

"Yeah, I heard you." The man on the other end didn't sound pleased. At all.

Not knowing how interoffice politics worked, I simply charged forward and asked, "Are you pissed at me? Or at someone else? For having your case taken from you?"

"I'm pissed that I wasn't told."

"No one told you they assigned me your cold case?"

"No one told me they assigned the cold case to a relative. Liv Bergen, as in Colonel Barbara Bergen's sister. You're Brianna Keller's aunt, right?"

I closed my eyes and cradled my head in my free hand. I realized I had just stepped in something. Probably not only getting Streeter in trouble, but getting Marshall's SAC in trouble, too.

"I know that case inside and out. There is no one who wanted to solve that case more than I did. Not even you, Special Agent Liv Bergen."

The frosty way he said my title and name made me feel worse than I already did.

"I understand. I am so sorry, Bo. Can I call you Bo? Yes, I am Brianna's aunt." From feeling like I was on top of the world to feeling like shit. Within seconds. A new record for me.

"So what the hell is this place coming to if they're turning a blind eye to the fox guarding the henhouse?"

That caught me off guard. "You think my sister was behind the abduction?"

Nothing.

"Shorty? Brianna's dad?"

The man sighed. "No, I wasn't saying that. I just think it's dangerous to have any relative reviewing or investigating a case. Active, cold, or otherwise."

"I agree," I said.

"Then why the hell is the Keller case lying on your desk, Special Agent Liv Bergen?"

"Will you quit calling me that?" No response. "Because they don't want me to quit," I answered honestly. "And call me Liv."

Special Agent Bo Marshall started chuckling and said, "Okay, now you've piqued my interest. What's this about?"

I told him how I'd been working as a limestone miner and how I had met the FBI on a couple of cases last summer before being asked to join the bureau as the handler for Beulah, how I'd finished my training at Quantico this past fall, and how I had jeopardized my nephew at Christmas. And I told Bo how I was tired of jeopardizing my family and was contemplating quitting the FBI.

"After only six months on the job?"

"Five months," I said, angry that he found this so funny. "And it would have been sooner if Streeter hadn't talked me into staying for six months before I finalize my decision."

I thought the pause meant that I had once again lost Agent Marshall until he said, "Streeter? As in Special Agent Streeter Pierce?"

"Yeah, he's the one who decided to let me run with this cold case. So I could see how being an FBI agent was helpful, not hurtful, to my family. Didn't your SAC tell you?"

"No, she didn't. But I'm not surprised. If she had, I would have refused," the man said, no longer sounding pissed. More like annoyed.

"You're not a fan of Streeter's?" I wasn't sure I really wanted to hear his answer.

"Oh, quite the opposite. I'm a huge fan of Streeter Pierce. Best field agent in the country. I would have refused to give up the cold case and demanded they let me work the case with him, if I'd known he was the one asking for it. So I could learn more about his investigative techniques."

Something stirred inside me.

"What the hell are you thinking?"

I was startled by the fervor with which he scolded me. "What do you mean, what am I thinking?"

"Don't you know how lucky you are working with that legend? I, for one, would give my right testicle just to observe him on one case."

I was starting to see a pattern emerge. I was running into fans of Streeter Pierce everywhere I turned. I could see why. I'd recognized my strong attraction and desire to work with Streeter the instant I first met him. But I never really considered that everyone else shared my sentiments.

"Well, I think giving a testicle would be a bit drastic, Bo, but thank you for pointing out my idiocy," I said. I felt quite foolish for thinking the way I had about giving up this opportunity at the bureau. "Look, help me out on some questions and maybe I can get you tickets to Streeter's concert the next time he headlines in Vegas."

"Smart-ass. You have no idea, do you? You joke about him, but seriously, Bergen, Streeter Pierce is a rock star in this line of work. And if I may be so blunt, you're an idiot if you don't recognize the opportunity you have to work with this guy."

"That I am."

During another long pause, I checked the clock. Marshall finally said, "And clearly he must see something in you to be working so hard to convince you to stay. So if I were you, I'd get this case solved and behind you before his ass is called on the carpet in John Chancellor's office in DC. Because if you're the cause for Streeter Pierce going down, you'll have more haters on you than ticks on a sorry mongrel. Do you hear what I'm saying?"

Agent Marshall's delivery showcased a Southern influence I hadn't detected earlier in the phone call. I appreciated his passion for Streeter's skill and experience. And agreed with him. Every word. Although Marshall's honesty stung a bit, the raw truth allowed me to see the predicament I had placed Streeter in from a different angle. And I was ashamed.

"So, help me get this cold case solved and maybe everyone can walk away . . . tickless," I offered.

"If I could have solved this case, don't you think I would have already?"

"When's the last time you ran the partial print through AFIS?"

"Just before I turned the files over to my SAC. Yesterday morning."

My heart sunk. Dodson would get no hits on AFIS. "How about manual manipulation of the print for enhanced diagnostics?"

"Sent it to DC and asked their best image analyst to work their magic. Nothing."

Discouraged, I hoped the brilliant Mitch Dodson would find a different angle to work. "Did you do any searches that led you to cases with similarities? Victim profile? Modus operandi? A possible repeat offender, especially in the Greater Las Vegas area?"

A long pause before Marshall answered, "Of course I did."

I waited a long moment, wondering what it was I detected in this Vegas agent's tone. Disgust? Concern? Impatience?

I heard the puff of breath he expelled before saying, "You do your own looking and then we'll compare notes. Maybe you'll see something I didn't."

Like the bunny, I thought.

Brianna despised bunnies, was scared to death of them. Yet nowhere in the case file did it suggest that Marshall or the Hawthorne investigator asked my sister about the stuffed animal found near my niece's body. And Barbara didn't indicate that she connected my line of questioning last night to Brianna's death, only to our brother Jens's childhood.

From the file, investigators must have assumed that my niece was clutching the toy when she was hurled from the car at a high speed and that she dropped the stuffed animal on impact with the ground. The bunny was assumed to have come with Brianna from her bedroom that night. But it didn't. I was sure of that.

"Okay, but first tell me where the evidence you gathered from the crime scene is."

"Headed your way. Addressed to your SAC. The boxes were sent overnight," Marshall said. "What is it you're wanting, specifically?"

Although my mind immediately jumped to the bunny, I thought I should be more discreet, in case the bunny turned out to be nothing. And if it turned out to be a critical clue he'd overlooked, I would find a way to give Bo Marshall the credit. He deserved that after investigating this case all these years. He was clearly passionate about justice for my niece.

"What exactly am I looking for?"

"Bovier."

CHAPTER 16

I HAD A NAME. And Marshall had had enough. He hung up.

I taped my niece's picture on the bare wall behind me to the left of the window and went to work on the keyboard at my computer. At first, nothing but articles on cows appeared and I realized that my autocorrect had changed my search term to *bovine*. Then I got nothing but dogs. Big, black, curly-haired breed known as Bouvier des Flandres. Then I typed in several different spellings and combinations of words—all failed attempts according to the content—until I typed in "Las Vegas Bovier." Twenty-seven matches flashed on my screen, most of which applied to the murder of a girl similar in age to Brianna.

This was the information Marshall had expected me to find.

"Jackpot," I said aloud.

Punching the print key, I listened to the printer whir into motion. The pages started discharging in rapid succession and within seconds I had printed everything in the print queue. By the time I glanced up at the clock on my computer, I had narrowed the "keep" pile to three articles and had tossed the balance.

As I scanned, read, and reread the articles for the last time, I finally decided to throw out one of the articles, cut out the color pictures from the second article, and keep the third article for my file. The quality of the color photos depicting a high school senior picture of Lance Bovier and the second-grade class picture of Tia Mulberry were fairly good, considering my new office printer was not best known for graphics output. I carefully trimmed around each of the pictures, dragging my finger lovingly along the two-dimensional dark cocoa cheek of the little girl known as Tia. She was younger than Brianna had been.

And somehow, according to Agent Bo Marshall, there was a connection between Tia and Brianna.

I placed the photos on the desk in front of me, the little girl on my right and the high school senior on my left, while I read the article for a final time before adding it to my file.

On the editorial page of the *Las Vegas Chronicle*, guest columnist Su Panini wrote:

> It seems incomprehensible how something so horrific can be so satisfying. In a bizarre turn of events in the tragic Mulberry murder case, last Friday Lance Bovier was given clemency by Governor Ubeck from the mandatory sentence of forty years in the state penitentiary for his conviction on second-degree murder, the strangulation of eight-year-old Tia Mulberry.
>
> A year ago yesterday, Bovier, a straight-A honor student from Washington High School, admittedly lured little Tia Mulberry away from her mother, who was playing the slot machines at a local casino. Bovier enticed Tia into the men's bathroom only a few yards away from where her mother sat by offering the little girl a surprise that he kept hidden from her behind his back. Once inside one of the bathroom stalls, he brutally raped and strangled her, for what Bovier himself called "just the thrill of it."
>
> The mind-boggling question might be how a seventeen-year-old, who should have been home preparing his valedictorian speech at graduation, was instead compelled

to lure a little girl into a casino bathroom and, ultimately, to crush the life out of her terrified, defenseless body. But an even more perplexing question is how Governor Ubeck found it necessary to grant this hideous killer clemency. Ubeck insisted that this young man's life was completely ruined by the excessive punishment of forty years of incarceration for one single, horrible mistake.

But what about the little girl's life? Gone. Not to mention her family's lives, which were also shattered by one single, horrible choice that Bovier made? Do they get clemency from their suffering? Are they less of the victim because this was his first crime?

I thought about my sister and her kids, knowing they never received clemency from their suffering. Ever. I continued to read the article.

Governor Ubeck also said that we must recognize that "this troubled young man with no previous record of any deviancy and with tremendous potential could contribute a great deal to our society with his staggeringly impressive intellect." That we must give him a second chance, or we are just as guilty as he is, only our mistake would be unforgivable.

Does the little girl get a second chance to live, Governor? Do her parents get a second chance to hold her and kiss her goodnight? Excuse me, sir, but in all due respect, how can you possibly criticize those of us who believe that Lance Bovier should be punished for his hideous crime— for brutally murdering little Tia, an innocent victim, and destroying her family—and then in the same breath allow the monster to go free, someone who brutally raped and squeezed the life out of that helpless, little girl, "just for the thrill of it"?

I glanced back at the name of the person writing the article, in case it was a name that should matter to me, strike a memory. Su Panini.

No, Governor Ubeck, we would not be guilty of an unforgivable mistake. It's called justice. You are the one who has made an unforgivable mistake by listening to Lance's father's plea for his son's freedom, by jeopardizing our children with your decision to release that monster last Friday. How could you do such a thing? It couldn't possibly be because the murdered girl was black and the murderer was white. We have evolved as a civilization way beyond that, haven't we? It couldn't possibly be because Lance's father, Vincent Bovier, was the single largest fundraiser for your campaign two years ago, could it, Governor Ubeck? That would be far too obvious even to those of us simpletons unfamiliar with the seedy inner workings of the political machine, wouldn't it?

My only solace is the hope that someone out there will recognize and correct your hideous mistake before it is too late. I am not suggesting that two wrongs make a right, but I cannot deny the overwhelming sensations I am enjoying, which include resolution, satisfaction, elation, and yes, even gratitude, for whatever repercussions come Lance Bovier's way after his release. What other choice are we left with other than to turn a blind eye to our so-called political leaders who have learned how to twist the judicial fabric to their own personal liking?

I smiled when I finished reading Ms. Panini's column, agreeing with every single word of her rant. I stared at the beautiful black eyes of Tia Mulberry in the second-grade picture. Her hair had been fixed in multiple braids and colorful ribbons. Her dimpled smile was wide and she was missing two of her front teeth.

Tears had welled in my own eyes as I imagined Tia's hideous and frightening death. As I imagined Brianna being pushed or falling—or jumping—from the speeding car. Jumping? Did I really believe that? Did my niece jump so she wouldn't have to experience the same fate as Tia? Was she that frightened by the man who abducted her?

Tia must have been so afraid, I thought. She must have felt so alone, so isolated, during those last moments of life as she stared into the angry eyes of that evil, bored teenager, a complete stranger. A single tear slid down my cheek and splashed across one corner of her picture. I cursed myself and dabbed the corner dry.

I carefully lifted her picture and spun in my chair. I taped Tia beside Brianna on my bare wall to the left of my window, studying Tia's face. Agent Marshall must have done the same thing for years, studying Tia and Brianna, wondering if somehow the cases were related.

I searched the computer for any listing of Lance Bovier in the Las Vegas area. Nothing. I expanded my search to include the entire state. Nothing. No one in the United States named Lance Bovier.

Knowing I had a few more minutes before I had to be in Streeter's office, I jotted down the name of the prison where Lance Bovier had last been held. I called only to learn that they had released Bovier two years ago but would give no other information to me about the case. Even though I told them I was a federal agent.

I called the newspaper so I could talk with Su Panini, the brilliant author of the article written just before Lance Bovier's release, only to confirm that she never worked at the paper, wrote the article as a guest columnist. Panini had asked to write the piece and they had never heard from her again. After that article was written, thousands of fans commented on Ms. Panini's op-ed, and the publisher wanted to hire her to write more. They spent six months looking for Su Panini and began the search again a year later when she won acclaim—an obscure newsprint award for best guest columnist piece in the western states—for her touching article.

When the newspaper tried to locate Panini to present her with the award, they had no luck finding her. According to the newspaper, after an exhaustive investigative search on the identity of Su Panini, their conclusion was that she never really existed and that someone was using the name as an alias. They'd also linked the submitted op-ed piece to a public library in Las Vegas.

I asked if they would be kind enough to send me their findings, and although the few people I had talked with at the newspaper said they would try, I got the sense they were reluctant to share anything with me, with law enforcement. I assumed it was because they didn't want to be accused of poor journalism, not validating or verifying the source of the guest article. I gave them my email address, just in case one of them thought of something more.

I stared at the picture of Tia, thinking through where to turn next in the investigation. I made a quick call to the only Vincent Bovier listed in Las Vegas, hoping he would tell me where I might find his son.

The man's voice was as hard and bitter as a weathered coffee bean. "Why do you people keep calling me?"

I wondered what he meant. Had Bo Marshall called him, too? Others?

"Haven't I lived through enough already without you people constantly digging up old bones?"

"Old bones?" I parroted, wondering why the odd choice of words.

"What do you want from me, anyway? Isn't it enough he's paid the ultimate price?"

"What are you talking about, Mr. Bovier? Who?"

"My son!" he hollered into the phone. "Wasn't it enough they killed him?"

"Who? Who killed him? Your son, Lance, is dead?"

But the man was mumbling as if I weren't even on the line. "My fault. I got him out of that rat hole. Only to get him killed."

"Your son was murdered?" I asked. "When? How?"

"Right after he was released. Strangled to death."

"In Vegas?" I asked, wondering why I hadn't seen anything like that in my search.

"In Atlantic City. We had encouraged him to get out of town, lay low for a while. Had him holed up with a false identity. Until the heat was off him," the man mumbled. "Barbarians."

I was thinking about how Lance had strangled Tia, a girl half his size, maybe even smaller. And I wondered if my view could ever become as distorted as Vincent's, even if I were a parent.

"Left him lying in the stall of a filthy bathroom," Vincent Bovier was saying.

"Isn't that what your son did to that little girl?" I thought my candor might cause him to hang up. Although my words were harsh, he must have detected the sincerity in my tone.

After a long pause, he said, "You cops are all alike. No respect. He was drunk. A child himself. Didn't know any better. I've spent the last two years trying to clean up what's left of his reputation. Scrubbing the Internet, threatening lawsuits over 'public' information."

I resisted the urge to argue with him. Instead, I tried to keep him focused. "Do you know who did this to your son, Mr. Bovier?"

"I know for a fact who did this to him."

I wasn't thinking he'd actually tell me. And found it incredible when he did.

"Su Panini."

CHAPTER 17

MAKING MY WAY UP the gray brick steps of the city-owned building that housed the police department, I couldn't help but think about Su
Panini, who she was and where she disappeared to two years ago.

I focused on every stone step, trying to get my mind moving from Brianna's case to the Douglass case. Expensive steps. I wondered if the citizens
of Fort Collins knew how fortunate they were to have a robust, healthy
local economy that afforded them such exquisite municipal benefits.

As quickly as I wondered if the citizens appreciated their riches, I
wondered what percentage of the many millions of dollars in the city cof-
fers were taxes coming from creative geniuses, academicians, and high-
tech businesses, for which the area was known, as compared to the less
glamorous but stable basic industries—ranching, farming, mining—that
had supported the area for over a century.

As I made my way through the large glass doors, I instantly felt the
rush of air blowing in my face. It had that new-car smell, too, which must
have come from the long stretch of light gray industrial carpet, expertly
trimmed in royal blue and maroon and unworn, as if it had been installed
yesterday. The matching maroon steel piping throughout the building,
fashionably twisted into stair banisters and balcony rails, gave the building

a contemporary look. The royal blue light fixtures that hung from the vaulted ceilings provided the artistic touch tying all of the color schemes together. The whole space was lighted naturally with the many windows and skylights.

Frankly, I thought the space looked more like an art gallery than a police department.

Locating the marquee that contained the department's directory, I ran my finger down the names until I found the listing for chief of police. The name behind it had been recently pulled from the board, and Theresa Fiero's name had not yet been inscribed. I took the stairs two at a time and walked down the expansive hall of the second floor. "Chief of" was etched on one door of the glass suite; "Police" on the other. I pushed my way through, hearing the slight whoosh of disturbance I had caused, and walked toward the receptionist.

The woman with long, dark hair pursed her lips as I approached. It appeared that the bespectacled receptionist was studying—with great regard—every inch of my body from head to toe. I felt suddenly very self-conscious and made a quick inventory of my attire, reminding myself I was indeed appropriately dressed in my dark suit, white cotton T-shirt, and solid blue silk blouse. I had pulled my long, brown hair into a loose French twist and I wore little diamond earrings in each lobe, as I always did. And I felt naked without my Smith & Wesson revolver or my 9mm Sig Sauer, having left both under the car seat, although I could have just as easily concealed either of them in the back of my waistband if I'd wanted to. I was, after all, law enforcement.

I said nothing until the receptionist was finished with her inspection of me. Maybe it was the boots.

"May I help you," the unpleasant woman whined.

"Yes. I am here to see Chief Fiero," I said confidently, to which the receptionist raised a suspicious eyebrow. "I have an appointment. I'm Special Agent Liv Bergen with the FBI. Special Agent Streeter Pierce was unable to come because of a last-minute issue that arose."

I wasn't happy that it was Jenna Tate who had raised the issue. She needed to leave town again. Suddenly. Needed a ride to the airport. From Street. Although Streeter's expression was apologetic as he told me to go on without him, the smile on Jenna's face would suggest she was not the least bit sorry for interrupting our plans. It didn't help that he shut the door behind me as I left, leaving the two alone in his office.

Thank God for the glass doors, was all I could think. Thanks to them, I wouldn't be tortured by what they might be doing in there.

The receptionist's skepticism all but disappeared. Her cheeks flushed and she stammered, "The FBI . . . oh . . . Ms. Bergen. I mean, Agent Bergen. Please, have a seat and I'll tell the chief you're here."

The woman ducked behind her large counter and pressed the intercom and whispered, "The FBI woman is here to see you, Chief. Liz Bergen."

I smiled at her calling me Liz instead of Liv. A common error. Within seconds, a professional-looking woman with short auburn hair and a dark blue dress suit emerged from beyond the receptionist's desk. She walked confidently toward me, wearing a friendly smile.

"Liv," the woman said, gripping my hand firmly. "Nice to meet you. Streeter told me so much about you. I'm Theresa Fiero."

"Nice to meet you," I said.

"And great smile. He told me about your dimples."

I felt my cheeks burn with embarrassment. Streeter talked to this woman about my dimples?

From the corner of my eye, I saw the receptionist shrink behind her counter, presumably to avoid retribution for her chilly reception or to avoid being reprimanded by her boss for getting my name wrong. Either way, I wasn't upset by any of it and thanked her.

"Bring two cups of coffee, please," Theresa instructed the receptionist. Then, turning to me, "Do you take cream or sugar?"

"Black is fine."

Theresa closed the door behind me.

"Chief Fiero, your office is fantastic." I was gawking at the vaulted ceiling, the beautifully decorated spaciousness, and the tastefully chosen Monet copies that added a hint of femininity to the otherwise masculine decor.

"Theresa, please," Fiero insisted. "Streeter called and told me he couldn't make it. Thanks for driving all the way up here. I know how valuable your time is and I appreciate you coming so early. Was the rush-hour traffic bad today on I-25?"

"No," I said. "I got a late start and avoided the morning rush-hour mess at the Mousetrap. It only took me about forty minutes. Planned on an hour and fifteen minutes to get here. So I found this great little restaurant downtown. The Silver Griddle, have you eaten there?"

"Definitely," Fiero answered. "It's a local favorite. Did you try one of their cinnamon rolls? They're the size of hubcaps, I swear."

"Next time."

"I think I've gained at least five pounds this past week since I got here." She patted her stomach as if she had just eaten one of the Silver Griddle's rolls. Fiero was a medium-sized woman in her mid-fifties, shaped like an apple, with thin, shapely limbs and hips accompanied by expansive breasts and waist.

I chuckled. "I behaved. Had a salad. You've only been here a week?"

"Salad? That figures. Just look at you." Fiero waved at my frame. "You're probably the type who forgets to eat. Me? I forget when to stop eating."

The conversations remained light as the grouchy receptionist entered with coffee.

Once she left, closing the door behind her, Fiero was all business. "I started a week ago. The old chief was fired. I've got a mess on my hands and I need your help." She let out a long sigh. "Where do I start? How much do you know about the Douglass case?"

"Mostly what I've read in the *Denver Post*," I answered honestly, which earned me a scolding look from Fiero.

"Anything else?"

"Streeter gave me the file this morning that you had sent him yesterday," I answered. "I read through it quickly but I admit, I haven't read it thoroughly. The chronicled events were very helpful, but I'm hoping you can fill in a lot of blanks for me. First of all, why did you call in the FBI?"

"Like I told you, I need your help," Fiero said, lighting up a cigarette. Then, as an afterthought, she asked, "Mind if I smoke? It's against city regulations to smoke in any municipal building. But what are they going to do? Arrest me?"

I smiled. I liked Fiero. Streeter would, too. I understood why they had picked her to replace the former chief, Bruce Schumaker, who the paper said resigned. But Fiero said he was fired. Probably asked to turn in his resignation or be fired. Fiero was tough and wouldn't take any crap from anyone. She would definitely be the candidate to pick for grabbing this raging bull of a case by the horns.

I had researched her background quickly before coming here and found out that Fiero had been the chief of police in Los Angeles during the rioting after the controversial Greg Richards trial that was so fraught with racial tension. She'd also been hired by New York City to get their gangs under control.

This lady took crap from nobody.

"Let me paint you a picture," Fiero said as she leaned against her desk and blew smoke at the ceiling. "On Valentine's Day, a six-year-old girl is found beaten, strangled, bound, and gagged in a toolshed in her own backyard several hours after the police had responded to a 911 call from her mother, saying her daughter had been kidnapped. The woman finds this ransom note, calls the police, and they come right over. We search their house and find nothing. This house is huge and has rooms and halls everywhere. It's like a maze."

"I heard somewhere that the Douglass family was quite wealthy," I said, watching as she drew more puffs on her cigarette.

"Filthy rich. And the ransom just happens to match the recent bonus paid Theodore Douglass. Nothing more. Anyway, we get the parents' statements and while we're searching the kid's room and the house for evidence, we send the father to look through the house again for anything out of the ordinary, something missing, broken, whatever. We really did it just to keep him busy. He's a type A, if you know what I mean, always needing to do something. So, they send him on a mission with a family friend, who had come to support the Douglasses. Within minutes, the father comes running in from the backyard, screaming and cradling his daughter's lifeless, stiff body in his arms. He's already removed the duct tape he said he found covering her mouth and he's untied the ropes that bound her hands."

I had a tough time imagining what that might be like. Finding your child. Dead. Bound and gagged. And again I heard the soft thump of the bunny against the desert sand. Told myself to focus on one case at a time.

Fiero took a long drag on her cigarette. "It's no surprise that three months later, we've got no arrest. The family is under an umbrella of suspicion. The parents refuse to cooperate with the department. Can't say that I blame them. We've done nothing but hound them as primary suspects. All we've got to show for our time is the near-total destruction of all evidence because of mishandling, the resignation of a senior investigator, and the filing of a defamation lawsuit by one of the officers. She was at the scene that day, the first officer to attend the father cradling the little girl. She claimed that she was defamed in the press by a fellow policeman who accused her of botching the evidence. Oh, and did I mention the no-confidence vote by the police union on their chief's performance, which subsequently led to his 'resignation'?"

"That's a lot going on in just a short time," I said.

"A lot of *bad* things going on. And that ain't all," Fiero said, leaning against her desk and hooking her ankles. "The backroom warring of a mayor and her city council. Missing or misplaced evidence. A request that the governor impanel a grand jury. Leaks all over the blooming place to the press. A town terrified that the murderer is still wandering their streets. Accusations that the department is on the take, has been bribed to look the other way from the millionaire father. An inexperienced police department handling the case. And an entire country outraged by the whole fricking mess."

Fiero sucked the last of her cigarette and twisted the butt into the ashtray she had pulled from inside her desk drawer.

"Did I forget anything?" Fiero asked herself. "Oh yes, and the case has the early signs of becoming one of the great unsolved mysteries of our time, at this rate. God forbid."

"You have your hands full, to say the least," I offered, feeling I had no response that would be worthy of her burdens. But if anyone could handle them, she could. She reminded me a lot of that actor Kathy Bates, which is probably why I liked her so much.

Fiero smirked, reaching for the scented aerosol spray, squeezing the trigger, and releasing liberal doses to chase the smoke. "Yeah, I've got my hands full."

Sitting at her desk and reaching into her top drawer, Fiero pulled out a stack of five-by-seven photographs and slid them across the desk toward me. I lifted them and studied them closely, flipping through slowly, one at a time.

The first picture was a close-up head-and-shoulder shot of the brown-eyed six-year-old, Rebecca Douglass, wearing a diamond-studded tiara in her salon-styled spun-gold hair, mascara stroked thickly on her lashes, eye shadow and liner around her sad eyes, mocha rouge streaking her chubby little cheekbones, and matching lipstick darkening her tiny, pouting lips.

The second photo was a full-body shot of Rebecca wearing a white ballet body stocking, white slippers, and a diamond-studded white silk cape that flowed freely to the ground, offering background for her bare arms and legs. A silver crown topped her golden hair, which was expertly curled, and her makeup was precisely applied once again. This time her lips were stretched across her face in a perfectly posed smile.

The third photo was of little Rebecca wearing a shiny gold two-piece and sitting on a beach towel with her arms behind her in a Farrah Faw-cett–like pose, her head thrown back, allowing her blonde locks to spill down her bare back. Her eyes had a haunting appearance and her seduc-tiveness appeared sadly misplaced on the juvenile's face.

"My word," I whispered.

"Toddler pageants, very popular. That's why her reality show had such high ratings. What can I say?"

"You can tell me why she looks so sad."

CHAPTER 18

I COULD HARDLY BELIEVE my eyes. I was staring at a six-year-old seductress. "What parent would allow this? She looks so unhappy."

"Allow it?" Fiero grunted with sarcasm. "They not only allowed it, the mother encouraged it, trained her to be the beauty queen she was at age six. She won more pageants in her short little life than I care to count, because each one makes me grow that much sicker to my stomach. That's how she got her own reality show."

I flipped to the next photo and flinched. Then I stared at it for a long time. The picture was of Rebecca, looking more like a six-year-old than in any of the other pictures I had seen.

She looked a dead six.

Rebecca's hair was tangled in a snarled mess behind her head on the wooden floor of her home's entryway, where her father had laid her. I knew this from scanning the report from that day, from Theodore Douglass's statement.

Her profile revealed bruises on the one side of her face and a slight red rash around her mouth where the duct tape had been removed. Her wrists red from where her hands had been bound behind her back. Her soiled, torn nightgown, which had been pushed up under her arms when her father first found her, was now pulled down to her knees, covering her naked buttocks, her panties missing. The dark, thin line around her neck from the obvious strangulation by some type of rope or cord had caused bruising from her chin to her tiny little shoulders and a slight bluing of her face.

I had unknowingly held my breath ever since Fiero handed me this picture, as if to ward off the stench of this hideously foul play. I let out a breathy, "Oh my," before taking in a deep breath. I felt inadequate to help Fiero and wished Streeter had come with me.

"This photo will give you nightmares, trust me," Fiero consoled. "That little girl has a haunting way about her."

"Don't you have any clue who may have done this to her?" I asked in disgust. Three months was nothing compared to the seven years that Brianna had already waited on us to find her killer, I thought. And it was far too long. And who was I to think I could help either girl?

"We had plenty of clues," Fiero stated bluntly. "But they've either been inadvertently destroyed by our own ineptness or lost somewhere in the process because of our own inexperience. Or have simply been made ineffectual because of the crippling statements made by disgruntled employees and by the district attorneys. Most of the evidence we have accumulated and used to direct our questions at suspects has been leaked to the damned press."

"The whole country learned about the ransom note left behind by the alleged kidnapper within hours of the child being found," I recalled.

"Leaked. Then there was the discovery of the enhanced 911 tapes. The latest find was that we had totally missed fibers found on the duct tape that Douglass ripped off his little girl's mouth. Those fibers may have helped us identify the killer early on in the case but would now be considered highly suspect if we introduced them as evidence in any trial. Hell, the whole world found out about that before we could even have them analyzed."

"Fibers? From what?"

"Theodore Douglass's bathrobe, but he denies ever wearing it. It was a gift years ago from his wife that he says he left in the spare bedroom, which is where we found it hanging." She sighed. "We're sinking faster than the *Titanic* because of all the leaks we have in our own department.

The problem is, there just isn't enough evidence to convict anyone in this wretched case." Fiero lit a second cigarette and drew a long breath.

"But you never answered my question. I understand your problem with convicting the killer. My question was, do you know who's responsible?"

Her expression said she did, but her words told me she was going to ignore my question. "And unfortunately, I don't see this getting any better."

"So how can I help?" I asked, knowing I wouldn't get her to tell me who she thought the killer was.

"For some reason," Fiero explained, "Bruce didn't want to get help from any 'outsiders.'" She moved both her index fingers in a quoting gesture when she said the word *outsiders*, and the long line of ashes dropped from her cigarette onto the carpet. She didn't seem to be bothered by that.

"When he resigned, the first thing I did was to call in the reinforcements. I asked Denver County's district attorney to help our Larimer County district attorney. I also asked two other counties to lend us their DAs. Then, I called in crime scene expert Dr. Richard Bentley, who will be flying in to meet with the district attorney and me next Friday at DIA, which, by the way, we'd love to have you join us. I've asked a prosecutor's task force to be established, including a DNA expert, a handwriting expert, a public relations expert. Hell, I think I'd even call in the Pope and a psychic if I thought it would help."

I smiled, wondering if Fiero knew how desperate she sounded.

"So where do you see me fitting in to all this?"

"I need you to help me with several things. First, I need access to your profiling capabilities. Independent of what we're doing. Which is why I haven't answered your question."

"I noticed."

"Then, I need some help from you on statement analysis, see what you think about all the statements we've taken so far and where you recommend we go from here. And finally, I heard you and Streeter did a great job with the abduction of that Williams boy at Christmas and I want you to go over all our files and see if we're missing something. The prosecution task force already has thirteen thousand pages documenting this case and we're not even close to completing our investigation. I need your expertise to look over my shoulder, see what we might be missing," Fiero explained.

I stood and walked over to Fiero's windows. Her view was westerly, toward the Rocky Mountains, just like my new office, but the distance to the mountains from Fiero's windows was much less than from mine. They were right there, close enough to touch.

I put my fists on my hips and turned to face Fiero. "Jack Linwood is one of the best profilers in the FBI. The best, in my opinion. I'll get his help on your first task. As far as statement analysis, I would be happy to see what I can do for you. But you and I both know there is no better analysis than that which is performed immediately after the crime, when the person is giving the initial statement. It can be done by studying the written documents, but it helps to direct the questions according to their response. To drill down."

Fiero pounded out the last of her second cigarette and pushed herself away from the desk. She walked to the other window and stared out at the traffic below. "I wasn't here and I can't tell you what Bruce knew or didn't know. I think we could arrange to have you meet with most of those involved, if you think more interviews would help. I don't know about the Douglass family. Like I said, they haven't been too cooperative lately."

"Why is that?" I asked.

"Our fault. Like idiots, we refused to release Rebecca's body to them so they could bury her after the autopsy was completed. We said we'd release her to them if the Douglasses agreed to cooperate with our department on some questions or assistance we needed. For cripes sake, what a thought. Why in the hell would we ever use a six-year-old's dead body as a bargaining chip for any reason? What in the hell were we thinking?"

I could tell Fiero was upset with the mess she had inherited from her predecessor and frustrated by how securely his mistakes had bound her hands for future investigations. She added more sympathetically, "I don't blame the Douglass family one bit. I wouldn't cooperate with us either if someone coerced me to cooperate by using my dead daughter's remains rather than just asking me to cooperate. That's just wrong."

I nodded and smiled.

Fiero changed her course. "Anyway, back to your original thought about the possibility of getting some of these people's statements in person. I'll work on that one. But tell me, do you want to do that first or is there a better angle here? What's your initial thinking on this?"

"I'd rather read through the files and statements first, see if I find anything unusual, any red flags. Then, I'll tell you what I find and maybe we can just bring in the individual or individuals who have questionable statements. Will that work for you?"

"That would be fine," Fiero said. "What about the overview, the second opinion on this whole situation?"

I looked away from her. "I'd be lying if I told you I wasn't interested to read through all of this and offer my two cents' worth. But Theresa, I have to tell you, I don't have any more experience than any of you. If you're looking for a fresh outlook, I'm your person. But if you're looking for someone to solve this thing, forget it. You don't need to know who did it. You already know that, don't you?"

Her mouth smiled, but her eyes did not.

I said, "You need someone to tell you how to resurrect evidence to *prove* who you think did this. Sounds like you've done the best you could. You want help convicting, not finding, the perpetrator. Am I right?"

"We're in a mess," Fiero said flatly. "I need to be sure—damned sure—before I make one move."

I nodded.

"Let me lay everything out for you, show you where all my files are, and we can get to work cleaning up this mess," Fiero resolved. "At least it's a start."

CHAPTER 19

THE OFFICE WAS ABANDONED this time of night.

I had buried myself in the Douglass files in Theresa's office for hours, barely noticing how much time had passed. I loaded some boxes into my car to bring back to the bureau.

Grabbing my sandwich and a cold bottle of water, I retreated down the hall and snapped on the light in my office. Beulah followed loyally at my side. I broke off a corner of my meal and fed it to my bloodhound, who was more interested in curling up and going back to sleep, not really keen on me waking her up and pulling her out of the canine day care.

The fluorescent bulbs glowed to life. I padded my way over to the desk and turned on my computer. Brianna and Tia met me face-to-face from the wall above my credenza and behind my desk, their smiles encouraging me to keep looking for answers. As I waited for my computer to power up, I slowly ate the sandwich, washing it down with water, and checked my text messages. Nothing from Jack. No text, no phone message, no email. Even though I had sent him a text about being assigned to the Douglass case. Nothing. I glanced up at the computer and clicked on the Internet browser.

The latest headlines grabbed my attention.

A twenty-six-year-old kidnapping case that Mitch Dodson told us about earlier in the week had finally been solved in Missouri. The missing girl's body had finally been found, buried in the yard of the man suspected of kidnapping her for ransom. The old man who'd been living under an alias—the suspect—was also found dead at his house.

"Good for you," I said to the photo of the Kansas City police chief making the announcement earlier today. She was quoted as saying, "Finally, peace can come to the Vanessa Greenwood family." And I wondered if Jack was the one who had helped her solve the case and in positively identifying Carl Halbrook as Clyde Hall.

A second headline grabbed my attention.

Breaking news, police lights flashing in the dark, a reporter live on the scene. I clicked on the video. Margaret Thurgood, the au pair on trial for the death of a toddler believed shaken to death, had been discovered dead in Cambridge, Massachusetts. The commentator said it was "a shocking end to the story that had dominated the news over the past year." No details were being shared by the investigators yet, but the taped-off scene behind the news reporter appeared to be a city park of some sort. No known cause of death, no speculation as to cause. Just that the mousy thirty-two-year-old Brit, who Americans had grown to hate over the last year, was now dead. The reporter speculated that the judge would declare a mistrial, ending the public outcry for justice in the Timmy Riley murder.

I sat back and studied the six-month-old boy's photo. And inexplicably, a peace settled over me with the knowledge that, at least in one case, justice seemed to be realized, even if the pressure of a public trial had caused Margaret Thurgood to commit suicide or have a heart attack or whatever it was that had happened to her in that park tonight.

At least Timmy Riley's parents had resolution. His killer was dead.

"Toodles," a voice sounded behind me, and I nearly leapt out of my skin.

I turned to see Jenna Tate sitting in a chair on the other side of my desk.

"How long have you been here?" I asked, my voice sounding much more wary than I'd intended.

"Long enough to wish I'd brought a sandwich, too. What are you working on?"

Her eyes slid to my computer monitor.

"Oh, nothing," I said. "Just catching up on the headlines before I go home."

"Mmm," she said, sounding unconvinced. "At one o'clock in the morning?"

"Weren't you supposed to fly somewhere?"

She smirked. "Been there and back already. And what have you learned so far on the Douglass case?"

My mouth opened automatically, but no words came out. Why was she here? What did she want from me? Had Streeter sent her? I hadn't been here all day, working the case alone with Fiero rather than with Streeter because of Jenna, yet here she was grilling me about the Douglass case I'd just been assigned.

"Not much yet," I said with a crooked grin. "But I'm working on it."

She stood up quickly and walked to the door with hurried steps. "Well, don't stay too long. Every woman needs her beauty sleep. Like I said, toodles."

And she was off.

I sat staring at the empty door for a long moment before glancing down at Beulah, realizing what a lousy guard dog she'd make. She hadn't even stirred awake when Jenna came in.

My inbox had a message from Special Agent Marshall in Las Vegas that read, "*Did you find Bovier?*"

I responded, "*On Douglass case. Lance dead. Father blames Su Panini. Who is she?*"

I didn't expect to hear from Marshall until the next day. It was nearly one o'clock in the morning here, which meant midnight in Vegas.

I clicked on the next email, which was from Dodson. "*No match in AFIS. Will work manually to enhance print.*"

I was about to tell him not to waste his time, that Agent Marshall had already asked the DC image analysts to manually manipulate the print, when an email popped into my inbox. From Bo Marshall. "*Panini doesn't exist. Alias. My opinion.*"

I typed a reply: "*Who's needing to hide behind an alias? Family member?*"

He responded with a question: "*Was Lance Bovier killed or given a death sentence?*"

I sat back and studied his reply. He already knew the answer. Bovier was given a death sentence for killing Tia. By some vigilante. He wanted me to come up with the same conclusion, which was easy to do.

If Su Panini, the adamant voice for those who didn't agree with the governor's clemency for Bovier, wasn't successful in keeping him behind bars, how far had she been willing to go? Panini grew silent after Bovier was found dead. Maybe she didn't want to be blamed for his execution. Or discovered as the vigilante. So she simply dropped off the face of the planet?

I typed, "*Are you at home or at work?*"

My direct line rang.

"Work," Marshall said when I answered the phone.

"Tell me about Su Panini."

"There is no such human being. Not in any system that we could search."

"What did the newspaper say about her?" I wanted to know if they told him the same thing they'd told me earlier today.

"Said everything they received from her was via email."

"How'd she cash her check? For the guest article?"

"She didn't. Only gave a PO box in Vegas, which was also a dead end."

"So we don't even know if Su Panini is a woman," I concluded. "Did you follow the IP address? For the emails?"

"ERT did. Led to the public computer stations at the downtown library," Bo explained.

"In Hawthorne?" I asked hopefully. I had so hoped there'd be a strong connection between Tia's death and Brianna's.

"Nope. Vegas. The day before Bovier was released."

"Vincent Bovier said Lance was killed in Atlantic City," I said. "Said he told his son to lay low. But the way I figured it based on the timeline, Lance Bovier was seventeen when he raped and killed Tia Mulberry. He was eighteen when he was tried as an adult and convicted. Pardoned by the governor a year later at age nineteen, right?"

"And killed a month after being given clemency. In a casino."

"How could that be? He was only nineteen. Not old enough to be gambling in a casino," I reasoned.

"His dad is connected, Liv. In Vegas. Which means he probably has connections in Atlantic City," Marshall said, exhaustion overcoming his earlier energy.

"Connections, as in political? Criminal?"

"Something like that," he said. "Organized crime remains prevalent in Vegas."

"Which allowed daddy to get his underage boy into casinos in Atlantic City."

"Can't prove it, but yes. That was my conclusion."

"So would it be a stretch to think Lance was killed because of his dad's connections? By mobsters? The Mafia? Panini sounds Italian. And Vincent Bovier was a little more than convinced that Panini killed his son." I was windmilling with my thoughts, hoping something would stick.

"First, not all organized crime in Vegas involves murder. Second, Mafia is Italian. And you're thinking of *panino*, which is 'sandwich' in Italian. Third, I don't think the Mafia killed Lance. I think the Mafia—or more accurately, Vincent Bovier—wants to find whoever did this to his oldest son. Even the score."

"Which would make more sense if Vincent Bovier was a mob boss of some sort, don't you think?"

"That's a leap."

"Isn't it a leap to think Vincent Bovier would want to even the score for someone killing his oldest son without any regard to the fact that Lance Bovier brutally murdered an eight-year-old girl for the thrill of it?"

Marshall sighed. "I can't explain it, Liv. All I know is that I don't even think Vincent Bovier grieved the loss of his own son, the pathetic offspring that he was. I think it's all about evening the score for him. Maintaining his power and dignity as the financial muscle in Vegas. Nothing more."

"Do you think Vincent had his own son killed?" I asked, wondering how this tied back to Brianna.

"Liv, I just don't know. And I really don't care. Because Lance Bovier won't be missed."

"Then why did you send me down this path?"

Marshall waited a long beat. "Before he was released, I paid a visit to Lance Bovier. He had been bragging about his daddy having pull with the governor the entire time he was in prison. A cell mate of his tried to plea bargain with some information Bovier shared about a cold case. Of another girl."

"Brianna?"

"Got me thinking. Two girls. Eight and ten. Same proximity."

"But he would have only been thirteen when Brianna was taken," I said, wondering how these two cases were connected.

"An impressionable thirteen," Marshall said. "With a mobster father. I got to thinking. What if he learned this abuse of young girls 'just for the thrill of it' from someone else? What if he was indoctrinated early into the criminal life of his father as muscle in Vegas?"

"By his father?" I gasped, horrified by the thought of a father teaching a thirteen-year-old how to abuse or rape a girl.

"No, Vincent Bovier is far too smart for that. But what if one of his henchmen was getting his son's hands dirty early? To keep him in line? Or as future leverage over Vincent?"

I couldn't imagine how horrible a life it would be as a child of a mobster in Vegas. "And what did Lance Bovier tell you when you went to visit him in prison?"

"Nothing. A big fat zero. He swore he had nothing to do with Brianna Keller. I showed him a picture. He claimed that he heard the name before, about the Brianna Keller case, from someone who had paid him a visit. A man. The man was trying to find a connection between Lance killing Tia Mulberry and this other girl's death."

"And it wasn't you?"

"Before me. And it wasn't the Hawthorne detective."

"Then who was it?"

"Lance mentioned that if he told me anything, the guy would kill him. He was scared stiff to breathe a word about the guy or about Brianna Keller, would deny he ever mentioned the name to me."

"And you think it was his father?" I asked.

"No, I think it was someone who was trying to investigate Brianna

Keller's disappearance, heard about Lance killing Tia, and had pieced the two cases together, just like we did."

"But who was investigating my niece's death, if not you or the Hawthorne detective? My brother-in-law Shorty maybe?"

There was a long pause. "My mind jumped to him immediately, too. I showed Lance a picture. He shook his head. I believed him. Someone else. And Liv, with all of Lance Bovier's blabbing, I highly doubt that the FBI was the only one to hear about his connection with the Brianna Keller cold case."

I thought about that, imagined seeing Brianna's killer face to face. I wondered who it was Lance Bovier was so frightened of seeing. "Did he tell you anything?"

"The only thing Lance kept repeating was that the visitor told him if he told me anything, told any authority, he'd end up like Cleveland. Seen the picture and didn't want to end up like Cleveland. If the visitor found out Lance was lying about having no connection to Brianna Keller's death, Lance would find himself ending up just like Cleveland. Was scared to death by the picture of Cleveland."

"Who's Cleveland? Or did he mean the city?"

"No clue. Never did figure out what the hell Lance was babbling about. I will tell you that I've never met someone so afraid in my life," Marshall said.

"Any name on the prison's visitor log ring a bell for you?"

"Thousands of names, many I recognized. Famous news anchors, entertainers, everyone wanting the inside scoop on the Bovier family." Bo hesitated, then added, "Around the time Lance clammed up? He had several visitors. Investigators, family members. But one visitor signed in as Su Panini."

"She was there? Wouldn't there be video or something?"

"That's the one thing I did manage to get out of Lance. He swore no one had ever visited him named Su Panini."

"But Su Panini signed the visitor sheet," I repeated.

"Yep."

"Bo, thank you. I mean for everything. I appreciate you helping me out with this case," I said, typing "Cleveland Atlantic City" into a search engine to see if anything came up. Nothing.

"Yeah, well, I'm doing it for selfish reasons. A fresh set of eyes on this case may be just the answer."

I typed in "Cleveland girl murder" and got several hits on various murders in Cleveland, Ohio, of different women.

"I'll see what I can come up with. By the way, thanks for sending the boxes to me." I glanced over at the stack of four boxes in the corner of my office, unopened. Streeter had stacked them there—or someone had—while I was up in Fort Collins today. Or yesterday, I thought, staring at the clock. I hadn't had time yet to open them; most of my time over the last sixteen hours had been spent on reviewing the Douglass case files. Then, I had a thought. "Bo? Tell me about the bunny."

"The bunny? You found it?"

My heart dropped to my stomach. "What? Is it missing?"

"You're talking about the toy bunny in the crime scene photos?"

I was looking directly at the photo of the bunny, covered in dirt and surrounded by desert cacti and shrubs, as we spoke. I'd taped it on the wall just below the photo of Brianna. "Yes, the gray, skinny bunny with the potbelly and long ears."

I held my breath, waiting for Marshall's explanation. "Hey, we've checked and double-checked. No one seems to know what happened to that bunny. Sometime between last summer and yesterday, when I boxed everything up, the evidence bag with the bunny came up missing. No one in the Vegas bureau checked it out. And I can't remember seeing it since."

"Well, that's weird," I said, staring at the rabbit's beady black eyes and squished face. "What do you know about it?"

"Well, we didn't find any evidence matching anything on our systems, if that's what you mean. No prints. Nothing but a few carpet fibers that we tested. Didn't match any car carpet that we could determine, so we assumed it was fibers that came with the girl from her home, since it was pink. But nothing panned out there, either. Your sister and brother-in-law were cooperative."

I had cradled the phone between my shoulder and ear, so my hands were free to flip through the files in the box marked "*EVIDENCE*" to find the carpet fiber. Extracting the plastic bag carefully, I saw the evidence number, held the clear bag up to the light, and noticed three fine strands of fiber, but couldn't tell with the naked eye that they were pink. "But you never asked them about the bunny, did you?"

"We wanted to keep specifics about evidence quiet. Why?"

"It wasn't Brianna's bunny."

"What?" croaked Bo Marshall.

"My niece hated rabbits."

"You must be mistaken."

"Bunnies gave her nightmares. It wasn't hers."

"Then whose was it?"

After Marshall told me where to search for the reports on the laboratory results from the carpet fibers, I hung up.

I focused on finding that file, opening the box lids and diving into more folders. I found the report, scanned in the lab results, and sent the findings to Dodson, wishing I had Jack to lean on: *Have time to check on fibers? Vegas bureau indicates carpet. Any similar leads on color, fabric, source?* I knew that as much as Dodson worked, he wouldn't be working this late.

I added Rebecca Douglass's photo to my wall, right of my window, opposite from Brianna's and Tia's. Cases needed to be kept separate. One active, two cold. It had been a long, productive day and I knew I was dreading going home alone. Without Jack.

At least Beulah would be by my side tonight. I didn't want to deal with Camera Casey or the banana bread from earlier or whoever it was messing with my psyche at my apartment. I didn't feel like running. I had too much weighing on my mind.

Before I called it a night, I did a final search, for "death murder Cleveland girl young," and struck gold.

I instantly understood what Lance Bovier was saying to Special Agent Marshall. Five years ago—two years before Bovier brutalized the sweet, young Tia Mulberry while her mother played slots—Daryl Cleveland allegedly raped and strangled a young black girl just like Tia. The story must have made an impact on Lance. And I could see why he told Marshall he did not want to end up dead like Cleveland.

Like Daryl Cleveland.

The man suspected of killing Kesha Ryan. Because someone got to Daryl Cleveland before New York City law enforcement and brutalized Daryl in the same manner he had brutalized the defenseless, innocent Kesha Ryan. Down to every detail, including stuffing Daryl's underpants in his mouth.

Lance Bovier was scared to death that somebody—another mobster, avenger, perhaps?—would get to him as they had gotten to Daryl Cleveland. Someone who wanted to see him dead, not alive behind bars. Somebody who wasn't the cops. Before he was incarcerated, protected by being behind bars.

Before the law could save Daryl Cleveland.

I smiled as I read the name of the lawman who had tried. Special Agent Jerome Schuffler.

CHAPTER 20

I QUICKLY RAISED MY right hand, not needing to steady it with my left, and shot six rapid-fire rounds into the approaching two-dimensional criminal.

As the pulley came to rest within an arm's length of where I stood, I reached for the flapping paper target that swung back and forth. I steadied the life-size paper criminal, who was dressed in black, held a sawed-off shotgun, and sported a menacing grimace. Through my yellow-tinted safety glasses, I examined the tightly spaced pattern in the crook's black leather jacket directly above the left breast.

My 9mm Sig Sauer automatic pistol was one of my favorite firearms. The clover-shaped pattern of bullet holes was no more than three inches in diameter, with only two shots straying completely outside the pattern, one hitting the crook's left shoulder and the other hitting his left collarbone.

I frowned in disappointment after seeing the stray shots and removed my earmuffs and plugs. "Too high," I mumbled.

A tinny voice sounded from the speaker above my head in the shooting lane I'd been assigned. "You want me to set up another?"

"No thanks, Kelly," I answered. "I just wanted to get a feel for the new shooting range. I must be getting a bit shaky or forgot my breathing in all the excitement. I had two this time that weren't mortal."

Kelly McDougal, the mustached man with the Boston accent sitting behind the control window on the floor above me, said, "That'll teach you to use both hands, Bergen."

I was surprised to find Jenna Tate watching me practice.

I draped the earplugs and earmuffs around my neck. "How long have you been there?"

She was standing with her arms crossed across her ample breasts, one toe tapping impatiently in her stiletto heels. "Long enough. Maybe if you'd stick to two hands you could protect yourself with that thing."

She grabbed my firearm, loaded the clip, and motioned for McDougal to repeat the setup I'd just worked. Stepping into the exact firing lane that I'd just occupied, Jenna rocked her pink earmuffs, her short tight skirt, and my Sig Sauer.

I thought I'd counted nine rapid-fire shots, in the same time frame I'd shot six, before the paper bad guy flapped to a stop nearby. I noticed the tight pattern, all of them fatal, as Jenna stepped past me without even looking, handing me my firearm as she did.

"Holy crap," I mumbled.

McDougal chuckled. "Haven't ever seen someone shoot like that."

"Thank you," Tate replied, taking off her earmuffs and glasses and primping her long blonde hair with her fingertips.

"Sorry to tell you, Liv, but she's got both you and Streeter," McDougal said, still laughing and wheezing.

"No shit," I said, grinning at Jenna.

McDougal was well aware of my marksmanship. He'd even called me "accomplished" once. It was not a secret that Streeter was the best shot of all us field agents and also no secret that I was a bit competitive. But I hadn't seen anyone shoot as well as Jenna Tate before either.

"Where did you learn to shoot like that?"

"From Street," she said, cutting her eyes toward me. "He gave me private lessons."

I knew that the comment—especially how she emphasized the word *private*—was intended to solicit my reaction, get a rise out of me. But instead, I said, "Well, you learned well."

Streeter had been ranked expert throughout his entire career in the US Army, had won all the competitions at Quantico, and had achieved the highest level of performance throughout his years with the bureau. His secret was his commitment to practicing on the bureau shooting ranges at least once a day. I'd been doing my homework, studying him. And, following in his practiced footsteps, I shot every day so I could stay sharp with my marksmanship.

I wondered if Streeter had already been down here to check out the new shooting range. And I couldn't help but think Jenna knew his habits as well as I did. Studied him, like I did. Hoped to find him down here, like I did. But she found me instead.

With mischievous intent, I stared up at McDougal, who was watching me from the control room above, then flicked my gaze toward Jenna and said, "If I start using a two-handed shot for better steadying, do you think I'll ever unseat Pierce as the top shooter of this bureau?"

McDougal's expansive girth jiggled when he laughed. Shaking his head slowly, he pulled the microphone to his lips and said, "One of these days? Girl, you left the old man in your dust weeks ago. You're hot. But not as hot as this babe."

"Babe?" Jenna said, sliding her eyes from me up to McDougal.

To defuse what I thought might be a brewing feud, I said, "Kelly, this is Special Agent Jenna Tate from HQ. Quantico. She's temporary assistant SAC. For Howard. Until his replacement's named."

"Holy shit," McDougal said. "Sorry, Agent Tate."

She softened and said, "No apologies. As long as you keep setting them up for me while I'm here and keeping my sharpshooting between you and me, then we're going to get along just fine. Wouldn't want to scare off any suitors," she said with a wink.

"You're single? How is that even possible?" McDougal gawked.

"Well aren't you a sweetie. I think you and I will get along just fine, won't we, babe? You don't mind if I call you babe, do you?"

"You can call me anything you want, Agent Tate. And your secret will stay between you and me."

How did she do that? I couldn't believe what I'd just witnessed. From an adversarial start to McDougal eating out of Jenna's hand. Man, she was good. A master manipulator of tools.

She turned her back on McDougal and held the paper perp in her delicate hands. She leaned in to me and whispered, "Don't you wish you could plug a pattern like that into whoever killed Rebecca Douglass? I do."

How did she know so much about me and the cases I was working on? Streeter had just assigned that case to me Tuesday. And he'd told me that Jenna and Calvin Lemley agreed that I should lead on the case. But how much more had Streeter shared with Jenna? I barely acknowledged my own rage, my own desire to step beyond the thin blue line of the law and take matters into my own hands. Yet here Jenna was reading my mind. Had Streeter shared this weakness of mine with Jenna? Did he talk to her about everything? *Everything*? I was about to ask her when she turned quickly on her heels again.

"Wonderful," she said to McDougal. "Let's start off on the right foot by making sure you never call my Street an 'old man,' okay?"

"Yes, ma'am. Sorry."

Hearing Kelly McDougal call Streeter an "old man" had upset me, too. But I think Jenna calling him "my Street" was worse. I didn't like hearing anyone make derogatory comments about Streeter. He was a fellow agent—my boss, as it were—and deserved to be treated with respect, as far as I was concerned. But more than that, as a person of great distinction, who *commanded* respect. My grin quickly disappeared and I waved to McDougal and Jenna before leaving the shooting range.

"Set up lane two with multiple perps, babe," I heard Jenna call.

From the corner of my eye, I saw McDougal hike his thick shoulders and heard him ask Jenna, "So, did you say you were single?"

As I stepped into the elevator and watched the lights climb from the basement levels to the fourth floor, I thought about Streeter's expert marksmanship. Although it probably should have bothered Streeter that I might become a better marksman than he, it wouldn't. I was sure of that. Even though I was not only a woman but also his junior by ten years, Streeter would likely consider my dedication to improving my marksmanship impressive. A source of pride, not jealousy.

A wide grin fell on my face at the thought of his talents and his amazing support of mine just as the doors opened at the top floor. I was startled when the man I'd been thinking about was standing on the other side. Streeter walked slowly toward me and placed his hand on the open door to prevent it from closing on me.

Seeing my attempt to conceal my grin, Streeter asked, "So, who's the lucky guy who brought that grin to your face?"

I could feel my face burn with embarrassment. I wondered how he knew I was thinking of a man—of him—and hoped his expertise didn't include the power to read minds. Like Jenna. As quickly as I had blushed, I suddenly realized he was simply firing for effect with no specific intuition directing his question. I had not, however, realized this quickly enough.

"You *were* thinking of a man, weren't you?" the receptionist mused, her eyes widening with the thought. I cut my eyes toward her.

Sitting behind the bulletproof glass that separated the waiting area—which was really nothing more than a glorified hallway—with the elevator from the FBI offices, the receptionist was wearing a smug smile on lips so close to the microphone I thought she might take a bite out of it. I watched as her entire body began rolling with laughter.

"Who is he? Do tell. You're among friends."

"Yeah, right," I said, sidestepping Streeter, moving toward the vault-like door. "Buzz me in, please."

Streeter casually suggested to the woman, "I wouldn't push your luck if I were you." He glanced down at my service weapon.

Unaffected by the threat, the large receptionist laughed even louder, until she was interrupted by the ringing of her phone.

I took the opportunity to ask, "Have you checked out the shooting range yet?"

Streeter was about to say something when the receptionist interrupted. "Agent Pierce? The eagle wants to see you."

"The eagle" was a nickname the receptionist had given Calvin Lemley. I imagined she fancied him as important as the president of the United States or something. And Streeter had been seeing a lot of Calvin lately. For some reason.

CHAPTER 21

ANOTHER LONG DAY WORKING through all the Douglass files. Since Tuesday, when I visited Chief Fiero, I had been trying to piece the timeline together as carefully as I could, working through the details. I stood and stretched, deciding whether to go get Beulah out of the pokey. She'd been there all day and I hadn't even gone to visit her, stopped to eat, gone down to the shooting range, nothing. I hadn't even given any thought to the odd offerings left at my door each morning, choosing instead to ignore the creepy gifts that came each day after the bread altogether. Instead, I stayed focused. I had been hunched over my desk. All day. For the last two days.

I stared at the framed picture I had chosen for the north wall that divided my new office from Streeter's. The forty-two-by-thirty-six-inch photograph taken by Thomas Mangelsen at sunrise depicted nothing more than a beautiful native tree in the foreground and the African wilderness in the background, highlighted in the warm colors of morning's first light, yet it was breathtaking. The shades of oranges, yellows, and browns in the photo had drawn out the natural colors of my office. On many occasions over the past thirty-six hours, I had looked to that picture for peace and focus as I pored over the documents, statements, and disturbing pictures of the Douglass case, but tonight all I could see in the African photo was confusion.

Was it actually a sunrise that Mangelsen had captured, or was it a sunset? Why had I been so sure it was a sunrise when I first saw the photo, and why now did it not seem clear to me anymore?

I shook my head and closed my tired eyes, rubbing them with the tips of my fingers. This complicated mess wore on me. My vision, not as clear as it had been.

Over the past three days, I had opened up so many different windows to the world of the underground that all I wanted to do was close and lock each one of them so no ill winds could continue to blow through my mind. But I knew closing out anything I'd learned about the cases—active or cold—would be a mistake. Unfair to the children. Those angels kept me moving forward, one step at a time. I looked over my shoulder at the wall to the west.

Tia Mulberry. Kesha Ryan. And my dear niece, Brianna Keller.

Under Tia's picture, I had taped a photo of Lance Bovier, slashing a red line across his photo and writing in the date he'd been found dead in the Atlantic City bathroom stall. Under Kesha's picture, I had taped a photo of Daryl Cleveland and written the date he'd been found dead in the New York City parking lot. Under Brianna's picture, I had nothing.

I stared at the wall, their smiles encouraging me, and then my eyes slid over to the space to the right of the window. To the active case. To Rebecca Douglass. And I contemplated the many faces that might be found taped beneath Rebecca.

I had diligently reviewed and studied the files that Theresa Fiero had given me. I had taken several boxes at a time to examine the documents gathered on the case to date and had sorted through much of it since Tuesday. Hadn't touched the cold case boxes on Brianna. Focus on Rebecca was crucial. There was so much information on the Douglass case that I had begun to draw outlines and flowcharts on all of the characters and the chain of events. My statement analysis was shallow at this point, but my speculations ran deep.

As if he had heard my wish to confide in someone about the case,

Streeter walked in to find me fully engrossed in the files that lay scattered on my desk and on the floor.

"Liv?" Streeter called in his soothing voice.

Sounding a bit too desperate, I said, "Just who I was hoping to see." I quickly rose and walked around the clutter to the other side of my desk. "I need company."

Streeter smiled and took a seat. I sat in the chair beside him.

He explained, "I was about to leave and saw that you were still here. I'm concerned about you. You've been here every night all week until well after eight o'clock. Sometimes much later, from what I hear."

I admit I was surprised he had noticed. I hadn't seen much of him. Of course, I'd been busy trying to understand every aspect of the Douglass case.

"I appreciate the time and effort you have been putting into the Douglass case, but we certainly wouldn't want you overdoing it."

We? Who was he talking about? He and Howard? He and Calvin? I said nothing. I was bewildered as to why Streeter would question my long hours. He, of all people, should know how important it was to stay focused and dedicated on a case like this.

Streeter added, "You aren't going home until late. You're coming in early. And I suspect you're working on this at home. Am I right?"

"So? What's the problem?"

Streeter's smile offered too much sympathy for my liking.

"The problem is burnout. You're trying to pedal too fast, when what you need to do is change gears and pedal more slowly, so you don't waste your energy. You're still going to get there in plenty of time, maybe even quicker."

"What's with the bicycling analogies? You're the one who taught me time was of the essence. Remember? Like with the Williams case? We didn't sleep for three days until we found him."

He patted my knee, which felt more like condescension than condolence. "That was different. We were assigned the case almost immediately after the child went missing. These are cold cases. The Douglass case, although active, is three months old. Your role is different."

I was annoyed by his reaction. "A kid missing or dead is still a heavy loss, no matter how old or cold the case."

My bewilderment became obvious to Streeter. He asked me, "It's only Thursday and you look exhausted. Did you know it's almost six o'clock? Have you eaten at all today?"

I shook my head.

"Didn't think so. Everyone else has knocked off for the day, except you." He paused for a second before adding, "You know how to eat an elephant, don't you?"

I answered with obvious frustration, "Yes. You've told me. One bite at a time."

"That's right," Streeter coached. "That means you can't sit here and try to eat it all at once, Liv. You'll get sick." I felt his eyes on me even though I had slid mine toward the photos on my wall. "Do you want to talk about it?"

My mood brightened with his interest. "It's so confusing. When Theresa Fiero said the whole thing was a mess, she wasn't exaggerating. I think everyone thinks they know who killed little Rebecca, but no one can prove it because of all the mistakes that have happened. If I didn't think it would be virtually impossible to carry out such a well-laid and complicated plan to make sure the killer goes free, I'd say these coincidences were all too far-fetched, too excessive, too convenient, too conspiratorial. Streeter, it's crazy."

I rose to my feet and started pacing in front of him without even realizing I had popped to my feet. I felt the tails of my dark suit flutter with each turn in my brisk pace, my plain white T-shirt underneath coming untucked. I suppose to Streeter I looked a mess, since I hadn't had time to launder my blouses. But the important point is that my mind was fresh.

"First, everyone tromped around in the house the day Rebecca was discovered missing. I mean, there must have been two dozen law enforcement and emergency response team personnel that went through the house at some point and to some degree. Not to mention a dozen of the Douglasses' closest friends and family that had come over to comfort the parents, Theodore and Cathy. Then, it took the police seven and a half hours from the time they arrived on the scene to find the little girl, who was lying dead in the corner of the gardener's shed near the garage in the backyard the entire time. And the officials weren't even the ones who found her. It was Theo himself, along with a friend, who accidentally came upon her body after Theo was told to see if anything had been stolen or was out of place."

I lifted my flowchart and taped it to the wall by the African sunrise. Streeter watched quietly as I pointed to different boxes on the flowchart. "I thought I'd try to identify mistakes made in the case to date. It's been nearly three months since Rebecca was murdered. I figured if I could sort through all the mistakes, then maybe I can see if there is a way to recover from some of them. Does that make sense?"

Streeter squinted and listened intently. "Sounds reasonable."

Encouraged, I continued, "First, the officers didn't secure the crime scene properly. They didn't even consider identifying the house as a possible crime scene, even though the crime of kidnapping had obviously occurred there, because they didn't find the girl. Needless to say, to prosecute meant obtaining critical evidence. And because of the contamination and missteps, most of the evidence hadn't been properly preserved, had been lost, or at best, had been contaminated, which meant the prosecution couldn't use anything anyway. At least not convincingly. It's all too easy for the defense to shred the case based on the flimsy preservation of evidence. There were far too many mistakes, too much contamination of the crime scene."

Pointing to the second box of my flowchart, I explained, "Then, the father found the body of his dead, battered daughter, who he thought had been kidnapped, not killed. How horrifying for him. He picked her up, cradled her in his arms, and carried her inside from the gardener's shed where he found her. I totally understand how a parent overcome by grief and shock would cradle their child in such a horrific situation. He wasn't thinking of evidence. Why would he? But by doing so, Theo managed to unknowingly destroy the last chance of preserving any helpful evidence that may have existed on her body or in that little shed. Those who believe he had something to do with her death claim it was intentional. But his actions would suggest he was experiencing a normal reaction to having discovered his daughter's dead body."

Brushing my finger over several boxes, I added, "Not only was the initial crime scene all but destroyed, most of the evidence that was collected in the house that could have helped investigators later turned up missing when they went to retrieve it, or at least a large share of it did. Theresa Fiero can't tell if her department somehow mislabeled it, stored it somewhere they haven't looked, or if someone has hawked it for financial gain."

My pacing sped up along with my heartbeat. I was getting worked up all over again.

"The former police chief, Bruce Schumaker, chalked that one up, along with the botched crime scene, to inexperience on his people's part. Which I assume played a role in him getting drummed out of there. Career suicide to admit your team is not so skilled, eh? Anyway, the tabloids, magazines, and television programs have been offering sizable amounts of cash for any exclusive photos or memorabilia from the Douglass murder so they can have something their competitors don't on this case. The story's dominating head-lines, capturing the country's attention. Which of course equates to ratings. Maybe someone in the department sold some of that evidence to the net-works or the rag sheets for a few extra bucks under the table. Who knows? It's a feeding frenzy, Streeter. That's another problem with this case. There are too many cameras trained on it, which has led to disaster."

"Forget about the media. What's at the core here, Liv? As you see it?" Streeter pressed.

I stopped and turned to look at him. He was right. The media frenzy is what had engulfed me in frustration, not the case itself. I had been disap-pointed in how easily those upholding the law had turned on one another. "Everyone is demanding a rush to judgment. The whole country wants to see someone punished. The easiest targets were Cathy and Theo Doug-lass. They were the two everyone loved to hate. They were rich, successful, beautiful, and had it all. Including their own reality TV show. Even if envy didn't strike a chord as it does with most people, then it was easy to hate the Douglass family for what they had allowed or directed their little six-year-old to do. She had captured more ratings and pageant titles in her short six years of life than most people could imagine. No one argues that she was a cute or talented little girl. The anger arises because she was made up to look like a seductive young adult at age six. That's what seems to be so offensive."

I buried my face in my hands, exhaustion settling into my shoulders.

"Is that what has you bothered? Personal judgment getting in the way of investigating?"

I looked up at Streeter. He was right again. I kept getting sidetracked with emotions. Personal judgment should be reserved for deciding which path to follow when facts don't clearly mark the way, not for deciding how to feel about the people involved in the case. "I admit I was upset with the Douglasses the first time I saw those pictures taken after Valentine's Day of Rebecca. Dead. And the other photos. From before. All the curls, the makeup, the costumes." I felt a chill. "It's just that her eyes are so sad. So unhappy. That's what gets to me."

I walked back toward Streeter and plopped down in the chair beside him. He laid his hand on my shoulder, started massaging my neck, and this time his gesture felt supportive. His hand was warm and firm, yet gentle, against my taut muscles.

"Streeter, maybe I'm not right for this case."

"You are."

"I thought you brought Jenna here to help you work this case."

"I told you and everyone on Tuesday morning, I brought Tate in because of Magnussen's retirement and to make the transition."

I glanced over at him. "And that's all?"

He grinned. "That's all."

"Not as a backup? In case I screwed up the Douglass case?"

He shook his head.

I believed him. "Then why does she keep asking me how it's going? What I'm learning? I actually caught her looking at my flowchart when I stepped out for a minute to use the bathroom today."

He smiled. "Tate's trained to assess you as an agent, Liv."

I sighed. "It seems more than that. Like she's checking up on me. And not in a good way."

I studied Streeter's expression, hoping he'd clue me in if there was more to Tate's prying. But if there was, he wasn't going to share what he knew with me. His hand slipped from my neck. Although I wanted to ask him to keep going, I pretended not to notice.

"Anyway, in the past three months it's just become easy for everyone to hate Theo and Cathy Douglass. The entire country wants to see them punished. It's become a trial by public opinion."

"High-profile cases involving a lot of media generally do," he said.

"The Douglasses have been guilty from the very beginning. Either of killing their baby themselves or covering for the older sister, Debra, who everybody also loves to hate. Mostly because she's so openly brash and condescending to the press."

"Debra was also a pageant girl, if memory serves," Streeter said.

"Right. And because her sister's death became such a media circus, with absolutely everyone joining in on the act, control by the investigation team was forfeited to the masses, which inevitably led to emotion-based, rather than fact-based, decisions. Theo and Cathy were asked to give a statement to the police, which they did twice, but when asked to repeat their statements for the third time, they requested the statements be taken after their daughter's funeral. They said they were doing everything they could to protect their two other children, Debra and a younger brother, both older than Rebecca. The Douglass family was grieving. I think they were totally reasonable to refuse, don't you think?"

"I'd want to bury my daughter, if I were them." His green eyes were fixed on mine.

"Some overzealous investigator whose ego was bruised by the request demanded the Douglasses give him the statement or he would not approve the release of their daughter's body for burial after the autopsy."

Streeter scowled. "Using her body to bargain with the parents? That's unconventional."

Exactly," I said. "So the Douglasses, who were emotionally charged to the max, refused to talk with the investigator, and the situation escalated out of control. The media, loving this drama because it sells magazines and boosts ratings, twisted the story for the public as the Douglasses' refusal to self-incriminate, when actually they're just pissed off about the police using their daughter's corpse as leverage. Since the public had already decided the Douglasses were guilty, then it stands to reason—with the help of the money-hungry media—that the police were not making any arrests because they were bought off by the filthy-rich Douglasses."

"Fiero has her hands full on this one," Streeter said, glancing toward my window.

"Once the focus of the media turned on the Fort Collins Police Department, the heat became too intense. One of the lead investigators in the case resigned because of public pressure to arrest the parents, who he believed did not murder the little girl. He wrote a scathing letter to the chief of police explaining how he refused to take part in a mob lynching of innocent parents who should be left alone to grieve the loss of their daughter."

"Mutiny," Streeter interjected.

"We have one female police officer who filed a lawsuit claiming she was defamed by an exposé piece that aired on one of the major networks, which showed an interview with a fellow police officer who blamed her for the destruction of the crime scene. She admitted being one of two dozen police officers who was there at the Douglass residence that day and being the first one to assist Theo Douglass when he brought his daughter's body in from the backyard. But she stated emphatically that she was not to blame for the destruction of evidence and countered that many people in the department and in association with the Douglasses were to blame for the destruction of the entire crime scene that morning. The infighting at the Fort Collins PD has gotten so bad, the local police union met and returned a no-confidence vote on their chief's performance. It was like a two-to-one vote, too."

Streeter said, "They turned on each other like a hungry pack of dogs and then blamed it on the one in charge."

"Exactly. Like I said, the cameras turned on them and the heat was too intense," I explained. "So then the cameras turned on the mayor and her city council, the reporters asking what they're going to do about the police department now that it's in total disarray and about the police union's vote showing no confidence in their leader. And they started bickering with one another."

"Feeding frenzy," he said.

"Eventually, we had more casualties and several others licking their wounds and reassessing why they chose to run for office. The mayor, forced by a four-to-three vote by the council, demanded Chief Bruce Schumaker turn in a letter of resignation. Two city council members resigned in protest of the council's action. A request was sent by one of the former city council members that the governor impanel a grand jury to look into the matter, which is being considered. Now the cameras are turned on him. We'll just have to see how he handles the heat. At least he has more experience with the media."

I don't even know when I had gotten back up, but I was pacing and pointing to my flowchart. Finally ending my rant, I quickly sat down next to Streeter again.

He asked, "So, where are you and Fiero on all of this?"

I sighed and answered, "I was supposed to review everything for Theresa and come up with a profile, a statement analysis, and my opinion on the case to date overall. I've sent an email to Jack asking him to come up with a profile on the murderer when he gets back into the office. And if you don't mind, since he won't be back for another week, I'd like to take a trip back to Quantico and discuss statement analysis with Bill Archibald in the ISU. And I want him to assess the funky ransom note."

"Demanding such a relatively small amount?"

"And coincidentally matching Douglass's latest bonus. Archibald's giving a lecture to the new class at the Academy that I'd love to hear. I'd be more comfortable talking with Bill about the conclusions I drew from my statement analysis before I present them to Theresa. Is that okay with you?"

"Sure," he said. "You know I'll support you."

His simple words of encouragement were uplifting. "Depending on flights, I'll either make it to the class offered tomorrow night or the one on Monday night. If I can't go tomorrow, I'll miss your Tuesday morning meeting."

"That's okay. I'll make you stay twice as long the next week."

Instantly, I felt compelled to confide in Streeter on a very personal issue. Without hesitation, I said, "Streeter, can I ask you something?"

His face seemed to relax and his eyes softened. "You can ask me anything."

"It's personal. I wonder if you could tell me if you think I'm crazy," I explained. "You see, there's this guy ..."

CHAPTER 22

MY WORDS TRAILED OFF as I searched for the best way to explain my situation. I almost missed the reaction I'd triggered in Streeter's face. From his expression, he hadn't liked the idea of having to hear about my problems with some guy. His jaw muscles had begun to tighten.

Afraid he might be getting the wrong idea, I quickly continued, "He's a man who lives in my apartment complex. At least I think it's him. Tuesday morning, I think he left a loaf of banana bread at my apartment door. It was tied with a blue ribbon and there was no note. I thought it might be from . . ."

I decided not to finish my sentence. I'd initially thought of Streeter, until I realized how ridiculous that would be. And Jack was out of town on his fishing trip. Instead I said, "I thought it wouldn't be wise to eat it, not knowing who had given it to me. So, I threw it away. Last night when I got home, I found a small teddy bear and a plate of chocolate chip cookies. This morning, a chew toy. I assume that was for Beulah, not me, unless my secret admirer thinks I'm a dog."

I laughed nervously. Seeing the seriousness grow in Streeter's expression, I continued, "And a bunch of handpicked flowers yesterday morning. Each gift has been wrapped in a blue ribbon, just like the banana bread on

Tuesday. It's not the gifts so much that bother me, but not knowing what this is all about. The phone calls are annoying and I feel like I'm being watched all the time."

Streeter's intense gaze held mine as he asked, "What phone calls?"

I furrowed my brows and answered, "They started Monday night. Before I knew about the bread. There was someone on the line, but they hung up after I said hello. I wouldn't have thought much about it until I had a call last night, too. Whoever it was didn't hang up after I said hello. So, I said hello again and 'Who is this?' Then they hung up. I assume I'll get a call again tonight. He doesn't say anything, but once in a while I think I can hear him . . . grinning. I know that sounds crazy, but it wouldn't be described as a laugh or a chuckle. All I can hear is the slight moaning sound someone makes when they're on the verge of laughing, beyond an overly excited grin. Am I making any sense? Or do you think I'm crazy to even give this a second thought?"

Streeter's eyes narrowed. "Who do you think is doing this?"

"There's this man who lives a few floors down," I explained. "I'm not exactly sure which apartment he lives in, but it probably wouldn't be too difficult for me to figure out. I met him at our apartment complex meet-and-greet this winter. Our neighbors have an annual get-together to make sure we stay connected to one another, watch out for each other. Anyway, there was this guy there, Stewart Casey."

"How old a guy is he?"

"Mid-forties? I'm just guessing. Everyone told me his nickname was Camera Casey, because no one has ever seen him without the cameras. He always wears three cameras around his neck. The rumor is the cameras are never loaded with memory. I remember leaving the party early that night because I had an uneasy feeling about him. I know this sounds weird, but I would swear he was taking pictures of only me that night. Well, he was taking pictures of others, but I got the distinct feeling he was focused more on me than would be normal by most standards."

I paused in reflection. Then I continued, "He was there with his parents. I met his mom. Might have seen his dad nearby, but that was a long time ago. Lots of new people to meet. I think he lives with his parents. Although I can't be sure, I think this man is developmentally disabled somehow. It may be enough of a disability that he still lives with his parents. Even though he's in his forties or fifties."

Streeter leaned forward and studied my face. "Why do you think he's disabled?"

"Just . . . ," I started, but stopped and shook my head. "It's just the way he grins and lays his head back all the time. It's the way he carries himself. His head cocked back at such a strange angle all the time. The way he talks. Something just isn't quite right. You know what I mean?"

Staring out at the darkening sky, I added, "Monday night, I met him again when I came back from running. The night before I found the first gift. The banana bread. I had just finished running my five miles and was stretching in the front lobby. It was raining outside. I heard the click of his camera and then he said hello as he approached me from behind. I remembered who he was instantly. He's unforgettable that way.

"We talked for a moment and something he said . . . or the way he said it, made chills go up my spine. So, I excused myself and went upstairs. But he followed me. Not on the same elevator. I saw him in the hall from my peephole once I was inside. He took a picture of my door. Streeter, it was so strange. He just stood there. I thought I could see his lips moving, like he was talking with himself for a moment."

"That is strange."

"And a bit spooky," I sighed. "Then, he left. Tuesday morning when I left for work, there was the banana bread at my door. Since then, I've gotten all these strange little gifts, almost like a child were leaving them for me. That's why I think they're from him. Childlike. Like the mental equivalent of a child."

Streeter asked, "Have you seen him since?"

"No," I answered hesitantly. "I haven't seen him."

"Because you're at work most of the time. That's why you've been staying here so late."

I shrugged. "I get home late, but I still have the distinct impression I'm being watched sometimes. When I'm walking into my apartment from the parking lot. When I get my mail. Even when I'm driving home. I know it's illogical but I feel like eyes are on me. I get chills. That's weird, isn't it?"

"No, not weird. Trust your instincts," Streeter said in a quiet voice. "Are you scared to stay by yourself, Liv? With Linwood gone?"

I shook my head, opting to stay clear of saying anything about Jack. "I have Beulah, like always. It's not that I think Stewart's dangerous or anything. I believe he's simply challenged and doesn't realize his affections toward me are making me uncomfortable. He may not even know how to deal with his feelings of infatuation. I'm pretty certain it's harmless."

"Pretty certain?" Streeter asked, with more seriousness than I had seen in some time.

I frowned. "I didn't mean to worry you. I just wanted someone else to know about this. Just in case. I just needed to talk with someone. It's been creeping me out."

I glanced at the children's pictures on the walls. "And these angels' cries for justice don't help."

"I can see why you've been staying so late at work."

"After dark, I have Beulah to protect me and no one's watching me from the bushes or anything like that . . . I think." I noticed Streeter raise one eyebrow. "So he got a few pictures of my backside while I was stretching Monday night. What's the big deal, right? Not my fault that Stewart's a crummy photographer."

My levity was not appreciated by Streeter, who grabbed my hand and said, "Liv, you have to take this seriously. Stalkers can be dangerous, even deadly. If this man is stalking you, there could be a reason. You can't take this lightly."

I thought I detected a crack in his voice during his warning. Streeter's hands were trembling as he held mine. Perspiration had begun to form on his forehead and above his lip. I had never seen him this way. He was more than worried or concerned about me. He seemed disturbed.

"It's okay. I'll be all right. The guy is just unstable. I'll be fine, really."

He squeezed my hand too tightly, but I didn't dare flinch. "Just be careful. Do you understand me?"

I nodded and started to ask why he felt so strongly when there was a knock on my glass door.

"Yoo-hoo," Jenna called into my office in her sweet Southern drawl. She was wearing her evening makeup, her long, blonde hair piled high and tamed into loose curls on the top of her head, and had on a tight yellow-and-black party dress that made her well-endowed chest look more so and her tiny waist look even smaller. "Sorry to interrupt, but I went home to get my overnight bag, Street. Are you ready to go?"

Ready to go? Overnight bag? What did she mean by that? And why was Streeter taking her anywhere, let alone somewhere that she needed an overnight bag? A lump had begun to form high in my throat and I tried desperately to swallow it.

Streeter released my hand and stood to go. He called to Jenna, "Would you mind waiting for me in the lobby, Tate? I'll be right with you?"

"Sure thing, Street," Jenna called over her shoulder. "Bye-bye, Liv."

She waggled her long, manicured fingers to us as she clipped a steady pace toward the elevators. I couldn't help but watch the swing of Jenna's shapely hips in the skin-tight dress, and I realized how Streeter could be attracted to her. Any hot-blooded male would be attracted to her.

I sighed and rose to meet Streeter, who was not staring at Jenna as I might have expected but was instead staring at me. He had a parental look of concern on his face, to which I responded, "I'll take it seriously. I promise."

"Thank you." As he turned to go, he called over his shoulder to me, "Sunrise?"

"Pardon me?" I asked, not sure what he had said.

Streeter turned in the doorway and pointed to my Mangelsen photograph. "I was talking about your photograph. It's spectacular. It is a sunrise, isn't it?"

I grinned and folded my arms across my chest. I answered confidently, no longer confused, "It's definitely a sunrise."

Streeter grinned and said, "See you when you get back from Quantico."

I waved, without waggling my fingers. "Sure. Have fun tonight."

I didn't want him to have fun tonight, not with Jenna, but I said it anyway. At least there was no longer any confusion. Wait, what? He'll see me when I get back from Quantico? That might mean Tuesday next week. Where is he going? More than an overnight. He'd be gone tomorrow and this weekend.

Well if he was leaving, so was I.

I spent the next half hour making flight plans for the morning, gathering the clutter, organizing files for the Douglass case. I sorted out what I would need in Quantico, grabbed files from Brianna's cold case, and changed my extended-absence message to let people know where I'd be. After packing my briefcase, I turned out the lights and made my way to the elevator. On my descent, the elevator stopped on the third floor.

When the doors opened, revealing Dodson on the other side, I said, "Hi, Mitch. You're working late."

As he stepped onto the elevator with me, Dodson smirked in a way that made me feel uneasy. "So are you. How have you been? I haven't talked with you since Tuesday. You haven't seen my emails, have you?"

"Busy on this Douglass case," I answered. "So what'd you find?"

"I did some manipulation on the print. Think I have some candidates," Dodson answered.

"What? Seriously?"

"I took the evidence gathered off the toy, too. The pink carpet fibers. Matched some unidentified fibers on another cold case from twenty years ago. In Washington."

"The state of Washington? That's not that far from Nevada."

"About seven hundred miles."

"You think there's a connection?" I asked.

"Both involved young girls found dead who'd been abducted."

"Did the FBI get involved in the other case like in Brianna Keller's?" I asked.

"Nope. Local law. You want the contact?"

"Please," I said. "And thank you, Mitch."

"No problem. It's what I do. Find the missing and bring the assholes responsible to justice. Hey, have you eaten dinner yet?"

"I haven't even eaten lunch."

Dodson's mood brightened. "Since Linwood's out of town, do you want to go to dinner? With me? I doubt if you already have plans or anything. I don't mean to imply that you—"

"No, but thanks," I said. Although I would normally be happy to have an excuse not to go home, I had no desire to spend time with Mitch Dodson. "It's been a long day and I'm headed out for the rest of the week."

"I just thought maybe you'd want to talk to someone about this Douglass case. I'm sure it's been driving you crazy. And with Linwood gone, I can help you with some thoughts before you go to Quantico."

As I stepped off, I stopped short. "Wait. How did you know about me going to Quantico?"

Dodson said nothing, stepping off the elevator with me, avoiding my questioning expression. All I had said was that I was heading out of town. How did he know where I was going? As my list of questions grew, so did my suspicion. I had tried to work with Mitch all week, felt sorry for him in many ways. Had he used my empathy against me? Leveraged my newfound reliance on him to learn more about me?

I turned quickly and faced him. I stood at least four inches taller than him. His moonlike face was far too close to mine and his smirk fueled my suspicion. "Seriously, Dodson. Where did you hear I was going to Quantico?"

I knew Streeter wouldn't have told him, and Streeter was the only person in the office who knew. And even if he had told Jenna Tate or the receptionist or Calvin Lemley in the last half hour, there would be no way it would have gotten back to Mitch Dodson that quickly.

Mitch answered, "From the email you sent Linwood. You asked him to work up a profile when he got back. And you mentioned going to see Bill Archibald at ISU."

I kept my anger in check. "What in the hell are doing reading Jack's emails?"

Dodson shrugged. "When he's gone, I make sure his emails and texts are automatically forwarded to me. How do you think I ended up doing all the testing on the Greenwood case?"

"The Greenwood case? What are you talking about? Does Jack know about this? That's a violation of privacy, Mitch."

"Not if it's bureau business, sweetheart."

"Don't call me sweetheart," I growled, stepping back from him, realizing I had fabricated an image of who Dodson was, not really sought to know the truth. I had never imagined him being a lecherous womanizer. Sweetheart? If I'd paid attention, I would have never relied on him. I'd brought him coffee, for Pete's sake. Hugged him. What the hell had I been thinking?

"Woo-hoo," he chortled, ignoring my growing fervor. "Somebody needs a little."

"Shut up, Dodson. You're starting to really piss me off." I was trying to sound tougher than I felt. Alarms were clanging. This situation between me and the old man was escalating out of control. I needed his genius, not his advances.

"And don't worry about the profile for the Douglass case. I'm working on it. Putting the data into the program tech installed last month. Who needs Linwood when you've got me?"

Dodson's hand slipped around my waist and I slapped it away.

"Come on. Maybe we started off on the wrong foot. Let's go have a few drinks and iron this out."

I felt him move closer to me, and I made three quick moves, pinning Mitch Dodson up against the glass in the lobby and slamming my forearm across his throat. "You crossed a line, Dodson. And if you want to find out how much it pisses me off to be called sweetheart, to be fondled, or to have some asshole like you think you're God's gift to women, then keep it up. Because I just may enjoy ripping that smirk off your sorry face."

His eyes were wide, but the smirk remained. For the first time, I detected alcohol on his breath. He'd been drinking. At work.

My cell phone chirped, yanking me from my red-zone reverie.

Before I released the pressure from his throat, I growled, "And quit following me. Quit calling me. And quit leaving shit at my door. Do you understand me?"

His bugged-out eyes grew wider and he nodded quickly.

I let up on his throat and walked away. I didn't really think he was the person behind the gifts and calls, but I couldn't be absolutely sure. So just in case, I wanted to warn him off. I got my point across.

As I made my way to the door that led out to the canine area, I called back as casually as I could muster, to make my defensive move seem effortless. "Thanks for getting those reports to me ASAP. Including the profile, so I can finish my statement analysis. Make sure you have that to me by Monday morning so I can go over all of it with Bill Archibald." And, ripping a page from Jenna's book, I ended by saying, "Toodles, Mitch. And have a great weekend."

I retrieved Beulah, feeling much more confident with her by my side. The second I got into my car, I sent a text explaining what Mitch Dodson was up to while Jack was gone, although I didn't get into too many details. Considering how Dodson might respond after seeing my text, I mentioned only that Dodson might be overworked, stressed without Jack here to help, alluded to the idea that it might cause me to drink a bit more than normal, if I were Mitch. I left off the detail about Dodson actually drinking at work. And I mentioned that Jack should take care with his emails and texts as they might further upset Dodson, avoiding the specifics of how they were being breached. A departure from my nightly texts about my progress on the Douglass case. And I hoped Jack Linwood would finally break his silence.

Because if Dodson ever tried something like that with me again, Jack was going to end up with a pissed-off girlfriend on his hands and a seriously maimed lab tech on his team.

Before I pulled out of the parking structure, I checked my cell phone to see who had called while I was overpowering the old man. Barbara, my sister. I hit the call-back number and she answered in one ring.

"Why were you asking?" Barbara's words were clipped.

"No hello?" I asked.

"Hi, Boots. Why did you ask? About Brianna? And no BS."

I pulled out of the parking lot, into dark and empty streets. The cool spring night made me feel empty. I sighed. "Just thinking about her."

"Why'd you ask about a bunny?"

My stomach growled when I pulled past the fast-food restaurant on the left. I was about to pull in to the drive-through when I noticed a light, old-fashioned car idling in the dark, empty lot, making me feel even emptier for some reason. I decided to keep going, find a drive-through closer to home.

"I don't know, sis," I lied.

"Bull. You're a terrible liar. What's up? Do you know something? Has something come up? Should I call Special Agent Marshall?"

"No, Barbara. Stop," I said, stomping on the brake accidentally in response.

When I did, I noticed the car trailing far behind on the empty street. The driver jerked to the right up a side street and sped off. The same light car from the fast-food parking lot? Had stomping on my brakes startled him? "Was that guy following me?"

"Who?"

I hadn't realized I'd said anything out loud. "Oh, nothing."

"Boots, if you don't tell me what's going on, I'm on the next plane to Denver."

I had no doubt she would be.

CHAPTER 23

STREETER SAT UP IN his bed, breathing heavily and sweating.

He stared wide-eyed into the darkness of his bedroom and listened for the echoes of the distant and terrifying dream, trying to regain some sense of reality and orientation. He could see nothing but the blackness and he could hear nothing but the early morning chirping of the birds outside his cabin. It was still dark, but the birds always started their day just before sunrise.

He lay back down on his pillow, which was soaked with sweat. He breathed deeply and tried to relax, knowing he was safe in his Conifer home, knowing it was all just a bad dream.

"What in the hell was that?" Streeter asked himself aloud in the dark, thinking of the wild dream he had just had. He hadn't had nightmares in a long time. For the first time, the nightmare wasn't about his wife, Paula, being in danger.

Instead, it was Liv.

He looked over at his clock. It was four forty-five. He didn't dare go back to sleep. He threw back the covers and snapped on all the lights in his bedroom, the bathroom, the hall, and the kitchen. He ground some coffee beans to drown out the words he still heard from the beast in his nightmare as it hissed to him, *Murderer.*

What did that dream mean, he wondered? He shook the ground coffee into the filter and filled the coffeemaker with water. He stood in his living room by the big glass windows, staring over the treetops of the caverns below to the north and over the tree trunks scattered on the rolling hills to the west.

As he listened to the gurgling of the coffee brewing, Streeter thought about his dream and wondered why, after all these years, the nightmares about Paula's death had returned. And why they had become so bizarre. Starring Liv.

His wife's death was certainly violent and horrific, but it didn't have anything to do with what Streeter dreamed just now. He wondered if something had triggered the nightmare and immediately thought of Liv and her stalker. That must have been the correlation, he thought. Hearing about the man in Liv's apartment complex had disturbed him more than he had realized.

When he had taken Tate to the airport last night for her return flight to Mobile, Alabama, Streeter had completely forgotten to ask her when he should expect her return to work. Maybe she had told him how long it would take her to move her things to Denver, but he hadn't been paying attention. She flew in Tuesday, back out Tuesday afternoon, back to work again Wednesday, and flew out again last night. He was wondering if Tate was planning plane trips just to get him alone on the drive to and from the airport. He'd suggest Howard Magnussen take her out and pick her up from now on. He had better things to do than to be Tate's chauffeur.

He was preoccupied thinking about Liv's stalker.

He remembered that the dream had taken place in an apartment, a new apartment, because he had left everything behind, taking nothing with him. Did that have something to do with Calvin Lemley's advice to him on Monday? About moving on with his life? Had he moved on by moving out? And what, he wondered, was the significance of the beast in his dream? He knew who the tenant and the building superintendent were. And he knew why the beast called him a murderer.

After nearly twenty years of blaming himself for Paula's death, and more importantly, for not being there with her when she needed him the most, he'd understood why his quiet mind punished himself with nightmares. But he thought he'd gotten over all that. So why had the nightmares returned and why were they so distorted?

"Weird," Streeter said aloud, shivering from a sudden chill that ran down his bare back.

The early mornings in the mountains were chilly, even in the summer. No matter what time of year it was, Streeter wore nothing more than his light linen pajama bottoms to bed. He rubbed his bare, muscular arms this morning to chase the chill out of him and smelled the coffee as it permeated the cabin. Running his thick fingers across his muscular chest, he massaged the tissue between each rib to ease the nightmare-induced tension that had crept into his muscles. He opened a window and drew a full breath of crisp, mountain air into his lungs. It was just above freezing outside, but somehow the air's freshness made him feel revived and warmer again.

As he poured himself a cup of coffee, Streeter told himself he had practiced enough pop psychology for one morning. He smiled and told himself to forget the dream. He didn't understand all of the hidden meaning of his bizarre nightmare, but he knew that the best way to get rid of the worst part of the dream was by convincing himself that Liv was in no danger.

Before Linwood returned, he was going to tell Liv the truth. How he felt about her. He'd have her determine their future. It was time.

Streeter had finally convinced himself after all these years that Calvin was right. It was time to move on. And he knew that Liv was the one he wanted to spend time with. If it wasn't for Tate arriving when she did to get her ride out to the airport last night, he would have asked Liv about going to dinner with him. Alone. To talk. She wouldn't have said no. Not last night. She wanted his company. She wanted to talk. He knew that much about her.

As he sat by the open window sipping his coffee and watching the darkness fade, the early rays of light worked their fingers through the treetops to the north like a woman's through her lover's hair. For the first time in a long time, Streeter was at peace. Even after the terrifying nightmare, he realized that he was experiencing deep and genuine feelings for Liv. And he intended to take action rather than ignore how he felt.

That was progress for Streeter, and he knew Paula would be proud of him.

He felt good about his decision to stop living in the past, to stop clinging to the safe, stable anchor of his wife's headstone. He was ready to share his thoughts with someone again just before falling asleep, to enjoy the warm feeling of having someone he loved fast asleep in his arms, and to hold hands on hikes through the woods. Streeter didn't want to celebrate another birthday or Christmas alone, to go out to dinner with only the company of a newspaper or magazine, or to sit by the fire reading a book without having someone on the couch beside him.

He finally realized there truly was a difference between being alive and living. He wanted more from life than to be alive. He wanted to live. He filled his lungs a final time with the crisp morning air.

The birds were particularly cheerful on this Friday morning, or maybe he simply appreciated them a little more than he had the day before. He wondered what Liv was doing this morning. He pictured her making her own pot of coffee and scratching Beulah's long, droopy ears as she drank her first cup. He pictured her retrieving the morning's paper from the apartment hallway so she could catch up on current events.

Then, he saw the little teddy bear with the blue ribbon wrapped around its neck propped against her door next to the newspaper. The blue ribbon unraveled all on its own and the bear's neck started stretching and slithering like the beast from his nightmare. The face on the bear contorted and revealed the sinister, snake-like eyes and piranha-like teeth of the beast in his dream. The bear was striking at Liv's hand as she reached for the newspaper.

Streeter shuddered and wondered why he'd had that thought.

He shook his head and closed the window. Heading for the shower, he decided to go to work early and hoped he could catch Liv alone. First thing. He made a mental note to research what he could about Stewart Casey as well. Regardless of Liv's belief that her neighbor was harmless, Streeter had to pacify his own mind.

CHAPTER 24

"**AGENT SCHUFFLER, IT'S ME,** Agent Bergen in Denver."

"Liv, how are you? And how's Streeter?"

We'd only worked with each other one time, on the Williams case, and that was months ago, and only via telephone. So I was glad that NYC bureau's finest, Special Agent Jerome Schuffler, remembered me.

"We're both doing well. Moved into the new Denver office this week."

"Pain in the ass to move, isn't it?"

"Definitely."

Schuffler was rumored to be even more dedicated to bringing criminals to justice than Streeter, but he did not have as good a record of arrests and convictions. No one was better in the entire bureau than Streeter Pierce was. Although Streeter mentioned Jerome Schuffler as being one of his closest friends, their shared love of work made it nearly impossible for the two men to ever find time for wives, let alone for one another's friendship.

"Word on the street is that the famous Special Agent Streeter Pierce is hanging his shingle on a new line of work," Schuffler said.

"New line of work?" I stammered.

"How are all of you taking the news?"

I didn't have a clue what Schuffler was talking about, but clearly he thought I did. I answered honestly, "Stunned."

"Well at least he's not leaving the bureau. Just leaving us field agents."

Leaving us? I had no clue. Streeter had told me none of this. I wondered what he was doing next or where he was going. "What's the word in your neighborhood?" I bluffed. "Any speculation on where he'll land?"

"I was going to ask you the same question. Odds are best that he'll be calling Quantico home."

Quantico? That was a long way from Denver. Too far. "And worst odds?"

"South Dakota, of course. No way would he take that SAC job."

"In Rapid City?" I asked. Was that why he was asking where I'd end up if I followed through with resigning next month? Was he testing me to see if I'd consider a part-time job out of the Rapid City office? I would have said yes if it meant he'd be the SAC. But I would have said no if Shank was staying. "So Shank isn't ever coming back?"

"Nope. That's public. But from your reaction, I can see I've revealed the part that isn't. That Streeter's been offered the position. So forget I said anything."

"Streeter told you?"

"He did. But that's not why you called me, is it?"

My head was spinning.

There was too much going on with Streeter that I knew nothing about. I wondered why he hadn't told me any of this. But now I knew why he had given me the Douglass case. And why Jenna Tate was spending more time in Denver. It was all starting to make sense. She was probably interviewing candidates to take Howard Magnussen's job as assistant SAC and to find a replacement field agent for Streeter.

"I need some help, if you can," I said. "Have you ever heard about the Tia Mulberry case? Involving Lance Bovier?"

"No. What was it about?"

I told him about Tia being found in the bathroom stall in Las Vegas, about Lance Bovier's conviction, and the governor's pardon.

"When the investigating agent from the Las Vegas field office interviewed Bovier, he clammed up because he said he didn't want to end up like Cleveland."

I heard Schuffler groan. "Daryl Cleveland, right?"

"Well that's what I'm thinking. Tell me about the Kesha Ryan case."

"How much time do you have, Liv? I know a lot. I was the one who worked that case," Schuffler said.

I looked at my watch. Five a.m. Seven o'clock Jerome's time in New York. I knew he was an early riser. "I have to leave to catch a plane in an hour. Think you can fill me in with most of the story by that time?"

"An abbreviated version, for sure. The New York office was asked to assist the NYPD on the investigation of a little girl who was killed by two boys even younger than she was. Her name was Kesha Ryan, as you know. But NYPD had it all wrong. The boys weren't the ones who killed her."

"Who did?" I asked, enlarging the clock icon on my computer so I wouldn't lose track of time.

"Here's the story. Eleven-year-old Kesha Ryan had been staying with her grandmother in one of the poorest neighborhoods in New York City. I'm forwarding you a picture."

The Wi-Fi in my apartment complex was amazing, and the picture came through immediately. A crumbling, dilapidated brick apartment building.

"What am I looking at? Is this where Kesha was killed?"

"This is where the Ryan family lived."

A low whistle escaped my lips. "Poor girl."

"Don't be fooled. The condition of the building was not indicative of the loving home and environment the working grandmother provided the girl, her only living relative. Although most of the tenants in the apartment complex were poor, working-class families who were simply trying to make an honest living, a few of the tenants had turned to less reputable means of earning a buck, including prostitution and drug dealing."

"And Kesha's grandmother protected her like a grizzly bear protects her cub, right?"

Schuffler said, "Exactly. Taught her which neighbors were safe and honest and which ones should be avoided. Late one evening, Kesha's grandmother called the police to tell them that her granddaughter never returned home from her trip to the store just before dark. Kesha had asked her grandmother if she could run down to the grocery store, which was less than a mile from their apartment complex, to buy some candy before the store closed. Her grandmother agreed, as long as she rode her bicycle and returned home within a half hour. Kesha agreed."

"Uh-oh," I said, not liking where this story was headed.

"After three hours, Kesha's grandmother called the police and rallied neighbors to search for the girl. The grandmother gave the officers Kesha's most recent picture. I'm sending it on."

I clicked on his incoming email, opened the attachment, and stared into the large black eyes of a beautiful child with a wide smile and shoulder-length black hair. It was a better picture of the child than the one I'd taped to my office wall. "She's adorable."

"And bright. Straight-A student. The next afternoon, Kesha's body was found in a weed patch outside an abandoned house only a block away from her home, her underpants stuffed in her mouth."

My stomach clenched. And I thought of Brianna. What might have happened if she'd stayed in the car? "That's horrible. How long ago did this happen?"

"Five years ago. Seems like yesterday. Kesha would be sixteen if she'd lived." Schuffler cleared his throat. "Within a few days of discovering her body, the authorities arrested and initially charged a seven-year-old and an eight-year-old, both boys, with the murder after they found Kesha's bike in one of the boys' family garage. After being questioned, the two boys falsely confessed to killing Kesha, which sparked a raging fire of controversy about juvenile detention laws and procedures."

"The controversy being that they were seven and eight and were coerced into a confession, right?"

"Proponents for juvenile offenders argued the two boys were too young to understand their rights under the Miranda Act and couldn't possibly comprehend the implication of their false confession, which was coerced by the officers who were first involved in the case. The news stories called NYPD Blue overzealous, brutally insensitive."

"Which must have made a profound impact on the investigators."

I could hear rustling on the other end. Schuffler had covered the receiver and was talking to someone. When he came back on the line, he said, "It did. But the case busted wide open after tests detected semen on Kesha's underpants. Medical experts advised prosecutors that it was unlikely that the young boys were old enough to produce semen, and the two were released."

"Semen? She was sexually molested?"

"Afraid so. After the charges were dropped, the attorneys for the boys demanded an apology from the prosecutors and from all the police officers involved in the terrorizing accusations made against the two youngsters. NYPD's chief of police refused to apologize. He publicly defended the department's actions during the investigation, addressed none of the accusations of harassment by police, and insisted that they behaved professionally."

"Did they?"

"The only mistake they made was a rush to judgment about the boys based on circumstantial evidence."

"The bike."

"Right," Schuffler said. "Otherwise, they followed the letter of the law and acted on the information provided by the two boys themselves. The chief insisted publicly that there had been no misconduct, nor had the officers coerced the false confession from the frightened boys."

"What do you think?" I asked, knowing that Schuffler was giving me the sanitized version.

"I think the fire of controversy over how the case was handled was so hot, the police chief got burned, and made a tactical error. Although the boys were released, the chief refused to declare that they were no longer suspects, arguing that Kesha's body was found in their neighborhood and her bike was found in one of the boys' garage. Because of the boys' ages and perhaps because they were two of the youngest people ever charged with murder in the country, the Kesha Ryan case had received notoriety and infamy. Not to mention the widespread media coverage."

"I don't remember hearing anything about this," I said. "So who killed Kesha? And how did the boys end up with the bike?"

"I think the boys stole a bike that was abandoned in an alley. End of story. Within a couple of weeks of the boys' release, the police came to that same conclusion. They had also discovered a similar match to the DNA found on the underwear in the state's criminal sex-offender database."

"Daryl Cleveland?"

"Yes, but it gets worse. The police learned that Daryl Cleveland had been sentenced ten years before Kesha's murder to twelve years in prison for a sexual assault."

"If he was serving a term in prison, how did his DNA get on Kesha's underwear?"

"Turns out, Cleveland wasn't in state prison. He had received a reduced sentence, had been released for good behavior, and was found serving a new sentence in a county jail on a charge of predatory sexual assault of a child. County wouldn't let NYPD get DNA samples once Daryl Cleveland refused. That's when the police involved the FBI. I decided to take a different approach."

I glanced at the clock. Just under half an hour had passed. I still had time.

"Knowing that DNA of family members can be similar, we found Daryl's brother, who gladly volunteered to give us whatever we needed. Cleveland's entire family had grown tired of the twenty-nine-year-old dragging the family through one crisis to the next. Daryl had been indicted, but acquitted many times. Nine years earlier on a charge of sexually assaulting a seventeen-year-old girl. Four years earlier for sexually abusing an eighteen-year-old mentally handicapped woman. The same year for aggravated battery, for choking a woman with his bare hands and eventually with a cord."

I thought of Rebecca Douglass and how she'd been strangled.

"And the bum was scheduled to appear in court the following week on charges involving another young girl, a ten-year-old."

I said, "Complicated. That poor family."

"You said it. Lots of victims in this case. Anyway, once DNA tests indicated a match, I arrested Daryl Cleveland for the murder of Kesha Ryan. He denied killing the girl, but did admit to engaging in sex with her the night before she was found murdered in the abandoned lot."

"That's so sick. The girl was only eleven."

"Yep. And he was claiming to have had consensual sex with her."

"Sick bastard."

Schuffler drew in a deep breath. "After further investigation of Cleveland, we saw that the charges filed against him with the ten-year-old girl involved similar circumstances as those in the Kesha Ryan case. That child, who had been sexually assaulted at gunpoint in an abandoned building less than a mile from where Kesha's body was found, had run home to her mother and identified Daryl Cleveland as the offender from both a stack of photographs and later from a police lineup. Having been accused of Kesha's death, Cleveland eventually confessed to sexually assaulting both young girls, but vehemently denied killing Kesha. As proof, Cleveland argued that he would have killed the first ten-year-old if he had been the killer of Kesha. The police testified that their reports indicated Cleveland was neither credible, nor believable."

"What a scumbag. So you had the right guy and plenty of hard evidence against him, right?"

Schuffler said, "Because NYPD screwed up so badly by initially arresting the young boys, they had been under tremendous scrutiny for their actions, accused of coercion, unnecessary roughness with suspects, racism—the works. So they were in the fishbowl, but not entirely deserving of the scrutiny. They did make a mistake by arresting the two young boys before all the reports were back, but the rest of the allegations were unfounded."

I looked at my clock. "So what was the problem?"

"The problem was, when we arrested Cleveland, the department put out a demand for secrecy on any further actions or information about his arrest until the public relations team decided how and when to release the information. The press knew nothing about Cleveland's arrest."

"That makes perfect sense."

"I caused part of the problem by using the brother's DNA to compare to the stains left on Kesha Ryan's underpants. The defense was going to suggest Daryl's brother killed the girl. Can you believe that? We never saw that coming. That twist plus the public sentiment about NYPD's rush to judgment with the two boys proved to be a recipe for Daryl Cleveland's acquittal. Again."

"And did he? Get acquitted?"

I heard him sigh. "While Cleveland was out on bail, someone killed him. Left his body in an abandoned lot not far from where Kesha was found."

"Payback? From the brother? Who?"

"Liv, someone had stuffed his underwear down his mouth. No one but the police and FBI knew that detail about Kesha Ryan's death. Even the press hadn't caught wind of that detail. An insider, my bet."

"That's what Lance Bovier was afraid of," I said. "Law enforcement or some whacky citizen on the inside of the judicial system had killed Daryl Cleveland. Before he went to trial. He must have been afraid the same might happen to him. That someone would kill him the same way he killed Tia. No wonder he wouldn't say anything."

Schuffler said, "The problem is, we never figured out who killed Daryl Cleveland."

"But you're sure Cleveland killed Kesha Ryan?"

"Positive. But as for how he died, even though I know it had to have been an inside job, I never could figure out who and how."

"And because Daryl Cleveland was found with his underwear stuffed down his throat, like his victim, you knew it was someone seeking revenge."

"That and the fact that no one ever knew we had him in custody. Not even the press. There were only a handful of people who knew."

"Do you have the list?"

"Why do you need it?" Schuffler asked.

"Because someone told Lance Bovier. And that someone knew Daryl Cleveland was killed as a payback for what he did to Kesha Ryan."

"That can't be. Seriously, Liv, other than where Jimmy Hoffa is buried, this might be the best-kept secret in the country."

"Someone knew. And told Lance Bovier. I need that list."

CHAPTER 25

THE WIZENED MAN PROPPED in the wheelchair near the window looked nothing like the photo I'd seen in the files down at Longview Police Department an hour earlier. The former Cowlitz County coroner had aged far more than the twenty years that had elapsed since the photo was taken. I almost didn't believe the woman at the front desk when she told me that the man in the commons area of the assisted-living home was Albert Duncan.

But she assured me he was.

From the files, I had gleaned much about Albert Duncan, even though the lion's share of the material was about the unsolved murder case of Rhonda Kuehl. Duncan, a confirmed bachelor, lived a simple life, had never been formally trained in medicine, yet had brilliant instincts and incredible talent for medical forensics. He had a lifetime habit of chewing tobacco, a strong sense of right and wrong, and a rigid work ethic that suggested to me how difficult it must have been for him to know that the Kuehl case was the only unsolved murder of his career. And fifteen years ago, Duncan had retired as a formidable man, even at age seventy, both physically and intellectually.

Yet here he sat, his body slumped against the chair, his eyes closed and his mouth hanging open.

"Mr. Duncan?" I said, standing nearby.

Heads turned my way as others heard me repeat his name a bit louder the second time. I touched his shoulder and called, "Mr. Duncan?"

His eyes fluttered open; his mouth snapped shut. He repositioned himself in the chair, saying nothing.

I extended my hand to him and his eyes focused as he reached out to take whatever it was he thought I was handing him. When he realized I wanted to shake his hand, his eyes moved up to mine, a quizzical expression on his lined face.

"Albert Duncan?" I asked, gripping his hand in mine.

"Yes," he said, sitting up in his chair.

"I'm Special Agent Liv Bergen with Denver's Federal Bureau of Investigation."

His eyes shone like beacons and the aged man before me morphed into the younger man of twenty years earlier. His voice strong, he asked, "FBI? What can I do for you, Agent Bergen?"

I looked around and pulled up a chair near his. The legs screeched across the linoleum floor and I noticed Duncan glaring at the other people in the room. Most turned away, and those closest to us toddled off when he shooed them with his bony hand. "Mind your business. We're talking."

I sat next to him and said, "I'm working a cold case from several years ago. Between Hawthorne and Las Vegas."

I noticed something shift behind his eyes, like a piece of a puzzle that had been eluding him. "Another young girl? Is she dead?"

I nodded. "I came across fibers in that case that matched unidentified fibers from the Rhonda Kuehl case. Do you remember that?"

"Huh," he snorted. "Remember it? I can't get it out of my head. It's the only thing preventing me from reaching the peace I'd always hoped for by this time in my life."

"Do you remember the unidentified fibers from that case?" I pulled a sheet of paper from the file the Longview Police Department had let me copy and handed it to him.

"I do," Duncan said, shoving the paper back at me. "But they're not unidentified. I know where they came from. But I could never prove it. And it's not what you think."

I didn't know what I thought and certainly hadn't a clue what he was talking about. "Then what is it?"

"Gary James killed that little girl as sure as I'm wasting away in this hellhole. Just like he killed that scientist's little boy in the neighboring county. And now James is dead and Cowlitz County has two open cases that aren't being investigated because they believe they have the answer for one, and don't care about the other."

"Yes, I read the file. I see Gary James was killed last year. He was your primary suspect twenty years ago. But you never brought charges. Wait, what do you mean 'believe'? Are you saying you know something the Cowlitz County folks don't?"

He slammed his palm down on the wheelchair's armrest. "One unsolved case. That poor little girl's murder. Dagnabbit, because of him, I have that blemish on my record and her injustice forever on my conscience."

"What happened? Why didn't you arrest Gary James?"

His eyes held mine for some time before sliding over to the window, a gaze that would suggest his mind had wandered. I wondered if senility or dementia was at work here, Albert Duncan drifting in and out of reality. But I wanted to know what he knew about the fibers, what it might indicate in Brianna's murder.

"Mr. Duncan?"

"Youth. So impatient," he said, his eyes staring far off into the wilderness beyond the yard of this deep inland port town of Washington. So I sat patiently until I was about to find a nurse, ask what his condition was, and try to arrange to come back when his mind was clear. "Just like your friend I talked to. Did he send you?"

"Who? What friend?" I questioned whether he even remembered who I was. And I was starting to wonder if anything Duncan told me could be trusted.

"From Denver. The agent."

"Do you mean Special Agent Bo Marshall? From the Las Vegas bureau?"

He shook his head and grew silent.

"Mr. Duncan?"

"Doc," he barked. "Pipe down. I'm trying to tell you a story."

I started to say I wasn't the doctor. But I decided I'd keep quiet.

"A small crowd had already gathered near the deserted lot where a gas station had once been on the two hundred block of East Bellevue Street. Morbidly curious, all those people. I just sat in my car staring out at the uniformed and plainclothes officers and deputies who were meandering about at the crime scene that day. I remember wondering if anyone was left to answer other emergency calls requested of the Longview Police Department or the Cowlitz County Sheriff's Department."

He frowned. I was trying to follow his ramblings. First, he scolded me about the agent who came to see him, confused by which bureau I was from. Or Marshall was from. Now, he seemed to be recollecting a crime scene. I just didn't know whose. Rhonda Kuehl's? Or Gary James's? Or the boy's from a neighboring county?

"I'd warned and scolded the citizens at town meetings for falling prey to gossip and for blowing every situation out of proportion before any official reports were ever released. And although their obsession with nurturing the town's grapevine disappointed me, I knew that it was beyond their control to behave any differently, since gossip in this small town is one of the only forms of entertainment."

"I understand. I grew up in Rapid City, South Dakota," I said, understanding now that he was telling me about the crime scene from twenty years earlier, about the nuances of investigating crimes in small towns, the locations from the files recognizable.

He sputtered a laugh. A smile fell on his tobacco-stained lips. "The Dakotas? Child, I knew there was a reason I liked you. That's where my grandpappy came from."

"Why were they gossiping that day?"

"Murder wasn't normal for us. In fact, as the county coroner, I can only think of three times, including that day, in the forty years I had served the community. That morning rumors were spreading from everyone's lips like wildfire during a drought."

It was my turn to chuckle. His analogies reminded me of my grandpa.

"My experience as coroner and medical examiner, however, was never more challenged than when I assisted the victims after the eruption of Mount St. Helens decades earlier. I was young. And it was May. May was not my favorite month. I'd lost fifty-two of my acquaintances and friends that May in the aftermath of that powerful disaster. I'd lost my mother in May a few years after that. And then there was Rhonda Kuehl."

"May seventh." Another fact I remembered from reading the files. My plane arrived in time for me to eat a quick brunch in Portland and read the files before driving the hour north to Longview.

His expression appeared far off again. "The only image that haunted me more than the carnage I saw in the aftermath of the Mount St. Helens disaster was that of little Rhonda's half-naked and battered body lying still and silent in that damned deserted parking lot."

"What's up with that? I drove by that parking lot and it's still deserted. Has this town's growth flatlined or something?" I asked.

He shook his head and raised an eyebrow as he stared. "That lot is bad news."

"I read in your files where some of the residents thought it might be haunted, a portal to hell or something. Is that still the sentiment around here?"

Duncan shrugged. "I wouldn't know. I don't get out much these days."

"What do you remember about that day?"

I saw him shift in his chair, swallow hard. "Tall, overgrown grass. A misty rain. My windshield wipers going back and forth, back and forth. I stared out my windshield for God knows how long at that empty lot and all those officers and sheriff's department people standing around. No dogs taking a crap or kids playing that day. I scooped an index finger full of snuff from my tin and stuffed it securely between my bottom lip and gums." I sat quietly, startled that he'd shifted his gaze from out the window to me. "I can still envision the old Shell gas station that has long since been torn down, underground tanks excavated and removed, from the northwest corner of that lot."

His eyes moved back to the window and I noticed a few nurses wheeling other guests out of the commons area. We weren't alone, but the nurses recognized we needed some confidential space for talking. "I'd spent hours and days—mostly nights—combing that lot looking for something that would help prove that Gary James had sexually assaulted and strangled thirteen-year-old Rhonda Kuehl. But there'd been too much rain."

I asked, "It had rained that May?"

He scoffed. "It rains every May. It always rains in Longview."

"What about the night before? When Rhonda went missing?"

"Good girl. You called her Rhonda. Not Kuehl. That's good. Means you care," he said.

I wondered if that was why Streeter called me Liv and others by their last name. Because he cared. "What happened? Do you remember?"

His eyes cut toward me. "Every detail. It was misty the night when Rhonda was last seen. Rhonda left a church social with two friends at a quarter to nine. About sixty teenagers from the Longview Middle School had attended the church-sponsored event. Rhonda and her friends left the party in time so the three girls would arrive at their homes before their parents' curfews of nine o'clock. They walked together for the first block, until Rhonda's friends went a different direction than she, to their homes. Rhonda was only a block and a half from her home. In an interview the next day, one of the tearful friends said, 'Doc Duncan, I looked back. Over my shoulder. Made sure to watch Rhonda make it home. So as not to get her parents mad about missing curfew. I swear, Doc!'"

"They call you Doc?" I asked, realizing he hadn't been confusing me with a doctor earlier. He was telling me to call him Doc, not Mr. Duncan. I wondered what else I had misunderstood. "And you believed their stories?"

He nodded. "Neither had seen anyone else on the well-lighted streets. Both were upset that they were probably the last ones to see Rhonda alive. The next morning, one of Rhonda's neighbors found her body in the tall grass behind the gas station on his way to work. The lot is empty now. Gas station was torn down years ago. Her corpse was within several houses of her home and the girl had been sexually assaulted and strangled to death."

"That must have been difficult for you," I offered.

"Her body was naked from the waist down. Her pants and under-wear were found nearby in the grass within a few feet of her body. Of the thirteen initial suspects who were interrogated, including the parents, which was standard practice with deaths of children, all but three of them, those who had no verifiable alibi for their whereabouts that evening, were quickly eliminated as possible perpetrators of the murder."

His recollection of details was quite sharp. I had underestimated Doc Duncan. "But someone heard something that night. I read your report."

"You pay attention." The gleam in his eyes when he smiled at me was a compliment. I was rewarded with more details, sharp and exactly matching what I'd read from decades earlier. "So I'm going to share a secret with you I've never told anyone. Not even your agent friend from Denver who paid me a visit."

CHAPTER 26

I WANTED TO ASK what agent friend but was afraid Duncan would tell me to pipe down again.

Everyone from the nearby tables around us had left the common area. The sunshine streaking through the window was trapping the particles of dust that hung in the still air. I noticed I'd been holding my breath, waiting for his secret, and was disappointed when all he recited was more facts from the file I'd read.

"During my investigation, I'd learned that one neighbor had heard voices around nine o'clock outside the back of her house, which was adjacent to the lot. She told me she awakened her husband, who got out of bed, went to the back of the house, and looked out into the darkness of the backyard and adjacent lot. He reportedly saw two shadowy figures and heard a male and female arguing."

"A man named Roger Croger. The neighbor, right?" I asked.

He nodded. "Croger said the female sounded upset, but explained to me that he didn't do much about it because he assumed it was likely a harmless squabble between two of the teenagers leaving the church social being held a few blocks down the street. The squabbling stopped when he yelled out to them something like, 'Hey, what's going on out there?'

Then, he said he went back to bed, thinking the two had resolved their differences."

"Frustrating. I bet that guy lived with a lot of regret."

"Until the day he died," Duncan said. "My recurring nightmare began when I first saw Rhonda's half-naked body in the grass, her prepubescent vaginal area smeared with semen and blood, her vacant eyes bulging, her black hair matted and tangled, the top buttons of her blouse ripped away, exposing a clear view of her deeply bruised neck where her fragile windpipe had been crushed. Crushed. But the worst parts were those small incisions overlaying the bruises where her fingernails gouged her own neck as she desperately clawed at her attacker's grip."

The room had fallen silent. I was aware I was holding my breath.

"The smell. And that milky bluish-gray translucence of her skin." He shuddered.

So did I. Although I had only seen photos of a body in the fully developed stage of rigor mortis, I dreaded having to experience that in real life. And couldn't imagine what that looked like on a child.

"The only image worse than seeing Rhonda at that moment was witnessing the expressions on the faces of her parents seconds later. The Kuehls had succeeded in pushing their way through the onlookers, curious about the commotion, and stood staring at their only child lying broken and still in the grass. Horrible."

"I am so sorry."

He looked back at me, his eyes wet with the memories. "They told me when they had awakened that day and saw Rhonda had not come home the night before, they assumed she had gone home with one of her friends, too afraid to walk home in the dark by herself. She had done this on several occasions, unusually fearful at age thirteen of what may be lurking in the shadows. Do you believe in premonitions?"

I stared at him, knowing he really wasn't looking for my answer, just my reaction. He wanted to know if I was open to the idea.

I must have appeared accepting, since he continued, "The Kuehls did. Anyway, I cursed at the policemen who were supposed to be controlling the crowd and quickly escorted the Kuehls away from the crime scene.

They only saw her for a brief moment, but they paid for it the rest of their lives. No parent should have to see that."

I thought of my sister Barbara and confirmed my belief that she should never see the crime scene photos of Brianna. Never. Not even if she did fly to Denver and beat me within an inch of my life or use whatever other interrogation tactics she'd learned in the army.

I tried to focus on how Albert Duncan's case twenty years ago related to Brianna's case. Not to confuse the facts with the active Douglass case that was waiting for my focus back home. All of them involved too much tragedy, with victims far too young to be a part of all the horror. "But fibers found in the cold case I'm working brought me here. To find you. Tell me about the fibers."

"Four days before Rhonda Kuehl's murder, the police had received a complaint from another teenage girl who said a man grabbed her and attempted to pull off her pants on the way home one night from the Longview public library. The young girl told police she had fought and screamed until a light came on at a nearby house and the attacker ran away. The police composite revealed a description strikingly similar to Gary James. Two witnesses also gave a similar description of James the night of Rhonda's death as the man who they saw walking down East Bellevue Street around nine o'clock and was assumed to be either drunk or well on his way to being drunk. In both cases, we found fibers."

He leaned closer to me and whispered, "And not unidentified. They're carpet fibers. An odd shade of pink. I know this for a fact because I've been in the house where they came from."

"Gary James's house?"

He shook his head.

My heart raced. I hadn't been wasting my time. This man knew about the fibers. "You know where the pink carpet fibers came from in the Rhonda Kuehl case. The exact same fibers found at the crime scene of the cold case in Nevada that I'm investigating. But they didn't come from Gary James's house. And Gary James is dead. Killed last year, from what I saw in your records. I'm confused. When I first got here, you mentioned that you believed Gary James killed Rhonda Kuehl twenty years ago, sure as you were sitting here."

"I lied. Self-preservation." He cut his eyes toward me, and then squinted. He reminded me of Festus from *Gunsmoke*.

I was so confused. He was talking in riddles. I wanted to know more. Wanted to believe that his mind was still sharp and focused, but the zigzag of his thoughts made me question everything. I waited, remembering his comment about my impatience earlier.

"You asked why I didn't arrest Gary James. Even with these eyewitnesses, I knew I couldn't press charges without some physical evidence to prove James's guilt. The rain washed away what little promise of hope I had for semen and follicles I might have found on Rhonda's body. I had a little, but back then the DNA testing wasn't so sophisticated on such scant evidence. Didn't matter. Gary James refused to offer a comparison sample, never put himself into any situation where a sample could be taken without his consent. I'd tried. In all that time, James never slipped up once. Never discarded a soda can, a beer bottle, or so much as a spoon from an ice cream treat into a public trash can. It was as if James knew more than I did about DNA."

"So after he died, you tested his DNA?"

He nodded. "Still know some people who owe me favors after all these years. I didn't want to believe my instincts on this one. But I was right. Gary James did not kill Rhonda Kuehl, did not attempt to molest the little girl four days before Rhonda's murder. But he did kill the little boy in the neighboring county. His DNA was a match on that case. But not on Rhonda's. That's my secret. Haven't told a soul."

"Then who killed Rhonda?"

He sighed and visibly slumped deeper into his wheelchair. "Even though the deputy sheriff hounded me every day to complete the autopsy, to complete my findings on every speck of evidence, tried to get me removed as county coroner, and eventually quit his job over my inaction on this case, I believe Gary James was actually an eyewitness to Rhonda Kuehl's murder that night, not the perpetrator."

"An eyewitness? How can you be so sure?"

"For one, he preferred boys, not girls. I tested the evidence from the other girl's case, a bite mark. DNA from James didn't match that either."

"But she identified Gary James."

"She'd identified someone who resembled Gary James. I searched Gary James's house, his vehicles, his work, everywhere Gary James ever visited. Found a lot of photos of little boys, but not one photo of a little girl. Never found any pink carpet."

"And you're sure the fibers found in Rhonda Kuehl's case were from a pink carpet?" The fuzziness of Duncan's world was beginning to come into focus. "Do you think the real killer of Rhonda Kuehl murdered Gary James last year?"

"No," he said, reaching into his deepest thoughts. "No, I don't think so. If he wanted Gary dead, he would have done it years ago when he had opportunity. But I do think the real killer of Rhonda Kuehl could very well be your suspect in the cold case you're investigating near Nevada. That's not far from here. Just a spell down the road."

My heart raced. Brianna's killer. He knew who Brianna's killer was.

"The coat he keeps folded up in the truck of his car would likely have stray carpet fibers from when he lived here in Longview."

"You know who the killer is? From twenty years ago? Whose house has pink carpet?"

"Not his house. His folks' house." Albert Duncan's eyes were bright. "He'd never wash that coat. It was his pappy's and it was cashmere."

"You know a lot about this man. Mind filling me in?" I said, anxious for a name.

Instead of answering me, he pulled out his wallet. He carefully unfolded the color photocopy he had neatly tucked where his dollar bills should have been. He slid the article across to me. "Did you see this in the files? At the Longview PD?"

I shook my head.

He said, "In the exact same spot of the lot in the tall grass in the same month of May on the twenty-year anniversary of Rhonda Kuehl's unsolved murder."

In the photo lay the half-naked body of Gary James, lying in a position identical to the one Rhonda had been found in. His pants and underwear were lying in the tall grass nearby. His shirt had been ripped open at the collar to reveal the bruises on the neck, chin, and shoulder area from the manual strangulation.

Gary James's face in the photo had a bluish discoloration along with small hemorrhages on the face and around his bulging eyes. The flies had already begun congregating and depositing larvae into the dark, moist areas of his head, concentrating in his agape mouth and wide nostrils. Seeing the small, linear abrasions on the bruised neck, it was obvious to me that James had struggled with his perpetrator, just as Rhonda had done, scratching and clawing for relief from the hands—or garrote—that gripped his neck and squeezed the life out of him.

"There's no semen. Not exactly like Rhonda's murder. But you get the gist."

I got it. Alarm bells were clanging in my skull. Another copycat murder of a suspect who'd apparently escaped the long arm of the law? Like Daryl Cleveland? Like Lance Bovier?

"Community justice. That's the term that came to mind when I saw it."

"Vigilante," I said. "An avenger."

He offered a knowing smile. "I don't have a clue who killed Gary James last year, but I've always suspected I knew who killed Rhonda Kuehl. Just didn't want to believe it. But you coming here, telling me the connection between Rhonda and another young victim near Hawthorne . . ."

His gaze swung toward the windows, his thoughts far off. I waited. I had no doubt this man's thoughts were crystal clear.

"I've been sitting on this horrible secret for years. It's worked on my insides as if I'd swallowed an octopus that wants out." He sighed and repositioned himself in the wheelchair. "There's only one man whose mother owned a house here in Longview, carpeted in pink. And there's only one man who resembled Gary James. I can understand how the first teenager could have been confused. But I could never get enough evidence to press charges. My one unsolved. And it was a doozy."

I held my breath and he held my full attention.

"Mrs. Kuehl died shortly after this picture was taken. After she spat on Gary James and cursed at him." He turned his face to the sun shining through the window. "She said, 'Wrath to the wicked.' And walked away. But Mrs. Kuehl was wrong about who killed her daughter. It wasn't Gary James. But he was wicked and deserved wrath."

I fought the urge to ask more questions.

He finally turned to face me. "You're looking for a man who has an insatiable hunger for young girls. A murderer. And hopefully you'll understand why I found it difficult to gather support for my theory. You're looking for a man named Wayne W. Wilson. He moved away from Longview a year after Rhonda Kuehl's death. But he still owns his mother's house. The woman's been dead for several years. And he returns to Longview on occasion."

"Thank you," I offered, ready to get started on my research of any Wayne W. Wilson, to track his movements since he left Longview nineteen years ago. "Albert Duncan, you're an amazing man. I'll let you know what comes of this. By the way, what was the name of the little boy who you think Gary James killed in the nearby county? And was his death ever vindicated?"

"Benji. Benjamin . . . dagnabbit. I'll think of it. Give me a minute."

He told me where Wilson kept a hidden key, gave me the address to his mother's house, which was only two blocks from here, suggested I check it out myself, take a sample for the lab to test. I shook his hand again and turned to go, thinking of one last question.

"You couldn't gather support for your theory and arrest Wilson because he was a hometown boy?"

He scowled and shook his head. "Because he was always tampering with any evidence I found on him. Wilson was my deputy sheriff. Oh, and the boy from the neighboring county who was killed, the scientist's boy? Linwood. Benji Linwood."

CHAPTER 27

MY FINGERS FLEW ACROSS the keypad of my cell phone, fumbling to call Jack Linwood.

Panic rose in my chest. It felt like I was having a heart attack. I didn't dare drive, so I just sat behind the wheel of my rental car in the parking lot of the elderly care facility. Could it be that Benji was Jack's son? Could it be that his son was molested, murdered by Gary James? Was that the torture that caused Jack's perpetual brooding, his deep introspection? If it was his son, had Jack known they'd discovered who killed Benji? Had he known that Gary James was murdered last May?

I lifted the phone to my ear and listened to the ring. Longer rings than I'd ever heard before. Long, numerous rings. I hit the end button. I typed a text. One that would get his attention. If I was correct in my assumptions. "*BENJI? CALL ASAP.*" I prayed he was within cell coverage rather than in the remote outdoors. I needed to hear his voice, to talk with him.

I drew in a deep breath and steadied my shaking hands by gripping the steering wheel. I turned the key in the ignition and shifted into reverse, maneuvered slowly out of the parking lot and onto the deserted streets of Longview.

I occupied my thoughts by recounting what Albert Duncan had told me, searching for a way to understand the connections in this web of destruction that had touched both my life and Jack's.

I started with the case furthest from either of us. Rhonda Kuehl.

I understood why Duncan never pursued the person he thought was the real killer of Rhonda Kuehl, since it was his deputy sheriff. I understood local politics.

No way Cowlitz County would ever allow Albert Duncan to accuse one of its own employees of murder unless Albert had indisputable proof. But I trusted Doc's instincts. And I could see how a deputy sheriff could redirect a sketch to Gary James away from himself, if they were that similar in appearance. The sketch was generic enough to look like both and with his direct involvement on the case with the girl, he or someone within the department could have easily steered her attentions toward James and away from a lawman. It was dark. She was young. He's the law. I could see how evidence might be manipulated from the inside.

I didn't give a rat's ass what Cowlitz County thought of me, so I was going to follow up on the strongest lead I'd discovered so far. And I'd been willing to bend my own standards to pursue the truth, including breaking and entering. I wondered if I'd still have Streeter's support if anyone ever found out what I was about to do.

I located the street within minutes of leaving the assisted-living home, glad I was driving a rental car. My mind flashed to the light, old-fashioned car that abruptly turned off my tail after work and I realized I might have seen a familiar rental car sticker on the window, just like the one I had today. I shook off the distracting thought and focused on my task at hand. The house was exactly where Duncan had instructed me to drive. It was small and tidy, like all of the homes in the neighborhood. The yellow paint was faded but not yet peeling. The lawn was as groomed as the neighbors', yet the house looked empty. Lawn service, I suppose. Or a willing neighbor, since Doc said the deputy sheriff only returned to his mother's home occasionally during the year.

The key was exactly where Duncan told me it would be. Hooked on a nail under the wooden deck, one foot from the house on the west side. I walked swiftly to the front door in broad daylight, as if I belonged, never swiveling to look over my shoulder or around the neighborhood.

I'd learned that guilty people, people who were doing something they shouldn't, tended to be more diligent about observing their surroundings than those who weren't. Stakeouts had been very helpful in crafting my own behaviors.

I slid the key into the lock, and it turned easily in my hand, as did the doorknob. I was inside within seconds. Stunned, I saw a sea of pink carpet. In the home of Wayne W. Wilson's dead mother. Pink everything. The house was in immaculate condition, as I imagined it had been when Wilson's mother was alive. The decorations, the furniture, the doilies appeared very much as I imagined Mother Wilson wanted. This was not a man's home. This was an old woman's home.

I glanced over my shoulder through the front windows to see if anyone might be observing me from a neighboring house and noticed that the lacy drapes allowed me complete privacy. I tiptoed carefully to the kitchen, sliding my sleeves over my hands, reminding myself to wipe down the front doorknob and the key before I left. Finding a paring knife and a plastic bag in one of the kitchen drawers, I knelt down near the living room corner and moved an end table aside. My hands were shaking a bit as I sliced some of the carpet and slipped it into the bag. Stuffing the bag into my pocket, I replaced the end table to cover up the swatch I'd cut.

Just as I was replacing the knife where I'd found it, my nerves were jangled by the shrill ring of a phone. I dropped the knife, cut myself as my instincts made me grab for it, and cursed as it clattered to the floor and I fumbled to answer my cell.

"Liv?"

"Jack! I—" My cell phone slipped from my bloody hand and clattered to the floor. I moved quickly to the sink to wash my cut and jammed paper towels against my index finger to stem the blood flow, cursing and mumbling along the way. I looked at the cell phone lying on the linoleum and called toward it, "Hold on, Jack."

I heard his voice but couldn't hear what he was saying.

I made quick work of my mess, wiped away any fingerprints and blood spatter, and scooped up my cell. "There. Phew."

"What are you doing? Are you okay?"

"Give me a sec. I've got to get out of here. So we can talk." I moved quickly to the front door, abandoning any thoughts of combing the house for more evidence, and slipped through the front door, replacing the key and returning to my car, head down without another word.

The entire time, Jack was asking if I was in trouble, was there someone with me, should he devise a code. I said nothing until I got into the car and pulled away from the curb.

"Sorry, Jack. I was kind of in the middle of something."

"Sounded serious," he said, his mood shifting from concern to irritation.

"I accidentally cut myself when you called and dropped my phone." I glanced in my rearview mirror, half-expecting to see the bubble lights of a cruiser behind me. Nothing.

"You okay?"

"Now I am. Jack, I'm in Longview, Washington." I waited to hear his response. His silence spoke volumes. Benjamin Linwood was definitely Jack's son. "I'm neck deep in something and I need your help. Tell me about Benji."

"First, is anyone with you?"

"No."

"You're alone?"

"Yes."

"And you sound like you got into a car. Whose car?"

"A rental. I'm headed to Portland. The airport. I have a flight in ninety minutes to DC."

"Good. Stay on the phone until you get there. Do not hang up. Do not let anyone stop you."

"Jack, what's going on?"

I stopped at a light that had turned yellow and listened to him breathing. I waited for almost the entire red light before I finally filled the void of silence. "I flew out this morning to talk to Albert Duncan about the Rhonda Kuehl case. Some fibers were found in that case that tied to another case I'm working."

"Douglass?"

I couldn't lie to Jack. Even to protect Streeter. "No, not that case. Another one that I shouldn't be working. Remember me telling you about my sister Barbara?"

"Barbara. Which one is that? The nun?"

"No, the army colonel."

"Oh yes. The one who lives in California, divorced, has two kids," Jack recited, like he was reading from a case profile.

"Three kids, actually," I said, feeling guilty for not sharing the whole story with Jack before now. "She had a third child, the youngest. Her name was Brianna Keller. She was abducted and killed seven years ago."

The noise Jack made was more than a groan, something sounding . . . wounded.

"I've kinda been working that cold case. Quietly. I don't want to get fired over this or get anyone else fired, which is why I hadn't told you about it. I'm sorry."

Jack chuckled. Something I rarely heard him do. "Don't apologize. I understand. Believe me. I have been doing a little moonlighting myself. I can't tell you how many times I've worked a case and wondered if it had any connection with my son."

"So your son was Benji?" I asked tenderly.

He talked a long time about his son, shared small moments between them, which spoke volumes about the love they'd shared. I hadn't heard Jack talk as tenderly about anyone before, even to me. The drive between Longview and Portland flew by, and I didn't want the sound of Jack's voice to end. His tone was a tonic that soothed. Jack had never shared so much about his life, himself, as he did in that hour as he reminisced about his life with Benji.

He must have noticed the time because he asked, "How close are you to the airport?"

"Just about there," I said, noting how his tone had changed.

"Duncan is smart. He spent years trying to solve Benji's case and I never knew it. I'm grateful to him for that. For caring, for never forgetting about my son."

The lightbulb clicked on about something Doc had said early in our conversation, when I'd questioned his mental faculties. He hadn't confused an agent visiting from Denver with one from Las Vegas, as I first thought. "You went to see him, didn't you? At the elderly care facility."

A long pause followed.

My heart ached for Jack. My heart weighed heavy from suffering chil-dren. I was crushed by not knowing what happened to Brianna. But I couldn't imagine what it would be like carrying that burden of not know-ing what happened to my own child.

I said, "I love you, too, by the way."

I heard him react. A smile? "Do you remember last Christmas? At DIA when you saw me coming in from a flight? I lied to you. About where I was."

I remembered. I knew he had lied to me instantly. At the time, I was worried that he might have a wife or girlfriend stashed somewhere and wasn't telling me. He told me he was with some college buddies and later added that he was working on an informal case behind the scenes, which is why he had asked me not to tell Streeter about him being out of town. And now, I had concluded what he was going to tell me. He had been hired as the private investigator on the Greenwood case, to help the KCPD solve that cold case.

"I can't live like this anymore, Liv. I can't lie to you."

"Then don't," I said simply, pulling into the rental car parking lot at the airport. I turned off the car and stepped out, waved off the rental company employee, and walked slowly toward the airport.

He drew in a breath. "I was on a fishing trip. Was following up some leads I'd discovered on a Kansas City case, a child's cold case."

My heart started beating faster. "The Greenwood case?"

"How did you know?"

"Dodson. He's been reading your emails. The investigators found the child unearthed on Monday, along with the man who owned the house. Apparently, he'd been killed in the same way as the Greenwood girl and they wanted to confirm both identities quickly."

Jack growled, "And Dodson never told me, never called."

"He said it came through on your work email so he was in charge of getting that work processed."

"Convenient," Jack said, but his tone was quite angry.

"What does that mean?"

"Nothing. Do you know what came of their discovery?"

"Check it out. There was a huge press conference on Tuesday morning.

Dodson verified the identity of both the Greenwood girl and the killer. Since then he's been building the case based on the files from the PI that Greenwood hired." I waited a beat, to let him confess that he was the PI.

"They found the killer?"

"Like I said, murdered in the same manner as he had killed the girl decades earlier." I had already added Carl Halbrook to the list of killers who'd been murdered in the same way as they killed children. To Daryl Cleveland, Lance Bovier, Gary James.

"How did I miss that this week?" Jack asked.

"Well, you have been off-grid all week. Probably weren't somewhere you could get reception most of the time." I walked up to the airline kiosk and punched in my reservation. With no bags, I grabbed my boarding pass and headed for security.

"Liv, listen," Jack said. "My annual fishing trips aren't about catching fish."

I stopped short. Of course they aren't. How dense did he think I was? He'd been investigating, fishing for information. About Benji. Hiring out as a PI to help on other unsolved cases.

"Then why did you go this year?"

"What do you mean? Isn't that obvious? Liv, my sole purpose for joining the FBI was to uncover what happened to my son. If they'd known that—if Jenna Tate had put two and two together during our interview— she would have never approved me being hired by the FBI."

I thought about how bad Jenna Tate really was with her interviewing skills, considering that Jack's past slipped through the cracks, as did my connection with a niece's cold case. That topic never even came up during my interview.

"And I could get fired for pursuing an investigation of my son's death, just like you could for investigating your niece's. We both have to be careful."

"But didn't Doc tell you?"

"Tell me what?" Jack asked.

"How long ago did you visit Doc Duncan?"

"Last year, about this time. I thought that maybe whoever killed Rhonda might know something about Benji."

My mind raced. Jack was in Longview this time last year during his "fishing trip." Jack visited Doc Duncan. If Doc told Jack what he had told me, his speculation that Gary James had killed the little boy in the neighboring county, but not Rhonda Kuehl, about the DNA testing Doc had finagled last year, then what would Jack have done with that information? How far had Jack gone on his fishing expeditions?

My heart raced. "Did Doc tell you who he thought killed your son?"

Jack hesitated. "He was tight-lipped. He told me he knew little about Benji's case, that he had focused his entire career on Rhonda's and determined there was no connection between the two abductions and deaths. He was absolutely sure of it. But I sensed he was protecting someone. I couldn't quite grasp who it was. But I think I've figured it out since."

"What? Who?" I asked, wondering what it was he was working on, considering Gary James was already dead.

Jack said, "Duncan had a deputy sheriff named Wayne Wilson. I have been hot on his trail ever since. The guy's a piece of work. Has a thing for little girls. I don't think he has any connection to Benji, but I do think I am building a case to nail his ass for Rhonda Kuehl."

"Then you don't know about Gary James?"

"Sure, he's the guy Wilson blamed for Rhonda's death. But I don't buy it. I talked with him last year, too. While I was in Longview."

And then Gary James was found dead in the parking lot. On Rhonda Kuehl's anniversary of being murdered. In May. Same time frame as Jack's annual fishing trip.

"What did he say?" I was almost up to the screening station at security, would have to end this call. Or miss my flight.

"He said he knew who killed Rhonda, had seen the guy do it. But he had been warned to stay silent or he'd find himself in jail, accused of killing Rhonda himself. I believed him, Liv."

And I believed Jack. He sounded like he was telling me the truth, like he didn't know that Gary James had been killed, probably within days or hours of his visit. Like he had nothing to do with any of this. Or was it that I wanted to believe he had nothing to do with it?

The security guard motioned for me to end my call, to step through security.

"Jack, did you ask Gary James about Benji?"

"Benji? Why?"

The security guard interrupted, "Ma'am you will have to get off your phone. Now."

"FBI, please," I said, flashing my credentials.

The guard nodded and shrugged. "Sorry, Agent Bergen. You have to keep moving."

Into the phone, I asked, "Jack, did you know that Gary James was killed? Found dead. In the same lot as Rhonda. Last May."

The guard's eyes widened and he grabbed my arm, pulling me from the line, repeating his demand that I hang up and step through security. Somewhere amid all the confusion, the call was ended.

CHAPTER 28

MY HEAD WAS SPINNING. I couldn't believe what I'd done over the course of the past few hours. I had used a hidden key to enter Wayne W. Wilson's lair and cut, bagged, and tagged some carpet fibers from his home. And I couldn't believe what I'd just learned about the true intent behind Jack's fishing trips.

But that was hours ago. And states away.

Now I was on the opposite side of the continental US, in a cozy, familiar classroom. And for now, I would treat my earlier questionable actions like that proverbial tree falling in the forest. No sound. I had to focus my attention on psychological profiling for the Douglass case.

"...So in conclusion, statement analysis is a technique many investigators use to direct questioning and to discern truthfulness in statements given by witnesses and suspects. When we are interviewing witnesses or interrogating suspects, we can use this technique to dissect the words used, examine the content of what is being said or what has been omitted, and analyze how the words are being delivered."

As former special agent Bill Archibald clicked through his computerized presentation, I had been scribbling furiously. I had been able to catch a direct flight from Portland to Washington Dulles International Airport and to drive to Quantico just in time for Archibald's evening class on Interrogation and Interviewing.

"I like to think of the technique as our way of getting the suspect to unintentionally provide us clues and insight, which could eventually lead us to his or her own arrest."

The students erupted in laughter and a few students clapped. I scanned the small auditorium-style classroom and estimated approximately sixty or seventy students in attendance. I studied Bill Archibald as he paced behind his podium.

An older man in his early sixties who retired after thirty years with the bureau, eighteen of which were spent teaching at the Academy, Archibald was asked on several occasions to return as a guest lecturer. His expertise was in interviewing witnesses and interrogating suspects. He had consulted on nearly every notable case investigated by the bureau over the past two decades, including several during the last five years of his retirement.

He was best known throughout the Criminal Investigative Division for developing the Archibald Technique, a regimented guideline for taking statements from witnesses and potential suspects with varying levels of intensity. His style encompassed statement analysis and skilled interviewing and had allowed the bureau to pry confessions from leading suspects on several occasions. I respected Bill Archibald—his techniques, his knowledge about human psychology—and appreciated his desire to continue teaching.

I watched him pace, his left hand clasped around his right wrist behind his back, the chalk clasped between the fingers and thumb of his right hand, and listened to the steady, methodical clopping of his heavy leather wing-tip shoes on the wooden stage of the small auditorium. The clopping echoed in the blank pauses between his statements.

Groomed impeccably, his neatly trimmed white beard, mustache, and closely cropped hair made him look like a professor. The small, gold wire-rimmed glasses and the dark blue houndstooth tweed jacket with leather elbow patches accentuated the academic look. He had a commanding presence, an attractive face, and a welcoming manner.

Archibald had been summarizing his two-hour lecture on statement analysis and I was looking forward to asking him specific questions about the Douglass case later tonight. He had agreed to meet and discuss my concerns over dinner. Other than mealtimes, his schedule was packed with various tasks, meetings, and guest lectures. I felt privileged he'd invited me to Georgetown, where he lived, to discuss the idiosyncrasies of the Douglass case and the statements given.

Archibald stroked his beard and announced to the class, "What I would like you all to do for our next class is to examine the statements given by Shelly Jones shortly after she reported her sons missing and the subsequent statements she made during television and police interviews. Based on what you have learned today about statement analysis, find ten different signals that could have suggested to the police that Shelly was not being forthright about the disappearance of her children. Bring it to class on Monday and we'll discuss it."

The rumbling of students as they gathered their belongings and departed the auditorium was like the distant roar of a buffalo stampede and yanked me back to late last year when I was a student here, anxious to complete my studies and focus on my new career as an FBI agent. I took advantage of the moment by jotting down a few additional notes and tucked them away in my briefcase. Archibald had not seen me approaching while he busied himself with removing his wireless microphone and shutting down his computer.

"Bill Archibald?"

My voice had startled him, and he turned with a jerk. Scowling, he removed his glasses and answered, "Yes."

"I'm Liv Bergen, special agent from the Denver bureau," I said as I extended my hand. "I graduated in December from the Academy and see why the bureau was begging for you to come back out of retirement to teach. You're amazing."

His warm smile and firm handshake signaled recognition. "Oh stop. My goodness, you surprised me. I thought you were one of my students. I didn't recognize you in the crowd, but I'm so glad you had the opportunity to endure my dry lecture."

"Enjoy, not endure, Dr. Archibald," I answered. "You can't imagine how helpful you have been to me already."

"Call me Bill, please," Archibald said. "And you flatter me. Are we still on for dinner? Chadwicks alright with you?"

"On the waterfront. My favorite." I was thinking about how much I'd enjoyed my time with Jack when we went there last November. We sat at a corner table in the quaint, old restaurant and the waiter handled us like the lovers I wanted us to be, despite Jack's distant mood. Maybe *distracted* would be a better word. Still, I had a great time because I was happy to see him. "And the clam chowder is amazing."

He chuckled and placed his large hand on the small of my back as we walked. "That's exactly why I chose that restaurant. See you at nine?"

I nodded. "Thank you for your help, Bill."

"I haven't done anything yet," he said with a wink as we made our way out of the auditorium and down the stairs.

"Yes, you have. The last hour was insightful." I couldn't possibly tell him how much.

He waved as he headed toward his office, and I headed to see a friend.

Coming here again made me reconsider the offer to work in the National Center for the Analysis of Violent Crime when I graduated. If Streeter was leaving Denver, maybe I should reconsider, move further from my family and the mining business to gain even clearer focus on my career at the bureau. I hoped I hadn't alienated them completely when I told them I preferred field investigations work at the Denver bureau.

"Hi, Andy," I said as I walked into the offices of NCAVC Investigative Unit.

Andy was a tall, young man, groomed and postured like a soldier.

"Liv Bergen," Special Agent Andy Shriver replied. I thought he might salute me. He walked a bit too quickly toward me and shook my hand vigorously. "Long time, no see."

"It's only been a few months. How're you doing?"

"Couldn't be better. And it's all because of you," Shriver replied. When I gave him a puzzled look, he explained. "When we graduated from the Academy, I was offered the job here after you turned it down."

"By Tate? The offer?" I was assuming, since she was the one who'd offered me the job.

He nodded. "And thank you for turning it down, because this is the best job I could ever have. You look wonderful. Are you married yet?"

I ignored his directness. "Is Christian still here this late?"

"Doonsberg is always here. I thought you knew him better than that." Andy's expression morphed to concern. "You're not here because you've changed your mind, are you?"

I ignored him, asking my own question. "Can you check to see if he has a minute to say hi?"

Andy eyed me, the suspicion growing more visible on his face. His fierce expression made me want to stay on the good side of him. "I'll take you back there." As I followed him down the hall, he added, "Don't screw this up for me, Liv."

Andy knocked on an open door. "Mr. Doonsberg, sir? Do you have a minute? There's someone here to see you."

The man was hunched over his keyboard, his back to the door, and he mumbled something inaudible. And kept typing. I took Andy's lead and waited quietly.

Christian Doonsberg finished his flurry of keystrokes and pushed himself away from his desk. Rising to his feet, he stretched and said, "Who would want to see me at this hour?" He spotted me and walked quickly toward the door, his arms open for a hug. "Liv! You're a sight for sore eyes. You get prettier every day, young lady."

I could feel the heat on my cheeks as he enveloped me in an embrace. Regardless of what was taught in the sexual harassment training, I, for one, never tired of hugs or those sexist compliments, particularly when they were given in the spirit of old-fashioned courtesy, unlike Dodson's lecherous advances.

"It's so good to see you, Christian. How are you? You're looking very healthy."

"A little cancer isn't going to keep me down. I'm through with treatment, hopefully clean, got all my hair back. And I'm enjoying my food again."

"Can't beat that." As I sat in a chair beside his desk, Andy said his goodbyes and left. "You gave me a fright when I heard you had cancer and were going through chemo. Are you feeling strong again? Honestly?"

He had sprouted a few more gray hairs and had lost about twenty pounds, only half of which were a healthy loss, and his cheeks looked slightly more hollow compared to the last time I'd seen him. But he still had that sparkle of mischievousness and life in his golden eyes. He was tall and slender with long lines that were accentuated by his long limbs. His curly brown hair was cut short and never combed, which was incongruously boyish compared with the deep and premature lines around his mouth and eyes, and with the bifocals worn low on his nose.

Christian was only ten years older than me, but I always felt a special connection with him, like a daughter with a father. We had been able to communicate easily and freely with one another ever since he taught me a behavioral science course during my Academy training. He was primarily responsible for all of the job offers I had received from Jenna Tate as a new Academy graduate and was most certainly responsible for getting me the job in Denver.

"Honestly," he answered with a gentle smile. "I feel strong. It's been four months since the end of treatment. I've never felt better. Cancer can't get me down, but you sure can. Devastating me like you do every time you turn down a job offer from me."

"Now wait a minute," I argued. "I never turned you down. Like I told Agent Tate, I just wasn't ready yet. I hadn't learned enough in the field to feel like I could really contribute to your unit." I grew serious and added, "But someday, I will. You'll see. That is, if I haven't discouraged you from asking me to come here."

"I think I prefer the chemotherapy to your rejections. So what brings you to Quantico?" Doonsberg asked.

"Bill Archibald," I answered. "I sat in on his Interrogation and Interviewing course and I'm headed to dinner with him."

"Lucky bastard," Doonsberg mumbled with a grin.

"I need some help on statement analysis," I added.

"What are you working on?"

"The Douglass murder."

"The little princess on TV? How'd you land that assignment?"

"Streeter Pierce assigned the case to me," I answered, proudly.

Doonsberg threw himself back in his chair and slapped both hands to his temples, shaking his head playfully between his long, slender fingers. "You have life by the tail."

"What do you mean?"

"You've got the best field investigator in the country as your mentor and coach. You've been assigned one of the most famous murder investigations in the country. And you're living in the Rocky Mountains of Colorado. No wonder I can't talk you into a job here." He pounded his fist on the desk and added, "And no wonder I lost Jenna Tate to you guys."

"Lost her? Is she permanent to Denver?"

My stomach twisted. If Jenna Tate became my new boss, my decision was final about turning in my resignation in June.

CHAPTER 29

CHRISTIAN SHOOK HIS HEAD. "Tate's temporary. But she might be in Denver awhile. Who knows? That woman flits around so much, I can't keep track of her comings and goings. You remind me of her. Headstrong. Independent. I offered her a job, too."

"Wait, what? You offered Agent Tate a job with the Investigative Support Unit?"

"Early in her career," Doonsberg said. "Rejected me, just like you did. Story of my life, rejected by the prettiest women. Tate is one of the best marksmen, has an excellent mind, and was top of her graduating class. Just like you."

I was trying not to think about Jenna with her overnight bag, asking Streeter if he was ready to go. "What kind of a boss would she make, Christian?"

"As a person, she's determined, like you. But unlike you, she has a bit of an aggressive bite that most don't know about. You don't want to see the business end of her fangs, if you know what I mean."

I didn't, but I wasn't going to ask.

He added, "On the plus side, Tate's got spunk, she's got manners, and she's got the power of persuasion."

And she's got Streeter, I thought.

"As a boss, I think more people would feel her bite. Let's just say I wouldn't get too close, if I were you."

I nodded. "At least you're honest. Why did she turn you down?"

"That was years ago, but she gave me the same reason you did," Doonsberg answered. "She wanted some field investigation experience. What is with you ladies? Field investigation is tough duty. Why would you want to aspire to do that?"

"I know I can help you out in this unit someday. But Christian, how can I support the field investigators if I don't understand what they're going through, what they do every day, what challenges they face?"

"You have a point. So how's your love life?" Doonsberg asked. "You know, all work and no play makes Liv a dull girl."

The heat returned to my cheeks. "Not that it's any of your business, but I am seeing someone and our relationship is developing nicely."

"It's about time Streeter started dating again," Doonsberg said.

"Jack Linwood," I corrected.

"Sure," he responded, but I knew he wasn't convinced. "Besides, Streeter's too old."

"No he's not," I protested.

He grinned, knowing he had backed me into a corner. "Tell me how you're doing with this Douglass case."

I blew out a long breath of air. "It's tough. Early on, there were a lot of mistakes made. There are a lot of problems internally and publicly. It's really like a big ball of barbed wire that somebody needs to untangle, which is no small task."

Doonsberg lifted a bottle of water to his lips and sipped. "So what's bothering you?"

"Because we made a mess of the early investigations, whoever did this might get away with terrorizing, torturing, and strangling the life out of such a weak, defenseless little girl," I answered. I could tell from Christian's skepticism he wasn't buying that my answer was the complete story of what was bothering me. So I added, "What bothers me is trying to get inside the mind of a monster who could do this to a child."

Doonsberg stared at me, studying my face intently. There was a long pause before he answered, "Unfortunately, imagining how a monster thinks isn't the worst part. What's the most frightening is to consider the sheer numbers in which the monsters exist."

I saw the change in his face. All of the jovial playfulness had disappeared. Christian Doonsberg was now focused and intense, yet peaceful. It was an odd contrast to his normal demeanor. I hadn't seen this side of his personality and wondered if this is what years of being with the bureau would do to me. I shuddered.

Eventually, he continued, "I can't keep track of them all. Some are worse than others. Last spring, a guy—Menendez, lived in Sacramento—had been divorced from his wife and had abandoned his young daughter, Carlita. Carlita Menendez. Isn't that a sweet name?"

I nodded.

"His ex-wife took him to court and demanded child support payments for the little girl, which of course, the courts awarded. This Menendez guy was so upset about having to make the payments until the kid's eighteenth birthday that he injected the sixteen-month-old baby with HIV so he wouldn't have to make them."

I grimaced, having a difficult time remembering that all people were God's children, even a piece of crap like Menendez.

Doonsberg replied evenly and softly, "That poor little girl is going to die an excruciatingly painful and slow death, all because her father didn't want to be saddled with child support payments. If she hasn't died already. Anyway, it turns out that this Menendez guy calls the cops one day a few months ago—around Thanksgiving—and complains that someone mugged him from behind, stole his wallet, stuck a hypodermic needle in his arm, and beat him senseless. The mugger tells Menendez that he's getting what he deserves and, of course, it turns out he tests positive for HIV."

"What kind of mugger carries around a hypodermic needle of HIV?"

Doonsberg shrugged. "Not a real mugger. A killer trying to make it look like a mugging."

"Isn't that second-degree murder?" I asked.

"Not until the guy dies, which was why Menendez wasn't behind bars in the first place for what he did to his daughter. All they could get him on was child endangerment, which by first offense only led to a restraining order being issued against him by the mother and child. Amazing how our justice system works nowadays. Seems like the benefit of the doubt for perpetrators has somehow morphed into reshaping them as victims now, doesn't it?"

"Did they ever find the mugger who injected Menendez?" I asked.

Doonsberg lifted his folded hands to his lips and added, "Why try? Whoever mugged Menendez might be more of hero, don't you think? Menendez got away with murder without any punishment."

I saw his eyes dart to the doorway. "Andy?"

Andy stepped around the corner, wearing a sheepish grin on his face. "Just checking to see if you two need anything before I head home."

From his obvious embarrassment, I concluded Andy had been eavesdropping on our conversation. And from Christian's sour expression, I deduced that this wasn't the first time.

Christian frowned and replied, "No, we don't. See you Monday."

After he'd gone, Christian mumbled, "I swear, sometimes I just want to smack that kid. Always eavesdropping."

So I had read the situation right.

"Okay, where were we? Oh yeah. I'm telling you, Liv, people all over this country are starting to get fed up with the weaknesses in our judicial system. I can't say I blame them. Think about how often we tout criminals' rights. Hell, whatever happened to victims' rights?"

"True, but we can't just sit back and let people take the law into their own hands. That's not right either. We'd have nothing but chaos," I argued, thinking about whoever killed Gary James. I thought about Schuffler's story of someone killing Daryl Cleveland. I thought of Lance Bovier's father accusing Su Panini, a phantom op-ed writer, of killing his son. And Vanessa Greenwood's killer in Kansas. Four killers, dead. I was thinking about Christian's latest comment when I mumbled, "Damned vigilantes."

"Like I said, I can't say that I blame them. Maybe it's because as a father myself, I just can't understand how Menendez could do that to his own daughter, his own flesh and blood." Doonsberg leaned back in his leather chair and stared at the pictures of his family on his desk.

I wondered the same about Shelly Jones. Drowning her sons, her own flesh and blood. I sighed and rubbed my eyebrows with my fingertips,

suddenly feeling every hour of this long day. "I don't understand how anyone could do that to any child, especially to an infant. Menendez's actions
are incomprehensible to me."

My mind flashed to Rebecca Douglass and how frustrated everyone in
Fort Collins was about the authorities not making an arrest in that case. I
wondered if the thought had crossed anyone's mind in that community to
take the law into their own hands, to become the vigilante. I shuddered at
the thought. Who might they kill? It wasn't clear cut, from my read on the
files and of the evidence. But Rebecca was everyone's child. At least that's
what the TV show's promotional ads boasted.

"But you do comprehend why vigilantes do what they do, don't you?
When the system fails to bring justice to the wicked, can you see why their
actions are justified?" Christian's piercing eyes bored through me.

I met his gaze, wondering about the purpose behind his words. Was
he challenging my ethics? Was he trying to tell me he agreed with vigilantism? Could Christian Doonsberg possibly believe that vigilantes were justified? That he was a wannabe vigilante, capable of taking the law into his
own hands? Just like whoever killed Lance Bovier, Daryl Cleveland, and
Gary James? First I questioned Jack. Now Doonsberg. Were Doc Duncan
and I the only people left in this world who believed that the judicial system was the only acceptable answer to justice? And who was I to question
them after reading Sue Panini's rant over Bovier and wishing the same fate
to whoever killed my niece?

I swallowed before answering, "What if a vigilante was wrong? Kills
the wrong man?"

Of course, I was thinking of Doc Duncan's secret, that while he publicly swore Gary James killed Rhonda Kuehl, he truly believed the real
killer was his former deputy sheriff, Wayne W. Wilson. A lawman. A man
of the law. I had to wonder if the vigilante had any idea he might have
killed the wrong man. Killed the witness, not the murderer, although Gary
James was no innocent man. He probably deserved to die, given that Doc
proved James had sexually molested and killed the boy in a neighboring
county. Jack's boy.

"Even if the vigilante exacts justice on those our system missed, even
if we all agree the victim is guilty, what does that do to our system?" I

asked. "The question then becomes, what can we or should we do about a vigilante?"

Doonsberg shrugged. "Not a thing." I could have sworn I saw a hint of a smile before he added, "All we can do is hope it doesn't become an epidemic, I suppose."

Something made me dig a bit deeper. Maybe it was the curious way Andy was eavesdropping on Christian during his story. Maybe it was Christian's firm hold on the goodness of vigilantism. But I had to press for more answers. "Christian, you said Menendez lived in Sacramento." I saw his smile falter. "Is that where he was mugged and injected with HIV last Thanksgiving?"

Christian drew in a deep breath and leaned back in his chair, his eyes never leaving mine. "No, actually it was here. In the DC area."

A grin spread across his face when he saw my stunned reaction. I wondered if Christian had anything to do with luring Menendez to DC. But if he had, why would he share the story with me when I knew nothing about it? Out of guilt? Hoping to get caught? Or was the story a warning that there was a vigilante among us? But who? Andy? Jack? Christian had asked about my love life. Jack was here in DC with me when Menendez was injected. Could he be capable of such a thing? Christian also mentioned Jenna having fangs and that few people knew that. Was he hinting that she might be skating close to the edge, blurring the line of the law on occasion?

Clearly I had secretly hoped vengeance would come to whoever killed Brianna, and I paid no mind to whether it was legal justice or not. Maybe Christian was testing me?

He must have known exactly what I was thinking, running all the scenarios through my mind. "Do you think I would have been strong enough to mug someone in my physical state last November, Liv?"

"Would you if you had been strong enough?" I challenged, wondering if I myself would cross the line if given the chance with Brianna's killer.

"Even if I could, I was never clever enough to think of such a grand scheme to trap Menendez the way someone else did." His chuckle was filled with sorrow. "Not as clever as someone like you."

"So who did?"

He stared at me for a very long time, presumably debating on whether to answer. Or how. "Have you ever heard the expression, 'If your right hand offends you, then cut it off'?"

"And cast it away. The book of Matthew, I believe."

"You know your Bible."

"A little. What's your point?"

"Doesn't the mind direct what the hand does? Yet the mind blames the hand, casts it aside?" Christian held my gaze. "Just think about it. I believe the mind is pinning the blame on the hand for what happened to Menendez. That's all."

"Two people? One who concocted the scheme, one who carried it out?"

"Just a theory."

CHAPTER 30

BY THE TIME I made it to Chadwicks, I was starting to wonder if I'd missed the memo about turning a blind eye to citizens who took the law into their own hands. Then I realized I hadn't needed a memo to ignore the law earlier today, when I broke in to Wayne Wilson's house to snip a sample of his pink carpet.

He who lives in a glass house and all . . .

Shook up and a bit discombobulated, I walked into Chadwicks and paused to send a text to Jack, telling him that I made it to DC and asking him whether we could finish our conversation. I'd explain what I learned from Archibald about the possible killer of Rebecca Douglass later, from my hotel room.

Before my finger ever left the send button, my cell chirped. Streeter had sent me a message that read, *"DON'T GET DISCOURAGED. TRUST YOUR JUDGMENT. YOU'RE NOT ALONE."* It was as if he'd read my mind. Either that or Doonsberg had called him already. I knew that if nothing else were true, two good men thought similarly to me. I considered myself lucky to be in great company with Albert Duncan and Streeter Pierce. My mood lifted until I realized that Jenna Tate was the company

Streeter was keeping. And I wondered how he found a moment to text me the uplifting message.

My cell phone rang and I quickly answered it, thinking it was Streeter following up after his text.

"You said you were going to call me." It was the Colonel, not Streeter.

"Barbara, I'm sorry. I had to leave town unexpectedly. I'm in DC."

"Brianna's case?"

"No, a different one."

"So you are working Brianna's case. I called Agent Marshall. He asked me about the bunny." Her words were clipped.

"He wasn't supposed to—"

"I lied," she said. "I told him you talked to me already and he told me everything."

"You shouldn't have done that," I said, spotting Archibald sitting alone as I scanned the restaurant.

"And you shouldn't have kept this from me." Her tone sounded hurt.

Archibald spotted me and I waved, pointing at the phone. He nodded and smiled.

"You're right. I shouldn't have. And you deserve to know what's going on," I said. "But Streeter's bending the rules by giving me this case and you don't want to get him or Agent Marshall in trouble for this, do you?"

There was silence on the other end.

"Especially if we have a chance of solving this case. Barbara, I may be on to something." I lowered my voice and met her level of seriousness. "But I can't talk about it right now. A man's waiting to talk with me as we speak, to discuss another case. Just trust me."

"See you soon," she said before ending the call.

Damn it. My sister wasn't one to be derailed if she had her mind made up. And she was most certainly heading to Denver, I was sure of it. Or here to DC. I couldn't avoid her for long.

I joined Bill Archibald at his table. The table next to where Jack and I sat last November. As we sipped our drinks waiting for dinner to be served, I sat quietly and watched Bill read the copy of the ransom note allegedly left behind in the Douglass mansion by the murderer of Rebecca Douglass.

When he finished, he cleared his throat before saying, "Interesting.

I see what you mean. It's definitely not consistent with a typical kidnapper's ransom note. The odd way it's worded, and demanding such a specific amount for the ransom."

"Theodore Douglass's year-end bonus. Exactly."

Archibald made a humming noise. "Then, of course, there's the length of the note. That is the longest ransom note I have ever heard of or seen in my entire career. Reads more like a bad television script."

"So, what do you make of it? Without knowing anything else, before I tell you what I've learned and all the statements I've analyzed, what's your impression of this?" I asked excitedly.

"It's . . . unusual. Amateurish." Archibald read through it again and scratched his head. "The way it's written makes it appear almost childish, innocent, simple."

I thought of Stewart Casey, the same words I'd used to describe him to Streeter. Could someone like Stewart possibly be capable of such a thing? Of murder? Of a little girl? Hard to envision an involuntary manslaughter charge, but insanity or diminished capacity as a defense for murder, I could.

"Yet the references to so many different lines from movies or books would make one think that this person is well read or at least has seen plenty of movies. The reference to the bonus amount and the small demands relative to Douglass's worth would not only make me wonder if a simpleton or child wrote this, but also that it must be someone with direct knowledge of the amount he was paid. An insider, like a family member, a banker, a coworker. Either that or someone wanted to make it *look* like it was an inside job. A mischievous attempt to leave evidence that pointed at one of the Douglasses."

"There's more," I said as I nodded in agreement with what Archibald had said. "It was written on a pad of paper from within the house."

"Hmm," Archibald said as he stroked his chin and read the note again. "That's odd. Who would kidnap a child from her own home, her own bed, take the time to write a lengthy note, and then strangle the child in her own backyard?"

"Would you buy the story that the ransom note was written first, the girl kidnapped and then murdered?" I asked, studying the professor's face.

"No. Why would the kidnapper stop, write such a lengthy note, before even getting the girl? It just doesn't make sense. The kidnapper would have written the note long before the kidnap if abduction had been the intent and ransom, the motive. And if the child was murdered accidentally? Would it make sense that the killer took her body out to the shed, then returned to the house to concoct a note?" Archibald asked.

He was studying my face and I could tell he wanted to learn more.

"I totally agree with you. So what is the most likely scenario in your mind considering what you know so far?"

"I suspect the girl was murdered and whether or not it was accidental, it would appear the whole purpose of the ransom note was to draw suspicion to one of the Douglasses in a very amateurish way. Either that or . . ."

"Or what?" I asked anxiously, shifting my weight to the edge of the chair.

"Or the note was actually written by one of the Douglass family members, and in the confusion and anguish that followed, mistakes were made. Maybe members of the family were covering up for a relative who accidentally killed the girl. Maybe they were trying to muddy the waters of the investigation that would be sure to follow," Archibald suggested.

"I thought that, too," I said. "But if that were true and the Douglasses were responsible for their daughter's death, they would have had plenty of time to remove Rebecca's body from the premises all together. They could have dumped her body elsewhere to be found by the police. They're both bright people. They had time and the brains to make it look more legitimately like a true kidnapping. It would make more sense, wouldn't it?"

"The psychology of a murder by a family member is very strange, Liv," Archibald explained. "Particularly when it involves a child. Normally, even after the child is dead, the parent or adult who murdered the child often straightens the child's clothes, brushes his or her hair, covers the child in a favorite blanket as if in sleep. A family member ultimately makes the child comfortable, even when dead. So if one of the Douglasses had killed the girl, maybe they could not bring themselves to dump her body elsewhere. Even if they had plenty of time and even if it would be prudent for casting suspicion away from themselves."

I thought about the report where Theo found Rebecca with her nightgown bunched up under her tiny armpits, the killer leaving her lower half exposed, naked. A father wouldn't make up such a detail, would he? If he was compelled psychologically to keep her safe and warm after her death?

"Handwriting analysis ruled out the other children and the father, who were in the house at the time," I offered. "But the handwriting by Cathy Douglass was inconclusive. Her handwriting had many similarities. Not enough to implicate her as the author of that ransom note. The investigators were particularly interested in Cathy's left-handed writing. They thought maybe that would explain the similarities and the inconsistencies with her dominant, right-handed writing."

"Interesting," Archibald said. "Was there any conclusive evidence found on the child, in the shed, or elsewhere in the house to indicate who may have been involved?"

I shook my head. "The problem is these guys in Fort Collins did their best with what little experience they had, but the crime scene was all but destroyed by their inexperience. We have very little and virtually nothing to go on for prosecution."

"Who would you prosecute?" Archibald challenged.

"That's what I wanted to ask you," I said as I handed him a copy of the statements taken from the Douglass family. "Did you get a chance to read what I emailed you?"

"Yes," Archibald said as he glanced through the stack of papers.

"Tell me if I'm wrong. I have pored over those statements, both the original and subsequent statements, and I can find nothing inconsistent or anything that would suggest deceit by Cathy or Theodore Douglass in any way."

"Nor did I," Archibald concurred.

"The parts of speech they used were consistent with people who were innocent. They gave no extraneous information. They had conviction in what they said. And there seemed to be a balance in how they described the events that night and the following day. They described what happened before they learned about Rebecca's disappearance, what happened when they found the ransom note and how they called the police, and everything that happened in the hours that followed in consistent detail and balance."

"Neither Cathy nor Theodore seemed to omit important details of the events."

I sighed and added, "I could not find anything that would raise a red flag for me if I had been interviewing them or that would make me want to question them again. They performed perfectly. How could a parent or parents be involved with the murder of their own daughter, handle the aftermath so amateurishly in the hours that followed, then give extremely consistent statements completely indicative of truthful, grieving parents? It just doesn't make sense."

"I agree with you completely," Archibald offered, just as the waitress brought us bowls of homemade clam chowder. "Would you like another drink with your dinner?"

I shook my head. I needed to keep my head clear.

"Did you see anything unusual or inconsistent in their statements? What did I miss?"

"Tell me about the other children," he asked, slurping his soup. "Why were they interviewed only once after they gave their original statements?"

"Theodore's attorney said that unless the law enforcement had a compelling reason or evidence that would suggest the children should be subjected to further questioning, then they were instructed to leave them alone and let them grieve the loss of their sister," I explained. "The attorney was at the house on the morning of February fifteenth when the police arrived. The Douglasses said they called him and another man because they were close friends of the family, not for his professional expertise."

"Why would the Fort Collins police honor the attorney's request to leave the other children alone?" Archibald asked, pausing between spoonfuls.

"Rebecca's brother was eight at the time. He seems to be having the most trouble dealing with his sister's murder. Her stepsiblings were visiting that holiday. Rebecca's half brother was seventeen and her half sister was twenty-two at the time," I described. "The stepkids were Theodore's by his first wife. The twenty-two-year-old was a child beauty queen, just like her half sister. But not a reality TV star. Apparently Theo really can pick the good-looking wives who give birth to beauties."

"Did you read their statements?" Archibald asked, raising one eyebrow in question.

"Of course," I replied. I squinted and asked, "Why do you ask? What did you see?"

"In the eight-year-old," Archibald said, "I saw an extremely frightened and distraught little boy. In the seventeen-year-old, I saw a tough teen, long on truth and not trusting of law enforcement. And he prefers brevity. But I saw nothing inconsistent or any red flags in either of their statements. It's the twenty-two-year-old who I have questions about."

"Debra Douglass?" I asked. I propped my arms on the table and leaned forward, toward Archibald, forgetting all about my soup. I wanted to hear this. "What did you see?"

"Areas that require a more directed interrogation," Archibald answered. "If you read her initial statement, Debra spent a great deal of time explaining the events that led up to the discovery of Rebecca's disappearance. She even described the relationship she has with her current boyfriend, which has absolutely nothing to do with Rebecca's murder. It begs the question of whether Debra was stalling or trying to justify her actions somehow for that night. Then, she had virtually nothing to say about the events as they occurred on Valentine's Day or when they discovered her half sister's body the next day."

"Early morning, February fifteenth."

"And the police questioned Debra almost instantly," Archibald said. "Did you see that? It wasn't even close to being a balanced statement. Also, during the first statement, the policewoman who took her statement made a note of 'little emotion.' Now, I don't know how well trained those Fort Collins people are on taking statements and the importance of observation. But in the report, the standard police form, there's an area that asks for the witness's emotional status at the time of the statement. The policewoman didn't write 'angry' or 'in shock.' She indicated 'little emotion.' That's a very odd observation, considering the circumstances."

The waitress placed the seafood we'd ordered in front of us. I ate as if I hadn't eaten in days. Around a mouthful of shellfish, I said, "It seemed strange to me."

As he ate, Archibald continued, "In the interview that followed a few days later, she did show emotion according to the policewoman and she did give a more balanced statement of the events leading up to and subsequent to the murder. But in the second interview, Debra kept repeating 'I think' and 'I believe,' which are qualifiers. She used these phrases just before the most critical statements, such as ... here, let me find it." He lifted the pile of papers and quickly flipped through them until he found the page he was looking for.

"Listen to this. 'I believe it was about one o'clock when I went to bed' and 'I think I hugged my father when I saw the body lying in the entrance-way.' It's as if she's trying to temper her actions as she described. It shows a lack of commitment on her part during critical moments. She would know if she hugged her father or not when she saw Rebecca's dead body. The other warning bell was how she referred to her half sister as 'the body.' It's as if she is distancing herself from Rebecca."

"I didn't see that before," I replied. "I guess I was so focused on the parents' statements that I didn't catch the most obvious. Was there anything else?"

Archibald nodded. "Yes. One more thing. In the original statement, when Debra described the events leading to the discovery of Rebecca's disappearance, she started out using the word *I* when she described what she did on Valentine's Day. But she switched to using *we* shortly into her statement, which would indicate no personal or individual involvement in the events."

"That's right," I said. My eyes widened and my thoughts wandered.

To allow me time with my thoughts, Archibald ate half of his dinner before asking, "What are you thinking?"

I shook my head. "It's just that I feel so foolish that I missed that. I was going down the wrong path. And because of it, I had blinders on. I assumed the mother must have written that ransom note. I just thought she was either covering for her husband or herself. I didn't think that she might have written the note to cover for her stepdaughter."

"Maybe she didn't," Archibald countered. "Maybe she didn't know who killed her daughter and thought she was covering for her husband. Or maybe her husband thought he was covering for his wife. Or the step-daughter for both parents."

"The evidence found on the duct tape suggested the fibers came from one of Theodore's bathrobes." I explained. "Maybe he found Rebecca in her bed. Strangled to death. Thought it was Cathy who did it. Or maybe he suspected Debra and was covering for her. So he carries Rebecca outside to the backyard into a gardener's toolshed to make it look like an intruder."

Archibald added, "And maybe Cathy sees or hears him carrying the child out the door."

I pushed my food around my plate and thought aloud, "Tragic. In that scenario they all assume the worst of one another and then cover for each other. Everyone has assumed up to this point that Theo was the one who murdered Rebecca and that his wife covered for him by writing that ransom note. An indictment of both parents for reckless endangerment was submitted, but was sealed by a judge. Please don't repeat that."

"I had no idea," Archibald said.

"No one does. The problem has been no evidence was found or collected properly to suggest that theory was true, other than the questionable comparisons of the ransom note with Cathy's handwriting and fibers from Theo's robe. Although the fibers that were found on the duct tape across Rebecca's mouth were consistent with Theo's robe, they weren't collected properly or in a timely manner. A defending attorney would have a field day with that evidence. All this time, I was so frustrated because I couldn't find any inconsistencies in their statements. But I hadn't thought that maybe they were covering for Debra."

Archibald must have seen the confusion on my face and asked, "Go on?"

"Well, we know the Douglass parents are very bright," I added. "If they were covering for their stepdaughter, wouldn't they have done a better job at coming up with a cover? Just like we said earlier, they had plenty of time to take the body elsewhere."

"But like I told you," Archibald repeated, "in child murders, the parents don't necessarily act rationally or predictably. Maybe they couldn't bring themselves to dump the body in some strange, unusual, impersonal place."

I was thinking about the fibers. From the bathrobe. And the thought of the pink carpet fibers crept into my mind from the other cases. Focus, I told myself.

"A toolshed is impersonal," I observed. "Maybe the Douglasses weren't covering for Debra. Maybe they didn't even know about this. And maybe

Debra intentionally tried to make her parents look guilty of killing her half sister. But the problem is I can't imagine why she would want to do that."

Archibald concluded, "If you figure that out, you may very well have enough to prosecute."

CHAPTER 31

STREETER HADN'T BEEN ABLE to catch Liv by herself. Not once all day. Since Monday, he had tried several times to find out how her meeting with Bill Archibald at Quantico went. He came in to work both Saturday and Sunday, hoping to find her in the office. But if she was working, it was from home.

After mulling the idea over all weekend, he was committed to finding a way to casually ask Liv out for dinner. Especially while Linwood was out of town. Before Linwood returned. A bold decision and he needed Liv's full attention. Unfortunately the situation had never presented itself and he was running out of time. It was already nearing end of day Tuesday and Linwood would be back at work after the coming weekend.

Someone was always around her. Or in his office. And the few times they had found themselves alone, someone inevitably interrupted them before he had a chance to ask. He'd had an opportunity earlier this afternoon down at the shooting range as they both finished target practice, but as they entered the elevator alone, Kelly McDougal, the shooting range manager, had called after Liv to ask her a question. She'd stepped off the elevator before the doors closed.

Streeter had been determined to ask Liv out on an official date, so he held the door for her, resolved that he'd wait until McDougal—the horny old goat—was done flirting with Liv. He waited until she waved Streeter off, saying, "Looks like I'm going to be a while. Go ahead, I'll catch up with you."

She never did.

When Streeter saw Liv walk toward the elevators just before five o'clock and overheard her tell the receptionist that she was going down to the cafeteria for a very late lunch, he knew this was his opportunity. Once the elevator doors closed, he rose to his feet and walked slowly past the receptionist, not wanting to look too anxious.

"I'm going to grab a Coke. Do you want anything?" Streeter asked the big woman behind the bulletproof glass.

"I'm on a diet. Can't you tell?" The large woman stared up at him with wide, expectant eyes. "Besides, I'm headed home. It's quitting time."

"You don't need to be dieting, my dear. There'll be less of you to love."

The receptionist giggled and jiggled, pushing her hand in his direction, playfully waving him on and saying, "Stop. You are so bad. And who do you think you're fooling, going for a Coke? There's a machine in the break room."

Streeter grinned at her just as the elevator doors closed between them. As the lights of the elevator blinked their countdown, he quietly hoped that there would be no stops. He did not want any distractions from his thoughts about what he was going to say to Liv. His heart was beating loudly in his chest at the anticipation of finally being able to catch her alone and away from the others in the office so he could ask her out, finally telling her how he felt about her.

As he stepped off of the elevator on the second floor, his eyes fell upon her at once. She was standing by the cashier, waiting for something. Just as he was about to approach her, Mitch Dodson moved in next to her and slid his hand around her waist. Streeter stopped dead in his tracks and watched as Liv stiffened and stepped clear of Dodson, forcing distance between them. Dodson leaned in to whisper something into her ear and she blocked his hand from her waist and sidestepped him. She ran her long fingers tenderly up the side of her thin face and into her long auburn hair, a haunted expression shadowing her eyes.

Streeter couldn't believe what he was witnessing.

His heart was pounding faster as it rose in his throat and his breathing had stopped. Where had Dodson come from? And what was he doing accosting Liv like that? Dodson worked in the lab, for Pete's sake. A coworker. Supposedly a professional. Why was he acting like this? What kind of a friend was he to Linwood, making a move on his girlfriend when he was out of town on vacation?

And the thought chilled him.

What kind of friend, indeed? Streeter was no different than Mitch Dodson, considering his earlier thoughts. And Liv would harbor the same contempt for Streeter that she appeared to feel for Mitch Dodson. Resentment.

He scowled. The indescribable feeling he was experiencing—foolishness—permeated his gut. As he turned quickly on his heels to abort his ridiculous mission, a familiar voice startled him in its badly timed delivery.

"Street?" Jenna Tate drawled. "What's your hurry? Wait up?"

Where had she come from?

He had been making a dash for the elevators but knew he couldn't pretend not to hear her. He squeezed his eyes tightly, breathed a quick, deep breath, and turned slowly to greet Tate with a feigned warm smile.

Tate grabbed his elbow, adding, "I'll ride up with you. You are going back upstairs, aren't you?"

Streeter pushed the up button.

"Wonderful, because I've been meaning to ask you something," Tate said as she continued to cling to his elbow like a hawk on its perch.

Streeter wasn't listening. His eyes were glued to the lights blinking above the elevator doors, his hopes pinned on the speedy arrival of the lift so he could escape this floor, the embarrassment he'd felt after seeing Liv's reaction to Dodson.

Tate continued, "I know this may seem forward, and I understand this may not be totally appropriate, considering our professional relationship, not to mention our past. But I was wondering if you would like to have drinks with me after work tonight?"

Beads of sweat formed on his forehead. Although he did not want to, he couldn't help but glance over his shoulder for one more look at Liv, not unlike the irresistible impulse he had when passing a car wreck. Just as he had turned, so had Liv, and from across the cafeteria their eyes met. Liv was holding her tray, alarm registering on her beautiful face. Tate's hold on Streeter was an anchor to stop him from punching Dodson, a chivalric action that Liv neither wanted nor needed. She could fend for herself. He knew that. He'd witnessed her self-reliance and strength firsthand, but he couldn't deny his desire to protect her all the same.

In that instant, Streeter saw Liv's alarm fade, her eyes fill with what he thought might be sadness. He impulsively wanted to go to her, beg her to stop seeing Linwood, and instead admit the natural attraction that was obvious between her and Streeter. But a woman's grip and the memory of Liv's reaction to Dodson's advances held him back. Streeter turned sharply from Liv.

The elevator had arrived and Streeter stepped in through the doors after Tate. He avoided looking outside the elevator again.

He didn't care if Tate had noticed what had just happened. He only cared that she didn't get any wrong impressions about the two of them, so he answered, "Thank you, but I don't think having a drink with you would be a good idea. Ever."

CHAPTER 32

THE CROWD IN THE cafeteria was beginning to thin as the federal employees returned to their work or left for home. I was hoping to enjoy my late lunch in peace, but Dodson appeared out of nowhere. He'd called my office so many times yesterday and today, I'd lost count. But I had read through all of his reports.

I scouted among the empty tables and chose one close to the windows. Unfortunately, Mitch Dodson had followed me. I walked slowly and steadily across the cafeteria, stalling for time as I thought about the vision of Jenna once again clinging to Streeter's elbow. Although I didn't like my possessive feelings toward him, it didn't stop me from having them. The adjective I'd use to describe the look in his eye just now when I saw him with Jenna would be *icy*.

Then, I reminded myself that it was only my imagination, and knowing Streeter, I had probably just detected his unhappiness that I'd somehow invaded his privacy by seeing him with his girlfriend. I had been trying to avoid him, burying myself in work so I wouldn't have to deal with my feelings about him going away with Jenna for the weekend.

I drew a quiet breath and put the thought of Streeter as far out of my mind as I could, or at least in a very dark corner of my mind.

For now.

Besides, Dodson had information for me, and it would take every ounce of my energy to barter with him and find out whatever he'd learned. And sitting in a public place, in the cafeteria, might keep him in line. As I sat across from Dodson, I picked up my fork and started shoveling food into my mouth to fuel my body.

"Aren't you going to ask me?"

I took my time chewing and swallowing before I answered, "Okay, what is it with you and your death wish?"

His tired eyes widened.

"Did you actually just put your hand on my waist over there just now? And didn't I tell you to never, ever get near me again, Dodson?"

His already-pallid face blanched. "I was . . . like I told you, I was just trying to share my findings. From the report you asked about. I tried calling."

"And I've been busy. You have email. Or have you been so busy reading Jack's email that you forgot you have your own account?" I scooped up more of the shepherd's pie and ate greedily. I was determined to finish this conversation as quickly as possible.

"You hugged me first."

That pulled me up short. "What?"

"When you brought me coffee last week. When you asked me to work the partial print. You hugged me. So I . . . I misunderstood your intentions." The way he swiped the wispy strands of white hair over his bald head, I could see he was speaking the truth. "That doesn't happen to me every day. Or ever." His grin was awkward and apologetic.

I had led him on by bringing him coffee, giving him a hug, and generally sucking up to him last week. He was right about that. Now I actually felt sorry for the arm-bar I'd put across his throat.

"Sorry, Mitch. I didn't mean anything by it. I'm a hugger. I was just grateful for your help."

He cleared his throat and closed his fingers around his own neck, a protective move. "I kind of figured that out after you slapped my hand away over there again. And after thinking about how you reacted to me last week when I asked you to dinner."

I dropped my fork. I'd lost my appetite. Apparently everyone's nerves were frazzled when Jack was gone. "Mitch, seriously. I'm sorry about that."

His smile was tentative and his fingers dropped from his neck, leaving himself vulnerable to me again. "You're scary."

"Can be," I said, pushing my plate away, thinking about Christian's comparison of me to Jenna, only she had a bite to her. Maybe I did, too. "Now what do you have for me?"

Dodson immediately started picking at the remnants of food on my cafeteria tray. "I worked up the profile, but I strongly suggest you wait on Linwood if you have the time. The Douglass case is too high profile to rely on my work when in a week, you'll have a much stronger expert in that area."

"I read the report and found it interesting that you suggested the killer is a man and might be trained by some branch of the military or law enforcement. What made you deduce that?"

"The house was full of people. No one heard the child scream, which would mean she either knew the perpetrator or he carried an authority that the child trusted. Plus the way the perp bound her hands and feet would indicate to me someone who'd been trained in restraint. Not an amateur or a common Joe from the streets. Just a theory," Dodson said, pressing his finger along my plate and licking off the juices from the shepherd's pie.

The smell of meat-and-vegetable pie, so enticing moments earlier when I was famished, had become sickening now that it was blended with the odor of his breath.

Not a woman. A man. Neither Theo nor Rebecca's half brother were former military. Far from it. I pondered how or if I'd break the profile news to Theresa Fiero, or whether I'd wait to confirm Dodson's findings with Jack. I was leaning toward taking Dodson's advice and waiting for Jack.

"And the other issue you asked me to pursue? The partial print from the Brianna Keller case, the one found on her nightgown?"

I nodded eagerly.

"Like I told you last week, I got a hit on the print I manually manipulated last week, but you're not going to like the results." He wiped his wet fingers on the breast pocket of his shirt, leaving a faint brown smudge near his pocket protector.

"Why not? Do I know the guy or something?" I asked, trying to quell the rising nausea in my throat. I had wanted this information more than I admitted, but Dodson's odd behaviors had distracted me from my focus.

He shook his head. "I doubt it. What I found isn't admissible in court. Because of how I worked the print. But I was trying to find you a good lead, let you accumulate other evidence to nail the bastard."

"And?"

His expression collapsed. "It's not good. Probably bad work on my part. This guy couldn't be a kidnapper. No way. But the good news is that the fibers you brought back from Longview and left in the lab this weekend definitely match those recovered during the Rhonda Kuehl case and in the Brianna Keller case."

My heart caught in my throat. "The pink carpet?"

My mind flashed to what Doc Duncan had said on Friday. Wayne Wilson, his deputy, had been upset that Gary James got away with murder, had demanded Doc provide something to prosecute. To assure Wayne Wilson a free pass for his crimes? To hush a potential witness to Wilson's crime? Or was Wayne Wilson innocent of Rhonda's murder, but guilty of tampering with evidence, leaving behind pink fibers in the files accidentally, his real intention to review the files personally so that Gary James could be prosecuted? This could easily be argued in either direction.

But one fact was certain. The pink fibers in both Rhonda Kuehl's murder case and Brianna Keller's case were consistent with the same source.

Wayne W. Wilson's childhood home. His deceased mother's home. Now *his* home. The home I'd broken in to for a sample.

I wondered how Wayne Wilson fit in to Brianna's case. Why was he looking in her files? Did he think Gary James may have killed Brianna, too? Or was Wilson the man who killed both Rhonda and my niece, as Doc Duncan believed?

I felt my neck grow hot.

The first call I'd make would be to Special Agent Bo Marshall at the Las Vegas bureau to find out if anyone from law enforcement named Wayne W. Wilson had ever checked out the evidence, which again might explain the pink fibers found on Brianna's nightgown. And the only reason I could imagine Wayne Wilson being interested in Brianna's case was if he thought Gary James was responsible. Wayne Wilson must have found something that convinced him of James's guilt, must have taken the law into his own hands once and for all.

And now Gary James was dead.

So I figured, if Wayne Wilson killed Gary James, wouldn't the chances be high that pink fibers showed up in the evidence file of that case, too?

"Want to fill me in here?" Mitch Dodson asked.

"Somebody killed Gary James last year, the man some suspected of molesting and murdering a thirteen-year-old girl named Rhonda Kuehl twenty years ago. His body was left in the same place Rhonda's was found, an empty parking lot in Longview." As I explained it, my mind flashed to Christian Doonsberg for some reason. He would fit the profile that Dodson worked up. And as quickly, I admonished myself for having such horrible thoughts about a coworker, an honorable member of law enforcement.

"And you're thinking that whoever killed Gary James must have known James was responsible for killing Rhonda Kuehl? A family member, perhaps?"

"Is that what your AFIS hit indicated? A family member?" I asked. He was shaking his head by the time I added, "Or someone with law enforcement, perhaps?"

He stopped shaking his head and eyed me. "How'd you know?"

"The name?"

"Wayne Wilson."

My blood boiled. Doc Duncan had been right. Wayne W. Wilson had a thing for little girls, had killed Rhonda Kuehl and had killed my niece. "There's been no mistake. You did well, Dodson."

"Don't thank me," Dodson said, pushing away from the table. "Thank Linwood when he gets back. He's the guy who taught me how to work prints manually and remain diligent about finding a match."

I grinned, knowing Jack had my back even when he was gone.

By the time I returned to my office, most everyone had gone home for the night. I left a message for Bo Marshall, asking that he send me a list of everyone who had checked out the evidence boxes for Brianna Keller's abduction over the past seven years, hoping he'd confirm that one of those names was Wayne Wilson. Otherwise, Doc was probably right. Wilson killed those little girls.

CHAPTER 33

"HEY, CAMERA CASEY. TAKE a picture of this," one of the boys at the junior high school yelled at him from across the bleachers of the softball field, just as he yanked his pants and boxer shorts down to his thighs, shooting Stewart Casey the moon.

Stewart smiled. He lifted one of his cameras to his eye and pointed it at the mischievous boy. The flash exploded to no avail, since he had no memory card in the camera. The group of boys encompassing the exhibitionist had not noticed the parent approaching up the bleachers as they laughed and whooped at their friend's deviancy. The parent grabbed the boy's arm before he could finish buttoning his pants and escorted him from the bleachers and away from the field.

Stewart giggled, then laughed wildly, and took several pictures of the boy being escorted reluctantly away from his friends to the punishment awaiting him at home. Of course, Stewart wouldn't use any of his precious development credits to capture the moment permanently in a photo. Instead, he would enjoy zooming in on the digital picture he took with his other camera—the one with the memory card—of the kid's humiliated face as his mommy escorted him away from his cackling friends.

Stewart was sure he was one of the guys now that he had shared in their deviancy and defiance of parental authority. He couldn't wait until the girls' softball game was over so he could meet all the kids down at the neighborhood burger joint and share in all their stories recounting the moment. He always went with them to their local hangout after school and after games to listen to their stories. Even though they ignored him most of the time, Stewart knew that secretly they thought of him as one of the gang. So he played it cool and occasionally snapped pictures of the girls when they came to the hangout, which made the boys laugh and the girls angry. He liked being one of the gang.

As the game ended and the stadium seats emptied, Stewart followed the kids down the street to the burger and ice cream shop. On his walk, as he hung back in the shadows of the fence, hedges, and lilac bushes that lined the sidewalks, Stewart wondered what kind of punishment the kid would get for mooning him. He wondered if the boy cared or if he would ever do something to defy them again. And he wondered if at home, Stewart's own mother would punish him for having the digital photos on his memory card.

His mother had punished him already last week for taking the banana bread she had baked and a few more times for sneaking out of the house over the past couple of nights. He refused to tell her where he was going and knew he'd be in big trouble if she ever found out. She had given him the ultimatum that if he left one more time after nine o'clock without her permission, he would be punished severely, but Stewart ignored her and went out last night anyway. He had to take the little plastic pony with the black mane and tail he had bought from the grocery store to Liv or she would think he had forgotten about her. He hadn't left a gift for her all weekend. And late last week, she hadn't picked up all the gifts he left for her, which made him mad and sad at first, until he noticed that her mail had bunched up in her box in the lobby, too. That's when he realized Liv had been out of town.

He was relieved to know Liv was still his girlfriend, that she wasn't mad at him or anything.

His mother had been so angry with him this morning about sneaking out again that she grounded him for a week, not allowing him out of the house except to accompany her to the store. She had tried to explain to him the importance of being safe and staying off the streets after dark, the concern she and his dad had for him when he didn't tell them where he was going, and the importance of following the house rules regardless of his belief in them.

But Stewart had not listened. He didn't like being punished. And he didn't like being treated like a little boy. He was a grown man. A man with a girlfriend. And that's what he told her just before leaving the apartment today to come to the ball field. That made her even angrier and she threatened to take away his cameras for a week if he did not follow the house rules. Until he started crying, explaining how important this softball game was to him and how all his friends would miss him. He could not bear the thought of being without his cameras. She caved and modified her punishment to being grounded at night.

Stewart decided not to push the issue for the time being. He'd stay inside at night. He would compliantly spend his nights in his room going through all his pictures of Liv and would pay particular attention to the picture he had put under his pillow. The photo he had taken of her from behind the bushes as she stretched on the front lawn of the apartment complex before one of her runs. It was not a centered picture, but it was a picture from her ribs to the top of her head, clearly showing her breasts against her gray T-shirt. In his excitement, he had cut off the top of her head in the picture, but overall he was pleased with the depiction of the clear round shape of her breasts beneath the thin, gray fabric. It was good enough to replace the picture of the nearly bare-chested redhead Cassandra sunning herself last summer. He was in love. With Liv Bergen.

On the long days when Liv was at work, he would hang out with his friends at the baseball fields and the local burger joint, listen to the junior high students talk about their girlfriends and their first kisses with them. Today he would listen intently from another booth as the young boys told their stories.

He sipped his shake, pretending not to be eavesdropping. He heard the kids swap horror stories about what Ricky's mother might be doing to him at this very moment. Ricky must be the kid who mooned him during the softball game, Stewart thought, since the kids had mentioned Camera Casey and the softball game. He lowered his head and grinned, glad to be the star he was to these kids. So famous. The topic of conversation changed quickly to the prettiest blonde in the seventh grade, who had developed early and generously.

"I'm telling you guys, I got to second base with her," said one boy, who appeared to be the natural leader of the gang of eight boys crammed into the booth.

"Oh, bull," another boy said as the others laughed.

"I took Sheila behind the concession stand near the bathrooms and first I kissed her. Then, she kissed me back. Hard," the leader said.

The others had stopped laughing and were now hanging on his every word.

"Her hot tongue pushed through my teeth and I could see she had her eyes squeezed shut," he continued.

"You kept your eyes open?" one of them shouted, which led the others to laugh and jeer.

Then silence.

He thought the boys finally noticed him, were going to yell at him. He heard one of them whisper, "Hey, who's that guy?"

The leader shouted, "Let's get out of here."

Stewart heard the rustle of boys elbowing one another to push themselves out the booth, rubber-soled sneakers squeaking across the tile floor as the kids made a hasty retreat out of the shop. He was about to grab his shake and follow them, fall quietly in behind them at a safe distance when a man appeared at his booth, looming over him and sliding into the bench across from him. The man was huge. And serious. And scary looking.

"Are you Stewart Casey?"

The man's voice sounded like the roaring rivers over sharp rocks. Low and rumbling.

Stewart's lips parted from the straw and he slowly lowered his shake to the table, nodding.

"And those are your cameras?"

Stewart nodded again.

"Can I see them?"

There was nothing in the world that could make Stewart Casey part with his cameras, not even his mother's threats. The cameras were his life. He said nothing. Did nothing. But tremble.

The man reached into the inside breast pocket of his suit coat and Stewart imagined him pulling a gun out and leveling it at his forehead.

"If it's about Ricky, I'll delete them. The photos. Are you Ricky's dad or something?"

The man hesitated for a moment, then continued to pull something out of his pocket. He slid it across the table to Stewart. The man's piercing blue eyes—ice blue—dropped down to the item. Stewart's eyes followed. The dark blue booklet had an official stamp, gold and official.

"Are you a cop? Am I under arrest or something?"

The man simply stared at Stewart and said, "Open it."

Stewart's long, thin fingers trembled as he opened the cover. The first thing he saw was the words "United States of America," then "Federal Bureau of Investigation."

"Will you let me see your cameras now?" the man growled.

Stewart quickly and clumsily removed the three cameras strapped around his scrawny neck and placed them on the table with a clatter. The man picked them up one at a time, finding only one with a memory card. He scrolled through hundreds of photos and popped out the card and slid it into his inside coat pocket along with his official booklet. At first Stewart thought he was going to wet his pants, he was so scared. He imagined he was under arrest and worried about how he was going to tell his parents. Would this man allow him a phone call? Weren't they supposed to allow him one call?

"Am I under arrest? Did Ricky's mom call you or something?"

"The photos of the naked bottom? That's Ricky?" the man said, motioning to the waitress.

Stewart nodded.

When the waitress approached, the scary man said, "Stewart would like another shake, please."

Stewart wondered why this man was being nice to him. He wouldn't be nice to him if he was about to arrest him, would he? Maybe he figured out that Stewart was famous, that he was Camera Casey. Maybe he knew about the pictures he'd taken of the man he'd seen following Liv Bergen, the tall man he imagined was a spy. Maybe this guy was a counter-spy.

After he slipped the waitress a twenty and she left, the man said, "Do you know it's against the law to have pictures of a naked person under the age of eighteen on your camera?"

The man with the white hair and imposing muscles slid the cameras back to Stewart. Stewart snatched the cameras and strapped them around his neck, disappointed this man wasn't a spy after all. Just some guy who wanted to laugh at Ricky's naked butt.

"These aren't any good without a memory card," Stewart said.

The man patted his breast pocket and said, "And this isn't any good to me without the copies of the photos you have in your bedroom, are they?"

Stewart didn't have any pictures of Ricky's naked butt in his bedroom. Just Liv. So what was he talking about?

The man must have read his mind because he said, "You know what I'm talking about. I'm not talking about Ricky. You have photos all over your room, hidden under your mattress where your mom won't find them. Of beautiful girls. Don't you?"

Stewart peed on himself. This scary man had been in his room, had broken into his parents' apartment just as Stewart planned to do to Liv's apartment. He swallowed hard, scared of the man's piercing eyes, and nodded.

"Here's what I'm going to do, Stewart. I am not going to arrest you." The man's words were clear, but Stewart had trouble believing him. "You are going to go back to your parents' apartment this instant and you are going to retrieve every single photo, every printout, every item you have ever taken belonging to any beautiful girl, and you are going to bring everything back to me. Immediately. If you do, I will give you back your memory card and we are going to make a deal."

"What kind of deal?"

"I won't arrest you. And you won't ever sneak photos of beautiful women ever again." The waitress put the shake in front of Stewart and the man waved off the change. "Take the shake with you. You have twenty minutes."

Stewart grabbed the shake and bolted for the door on rubbery legs.

The scary man called after him, "And Stewart?"

He paused and turned to see the man motioning for him to return. His knees shaking, Stewart inched back toward the imposing hulk in his booth. Once he was closer than he wanted to be, the man reached up and grabbed a camera strap, pulled Stewart closer to his face, and said, "I know about the pony you left last night at ten o'clock. I know everything. And if you ever have anything to do with her again, anything . . ."

His words trailed off but his eyes stayed fixed on his. Stewart was frightened.

"Don't you dare bother, sneak around, take pictures of, or call Liv Bergen again. Or leave anything at her door," the man growled. "Or I'll find you."

CHAPTER 34

FORT COLLINS POLICE CHIEF Theresa Fiero explained, "Liv, I can't force the Douglasses to cooperate. They refuse to deal with anyone from our department anymore. Their attorney is saying that until we issue a warrant to arrest someone or unless the governor decides to let a grand jury handle the case, they have complied with their obligations for giving this department their statements and their earlier statements stand."

I asked, "They won't let me talk with any of the Douglass children either?"

"Not unless you're appointed to the grand jury," Fiero repeated.

I sighed audibly into the phone. "But Debra's a grown adult."

Fiero added, "I told you how frustrating this has been for us. Welcome to our world."

I told Fiero that I would finish up my analysis by the end of next week. I wanted Jack's help on the profiling before I sent anything up to Theresa. I had spent most of my time reviewing every piece of paper in the Douglass files for the second and third time since my original perusal last week. I had pieced together more flowcharts on events as they occurred, and the charts were now plastered all over one of my blank office walls. And I had documented the mistakes that were made with evidence and with key witnesses in the case. On the last pass through the files, I had been focused on gathering data and reviewing evidence only as it related to Debra Douglass, the twenty-two-year-old half sister of Rebecca.

Everything I had gathered and reviewed indicated that Debra was indeed the most likely suspect, just as Bill Archibald had suggested from his review of the statements, but I had not produced any solid evidence that would withstand the challenges of a defense team. Plus, something didn't sit right with me.

My instincts suggested that I'd missed something. I could, however, clearly show through circumstantial and arguably tainted evidence that Debra was the likely murderer, but I had not shared my thoughts or findings with anyone, not even with Jack in my nightly texts, fearful that Dodson might be intercepting them. Still no word back from Jack since our phone call was cut off last Friday.

Damned fishing expedition.

If only I could determine a motive, I may have enough to convince the Douglass family to confess to the true events of Valentine's Day. Or at least Debra, who was obviously holding something back in her initial interviews.

Although I had not shared my suspicions with Mitch Dodson, I had been asking him several questions, primarily about the assumptions he used when he developed the profile on the Douglass murderer. His profile suggested that the murderer was likely male, but didn't necessarily have to be a man, and likely had military or law enforcement training.

But Dodson went on to calculate that the killer was someone either in the family or very close to the family and that the murder was spontaneous, unplanned, and not sexually motivated. I thought about the television crews, how I'd read that they had been dismissed for the holidays, banned from being around the Douglass family until after the first of the New Year.

Dodson's profile indicated that the perpetrator was disorganized and had lashed out at the victim for specific reasons or motive. The profile suggested that the motive was not for excitement, sexual gratification, perversion, or monetary gain, but more likely was for personal reasons, revenge, or possibly mental illness. Dodson's profile, which he reminded me was an artful tool, not a scientific tool, had not ruled out any members of the Douglass family.

Suspecting that Cathy Douglass, the mother, had indeed written the note with her left hand and that Theodore Douglass had carried his daughter's lifeless body to the shed in the backyard, my task was to determine why they would have done those things if Debra had killed Rebecca. Were they trying to cover for her? Had they lost one child already to a terrible tragedy and couldn't bear to lose another child to incarceration?

If I believed the profile that Mitch Dodson had compiled was accurate, then Debra likely killed her half sister for personal reasons, for revenge, or because she was mentally ill. From my research over the past few months, I could find no records or notations indicating that Debra had been treated for mental illness at any time. I had not discovered any reason why Debra would seek revenge on little Rebecca, nor would she benefit personally from her half sister's death. If only I had an opportunity to interview Debra for myself, I could pursue some of the red flags from Debra's earlier statements to police.

I decided to take a long shot.

I spent the rest of the day in Fort Collins, shadowing Debra Douglass. Within a few hours, I noted an opportunity and decided to act. Debra had left her house at noon. She lived in a small but obviously expensive lakeside home north of town. It appeared she wasn't working and, considering it was the middle of the day in the middle of the workweek, I assumed she was probably living off her father's wealth.

Debra met friends for lunch, followed by shopping. Never alone. At three, she worked out at an exclusive private club for two hours. Again, never alone. Then, she returned home. Just as I was about to stop my stakeout, get out of my car, and knock on her door, Debra emerged dressed for the evening. I followed her to a popular nightclub in downtown Fort Collins, where she ate a light dinner with friends, and then followed her as she drove into Denver to a hot nightspot in Larimer Square.

Her friends were not with her. Debra appeared to be waiting for someone. I sat at the bar next to her and ordered a beer, which I nursed, hoping to strike up a conversation naturally. But being around Debra Douglass was like being around a movie star. People were approaching her in waves or pointing and talking about her. She dismissed them all, ignored their attentions.

It was the bartender who gave me my opening when he asked, "You're not from around here, are you?"

He was scanning my boring outfit, black suit pants and a white button-down shirt. At least I thought to ditch my suit coat.

I noticed that Debra Douglass had snuffed out her cigarette and was pretending not to be interested in our conversation, yet I knew she was. Apparently she wanted to know if I was from around here, too.

"Nope," I lied. "How'd you guess?"

"Rockies, not Cubbies around here," he said, jerking his chin at my baseball cap with the Chicago logo and toward the bank of televisions that were playing the local baseball game featuring Denver's MLB team. "So what brings you to town?"

"Scouting," I said. "Checking out venues for a band."

"Have I heard of them?" the bartender asked.

From the corner of my eye, I noticed Debra's smoky eyes dart toward me. I assumed she was a music lover, so I played up my story.

"Absolutely," I said, offering nothing about who they were, simply lifting my finger to my lips as if keeping a secret.

Debra's sculpted body, hidden beneath a skintight black bodysuit and expensive black leather jacket, shifted closer to me. I understood how men could be so readily taken by her and how easily she captured various beauty pageant titles as a child contestant, just like her dead half sister had done.

Debra leaned against the bar and shook her empty tumbler, the ice rattling. In a husky, sexy voice, she asked, "Another one, Reggie?"

The bartender said, "Have you two met?"

I stuck out my hand. "Liv Bergen."

Debra grabbed my hand but did so delicately. And she didn't offer her name.

The bartender said, "This is Debra Douglass."

She shot a look at the bartender and then studied my face. "Debbie," she said, raising one eyebrow. "Liv?" she said mockingly.

The bartender continued, "Liv's a scout for a famous band that's planning on playing in this area. She's supposed to inform them about the best place for their show and the best places to party afterwards. Right?"

I nodded. "Red Rocks would be my recommended location at this point."

Debra waved me off. "Maybe if your band is popular with the geriatric crowd. There are cooler places around."

"So where's the best venue?"

Debra was on her fourth recommendation on the hottest spots in Denver by the time the bartender finally left us to ourselves. My heart was pounding in my chest, despite my efforts to appear nonchalant and cool to the woman who was assessing me. I knew this was my only chance to get candid information. And we kept getting interrupted by random strangers approaching Debra. I had to get her out of here. Alone.

I pretended to pay my tab and leave, saying, "Well you seem to have a lot of friends waiting on you. All your ideas sound great, but my job is to scope out my recommendation. My plane leaves tomorrow morning, so I don't have a lot of time to check these places out. I better get going. Thanks, Donna."

I watched Debra look me up and down from head to toe as if I were from Mars before she corrected me. "Debbie. You really don't know who I am, do you?"

"Yeah, you're the nice lady who knows where all the coolest venues are for my band. And I really appreciate all your help. But I don't know this town well and I have a shitload of work to do tonight, thanks to you." I grinned and left money on the bar to pay for my unfinished beer.

A drunk elbowed his way through the crowd to Debra and asked, "Well, did you do it?"

Debra Douglass ignored the drunk and asked me, "Why don't I show you around? I owe you, after all, since I'm the one who foiled your plan at Red Rocks."

I couldn't have hoped for a better opportunity and, trying not to sound eager, responded, "No, I don't want to put you out or anything. I'm sure you have better plans than to be my tour guide."

"Hey, sounds like a party," Debra said casually. "But if I show you, then you have to promise me an introduction to the band backstage. That is, if they're as famous as you pretend."

I tried to appear as casual as Debra. "Deal. You've been so nice to me, you deserve a backstage pass. But you have to promise not to mention I was here or what you told me until after they play in Denver, okay? Because if this leaks out, the news of them coming to Denver would be all over the headlines and they're just not ready to commit yet. Happens all the time. I'll get you tickets for the concert and backstage passes, and I'll get you into one of their private parties."

"Then let me show you the town." Debra waved good-bye to Reggie and quickly jumped to her feet and hurried after me.

After spending time driving around to venues, in four different nightclubs in downtown Denver, all around Larimer Square, and after watching Debra consume dozens of shots and mixed drinks, I knew I was drawing closer to my opportunity with her. I nursed several mixed drinks, leaving full ones behind and swapping for empty glasses at each opportunity to make it look like I was keeping up with her.

On our way to the fifth nightclub, as we sat in the backseat of the Lincoln Continental taxi I had paid to chauffeur us around Denver, Debra asked, "How old are you, Liv?"

"Thirty," I answered. "And you?"

"Twenty-three," she answered. She added with a slight slur, "You're pretty cool for a thirty-year-old. You don't act like all those middle-agers I know."

Middle-aged. Great.

Debra pulled out a joint and lit it. She asked me, "Have you ever done a Jim Jones?"

I shook my head and frowned disappointedly. "No, I've never heard of it. But even if I want to try it, I can't. It's my job. They make me piss in the bottle every week to make sure I'm clean. And if not, I'll lose my job. They do that with every staffer for this band. But I'm from LA, and I've never heard of a Jim Jones. What is it?"

Debra drew hard on it before answering, "It's a joint that's laced with cocaine and dipped in PCP."

"Shit, oh dear," I responded. I glanced at the driver to make sure he couldn't hear us—or smell us—through the raised glass partition. "You people in Denver really do know how to party."

Debra smiled proudly. "We sure do, sugar." She sucked greedily on the stick and added, "And by the way, I'm not from Denver. I'm from Fort Collins. Didn't you know that?"

"No, I guess I just assumed you were from Denver since so many of the people at that bar knew you and since Reggie told me you knew everything about the Denver hot spots," I casually answered, trying not to breathe the sickeningly sweet, thick air that was becoming even more so. "How far away is Fort Collins?"

Debra laughed. "You really don't know who I am?"

"Sure, you're Debbie," I said, shrugging my shoulders. "I'm not that drunk."

"My face has been in every newspaper every day since Valentine's Day."

"Valentine's Day?" I looked blankly at Debra, who snuffed out the joint after I refused to take a hit for the second time.

Debra stared at me and said, "Haven't you ever heard of the Rebecca Douglass murder?" Seeing the blank expression I glued on my face, she continued, "God, you must have been living under a rock for the past three months. You know, the six-year-old reality show star who was killed? Strangled?"

I closed my eyes for a moment and said, "Oh, yes. I think I remember something about that. She was that little girl they showed on the television parading around on the runways like a midget hooker, all painted up and wearing skimpy clothes and feathers."

Debra frowned.

Knowing I'd hit a nerve, I continued, "I do remember something about that. The father getting her into a kiddie porn thing or something? Made his own daughter strip for him? Something like that, wasn't it?"

She scowled. "Idiot."

"I'm just telling you what I read."

"Well the media is a bunch of idiots, too. It wasn't like that at all. My dad wouldn't hurt a fly."

I snapped my head in her direction. "Your dad? Oh, I am an idiot. Sorry."

She shrugged. "It was that bitch stepmother forcing the little girl to take on the reality show thing and to win all those trophies and pageant titles. Living vicariously through that kid to win titles and trophies she couldn't win herself. She did the same fricking thing to me and I hated her for it."

I gasped. "You were in beauty pageants? I mean, not that you aren't beautiful or anything, but I just can't picture you being in one of those things."

"*Those* things?" Debra said as she snatched the joint from the ashtray and lit it back up. "They're called pageants. And I hate them. They're disgusting. They're hard work, a pain in the ass." She blew out the smoke in a long breath before adding quietly, "And they rob you of your innocence, your childhood."

I quickly thought about the direction I should take. I detected Debra's disdain for her stepmother and her adoration of her father and finally asked, "What kind of mother would do that to her own kid?"

"A shitty one," Debra answered. "An evil stepmother."

"Wait, you had the evil stepmother? Or did that little kid who was killed have a stepmother?"

"My dad remarried when I was young. My stepmother is evil, made me participate in pageants. Hated them," she said with frustration. "My stepmother is the biological mother of Rebecca Douglass, my half sister."

"Oh my word," I gasped again, pretending to be surprised by all the twists and turns of her story, knowing every detail from the files. "Rebecca Douglass was your sister? I am so, so sorry. That must be a horrible burden to carry."

"Not my burden," she said flippantly. "I know burdens. Rebecca got off easy."

"Being killed?" I asked. "That's getting off easy?"

She shrugged. "My mother died when I was only five years old, my brother was a baby, and my dad married that bitch of a stepmother almost immediately. She had me parading on the runways in no time, showing off my undeveloped body to every child-molesting pageant follower who cared to watch me strut my stuff. What a bitch."

Motive with this woman was overwhelming. Debra may have had strong reasons to forge the ransom note to make it look like her stepmother's hand-writing, to implicate her in the murder of her half sister. I decided to see if Debra was going to be as talkative about the murder. "Hey, now I remember. Wasn't Rebecca Douglass shot to death or something by her dad?"

Debra laughed. "I guess it's working."

"What's working?"

"The media smear campaign on my dad," she said. "Rebecca goes and gets herself killed and my poor dad is the one who suffers for it."

"I still can't get over it. So that famous kid, Rebecca Douglass, was your sister? Were you on all those TV shows, too? So all this time, you're famous and never mentioned it?" I knew Debra was so wasted she'd find my comments flattering rather than stupid. Playing dumb wasn't my stron-gest talent.

"I'm not famous. More like infamous. And she was my half sister," Debra quickly answered with a curl in her lip. "I told you. We only share the same father. I have nothing to do with that bitch he calls his wife now. And she refused to let me be a part of the reality show. Just like she refuses to let me be part of the family. I am so sick of all the accusations, the ques-tions, the cameras being shoved in my face every day. If those idiot police don't figure out who killed the little bitch soon, I might just puke. She's dead. Get over it. The world keeps spinning. Imagine that."

"Seems harsh."

"Life's harsh." Her head swiveled to stare into the darkness beyond the window.

"Why was your half sister a bitch? I thought you said it was your stepmother you hated?" I asked, recognizing she was not only drunk but stoned. I worried she might be losing sight of her source of anger. And I wanted to know clearly what that source was.

Debra cut me a suspicious glance, then said, "My daddy was so wrapped up in that little bitch and all her stupid TV show stuff that I never got an ounce of his attention. I thought it was bad when he mar-ried that bitch, Cathy, but then it got ten times worse when that little Rebecca was born. And even worse when she scored a TV pilot. I was only twenty and it was like I didn't even exist anymore. He spent all his time with her, cameras rolling."

Jealousy, another motive. This time for murder? I said nothing, fearful of sounding too inquisitive for a total stranger.

"He used to spend all of his time watching me stroll up and down the runways. I was his little princess. Until Rebecca came around." She turned her bleary eyes on me and sported a sloppy smile. "Now, I'm his princess again. He has spent more time with me in the past few months than he has in years. And that bitch, Cathy, is still trying to keep the police off her fat ass."

Risking that she might shut down, I asked, "Were you there the night Rebecca was shot?"

"She wasn't shot," she snapped. Then a smile fell on her full lips. "She was strangled to death. And yes, I was there, but just by chance. I hate my stepmother more than life itself and she was the reason I was there that night. She told Daddy I was too stoned to drive that Valentine's Day. Daddy had called me that evening to ask if I wanted to come for dinner. A dinner with just family. No TVs. I stepped outside after dessert and the she-devil found me on the porch smoking a joint. It was one joint. I wasn't that stoned."

I recognized the rage in Debra's eyes. Clearly, she loathed her stepmother.

"She got all hysterical like she always does and told my daddy about it. He told me I had to stay overnight. That wouldn't have been so bad because my brother was there, too. But it was that bitch Cathy and her evil little princess mini-bitch that I couldn't stomach. They were all condescending towards me with their holier-than-thou attitudes. Rebecca refused to talk to me."

I sat silently beside Debra Douglass in the dark. Debra had shown little emotion during her statements to the police, and it was clear to me now why she hadn't. It was because she genuinely had little emotion for Rebecca, except maybe jealousy and misplaced anger.

Debra chuckled. "Now everybody thinks my stepmommy is somehow involved in her little princess's murder. What a kick!" She took one last drag on the Jim Jones before snuffing it out a final time. "And she's the one who keeps shoving the limelight back my way, the bitch. If it wasn't for Willie, I'd probably have blown my brains out by now."

"Who's Willie?"

"My knight in shining armor," Debra slurred. "The only man who believes I didn't have anything to do with Rebecca's death. The only person smart enough to prove my stepmother killed Rebecca. Not me."

"How can he prove it?"

"He saw her do it."

My stomach flew into my throat. "Saw her? Was he there that night?"

"Shhh," she said, her eyes not tracking with one another, but trying to lock with mine. "I haven't told anyone that. Since that bitch made me spend the night, I asked Willie to spend it with me. My parents don't know. So shhhhh. Our secret."

Theo's robe. Maybe Willie wore it? Nowhere in any of the files was this "Willie" ever mentioned. A key witness? Or the murderer?

"Willie who?" I asked.

"Willie, my bodyguard," she said, her head lolling back on the seat and her hands moving to the inside of her thighs. "He used to work for my dad. Until Daddy found out we were screwing. Then Willie got fired. And I hired him."

Motive. The man had been fired by Theo Douglass.

"Willie and me laughed about it. The note. I did my best to make it look like the bitch wrote it. Forged it as best I could with her loopy style. To help the police. So she wouldn't get away with murder."

"What's his last name? Debbie?"

But I was too late. Debra Douglass had passed out cold.

CHAPTER 35

AS THE DRIVER OF the Lincoln Continental headed back from Fort Collins—Debra Douglass safely tucked into her bed—I thought about what she had said and was convinced now more than ever that, although she hated her stepmother and half sister, she wasn't the one who had killed Rebecca. But I admittedly hadn't digested everything I'd learned tonight.

One mystery solved was that Debra was hoping to pin Rebecca's murder on her stepmother. Perhaps at Willie's urging. But she'd implied writing the ransom note.

In between bouts of unconsciousness, she had joked about forging penmanship to make it look like Cathy Douglass was involved in or guilty of Rebecca's murder. And the note had referred to her father's bonus, which I could only assume Debra might know. Maybe even Willie knew that. Adding the amount to the note would cast more suspicion of an inside job. Maybe Willie had put Debra up to writing the note, pinning suspicion on poor Theo and Cathy for something he had done. After all, how would Debra know? She was stoned the night of Valentine's.

And fibers from Theodore's robe ended up on the duct tape that covered Rebecca's mouth, which I'd assumed meant Theo was involved. Debra could have easily given the robe to Willie to wear, since neither had known they'd be staying the night at the Douglass house, which meant nothing to wear to bed or any clean change of clothes.

All of my speculation fit much better with the facts, and with my suspicion of the Douglass family's innocence, if this bodyguard Willie truly had spent the night. And I believed that Debra had never told anyone before, because there was absolutely no mention of Willie in any case file. Anywhere. I'd never heard anyone mention him.

I tried to remember if there was a list of employees, current and former, who worked for Theo in the case files. If so, maybe I could find anyone who might be nicknamed Willie.

Who was he? Besides being an ex-employee of Theo's and a bodyguard for Debra. And how did he fit in to all of this? Another barnacle clinging to Debra's infamy in search of sharing her short-lived spotlight? As Kato was to O.J.? I would have to search the tabloids to see if anyone snapped a photo of Debra with a man named Willie in recent weeks. Or maybe the bartender, Reggie, would know. I was headed back there to get my car anyway, so I could stop by and ask.

Then doubts crept into my mind, weighing down my perfect theory. I thought about what Debra said. Maybe, since this was an unplanned overnight and her father had forced her to stay at their house against her will, Theo gave Debra his robe to sleep in. She had mentioned that her brother was there, too, as if he wasn't normally at home. Had he stayed because Debra was there? Was the brother the one using Theodore's robe?

Maybe one of those two children hadn't intended to implicate their father in the murder. Maybe it was just an oversight. After all, Debra admitted to smoking a joint that night. If it had been a Jim Jones joint, maybe she was too stoned to remember killing Rebecca. Certainly it would make sense that Debra would be too stoned to think about leaving fibers from her father's robe on the duct tape that covered Rebecca's mouth.

Assuming the motive for Debra to kill Rebecca was revenge for having stolen all her father's time and her desire to implicate Cathy—removing any obstacles between Debra and her father—I still didn't believe that Debra killed her half sister.

On the long drive back from Fort Collins, I constructed my text to Jack carefully, saying only that I spent the evening with Debra Douglass and gained keen insight on who likely killed Rebecca. I hit send just as the limo driver dropped me off at the bar where I'd started the night. I offered the man my credit card to pay the small fortune owed him and headed back inside, minutes before closing time.

I threaded through the crowd and sidled up to the bar, where the bartender instantly recognized me. "Where's Debra?"

"Home. Passed out in her bed," I answered honestly. I laid her car keys on the bar. "She told me to give these to Willie. Is he here?"

He shook his head.

"Do you know him?"

"Sure do," he answered, snatching up the keys.

I grabbed his hand before he was able to get away. "Not so fast. It's been a long night. How do I know you're going to give these to him?"

"Why wouldn't I?" he said, surprised by my strength.

"Because maybe you'll use those keys to take advantage of my new friend?"

"She's my friend, too."

We stared at one another for a long time. "Prove it. Willie's last name?"

Reggie grinned. "Some friend you are."

I released my hold on his wrist, sensing I'd said something wrong.

"If you were, you'd know Willie's the only name he ever gives. I don't think Debra even knows what his last name is. Never will, if you ask me."

"What do you know about him?"

"He's an old guy. Even older than you."

Older than me? I was only thirty. "Where's he from?"

"Somewhere west of here. Not much of a talker. Works security, as a bodyguard."

"Does he really have Debra's best interests at heart?"

Reggie hesitated, shook his head, and stuffed the keys into the front pocket of his jeans.

"Didn't think so. You're a good friend," I said. At least I had something to go on—he was older than me, from the west—and I was now anxious to get on my computer to do some searches.

As I drove home, I assessed my energy level and how much work I could still get done tonight.

By the time I trudged through the parking lot and up the stairs to the apartment complex lobby, I'd finally identified the feeling that was weighing me down. Dread. I dreaded coming home alone to whatever crazy gift Stewart had left at my door. Last night it was a plastic pony with a black tail and matching mane, confirming my suspicion that he was indeed challenged somehow. What grown man with a mature mind would think a toy horse would impress me? Maybe I should talk with his parents if this continued, I thought. I didn't want to hurt his feelings. I just wanted him to stop.

As I stepped into the elevator, a chill went up my spine. The thought of being alone tonight, since I hadn't made it back to the office to retrieve Beulah from the canine kennel club, made me feel empty. Just like my stomach. I realized I hadn't eaten all night. Dragging myself off the elevator and down the hall to my apartment, I glanced at my cell phone, hoping to see a message from Jack and finding none.

My spirits lifted as I found nothing waiting for me outside my door. No chocolates, no poems, no toys, no flowers. Nothing. I let myself in, flicked on all the lights, and foraged for something to eat, finding a frozen turkey potpie.

Just as I was sticking my dinner in the microwave, I heard a faint knock on my door. I walked over and peered into the peephole. Camera Casey. I grabbed my pistol from the counter, left the chain on the door, and opened it.

"Do you know what time it is?" I asked him through the crack of my door, holding my loaded pistol just out of sight.

He looked at his watch. "Two thirty-five. In the morning."

Apparently he didn't understand my question, took it literally.

"Uh, Liv. I do not want to bother you. And I know I am not supposed to be here, or call you, or leave you anything ever again or the scary man will find me, but there's—"

"Scary man?" I asked.

He nodded rapidly, his eyes darting down the hall. "A real life Stretch Armstrong. But this is important. There's something I have to tell you. And you said we were friends."

"Stewart, I like you. Really, I do. But I already have a boyfriend."

He shook his head and frowned. "No, not that. The scary man told me to never bother you again, but I am afraid for you. Someone is following you. I've seen him. A tall man."

I closed the door and unhitched the chain, stepping out into the hall with Stewart. I followed his eyes down the hall toward the elevator. "Here? At my apartment?"

"Here. In the hall. In the building. Outside the building. In the parking lot. I thought he might be a spy or something."

Just then he noticed my gun, his eyes growing wide.

"When?"

"Almost every night. When you come home."

"Do you have a picture of him, Stewart?"

He lowered his eyes, his cheeks blossoming with embarrassment. "I did but another guy took my memory card."

"What's he look like?"

"The guy who took my memory card?"

"No, the guy following me."

He shook his head. "I don't know. He dresses in black. He stays in the bushes. In the dark shadows. Around corners or behind cars. He's taller than me."

Taller than six-two. That was something. "Is that why you call him the scary man?"

"No, the tall man and the scary man are two different people. I've seen the scary man but once. When he took my memory card. He's not as tall. Please don't tell scary man I was here. He said he'd find me if I ever bothered you again. He's with the FBI. I saw his badge."

The only person I'd ever told about Stewart was Streeter. "Does scary man have white hair? Sound like a broken-down lawn mower when he talks?"

Stewart nodded rapidly, but didn't grin.

Streeter. God love him. "But scary man isn't the one following me?"

He shook his head.

"Stewart, I'd like to be friends. But you have to quit leaving me gifts and taking pictures of me."

"I know. Scary man told me. I like you."

"And I like you, too. But not as a boyfriend. Just as a friend. Can you handle that?"

He nodded. "Friends warn each other, right? When someone's following them?"

"Yes, thank you." I looked down the empty hall, stuffed the pistol in the waistband of my pants, and stuck out my hand to Stewart. "Thanks for the warning. I'll be okay."

"You're welcome," Stewart said, his smile nearly splitting his long face.

"Now go home before you get in trouble with your parents," I guessed. "Quit sneaking out. You're causing them to worry. And you don't want that."

His smile faltered and he shook his head. "Okay."

As he hurried down the hall to the stairwell, I called after him. "Stewart, did you happen to see the car he was driving? Tall man?"

"A car with two doors. Old-fashioned. The color of bologna."

I knew exactly which car he was talking about. The car that had been following me the night I was talking with Barbara.

"Be careful," I said. And he was gone.

I latched my door, setting my pistol back on the kitchen counter. As I padded back to the microwave, I smiled thinking about how Streeter had warned Stewart off me. I smiled wider that Stewart braved his wrath by warning me about the man in the bologna-colored two-door car. Who would be following me? Taller than Stewart Casey? Ruled out Dodson. Ruled out most people I knew.

I powered up my laptop as the microwave whirred, and within minutes I was filling the void and searching for tabloid pictures of Debra Douglass and the mysterious man with one name: Willie, the bodyguard.

An avalanche of photos with stories vilifying Debra filled my screen. I found it odd that nothing came up under "Willie," particularly given how enamored Debra was with the man. I tried typing "bodyguard" and found references made by Debra to a bodyguard she had hired since the Valentine's Day murder, but no recognizable images popped onto the screen. No group shots, no paparazzi candids, no selfies, nothing.

I decided to cyber-stalk Debra on social media and found numerous entries about hiring a bodyguard and referring to Willie. I tracked backward on her posts to the earliest reference to either having a body-guard or to dating Willie. The first mention of hiring a bodyguard came in mid-January. Debra referred to being angry that her father had fired the hottest guy she'd met in a long time, all because the evil stepmother—"ESM" as Debra called her—didn't like him. She mentioned using her "allowance from daddy" to hire a bodyguard, the very man Daddy had fired, just so Debra could fan the flames of ESM's ulcers. A week later, Debra suggested she'd found love. And a few days after that, a man named Will participated on her posts.

When one friend suggested that Debra's mysterious man was nothing more than an April Fools' prank—an imaginary friend similar to the vol-leyball playing the role of friend to marooned Tom Hanks in *Cast Away*—Debra cursed crass expletives. Debra explained that Willie was not only very much real but also profoundly professional. So professional that he believed that if he allowed pictures to be taken of himself, the very act may compromise his ability to protect her.

Was Willie short for something? Like William, Willard, or Wilson, as in Wayne Wilson, hence the reference to Tom Hanks's volleyball?

Not an imaginary man, but certainly elusive.

I was kicking myself for not spending a few more minutes in Deb-ra's home tonight after tucking her into her bed, for not riffling through the drawers and cupboards. Maybe I would have found photos or docu-ments or something that would tell me more about this Willie character. I decided my efforts were being wasted and glanced at the clock, trying to determine whether I was tired enough to get some sleep.

Three o'clock in the morning.

I decided to check my inbox before hitting the hay.

The first email that caught my eye was from Bo Marshall. He had attached a list of everyone who had ever checked out evidence on Brianna's case. I glanced through the list, recognizing only one name. The cursive handwriting was impossible to decipher, but it appeared to me to be W. W. Wilson, even though only the W could be determined for sure.

Wayne W. Wilson. Had to be.

Then I noticed a second email.

"Hello, Jerome," I said aloud, noticing he had sent me an email earlier in the afternoon. I opened Special Agent Jerome Schuffler's email and read his brief note, which apologized for taking so long to get me the list of the individuals who knew that Daryl Cleveland had been taken into custody but was out on bail before his trial in New York for the murder of Kesha Ryan. I had almost forgotten about my conversation with Jerome last week and his speculation that only an insider could have killed Cleveland. I wanted to know who had that inside information—and who may have used it to threaten Lance Bovier.

Lance had been so convinced that someone was after him—a vigilante who was willing to take the law into his own hands—that he fled to New Jersey. Not paranoid after all. Bovier was found strangled in a casino bathroom exactly as his victim Tia Mulberry had been found. He'd been murdered, just like Cleveland had been murdered.

Either by a competing mob member or by some vigilante.

I scanned the list quickly for Su Panini, who Lance's father believed was responsible for his son's murder. But there was no Su Panini on Schuffler's list, nor in any of the Daryl Cleveland articles. I wasn't really thinking it would be that easy. But the list did include a name that was vaguely familiar to me, and I wasn't sure why I recognized it.

So I turned to the search engines and typed "Morris Kuchenberger." Few results appeared, which told me Morris wasn't all that active in cyberspace. But I clicked on the images tab when something caught my eye. I scrolled through the first few photos until my eye landed on a group photo of several men. I scanned the text attached to the image and noticed it was a listing of all the men in the photo. My eyes landed immediately on Morris's name and I searched for him in the photo. He was in the back row, three from the left. I zoomed in on the image and studied Morris's face. He was a man of about fifty years, a paunchy stomach, saggy jowls, and narrow eyes. His hair was sandy brown with gray around the temples.

Nope, meant nothing to me.

But as I scanned the rest of the photo, my eyes caught on the man two people over from Morris, on his left, the photo's right. It was none other than Mitch Dodson. I scanned the rest of the names and realized that many of the fellows in the photo were names I recognized. Christian Doonsberg was sitting in the front row, four from the right. As was

Andy Shriver, wearing a military uniform. Then I noticed the classroom they were in. This photo was taken at Quantico. These men were primarily graduates of the Academy or invited guests of law enforcement. I scanned more of the text but found nothing more than the word *BOLO* hand written in the corner of one photo.

"A police term," I said to myself. "Be On the Look Out."

I searched for "BOLO" and found the usual references to police jargon. I then typed in Morris Kuchenberger's name and the moniker BOLO and got one result. Someone had written a scathing blog about police brutality in New York City and included as the last line "Be on the look out, alright. For the Brotherhood of Law. They're dangerous."

"Brotherhood of Law?" I asked aloud.

I typed in "Brotherhood of Law" and found IBPO, the International Brotherhood of Police Officers, and the Brotherhood of Law Enforcement, but no Brotherhood of Law. Maybe the blogger was trying to draw attention generally to the law enforcement as bad, but from how he wrote the article, it appeared he was against rogue law officers, not all law enforcement. So I tried to imagine what BOLO might stand for. I typed "Brotherhood of Law Officers." I got the same results as before. I couldn't think of any other O words to try.

It was late and I was tired. I gave up and headed to bed.

Before my head hit the pillow, I thought of the word I was looking for, something that would sound official yet more covert. *Operative.*

I threw the covers back and padded in the dark over to my laptop, powered it up, and typed "Brotherhood of Law Operatives" into the search engine. The image I had seen earlier popped up, as well as others. Police officers. Judges. Special agents. Marines. Other military personnel. There must have been images of nearly one hundred individuals from all over the country in various photos. The largest grouping was eighteen, the initial photo that showed Morris Kuchenberger standing in a classroom at Quantico with my friend Christian Doonsberg, my classmate Andy Shriver, and my coworker Mitch Dodson. I scanned the faces again to make sure there wasn't anyone else I might recognize. I dashed off an email thanking Jerome Schuffler for the list and asking if he knew anything about

BOLO or the Brotherhood Of Law Operatives, some secret society of law enforcement personnel.

And just as I was about to power off the computer, a familiar name caught my attention amid the BOLO results. The man who Doc Duncan believed had something to do with Rhonda Kuehl's death and who'd blamed Gary James for committing the same crime. And the man who owned the house filled with pink carpet. The source of the fibers found in my niece's murder file.

Wayne W. Wilson.

CHAPTER 36

THE BLINKING LIGHT ON my office phone the next day was insistent.

I hit the button to listen to the message. "Liv, it's Jerome. Call me when you get in. First thing."

I looked at the clock. It was seven o'clock Mountain Standard Time, nine in New York. I dialed Jerome's number.

"What in the hell have you gotten into this time, Bergen?"

"No 'Hello'? 'Good morning, sunshine'?"

"That brotherhood is dangerous. Something you don't want to mess with. Stay away from them. They will ruin your career."

"Did it ruin Morris Kuchenberger's career?" I asked.

Schuffler's hesitation spoke volumes.

"Morris was on your list."

After some rustling noises on the other end, what I thought sounded like fingers clacking against a keyboard, Schuffler said, "Ah shit. We missed that. The BOLO connection, I mean. We believed he had cut all ties. Damn it."

"Jerome, what's going on? Who's BOLO?"

"Let me call you back."

And Schuffler was gone.

My curiosity piqued, I stared at the phone, deciding whether I should talk to Christian Doonsberg next or Mitch Dodson. I opted for Dodson since I preferred talking face to face.

I quickly printed the BOLO image, grabbed two cups of coffee, and headed down a level to ERT. Dodson was hunched over a microscope again.

"Coffee, no hug," I announced, pleased that I'd made him smile.

I sat on the stool in front of the Bunsen burner nearby where Dodson was sitting. I didn't want to sit too close to him. He wore a white lab coat and, in stark contrast, I wore my black birth-control bureau suit. And matching steel-toed boots, as always.

Dodson and I had navigated through some rocky terrain in our working relationship this past week, and I needed him to be forthcoming with me now more than ever. I had to know what he knew about BOLO, yet I had to be cautious, lest he misread my intentions again.

"Help me with something, will you?" I said, offering him a smile.

"The Douglass case?" he asked, wiping his hands on his lab coat and spinning on his stool to face me. Our knees touched. I scooted my stool back.

"Sorry," he mumbled.

I handed him a cup of coffee. "Do you think the Douglass investigation is so far gone that the killer will get away with murder?"

Lifting the cup to his lips, he closed his eyes, breathed deeply, and caressed the rim of the mug. I waited. Eventually, he sipped and lowered the cup. "That's exactly what's going to happen."

"And do you know who killed Rebecca Douglass?"

His confusion was genuine. "No, why do you ask?"

"You seem to know so much. I was just hoping you could share some insight with me."

I was surprised when he asked me, "Do *you* know who killed Rebecca Douglass? And do you think the investigation has been so botched that no charges will ever be filed?"

I took the same care to answering, just as he had done. "I thought I knew who might have killed Rebecca, but now I'm not so sure. I have two very believable suspects, but my instincts say I'm wrong about one."

"And right about the other. And do you have enough to help Fiero bring charges?"

I shook my head. "Not anytime soon."

"Does Fiero agree with you about the leading suspects?"

"I haven't told her my theories yet." His awkward grin unsettled me.

"So you haven't shared my profile with her," he said, his eyes sad.

"Not yet, but your findings were quite helpful to me."

"But you're taking my advice and asking Jack to conduct an independent profile?" Dodson asked. I nodded and he continued, "Mind if I ask who you suspect?"

"I do mind," I said. His expression of shock pleased me. I needed him off balance for my next question: "When you were telling me about the partial print and the match you found to Wayne Wilson, you mentioned that he couldn't be the one who killed Gary James. Why do you think that?"

He sipped, yet his eyebrows buckled. I braced for a lie. But he didn't. "Like I told you already. Because he's law enforcement. Or was. Which means his print must be a mistake, contamination of evidence or something."

"Was?" I asked.

He nodded. "Has been most of his career. Started in Longview. But you know all that. Doc Duncan told you about it, right? His deputy sheriff. Wilson's retired now."

I decided that if Dodson was being straight, I would be, too. But I'd start the story the way Duncan did. With the premise that Wilson was a good bad guy, killing the murderers, not that he was a bad bad guy, the murderer of little children.

"Albert Duncan believes Wayne Wilson is responsible for Gary James's death. The carpet fibers you tested—the pink carpet fibers—were found at the Rhonda Kuehl crime scene twenty years ago and at the Brianna Keller crime scene seven years ago."

"But not at the Gary James crime scene last year, right? Did you ask Duncan that question?"

He was right. There were no fibers at the Gary James crime scene.

"How would you know that, Mitch? I never told you. Are you friends with Wayne Wilson?"

He pursed his lips. "Wilson and I don't see eye to eye. Not at all. In fact, I might wish I could fabricate evidence that would implicate Wilson in the death of Gary James."

"Did you? When you manually manipulated the partial print that was lifted from Brianna's nightgown?" I was hoping if the print matched Wilson and the pink fibers found on the bunny from Wilson's home tied him to the Rhonda Kuehl case, maybe I could convince Cowlitz County to press charges against Wilson for killing James. Wilson couldn't possibly convince anyone that he mistakenly contaminated evidence in two murder cases of little girls, could he? And I certainly didn't need yet another case of manipulated evidence. "Mitch, tell me you didn't manipulate the partial print."

"No, but if I did, would that help you and Doc Duncan throw him behind bars?"

I was standing on the edge of a very slippery slope. Dodson knew far too much about this case. About so many cases he had no business knowing. Several alarms sounded in my head. I tried to plaster that familiar placid, naive expression on my face to cover my "holy shit" reaction to what I was hearing. Why would Dodson so dislike Wilson?

And was it possible that Debra Douglass's Willie was actually Wayne Wilson? Could he really be the avenger of all these cold case murders, going around the country and killing people like Gary James, murderers of children, those who slipped through the system? An avenger worming his way into unsuspecting Debra Douglass's life so he could plan his next attack?

"Do you know if Wayne Wilson is hiring out as a bodyguard these days?"

He scoffed. "I've heard a rumor he's in security."

I made a far-fetched speculation, to get a rise out of Dodson. "Have you seen Wayne since he moved to the Rocky Mountains?"

He shook his head, his eyes flicked in my direction. He was studying me. "Like I told you, we don't see eye to eye. I believe in the sword of

Solomon. He ascribes to the philosophy that all will be forgiven. There's a difference."

"And what is that difference?"

The old man in front of me withered. "If you don't know, how do you choose which side you're on?"

"I'm on the side of the law," I said, holding his gaze and willing myself calm. "If fabricated evidence would help me and Duncan arrest Wayne Wilson for the murder of Gary James, would you really do that for me?"

Dodson's eyes wandered through the lab, calculating whether any of his coworkers could hear what we'd been saying. When he was convinced they couldn't hear a word, he answered, "Are you asking me to?"

Mitch Dodson was crooked. For good reasons? Did he want to see the bad guys do time? Or was he the bad guy? He was crooked either way. He had crossed that very thin blue line everyone was afraid to draw near in law enforcement. The temptation had been too great. He couldn't resist the pull toward the wrong side.

"Is that why the Kansas City bureau involved you in the Greenwood case? They needed you to fabricate evidence?" I was referring to a casual conversation Dodson had with some of us field agents last week in the break room. He had gloated about working 24/7 to confirm the findings from the most notorious kidnapping in recent history. The unearthed remains of Vanessa Greenwood, who was kidnapped from her school decades earlier, had been found buried in the backyard of Carl Halbrook, along with the body of Halbrook himself.

When he said nothing in response and instead sipped casually on his coffee, I asked, "Why didn't the Kansas City bureau have their lab do the workup on the findings?"

"Ask your boyfriend," Dodson said, savoring my reaction far more than the coffee. His demeanor was not that of a guilty man, but he was also a trained professional. He knew I was questioning him for a reason. "They sent the request to him. Maybe he was supposed to fabricate the results for them. Since he and the police chief go way back."

The news stunned me. I thought I was hemming Mitch into a confession of his involvement, not hurling myself against a wall to implicate Jack.

I suspected Jack was the PI Mrs. Greenwood had hired. But I didn't know about his connection to the police chief. "Why would KC do that?"

Dodson shrugged. "Because the case was so controversial, so emotional, maybe they knew Linwood would create a case for them once and for all, get it behind them, by positively identifying the Greenwood girl and her killer with irrefutable evidence."

"And did you fabricate those results, Mitch? In Jack's absence?"

He shook his head. "Didn't have to. Someone got this right. Clyde Hall was Carl Halbrook, who killed Vanessa Greenwood and buried her in his backyard so no one would ever find her. He changed his name. He led a meager life, never spent the ransom money. Lived like a pauper because he was deathly afraid of getting caught. Until someone figured out who he was and what happened."

"Someone from BOLO?" I asked.

His demeanor shifted. "Don't talk about that here. It could get both of us fired."

"Not me," I said. "I've got nothing to do with BOLO."

"I wasn't talking about you," he said. His eyes flitted around the lab and his hands trembled as he set his coffee cup on the counter.

Who did he mean by "both of us," then? What was this BOLO group? I had gotten nearly the same damned reaction from Jerome Schuffler a few minutes ago. "Don't talk about what? BOLO?"

He glanced around the room. "Later. Tonight. Meet me at the Country Buffet. At seven."

There was no doubt in my mind he was not coming on to me. He was nervous. "Do you drive a tan car? A classic?"

"What the hell are you talking about?" he growled.

I decided to keep the picture I had folded up in my back pocket for later. This was clearly not the time or the place to tell him it was no secret he was a member of this underground group.

As I rose from the stool, he reached out and laid his hand gently on my arm. "Do you know for a fact that Wilson has moved to the Rocky Mountains?"

His pleading eyes—maybe even fearful—gave me pause.

I said, "I made that part up. To see what you knew. And do you?"

"Know if Wilson's here? In the Denver area? I don't." I believed him. "But if he is, God help us all. And spare us the sword of Solomon."

I thought about Dodson's quirky way of speaking in code and wondered if I had been conversing with a criminal or a genius. And my instincts told me that Dodson and Wayne Wilson were on two different sides of the law. If Doc Duncan was right, Wayne W. Wilson might be a serial killer of little girls. Rhonda, Brianna, maybe even Rebecca Douglass. If Wilson was Willie, an employee fired by Theo and attracted somehow to the princess toddler, it would explain why Wilson snuggled up close to Debra, to stay connected to the case just beyond the spotlight's glow. If I understood Dodson's cryptic discussion, Wayne W. Wilson took the law into his own hands, whether it be as a criminal or as a vigilante, when the justice system failed.

Dodson all but told me he was willing to commit criminal acts and alter results with evidence. To convict criminals. So was he saying Wilson was a criminal or a vigilante? Both possibilities indicated a different perspective than Dodson's. I'd argue that both men were clearly on the wrong side of the law, not opposite sides. So what had Dodson meant by that?

Did Dodson believe that Wayne was wrong for murdering murderers, but that he himself was justified in tampering with evidence to convict criminals? What was it Dodson said? He believed in the sword of Solomon, and Wilson believed all would be forgiven? One was decisive with his rulings, the other set his own rules? I wasn't sure.

I took the stairs two at a time and avoided everyone as I made my way to my office. I had so many questions, so many avenues to turn down.

The fear in Dodson's eyes propelled me. Why was he scared? Was he afraid someone else would be murdered by Wayne Wilson, someone who had gotten away with a crime? Or was Dodson personally afraid of Wayne Wilson? Did that mean Mitch Dodson had committed some crime that Wayne Wilson might have discovered? Like tampering with evidence? And Wilson might kill Dodson for that? And what was the connection with the two men through BOLO? I was getting totally confused.

Luckily, the message light was blinking again, and it was from Jerome Schuffler.

"What's up?" I asked when Schuffler answered his phone on the first ring.

"You were right. I just hung up with the NYPD chief. She talked with Morris Kuchenberger. He swore to her that he had turned his back on BOLO years ago when the former police chief found out he was a member. He signed an undated resignation letter that the NYPD chief found in her predecessor's files along with a sworn statement that Kuchenberger would have nothing to do with BOLO ever again in exchange for keeping his job as a police officer with NYPD."

The pause was intense. "And?"

Schuffler sighed. "The chief dated Kuchenberger's resignation with today's date. He admitted receiving a call from a BOLO member three years ago asking for the status of a Daryl Cleveland who was awaiting trial for murdering Kesha Ryan."

"And Kuchenberger spilled the beans about Cleveland being out on parole."

"Right," Schuffler said.

"So he violated his agreement with NYPD. And the chief fired him."

"Right."

"What the hell is BOLO and why did you tell me earlier to stay clear of them?" I asked.

Schuffler answered quickly, "I told you. Because BOLO kills careers. Just like for Kuchenberger."

"What is BOLO?"

"They're an informal underground group of law enforcement professionals who are tired of the judicial system letting criminals back on the street. BOLO's a secret society that believes justice must prevail, even if the long arm of the law must reach beyond the walls of the judges' courtrooms."

"Rogue police officers?" I asked.

"And special agents. And judges. And military personnel. And sheriffs." Schuffler sounded exasperated. "Look, Liv. I admit it's tempting some days. I work hard to bring dirtbags in, only to see guys get off on a technicality or because of shoddy work by an overworked, underpaid prosecutor. Sometimes I just want to strangle someone. But I don't. That would be wrong. What BOLO advocates is wrong."

"What do they advocate? Strangling criminals?"

"Bending the rules. They educate each other on throwdowns and ham sandwiches."

"Guns and planted evidence," I said, recognizing the slang. I thought of Dodson. He flat-out asked me if I was asking him to falsify evidence to convict Wayne W. Wilson for the murder of Gary James. "How far is BOLO willing to go? Did they kill Daryl Cleveland? Lance Bovier? Gary James?"

"Who's Gary James?" Schuffler asked.

"Oh, sorry. I didn't mention him the last time we talked. Gary James was suspected of murdering a young girl in Longview, Washington. Similar to Kesha Ryan's situation. The guy was found last year dead in the same vacant parking lot, staged in the same fashion as the girl he killed."

The long pause disturbed me. My stomach felt tight. What had I said?

"Liv, how many of these cases have you uncovered? Where the suspected murderer was found dead in the same position, same place, as the victim?"

I looked up at the wall of children staring back at me. "Gary James was murdered last year. He was suspected of killing Rhonda Kuehl twenty years ago in Longview. Lance Bovier was found dead in an Atlantic City casino bathroom two years ago. He was convicted and pardoned for killing Tia Mulberry in Las Vegas. Carl Halbrook was unearthed in his own backyard last week. He was suspected of kidnapping Vanessa Greenwood twenty-six years ago, although she was never found. Until last week. Vanessa's body was found buried nearby."

When I paused, Schuffler added, "Daryl Cleveland was murdered and had his mouth stuffed with his underpants two years ago while out on bond. He was suspected of killing Kesha Ryan five years ago. Liv, we don't have vigilantes out there. We have a serial killer."

"The same person?" My mind flew to Wayne W. Wilson. "Killing five murderers?"

"Five? You mentioned three, I mentioned one. Who's the fifth?"

"One isn't dead yet. Ramir Menendez from Sacramento, California. He admitted to shooting his daughter Carlita with an injection of HIV so he could escape child support payments. Last Thanksgiving, someone mugged him during a visit to DC and injected him with what appears to be the deadliest strain of HIV. He's a walking dead man."

"But it fits the same profile," Jerome said. I heard him clicking his pen. Rapidly.

"Only Menendez might be able to ID our serial killer," I said, taping Carlita's photo on the wall, something I hadn't had time to do since I'd returned from DC. I had confirmed she had died, which meant the charges against Menendez would become much more serious now.

"There's more," Jerome said. "Now that you have me thinking in this direction. Have you heard about the cases last week? Margaret Thurgood and Shelly Jones?"

I typed furiously on the computer as Schuffler spoke. "I heard Shelly Jones went missing early last week."

"They found her. Dredged up her car earlier this week from the same pond she had drowned her kids in. She was strapped in her seat, just like the boys had been."

The boys' smiling faces greeted me on my screen and I hit the print button. I clicked on the articles about Shelly Jones. "Oh, Jerome. This is horrible. I haven't been paying attention to the news. Too busy. Clearly this wasn't suicide, as this article is suggesting. The trial may have been too much for someone, but not Shelly Jones."

Just as Shuffler began to answer, I saw a crime scene photo snapped by the paparazzi. "Murdered. Her hands were bound to the steering wheel with duct tape. Someone forced her to face the same fear her boys faced. Her car coasted down that ramp, floated out in the water, and sunk. Any doubt Shelly Jones had about how much her boys suffered was erased in those final minutes of her life, I'm sure."

"If she ever wondered," I said, taping the Jones boys' picture on my wall, my eyes falling to my beautiful niece, Brianna, and the picture of the bunny that had been found with her. "Six murderers murdered. Who's Margaret Thurgood?"

"The nanny case. In Massachusetts. Have you heard of it?"

"Oh yeah, the nanny who shook the baby to death. The one where they found the woman dead in the park. During the trial, right? Someone killed her, too. Right? No suicide, no heart attack," I said, staring at the children's faces on the wall. I printed off a picture of baby Timmy and stretched the phone cord to tape his photo at the far end, to my left.

"Nope. She didn't show up last Wednesday in court. They found her body discarded in the bushes outside the courthouse."

My stomach clenched as I studied the sea of faces, the little sacrificial lambs, landing on Timmy's and not really caring how Margaret Thurgood died. Whatever happened, it served her right. She deserved whatever she got last week for killing that adorable baby boy. But curiosity got the better of me. "How'd she die?"

"The autopsy on Thurgood revealed that the cause of death was from irreversible damage to the brain stem and lack of oxygen and blood to the brain."

"Strangulation? Asphyxiation? Overdose?"

"None of the above. Her brain swelled and she died. No other injuries, no bruises, other than bruising to her upper arms and chest. My guess after hearing all of the dirt you've dug up this morning is that Margaret Thurgood was strapped to some kind of machine and shaken to death."

I was typing furiously, inundated with news articles speculating on why the English nanny had been found dead outside the courthouse.

"The case was being tried in Cambridge, Massachusetts, which isn't all that far from here," Schuffler said. "Thurgood and Jones have dominated the news. *Vigilantism* is the new buzzword."

"Oh no," I said, understanding how contagious such a notion might be. Citizens taking the law into their own hands. Reverting to the days of pitchforks and torches. Or public lynchings.

"That would make the count go to seven, Liv."

"Seven dead murderers. Eight dead children," I corrected.

"Suspected murderers. Only one was ever convicted, and he was pardoned," Agent Schuffler said. "What does Streeter think about all this?"

"I haven't told him. I didn't piece this all together until now. With you."

"Find him. I'll hold."

Within minutes Streeter and I were in his office on a conference call with Special Agent Jerome Schuffler. It took only a few minutes to get Streeter up to speed on the children who'd been murdered. We explained how the prime suspect or convicted murderer was always found dead in the same position and same location as their victim. While Jerome got Streeter up to speed on BOLO, I unfolded the photo I had in my back pocket. Streeter studied the faces and names as he listened to Jerome explain that the MO appeared to be that of one killer, one person.

Streeter looked up from BOLO picture and at my face. I knew what his unspoken question was. Did I think that Mitch Dodson might be involved? I held his gaze and waited for Jerome to finish his explanation of BOLO and the firing of Morris Kuchenberger that morning.

Streeter held my gaze and asked, "Schuffler, do we have a suspect?"

"Not that I know of. Liv?"

I said, "The rumor is that a former deputy sheriff, Wayne W. Wilson, killed Gary James in Longview, Washington. James was rumored to have killed Rhonda Kuehl. The pink fibers from Wilson's deceased mother's home were found as evidence in two cases, but not in the Gary James case."

Streeter's eyebrows buckled slightly. "Which two cases?"

I cleared my throat. "Rhonda Kuehl and Brianna Keller."

"Rhonda, the child who was killed and discarded, half-naked, in a vacant lot in Longview?" Streeter asked, his eyes growing sad.

"Who's Brianna Keller?" Schuffler asked. "You never mentioned her."

I swallowed hard, preparing to explain.

"Another unsolved abduction. Hawthorne, Nevada." Streeter left out the detail that she was my niece. "Evidence was found in two children's deaths that points to Wayne Wilson, but not in any of the murderers' deaths?"

"Not yet," I said. "We haven't asked for those files yet. Similar fibers might have been found at any or all of those crime scenes. Time will tell."

"But no pink fibers were found at the Gary James crime scene, in Wayne Wilson's hometown?" Streeter repeated.

I shook my head. "And they were thorough. They looked specifically for pink fibers, thanks to a call from former county coroner Doc Duncan. He insisted the forensics team scour the crime scene with a careful eye toward finding the fibers."

"And they found nothing?"

"Duncan thinks his former deputy, Wayne Wilson, might be the pervert who killed Rhonda Kuehl." There, I'd said it. "It's just easier for me to believe a lawman crossed the line to kill the murderers of children than it is for me to believe he crossed it to diddle little girls."

"We really don't know if Wayne W. Wilson is our prime suspect for murdering murderers or if he might be the pervert who killed two young girls, but we do believe he's involved up to his elbows in all this, right?" Streeter summarized.

"Plus, he's part of BOLO," I added. "And if Wilson's innocent, the only logical explanation of the pink carpet fibers showing up in both girls' murder cases would be that he was investigating the cold cases and the fibers were from contamination, from reviewing the evidence files." As soon as I said it, I knew how ridiculous I must sound, considering how much of my theory was based on criminal acts. Dodson, possibly manipulating a partial print to implicate Wilson. Me, breaking and entering just to get a sample carpet fiber. But if Wayne W. Wilson killed my niece, I wanted to be the one who confronted him. "According to Dodson, who personally reviewed a partial print left at Brianna's crime scene, Wilson was the one to leave the print."

I noticed Streeter shift uncomfortably. And frown.

"Where do we go from here?" Jerome asked.

I said, "I say we pay a visit to the one man who might be able to pick Wayne W. Wilson out of a lineup. Ramir Menendez."

CHAPTER 37

WITHIN AN HOUR, STREETER and I were on our way to DIA for a direct flight to Sacramento, a recent photo of Wayne W. Wilson in hand. Wilson reminded me of one of the beach boys, long wavy blond hair and a carefree smile, the crinkles around his eyes gentle. The photo was from Doc Duncan, and just to be safe, I also included photos of Christian Doonsberg, director of NCAVC Investigative Unit at Quantico; Mitch Dodson, assistant at ERT Denver; Morris Kuchenberger, the man from BOLO who knew of Daryl Cleveland's release from prison in New York just before he was murdered; and photos of convicted criminals and random men within BOLO taken from the Internet.

While we were checking in for our flight, my cell phone chirped. Streeter looked at me inquisitively. I looked at the display. "It's Jack."

Streeter's mouth tightened and his eyes hardened. He grabbed the phone from my hands, punched a button, and lifted the phone to his ear. "Check your emails, Linwood, and get your ass back from your fishing trip. Now."

He handed me the cell and stepped away, leaving me stunned. I watched as Streeter moved toward the airline counter and began arranging for our flights before I lifted the phone to my ear.

Jack sounded worried. "Liv? Are you there?"

"Wow, sorry about that, Jack. Things have been a little tense around here since you left."

"Sounds like it," he said. "You okay?"

"Where are you?"

"On my way back. Now," he mocked. "Where are you?"

"At the airport," I said. "Streeter and I are flying to—"

"Liv, let's go," Streeter called, hurrying toward the security area.

"Gotta go, Jack."

And just as I hit the end button I heard Jack say, "Be careful, Liv. Everything's stirred up and—"

I ended the call, trying to catch up with Streeter. Once we were through security, we ran down the stairs to catch the train to Concourse B, back up the escalator, and to our gate. We arrived just as they were about to close the doors. Finding my seat quickly, I hurried to search Debra's social media accounts to see if the picture of Wayne W. Wilson matched any of her connections or any of the photos she'd uploaded. I flicked through the tiny images on my smartphone, squinting at the faces. But I found nothing. The flight attendant glowered at me and reminded me to power down my phone.

Apparently, airplanes are to me as rockers are to babies because the next thing I knew I was jolted awake by the tires touching down in Sacramento. My head had been resting on Streeter's shoulder and I was embarrassed to be sleeping on the job. I was grateful that Streeter pretended he had no idea I had dozed off or that I had been using his arm as a mattress. I sat up, extended my toes to retrieve a boot that had gone askew, and smoothed my bureau pantsuit, ignoring the impish grin on Streeter's lips. I powered up my phone and resumed my search for a picture of Wilson with Debra Douglass, scanning the images more closely.

Maybe I had jumped to conclusions too soon. Willie was a common name. I'm not sure why I assumed so readily that Willie and Wayne Wilson might be the same man. Foolish of me to speculate.

"What are you hoping to find?" Streeter asked.

"A picture of Debra Douglass's bodyguard," I said, flicking and flicking and flicking through the hundreds of images.

"Rebecca Douglass's half sister?"

I nodded.

"Try scanning the background in the photos," he said, leaning into the aisle and waving at the flight attendant.

I glanced over at him. He was grinning. I wondered what had happened while I was asleep.

I flicked through the images again, focusing on the people in the background, and just as we were about to embark, I found what I was looking for. A man in the background was watching something or someone beyond a reporter, who had a microphone shoved in Debra's face. It looked like she was at a press conference or something. March 14. A month after Rebecca was murdered.

I zoomed past Debra's head on the man in the background. He was wearing a suit, his eyes staring at something beyond the reporter, his hand to his ear—probably an earpiece—his lips slightly parted. He looked like someone who might work with the Secret Service, all serious, professional, yet blending into the background. And the man resembled the photo of Wayne Wilson, heavier, same crinkling around the eyes only more pronounced and the hair was darker, shorter, and curlier with gray. But given the different angles of the photos, it was hard for me to say for sure if Willie the bodyguard was one and the same as Wayne W. Wilson the murder suspect.

I felt Streeter's nudge, shoved my phone into my pocket, and followed.

Because we had nothing but a briefcase, we were at the taxi stand in no time and quickly thereafter headed to the California State Prison in Represa. Within an hour, the warden was leading us to an interrogation room where we could meet in private with Ramir Menendez.

A guard escorted in a man wearing blue denim pants and a blue denim shirt, his wrists and ankles restrained.

"Ramir?" I asked, standing to shake his manacled hand.

Menendez lifted both to return the gesture but the guard blocked his chest with his forearm, warning me, "Don't touch the prisoner."

I dropped my hand and sat back down in my chair beside Streeter. The guard steered Menendez across from us and anchored his ankle shackles to the floor bolts.

I said, "Geez, serious business here."

The guard peered at me, straightening, looking more like a soldier in his forest green slacks and tan shirt. "You have ten."

"We have twenty," Streeter growled. "According to the warden."

The guard hesitated a moment before retreating to the door.

"I've already told the whole story," Menendez said. "What more do you people want?"

"The whole story," I said. "Start from the beginning."

"I was convicted of first-degree murder. Serving life."

"And?" I asked. "I thought you were charged with reckless endangerment?"

"That was before."

"Before Carlita died?" I saw Ramir flinch at the mention of his daughter's name. So I said her name again. "What made you want to kill Carlita?"

He squirmed in the wooden chair, looked at his feet. I took the moment to pull a file from the briefcase and started reading some papers.

Without looking up, I said, "I'm Special Agent Bergen, by the way. For Special Agent Pierce's benefit, let me summarize. You injected your sixteen-month-old daughter, Carlita, with a deadly virus so you wouldn't have to pay your estranged wife child support. You were convicted of reckless endangerment, served your short term, and then were released." I waited a beat and added, "Carlita, wasn't that her name? Your daughter? Carlita?"

I saw the muscles of his jaw bulge as he stared at me. He was balling his hands into fists.

"Am I bothering you, Mr. Menendez?"

"Lady, do you know why they have me in these shackles? Because I have nothing to lose. I'm already a walking dead man, so I have no problem killing again. Killing you, if you don't stop talking about my baby girl."

I noticed Streeter shift in his chair.

"But you won't. Because I can do something you can't," I said, my sense of calm spreading through the room like mustard gas. His hands relaxed but his eyes were hard. "I can find out who put you into a position of having nothing to lose. The man who mugged you, injected you with HIV last year while you were vacationing in DC."

Menendez relaxed and sat back in his chair, eyeing me.

"And all you have to do is answer a few questions for me." I set the papers on the table by the briefcase. "Carlita died. That means a whole lot of shit's about to rain down on you."

Menendez said nothing.

"Why would you do such a thing? Kill your own child?"

Menendez sat staring at me, his shackled hands in his lap.

I stuffed the papers back in the file, making sure the corners of the photographs peeked out at him as I did. "No answers for me, no answers for you. That's fair."

I saw his eyes dart down to the file, to the photos.

As I slid the file into the briefcase, Menendez said, "She died. I was convicted of first-degree murder. A life sentence. And you already know why I did it. My ex-wife took me to court on child support. She convinced the judge I was made of money and he ordered me to pay a small fortune until the baby turned eighteen. I couldn't do it. Couldn't pay that bitch one dime for what she did to me."

I hung on his every word, knowing he wanted to see the photos in my file.

"So you chose a torturously slow and painful way to kill your own daughter, just to get back at your ex-wife? Your own daughter?" I asked. He didn't flinch. "Did he say anything to you? The guy who mugged you in DC?"

He hesitated before shaking his head. "I didn't even see him coming."

"By the way? Why did you choose DC for a vacation? A history buff or something?"

Menendez scoffed. "I won a prize. Beer for life. From some brewery. All I had to do was show up in person to claim my winnings and they'd set me up for life."

"And did they? Set you up for life?" I already suspected the answer. Whoever injected Menendez had likely lured him to the DC area using something that would appeal to him. A lifetime supply of beer.

"Nah, I never made it to the brewery. I was mugged before I got there." The tic below his right eye was evident. Obviously he was still shaken by what happened to him in DC.

"How close were you? To the brewery?"

"I had just parked my car. I was a few minutes late for the time I was supposed to meet the guy, and the caller had said I had to be prompt, on time, or I wouldn't get to claim the winnings. So I wasn't paying attention. Didn't see the mugger come at me from behind."

"Hiding behind cars in the lot?" I speculated.

"That's what I figured. I just know I never saw the bastard."

"Do you remember the guy's name? The one who called you?" I asked.

He shook his head. "She didn't give her name and didn't tell me the name of the guy to meet."

"A woman?" This revelation stunned me. I'd heard he wanted to find the guy who injected him, but maybe I'd misunderstood. Maybe a woman was behind all this. My mind jerked to Su Panini. "But it was a guy who injected you? You're sure?"

He nodded. "Yeah, I'm sure. You don't forget something like that."

Two people involved. A woman and a man. Maybe Menendez's wife hired a hit man, set up the scam? Or maybe Christian Doonsberg was right about the mind and the hand. One directing another. Two people. "Do you remember the name of the brewery?"

He shook his head.

"Where you were in DC? Streets? Anything?"

"I landed at Washington National, rented a car, and it took me about an hour to get there. South."

I sensed Streeter bristle.

"South to where?"

"I told you, I can't remember. I woke up in the hospital. The guy had beaten the shit out of me and left me for dead." His tic had intensified and Menendez became irritated. "Excuse me for not remembering the name of the brewery. I had more important things to be concerned with, like if I had brain damage from the beating and what the hell he injected me with," Menendez said, visibly shaken by the memory.

"So you were conscious when he injected you? You remember specifically having a needle poke your skin?"

"Hell yeah, I remember. The asshole jumped me from behind, slammed me to the pavement, and lay on top of me. He was huge, twice my size. Military guy, I'd guess."

I was relieved to know he wasn't describing Mitch Dodson.

"Slammed my face into the ground and told me to stay still. While he held both my wrists with one hand, he put his lips against my ear and I felt the needle slide into my arm. I started fighting again and he must have dropped the syringe because he grabbed the back of my head and slammed my face into the pavement. Next thing I know, I wake up in the Washington Hospital Center two days later. Took me a week before I was released. Came back to California and forgot all about the damn beer. Wasn't worth going back to that crazy place and explaining what happened."

I realized Menendez hadn't understood it was likely a scam designed to draw him out for the attack, a common approach federal agents took to drawing out criminals. "And you told all this to the police?"

"Yeah, the police in DC. The police in Sacramento," he said, sneering at me. "But what good was that? Those guys were probably cheering the guy on, if they hadn't put him up to it."

"Because whoever jumped you gave you what you deserved?" I asked.

He nodded and dropped his eyes to his ankles, the anger all but gone. "Smallwood Park."

"Excuse me?" I said, surprised because I knew the place. Quite well. It was only eleven miles from Quantico. Many of us attending the Academy hiked around in Smallwood State Park in Marbury, Maryland, on our days off. Jack and I had rented a boat and floated the Potomac off Sweden Point Marina one day last fall when he visited me.

"The brewery. It was near Smallwood Park. That's all I remember."

I noticed Streeter cut his eyes at me and then back at Menendez.

My mind raced to my time with Christian Doonsberg and his association with BOLO. His office was a short eleven miles from where this man sitting in front of me had been left for dead. Injected with HIV. Just as tiny little Carlita had been. Christian was a big man. Not fat, but tall. And was former military, knew martial arts. This tiny man would be nothing for Christian to subdue. Even as weak as he'd grown just before being diagnosed with his cancer. I had a more difficult time placing Mitch Dodson in the role of attacker, but even I could have taken Menendez. Maybe. And who knows about Wayne W. Wilson?

"Did you get a good look at the man who jumped you from behind?"

"Not a good look, just a glance." Menendez's eyes slid to the file that was poking free from the briefcase. "Can I see them now?"

I couldn't think of any other questions at the moment. I glanced at my watch, realizing our time with Ramir Menendez was almost over. I reached for the file to retrieve the photos when Streeter laid his hand over mine.

He leaned forward on the table and asked, "Why did you lie?"

Menendez appeared as confused as I felt. "I didn't lie. Why would I lie? I have nothing to lose."

Streeter lowered his voice to a near whisper. "You have the most to lose now, more than ever in the past year." As he pinned Menendez with his stare, he slid the file from my grip and held it up. "You will lose the chance to see some photos of men who might have been responsible for sentencing you to a death as painful and torturous as the one your daughter suffered. Unless you tell us the truth."

Menendez swallowed hard and licked his lips as his eyes fixated on the file. "About what?"

"You said the man who jumped you from behind put his lips to your ear before injecting you. You know and I know that man said something to you. What did he say?" Streeter asked.

"He . . . he asked my name," Menendez said, his tongue rimming his lips.

"He asked your name, or did he ask if you were Ramir Menendez?"

"Yeah, he asked if I was Ramir," he said, his eyes darting between the file and Streeter's eyes.

The muscles in Streeter's shoulders relaxed a fraction, but I could tell he hadn't gotten what he wanted from Menendez. "And?"

"And he said . . ." Menendez looked down at his shackled hands and then glared at Streeter. "He said, 'You sentenced your little girl to death. An innocent little girl, you coward.'"

I held my breath, waiting for more. Apparently Streeter also knew there would be more, because he said nothing and waited, too.

Menendez added, "Then he said, 'It's your turn to suffer the sword of Solomon.'"

Dodson. I'd heard him say that phrase many times.

I grabbed the file from Streeter and flipped to Mitch Dodson's photo and slid it across the table to Menendez. "Is this the guy?"

He barely looked at the photo and said, "No. Are you kidding me? I could take this grandpa. I said the guy was big, military."

I couldn't believe my ears. Certainly the phrase "sword of Solomon" was unusual enough that Mitch Dodson must somehow be connected. So I fished out Christian Doonsberg's photo.

Menendez shook his head.

"Are you sure?"

"That's not him." Menendez's mood was beginning to sour.

I slid all the photos over to Menendez one at a time, each BOLO character, including Morris Kuchenberger and finally Wayne W. Wilson.

"That's it? That's all you've got? You incompetent bitch," Menendez said, jerking to his feet. He lunged at me, but I was too far out of his reach.

I barely noticed the guards rushing in to remove Ramir Menendez from the room, my head still swimming from the concept that we had been so close yet had fallen so short of the mark.

Who had injected Menendez in DC? Not one of the people from my suspect list.

Then I had a thought. "Wait! Just a second."

I fished for the folded photo from my pocket, the one with several BOLO members in the Quantico classroom, and thrust it toward Menendez over a guard's shoulder. The guard shoved us out of the way, but recognition brightened Menendez's eyes. He pointed. "That's him! The bastard. What's his name? What's his name?"

The guards had maneuvered him through the door against his will, Menendez fighting their every move.

"Which one?" I called after him.

"Standing in the back row. Next to the guy from the first photo. Who is he? What's his name?"

The shouts echoed with desperation down the bare hallway.

Streeter looked over my shoulder at the well-worn photo I had folded in my pocket. The first photo I showed was Mitch Dodson. On either side of him stood men who fit the description of his attacker: one I knew, one I didn't.

CHAPTER 38

I WAS DRIVING TOO fast. Adrenaline pumped through my veins.

"At least we narrowed it down to two," Streeter said.

"Streeter, I've heard Mitch Dodson use the term 'sword of Solomon' at least three times in the past two weeks. That can't be a coincidence. Do you suppose it's some kind of BOLO mantra or something?"

I'd been so sure Menendez would identify his attacker from my stack of photos. I just missed who it was he'd finger.

"We'll ask Mitch about where he picked up that phrase when we get back to Denver." Streeter's nonchalance was pissing me off. I was starting to wonder if maybe *he* was behind this entire macho vigilante shit. And as quickly as I had the thought, I admonished myself for being so paranoid, so wrong, recognizing that my anger was truly blinding me. Besides, if Streeter was the one who injected Menendez, even the shackles wouldn't have stopped Menendez from launching himself across the table at him.

"Who's the guy in the photo you recognized?"

"A recent graduate from Quantico. He was in my class. His name is Andy. Andrew Shriver. He got the job at Investigative Support Unit that Christian Doonsberg had offered me."

"And the other guy?"

"No clue."

"But Doonsberg would know," Streeter said.

"Do you think he'll tell us? Being BOLO and all?" I asked.

"Let's find out. Why don't we talk with Doonsberg?"

I pulled in to the airport parking lot, nearly yanking the door off the rental car, I was so steamed.

Streeter moved quickly between me and the door to the airport. "Liv, calm down. You're letting your emotion take control and you won't find any answers that way."

I drew a breath and tilted my head as far back as I could, staring at the clear blue skies above me. I felt Streeter's hands grip my arms to steady me. I gulped in the summer breeze as I closed my eyes to calm my nerves, knowing Streeter was right.

"Okay, but I want some answers."

"Go get 'em, cowgirl," Streeter said, opening the door and stepping aside.

I sat on a bench inside the airport terminal and punched in Christian's direct line.

"Liv, how's that Douglass case coming along?"

"Not good," I answered honestly. "Keep getting sidetracked on other cases."

"What could be so important that you'd be distracted from the highest-profile case in the country?"

"I'm going to put you on speakerphone, Christian. I have Streeter with me. We just met with Ramir Menendez," I said, punching the speaker button.

"Oh," his voice sounded small. "Hey, Streeter."

"Doonsberg," he answered. "Back to full steam after your chemo? Clean reports?"

"Yes and yes," Christian answered. "So what's up with Menendez? And how's his daughter?"

"Carlita died and Ramir is in prison. For life," I said.

"And his attacker? Have you figured that out yet?"

I could almost see Christian's long face, his limbs, and the constant twinkle in his eyes like a stretch of starlight. I drew in a breath and said, "Tell me about your role in BOLO, Christian."

"BOLO? What does the Menendez case have to do with us?"

"Us?" I asked, looking at Streeter, who shrugged.

"What do you want to know?" he asked, unfazed by the mention of the underground group.

"Did you have anything to do with injecting Menendez with HIV?" I asked.

Christian chuckled. "I told you before, Liv. I was in no condition last Thanksgiving to subdue anyone, considering how sick I was. And what kind of man do you think I am, arranging an execution? A killer?"

"Why would you support those who are?"

"You mean by being supportive of the Brotherhood Of Law Operatives?" Christian asked. "I told you. I may not be a vigilante myself, but I find it very difficult to condemn those who are. I applaud whoever gave Ramir Menendez a taste of his own medicine. Otherwise, he might have enjoyed a long life of luxury behind bars at taxpayers' expense. And at Carlita's, of course."

"Why do you openly harbor criminals, murderers, Christian?" I asked. "And how is it that you manage to keep your job?"

Christian laughed. "Oh, dear Liv. I am not a criminal, nor am I harboring murderers, just because I secretly enjoy the creativity of some poor stiff who did to Ramir Menendez what he had done unto Carlita, his infant daughter. She's the innocent. And it's not like I publicly condone vigilantism. I work hard to put the bad guys behind bars and that's how I keep my job."

"It would seem to me that you'd at least pretend to be more offended by my accusations, surprised by my assault on your character," I said, noticing that Streeter seemed amused by my conversation and unwilling to join in on my attack on Christian.

"You are captivating," Christian answered. "Streeter, you old bastard, I am so jealous Liv chose only you to work with, even after I tried to spirit her away from you."

Streeter raised an eyebrow.

I was getting even more pissed off by the minute. "Christian, I'm serious. Who injected Menendez?"

"How would I know that?"

Frustrated, I asked, "What's the BOLO motto?"

"Motto?"

"The general motivation for BOLO. You know, the secret handshake, the telltale sign, the code, the hush-hush knock—the thing that only BOLO members are allowed to know. A statement you all share in common to let one another know you're in on the secret," I rambled.

"Breathe," Streeter whispered to me.

Christian quickly said, "Liv, you have this all wrong. It's not like BOLO meets on a regular basis or has a secret handshake. We're not even a formal organization. Some blogger dubbed those of us in law enforcement with the moniker BOLO to describe anyone who believes in justice, whether our system delivers or not. We don't advocate vigilantism. We don't have a motto or dues. We don't have clandestine meetings. We don't even have a 'we.' There is no list or code of ethics."

"I have a picture. You're in it. Along with Mitch Dodson."

"A picture?"

"It was taken there at Quantico. I recognize the style of classroom."

"Probably. We have lots of pictures taken in the classrooms. I have lots of Academy graduates just like you who want class photos. Mitch Dodson?"

"Along with several others. Do me a favor. Get on your computer and search for 'BOLO Morris Kuchenberger.' Click on the images. See it? You, Mitch Dodson, Andy?"

"Got it," Christian said.

"See the guy three from the left in the back row? That's Wayne Wilson. Know him?"

"Heard of him. Looks vaguely familiar. Seems to be a loose cannon, from what I hear. You know him, Streeter?"

"I don't," Streeter said. "What have you heard about him?"

"Just that he has a temper, left law enforcement when he didn't get his way as a deputy somewhere out west. He seems to be one of those superhero types who have to save the universe. Swoops in wearing a cape and saves women in distress."

"And who are you hearing that from? Your fellow BOLO members, like Mitch Dodson?" I asked.

"Liv, seriously. BOLO simply describes people who believe those who have committed crimes should pay a price to society. There's nothing mysterious or covert about this group."

"Then who's killing all the murderers?"

"What murderers?" Christian asked, a tone of seriousness entering his words for the first time since I'd started this call.

"The killers of children. Those who escaped punishment for their crimes. Someone is going around the country killing those killers exactly how they killed the children."

"Oh my word. Like Ramir Menendez."

"Like Gary James. Like Daryl Cleveland. Like Lance Bovier. Like Carl Halbrook. Like Shelly Jones. Like Margaret Thurgood," I said, accounting for all the murderers who I knew about to date.

I heard Christian's sharp intake of breath. I glanced over at Streeter, who'd noticed the same and leaned toward the phone.

"Christian?" Streeter said.

"They're all . . . dead?" Christian's voice had become thin. "Margaret Thurgood? How did she die?"

"Shaken to death, just like the infant who was in her care," I said, holding Streeter's gaze. "Schuffler and I think someone used a nearby excavator, strapped Thurgood to the bucket, and shook the hell out of her. Until her brain swelled, just like baby Timmy."

"The trial . . ."

I held up my hand in surrender, wondering where to lead this conversation.

Streeter took over. "What is it? What's wrong, Christian?"

"When?"

"When what?"

"Margaret Thurgood? When was she killed?" He didn't sound himself.

"Tuesday or Wednesday," Streeter said. "Last week."

"Probably Tuesday night," I said. "She was at the courthouse Tuesday, but didn't show up Wednesday. Was found in the bushes outside the courthouse."

Streeter said, "Why do you ask, Doonsberg?"

"Take me off speakerphone," Christian said.

This so surprised me that I froze, simply staring at my phone.

I heard Christian's voice crack when he repeated, "Take me off speaker."

"Who's the guy standing on the other side of Mitch Dodson, opposite of Andy?" I said, panicked I was about to be left off the conversation.

"I . . . I don't know, Liv. It might have been Andy. It doesn't matter."

"The hell it doesn't. Did Andy Shriver inject Menendez? You know who did, don't you. Menendez fingered either the guy I don't know on the other side of Dodson or Andy as his killer." I was taking a leap, but the obvious groan from Christian told me I was losing him. "You know something. Andy killed Menendez, didn't he?"

I heard Christian cover the phone, followed by some mumbling, rustling, shouting. "We've got a runner. Andy just took off. Must have been eavesdropping again. Streeter, let me talk with you for just a minute. Alone. Sorry, Liv."

Streeter lifted the cell phone from my hand, pushed the speaker button, and held the phone to his ear. "Speakerphone is off."

Streeter watched me as he listened to whatever Christian was telling him. Sadness hooded his eyes, his expression pained. Within a minute, he stood and walked away, turning his back to me as he rubbed his forehead and eyes, plowed his fingers through his shortly cropped white hair. I had no clue what Christian was telling Streeter, but I could see the burden being heaped on Streeter's shoulders as the seconds ticked away.

I was growing angry again. At Christian. For whatever he was doing to Streeter. Yet I was secretly relieved that it was not me who had the phone to my ear. I dreaded shouldering the burden of what Christian was telling Streeter. Whatever it was.

After a few minutes, Streeter returned to where I sat, handed me the phone—Christian long gone off the other end—and headed toward our flight back to Denver.

Without another word.

CHAPTER 39

STREETER HAD CLOSED HIS eyes the instant he strapped into his seat. I knew he was thinking, not sleeping. I waited until the plane had finished its ascent. We had the row to ourselves and I was grateful for the privacy.

The canned air blowing between us wasn't enough to stop me from relocating from my aisle seat to the center, closer to Streeter so I could talk low enough for surrounding travelers not to hear.

"What did he tell you?"

Streeter didn't open his eyes. I nudged his arm off the armrest. He continued to ignore me.

"Talk to me."

"I'm sleeping."

"Talk in your sleep," I insisted.

I noticed a hint of a grin on his rugged face.

"Please? What upset you so much about what Christian said?"

He opened his eyes and lifted his head, our faces inches from one another. "I have to digest all of this first, see how it all fits in."

"Digest what and fits in where?"

He stared at me for several beats and then asked, "Have you constructed a timeline?"

I stared at his green eyes that seemed to change to blue as we broke through the clouds into cruising altitude. I understood what he was asking, but the intent behind the question made me wonder what Streeter was thinking.

He added, "What you and Schuffler told me about this morning. Your theory that we might have a serial killer on the loose. Have either of you laid out a timeline of those murderers being murdered? When each of them happened?"

"Is that what Christian told you? That there's something relevant about when each of the killings occurred?" I asked, smelling sweet mint on his breath, which blended nicely with the hint of citrus in his aftershave.

When he didn't answer, I reached up and turned off the air vent, so I could savor the aroma that was uniquely Streeter.

His eyes dropped to the briefcase beneath my assigned aisle seat. I reached over to retrieve the case and lifted it to my lap. "I have a timeline. It's crude. But if it will help, let me share it."

I fished out my notepad, flipped to the later third of my notes, and started reading. "Starting from the beginning . . ."

I flipped back and forth between my pages of notes, searching for the first killings.

A small notepad appeared in Streeter's hand and I saw him jotting notes.

"Daryl Cleveland and Lance Bovier seem to be the first and second killers murdered. That was two years ago."

"Cleveland in New York. Bovier in Atlantic City," Streeter said.

"And Morris Kuchenberger was fired this morning from NYPD for giving the information out on Cleveland's release."

"Do we know who it was Kuchenberger told?"

"Schuffler didn't say."

I saw Streeter power up his phone and call Jerome Schuffler. The flight attendant immediately approached and Streeter flashed his credentials and a smile. She smiled back and said, "Make it quick."

Streeter told Schuffler to get Kuchenberger to talk and ended the call.

"And Bovier's dad credits Lance's death to an activist named Su Panini, but Agent Bo Marshall at the Las Vegas bureau and I couldn't find anything out about Panini. Schuffler thinks she doesn't exist."

"Panini?" Streeter asked.

And when I nodded, I caught the recognition that touched his eyes and lips. He said, "And Su, S-U, as in Sukanta."

"What? Who's Sukanta?"

"Nothing. Marshall and Schuffler are right. Su Panini is a fictional person but the name comes from a very real place."

"What place? Who is she? Same woman who set up Menendez?"

He ignored me and said, "Focus on the timeline. First Cleveland, then Bovier. Both killed two years ago. Then who?"

I studied my notes. "Gary James in Longview last spring. Ramir Menendez last Thanksgiving."

"What time of year were Cleveland and Bovier killed?"

"May and December," I said.

"Spring and Christmas holiday," Streeter repeated. "Who else?"

"Last week Margaret Thurgood was shaken to death, and Shelly Jones was strapped to her car and submerged in the lake. Also last week, Carl Halbrook was found buried in his backyard."

"That's when he was found. When was he killed?"

"I'll have to ask Dodson. But you're saying there's a pattern? All the killings happened in May?"

"And holidays. Why would Dodson know when Carl Halbrook was killed?" Streeter asked, his eyes sliding toward me.

"Because he's doing some work for the KCPD. You didn't know that? I thought I mentioned it. Dodson assumed there might be too much emotion in the Vanessa Greenwood case for the KC bureau to remain impartial. Plus he said Jack had a personal connection with the chief of police." I noticed the skepticism in his eyes. "What? That's what Dodson said when I asked the same question."

"They're professionals, Liv. KC bureau's ERT would have been fine doing the forensics work on this case. There's something deeper at stake here," Streeter said, probing my face, seeking my reaction.

Confusion was all I offered. "So you think Mitch is involved some-how? Maybe tampering with evidence for whoever is killing these people?"

"What did he tell you about the case? How did he get involved?"

I shrugged. "Mitch all but admitted to me this morning he'd tamper with evidence for me to get one of the bad guys off the streets. He felt jus-tified as long as he believed in the 'sword of Solomon.' That's why I was so sure Menendez would have pointed out Dodson in the photo lineup. Who uses that phrase? Sword of Solomon?"

"Liv, focus. What did Dodson tell you about how he came across this case?" Streeter had completely ignored my accusation that a coworker was willing to tamper with evidence.

I was missing something. Something big.

And I thought of Wayne W. Wilson. And the ticking time bomb for whoever killed Rebecca Douglass. Because someone was out there kill-ing the killers. One by one. And Debra said Willie saw her stepmother kill Rebecca. Was Wilson planning on killing Cathy Douglass? Despite Menendez not recognizing him in the individual photo, maybe it was Wil-son he recognized in the group photo. If Wayne W. Wilson was the serial killer of murders, not Andy Shriver, that meant wherever he was, he might lead us to a murderer of children. But if Wayne W. Wilson was diddling little girls, we could find him and use him to bait the killer of murderers.

Dodson was insistent on knowing whether Wilson was in the Denver area. Had Dodson provided Wilson with information about the Rebecca Douglass case? Evidence I might have asked Mitch for help with over the past week? Surely if Dodson was knowingly involved with Wilson, he wouldn't have manipulated the partial print on Brianna's case to implicate him. Or would he? Mitch seemed at odds with Wilson, on opposite sides of the spectrum. 'Sword of Solomon' as opposed to 'all will be forgiven,' but I was starting to wonder if the philosophies applied to both. If I were a vigilante, I might subscribe to the idea that if I had to invoke the sword of Solomon, a deadly decision, all would be forgiven.

"Liv?"

I cleared my mind. Thinking about my promise to meet Dodson at the Country Buffet later that night, I said, "I could try to get more out of Mitch when I meet him later."

"Like what?" Streeter asked.

"Mitch said that while Jack was gone, he was doing some of the work that had piled up." I debated for a moment, then added, "He said he was reading Jack's emails and getting ahead to earn some brownie points with his boss."

Streeter's jaw muscles twitched. "Linwood's emails? Does he know about this?"

"Who, Jack? Not until I told him."

"When? How did he take it?"

"Uh . . . Friday. And you know how he is about his privacy. And about confidentiality. I can't imagine Jack giving Dodson his password," I said, thinking of how wolfish Dodson had become finding some personal texts from me that were showing up on Jack's inbox as well as on his cell phone, warning him about Dodson's doings. I was as subtle as I could be, but I knew I wasn't fooling Mitch.

"And how often have you been talking to Jack?"

"I've been texting Jack each night about what I've been finding. On these murders as well as on the Douglass case. He has those texts synced with his email account."

I noticed the muscles in Streeter's jaw tighten. I felt terrible.

"You don't suppose I'm the breach, the one feeding Dodson all the evidence pointing to a possible suspect in the Rebecca Douglass case? If so, I've been handing evidence and findings over to Wayne W. Wilson—assuming he's the vigilante—through Dodson and unknowingly may be sentencing someone to death."

Streeter leaned back in his chair and closed his eyes. But I could read the concern etched on his face.

"What did Christian tell you?" I insisted.

Streeter kept his eyes closed, which allowed me to study every line on his face.

"Has your neighbor bothered you lately? Called you?"

"No," I said. "And thank you. I know you were the reason his unwanted advances stopped. Seriously, thank you."

"And do you still feel like someone's following you? Been watching you?"

"As a matter of fact, yes," I said. "Anyway, I don't think they were related. In fact, I'm sure of it. Someone at my apartment told me a tall man has been following me. Someone they hadn't seen around before."

"They're right. Be careful," Streeter said, his eyes still closed. I waited patiently for him to explain. He opened one eye to see if I was interested. "I have the memory card from Stewart Casey's camera. And he did snap some shots. Someone has been following you. We have proof."

"Who?"

"I'm still working on that."

"Then thank you for whatever you said to Stewart Casey to make him stop crushing on me. But screw you for not telling me what Christian said to you. Or who's following me."

His breathing slowed and I thought he'd fallen asleep. I glanced at my watch, deciding whether to wake him up or give him his peace like he'd given me on the way to Sacramento earlier today.

I thought about my friend Christian and his passion for justice. I was ashamed at how judgmental and accusatory I'd become of him over the past week. I realized now why he laughed at my gullibility, as I ranted about BOLO earlier. If I were truly honest and allowed myself the guilty pleasure, I would gladly break the law to find my niece's killer. Like I did in Longview. After all, I had broken in to the empty house of Wayne W. Wilson's dead mother to get a sample of that pink carpet, hadn't I? Doc Duncan showed me where the house was and told me where the key was hidden, hadn't he?

Yet I respected Doc and justified my own actions while chastising Christian and Dodson. Wasn't I tampering with evidence? Who was I to judge my friend Christian for his views on turning a blind eye toward vigilantism when secretly I wish someone would do the same to whoever killed Brianna? I dreamed of finding my own personal justice, of blowing the killer away and spitting on the carcass.

So what kind of a person did that make me?

I understood Christian Doonsberg's position on vigilantism.

"About Dodson," Streeter said, startling me from my thoughts.

He was staring at me, must have been studying me when I thought he was sleeping.

"Dodson had a son who had Down's syndrome. One day after school, some bullies led his son to the local graveyard. He was found dead with a shovel handle up his rectum. Dodson's wife committed suicide a year later. That was twenty-five years ago."

I studied his face, saw the angst etched around his eyes.

"Christian reminded me that it was cases such as these that led so many of us into careers with law enforcement. And so many to embrace BOLO."

His expression of torment intensified. Was he worried about the questions I might ask him? Or pleading with me to blurt them out, get it over with? I knew that Streeter's wife had been killed while he was an FBI agent. And I knew she looked a lot like me. But I didn't know much more than that. Or was he trying to tell me something far more personal. About Brianna?

"And Christian hoped you and I, in particular, might understand how someone might be tempted to ignore the thin blue line that separates us good guys from the bad guys."

I nodded.

He held my gaze. "And Christian hoped you'd understand more than anyone, considering it is his best friend—your boyfriend—who suffers most each time a murderer escapes the long arm of the law after killing innocent lambs like your niece Brianna."

A haze filled my brain. Jack's son didn't just die. Wasn't just killed. There was something more, but I wasn't sure I wanted to know. "They . . . they never found out who killed him? Jack's son?"

"He was brutalized, Liv. Tortured."

"He was only six. Doc Duncan believes Gary James killed Benji." My breathing heaved, heavy with sorrow, and Streeter reached up and pulled me to his chest, just like my dad would have done.

"Christian wanted us to understand the people of BOLO. Considers us part of them, Liv."

"I don't want to be," I said, closing my eyes.

"None of us do." He patted my arm. "Right now, the most important thing we must do is not let the killer amongst us know who we think murdered little Rebecca Douglass."

I sat up, swiping at my eyes. "I know. And with a breach in Jack's email account, maybe I have pointed them in the wrong direction."

"In your texts to Linwood," Streeter asked, "who were you suspecting?"

"Debra Douglass."

"Rebecca's older sister?" Streeter asked.

I nodded. "But she didn't do it. She admitted to me that she wrote the ransom note. To set up her stepmother. But she didn't kill her half sister."

"You know that for a fact?" Streeter asked.

"Not for a fact, but I am fairly sure. Her boyfriend spent the night that Valentine's Day. I haven't told anyone that, but I think he killed Rebecca. It explains everything. But he told Debra that he saw Cathy Douglass kill Rebecca."

"But our vigilante doesn't know anything except that you think Debra Douglass is the prime suspect, based on your texts to Linwood?"

"Right. I haven't had time to research that case as thoroughly as I'd have liked. I've been too wrapped up in these other cases. I was hoping to corner Wayne W. Wilson, find out what he knows about these cases, since I seem to keep bumping into his name as I research." I wasn't about to admit the real reason I wanted to talk with him. About Brianna. Since Wilson was one of the people who'd been poking around Brianna's case, checked out the files, according to Agent Marshall in Las Vegas.

Maybe they were right. Maybe if Wayne W. Wilson told me he found Brianna's killer and made fast work of him, I'd turn a blind eye, too. Not maybe. Probably.

"No, the first thing you need to do is something for me. I need you to send one more text to Jack. Let's see if we can't bait our killer from his hiding place, shall we?"

CHAPTER 40

MITCH DODSON HAD STUFFED himself into a corner booth in the farthest reaches of the Country Buffet.

Alone.

The isolation triggered alarms in my head and I dulled their warning by reminding myself that we were in a public restaurant and Dodson chose this place intentionally to talk quietly. So what was I worried about? What could possibly go wrong?

I thought Streeter would argue with me about meeting him. But after we landed at DIA, he had received a text from Schuffler and seemed distracted. So we went our separate ways. He told me to stick with our plan for flushing out the serial killer of murderers later that night. If he or she existed. I still wasn't convinced that we were faced with one serial killer. My bet was on several spree killers ignited by the common spark of BOLO. And I was hoping Dodson could convince me, one way or the other.

Whatever the case, I hoped to find Wayne W. Wilson at the end of my Glock tonight. But first, I had to find out what Dodson knew about him.

I slid into the booth across from Mitch and said, "Dodson, I've had a long day. I don't need any more of your crap."

Dodson was fidgeting, a behavior I hadn't seen in him before now.

Normally he was a curmudgeonly, unexcitable, fact-based researcher. I wondered if he'd been drinking a steady stream of caffeine since I'd seen him last, which was early that morning when I brought him coffee.

"It's not bull. It's BOLO. I wanted to tell you about them."

I couldn't help but notice the way his eyes darted around the restaurant as he talked, particularly as he whispered the group's name.

"I've already heard. Been talking with Christian."

"Doonsberg?" Dodson's eyes widened. His shoulders seemed to relax. "Then you know there are people out to get us. Those of us with BOLO." He leaned forward and whispered, "They fired Morris Kuchenberger this morning over an alleged BOLO incident two years ago. Can you believe that? He didn't do anything, and they canned him after twenty-seven years with the force."

I raised an eyebrow. "That's not what I heard. I heard they fired him for breaching a code of silence during a case. For telling someone about a prisoner being released."

His mouth fell open.

The waitress arrived and I ordered a Diet Coke. As she walked away, I told Mitch, "Close your mouth. You're gathering flies."

"Doonsberg told you that?"

I shrugged.

Dodson fidgeted some more, drank from his nearly empty cup of ice, shaking it to free up the dark cola, presumably deciding where to take this conversation that had already gotten away from him.

The waitress set the drink in front of me and when she reached for Dodson's empty, he waved her away.

"Look, Mitch," I said, gripping the liquid energy between my palms. "I'm not here to bust your balls about the ethics or lack thereof in being with BOLO or tampering with evidence. I ain't your mother or your priest. And I understand why you feel the way you do about wanting justice."

The corners of his eyes sagged.

"I don't want to see you fired, either. Although your ass would already be out the door if I'd told anyone about your macho maneuver on me last week, considering you hit on your boss's girlfriend, not to mention a coworker." His eyes grew wider. "But we're past all that, right?"

He nodded.

"I just want some straight answers," I said. "Did you have anything to do with Andy Shriver injecting Ramir Menendez with HIV last Thanksgiving?"

"What? Who?" Dodson's confusion was genuine. "HIV? Are you kidding me? Who's Andy Shriver? "

"Had you heard about it?"

"No, why would I know about some guy injected with HIV? And what does that have to do with BOLO?"

I hadn't mentioned Menendez in my texts to Jack this week, so unless Mitch was the killer, he wouldn't have known about Carlita or Ramir. Unless the killer had told him about it. He seemed genuinely surprised by my question. And at least I'd established that Mitch Dodson and Christian Doonsberg weren't talking to one another regularly, because I'd originally heard of Menendez from Christian when I visited Quantico earlier this week.

"I tied him to you, not BOLO," I said.

"Me? How?"

"Because he said that whoever injected him last Thanksgiving whispered the words 'sword of Solomon' before beating the mess out of him," I said, pinning him with my gaze.

For the first time since I'd walked in the restaurant, Dodson appeared to be on the verge of smile, rather than about to crap his pants. "Me? Beat someone up? That's rich. But thanks for thinking me capable, Liv. Where was it that I supposedly beat him up? At a Bronco game? In LoDo on the 16th Street Mall?"

"No, he was in DC."

He scoffed. "Even if I had the physical wherewithal to beat someone up, which I don't, I was stuck working last Thanksgiving because my boss went to visit you for the holidays. Remember?"

I did. Jack had come to see me during the holidays and we shared Thanksgiving dinner together before going on a short boat ride on the Potomac River to watch the sunset. It was beautiful. So was Jack.

"So where does the saying come from? Sword of Solomon?"

He shrugged. "It's just a saying. To be careful of the repercussions of your decisions. It's the sign-off this anonymous blogger uses, writes for a website a bunch of us BOLO members follow. Encouragement to do the right thing, even if it's not right by the law."

"And it's intended for BOLO only? This secret website?"

He nodded and grabbed a napkin, jotting down the web address, login, and password. "Check it out yourself."

The website was www.sos.com. "Let me guess. The name of the website is 'Sword of Solomon.'"

He nodded. "It's about supporting those of us who believe in justice, who sometimes find ourselves in Solomon's situation, where a decision must be made that appears to be harsh, yet is designed to ferret out the truth so real justice can be delivered."

I thought about King Solomon's decision to split that baby so that the true mother would step forward and spare its life. And I heard Sister Delilah give the "moral of the story" to us third graders, warning us that we would be faced with difficult decisions in our lives and that we had to think carefully before making them.

Dodson was right. The sword of Solomon was so much more complex than what I'd learned from Sister Delilah.

"And the Carl Halbrook case," I said. "You said you didn't manipulate the evidence in any way. Were you telling me the truth?"

He nodded, a look of puzzlement draping his moonlike face.

"And you don't know who killed Halbrook, Vanessa Greenwood's murderer? Or Shelly Jones?"

He hesitated, then shook his head.

"But you suspect someone?"

He nodded, almost imperceptibly.

"Mind telling me?"

"No point."

"No point, because you agree with what he is doing?" I asked.

"Don't you?"

"What I need to know is whether this is a rash of killings spurred by BOLO or whether this is a serial killer acting alone, as a vigilante."

"Why?"

"Because it may affect the outcome of the case I'm investigating," I said.

"Rebecca Douglass's case? Or your niece's cold case?"

"Does it matter?"

"It might," he said. "Because if it affects the outcome of the Douglass case, then Debra Douglass is in serious danger, isn't she?"

Clearly, Dodson had intercepted my text to Jack. I gritted my teeth. "So you believe we are dealing with a single vigilante? Is it Wayne W. Wilson?"

"No. Just like I told your sister a couple of hours ago," Dodson said, draining the last of his soda and glancing around the restaurant.

The smell of old grease and fried onions that wafted from the nearby kitchen had finally gotten to me. My head was spinning. "My sister?"

"Colonel Bergen," he said. "Isn't she your sister? She said she was."

"She called you? Why?"

Dodson's cocked his head back. "She came to the federal building. Looking for you."

"Today? Barbara's in Denver?" I frantically scanned the restaurant to find the nearest bathroom. My stomach was about to purge even though I knew this was going to happen. I'd managed to put it out of my mind with everything else that was going on.

"Nice lady. Tiny little thing. Doesn't look anything like you," he said, his eyes probing mine. "She said you talked to her about the Keller case, told her about the bunny, and she showed me some notes you'd shared with her."

"I didn't . . . damn it." My sister Barbara got her first promotion with the army by showcasing her brilliant ability to hack computer systems. She must have gone to my apartment today while I was out of town with Streeter. And hacked my laptop, probably read my files.

"I assumed she was telling me the truth. That you'd finally come to your senses about fabricating evidence to convict Wayne Wilson on the Rhonda Kuehl case. On your niece's case."

"I didn't. And she wasn't. I would never involve her in something like this. And I don't believe she has a right to know what we're investigating until we're ready to tell her," I said, fuming about my sister's intrusion. I couldn't believe she'd gotten into my apartment, read the files, and visited Dodson at my work. "What did you tell her?"

"Nothing. She asked me about Debra Douglass. About Wilson. Where she could find them."

Barbara had definitely accessed my apartment while I was in California today.

"I told her I thought Wilson was scum. Why? What are you worried about? Wilson's a walking dead man, just like Menendez after being injected with that super strain of HIV," Dodson stated. "Yes, I know about the fast-growing strain. He's screwed."

My cell phone chirped and I instinctively said aloud, "It's Jack."

Dodson slid out the booth to leave.

I watched his backside as he ambled through the diner toward the door. "Jack?"

"Where are you?"

"Near the office," I said. "Why? Where are you?"

"Just landed. Want to have dinner?"

I looked at my watch. Seven thirty p.m. The plan Streeter and I had concocted was about to begin. And I had to find my sister. Before she stepped in the middle of everything. "I can't. But how does breakfast sound?"

"I really want to see you, Liv," he insisted. "Sure you can't meet me tonight?"

"Can't. I'm working on the Douglass case and have to meet up with Fiero in Fort Collins," I said.

I was also meeting up with Streeter and was excited that Fiero was included in our plan. We hadn't told many people because we were afraid that with BOLO connections potentially all around us, word might spread about our real intentions. And we had to keep the number involved to a minimum. Even Jenna Tate. Streeter told her just enough to convince her to play the role of Debra Douglass for the evening. Tell no one. Including Jack.

Hopefully a serial killer would take the bait.

The last thing I needed was for Jack to be concerned about me and try to tag along. Then I'd have both Jack and Barbara to worry about tonight. And if I didn't hit the road soon, I wasn't going to be in position in time.

"What about later?" I suggested. "Want to meet me at my apartment, say around eleven?" If I got tied up in Fort Collins, I'd just call Jack and tell him plans had changed. That I'd been delayed. Besides, I wouldn't mind him meeting my sister, who was probably at my apartment waiting to ambush me with hundreds of questions. But right now I didn't have time for either one of them.

"Perfect," he said. "Liv, did you really find evidence that will break the Douglass case wide open?"

"We did," I lied, not willing to share the truth with him quite yet. At least nothing more than what I'd already told him about the case in the emails and texts I'd sent him. The communications that undoubtedly continued to be compromised by Dodson. And whoever else.

"Can you prove it? Do you have enough evidence to make it stick?"

"No," I answered honestly. "But we're hoping to draw out the killer, maybe even get a confession or a slipup of some kind that we could use for an indictment in Rebecca Douglass's murder."

"And Debra's bodyguard is the killer? You're sure of that?"

Hoping Streeter and Theresa were already in position, just in case Willie bolted, I said, "Dead sure."

CHAPTER 41

AS THE SUN DIPPED behind the Rockies to the west, I was glad I had brought my oversized sweater to ward off the chill from the late-spring winds. I wrapped the coffee-colored rag wool tightly around my frame and folded my arms snugly around my waist. When I had first arrived here near Terry Lake shortly after eight thirty, Streeter and Theresa were already in position, had already searched the house and made a sweep for bugging devices. They'd been waiting for me and for Jenna to get into position.

It didn't take me long to set up on the back side of Debra Douglass's house, where I had a great view of the back door. A few fishermen were scattered along the rocky banks of the lake. Bicycle enthusiasts peddled and joggers pounded their way along the winding path that encircled the water in the Fort Collins neighborhood. Since the wind weaved its way through the rocky canyons to still waters, many of the recreationalists had since called it a day.

Pulling my knees to my chest and wrapping my arms around them, I sat near a large rock at the water's edge, watching the backyard, listening to the tiny waves lap at the rocks.

Until I got the signal to move in.

I would certainly do just that the second Streeter told me to. Until then, my job was to make sure no one—especially not the vigilante—came near Debra's house from the rear. We had the house flanked. Streeter on my left, positioned near the driveway on the right side of the house, facing the front door. Theresa on my right, positioned in the hedges to the left of the front porch.

I noticed that within fifteen minutes of my arrival, all of the fishermen had called it a day and left. Except for one stray dog, whose nose was deep into the grassy swamp near the rocky beach, I was alone. I saw black clouds on the northwestern horizon moving rapidly in our direction and cursed.

Streeter's voice sounded in my earpiece, "What?"

"Storm rolling in," I said, covering my mouth with my sleeved hand when I spoke, in case any neighbor was watching. The message reached Streeter, Theresa, and Jenna based on the clicks, and the mic was hidden carefully in the collar of my shirt beneath my sweater. I would be making a quick wardrobe change once it was time and needed to be wired carefully so that Wilson wouldn't know.

I heard the click of Streeter's acknowledgement. And two more. One from Theresa and one from Jenna, who hadn't made her grand appearance yet. She was the decoy. Hopefully, the person luring our killer into a trap.

The theory I'd shared with Streeter was that I thought Debra Douglass's bodyguard, Willie, was actually Wayne W. Wilson. I believed Wilson accidentally killed Rebecca Douglass on Valentine's night and devised a hurried plan to cast suspicion on the entire Douglass family. I believed that if I sent a text to Jack Linwood stating that I knew Wayne W. Wilson was the real killer of Rebecca Douglass, my thoughts would likely spread through BOLO via Dodson.

One of two consequences might occur: the first was that Wayne W. Wilson might get nervous and make a move to frame Debra for Rebecca's murder, plant evidence of some sort, and the second was that we might be able to flush out the vigilante. My statement to Jack might finally get this vigilante to go after Wayne W. Wilson, to take the decisive action that a previous lack of evidence had prevented.

Either way, we needed to be here at Debra's house since no one had been able to locate where "Willie" lived, other than with Debra from time to time. Wilson was elusive. Thank God we'd convinced Debra to cooperate.

And thank God she was in the care of Special Agent Phil Kelleher, far, far away from here, in a safe house. It took me awhile to convince her why I had pretended to be scouting for a band and what a schmuck Willie really was, but once I did, she was happy to set up her boyfriend.

Our stakeout was designed in hopes that either Wilson or the vigilante would act sooner rather than later. But we had concocted a plan to continue this stakeout for days, which meant Jack's return to Denver and Barbara's ambush of my apartment were ill-timed for me, to say the least. I might be sleeping in my car for the next few days, not able to tell either the truth about what I was up to.

I inhaled the cool, crisp air as the wind blew in my face.

Everything was quiet except for the rumble of dark clouds rolling in overhead and the winds blowing off the mountains. I noticed movement from the corner of my eye where the tall grasses and soft mud met the cool water of the reservoir. A duck waddled slowly and cautiously from the tall grass and cattails.

I smiled when I saw the little dusty yellow chick that followed its mother from the grasses that concealed their hiding place. As the mother gracefully stepped into the cold, black water, the little chick hesitantly followed, as did the other eight that emerged in a compliant line from the grasses. The fuzzy chicks were reluctant to step into the water, and I suddenly realized that this was the mother duck's attempt to take her newly hatched chicks on their first swim. Just before the storm. Fascinated by the evolving miracle of nature and instinct, I smiled and sat perfectly still near the rock so as not to startle the mother or her chicks.

By the time the mother duck made her way over the first large wave that eventually slapped against the muddy bank, three of her chicks had also successfully maneuvered over it and three more were not very far behind. As the other three chicks stepped into the water from the muddy bank, one more chick appeared from the tall grasses. The littlest chick straggled far behind its compliant siblings, who were already falling in line behind their mother. As the remaining chicks made their way over their first wave, the mother and the two chicks in front were already maneuvering over the third wave. The tenth chick was still standing on the muddy bank, reluctant to follow. With determination, the last little chick took a quick and daring hop into the cold waters. Within minutes, the winds had picked up and the sky had darkened.

I watched with interest as the mother duck led her ten little chicks into the cold and tumultuous waters for their first swim. That last chick was desperately trying to get over the waves as they slapped against the muddy bank. The others were pulling out into the lake while the water was overpowering the littlest chick and tumbling it back to the bank repeatedly. Instinctively sensing the distance growing between her and the tenth chick, the mother duck started quacking loudly and continued her swimming lesson with the others. For a third time, the littlest chick stood on the bank, chirped back in reply to its mother, and braved the waters to join the family, only to be thrown back onto the muddy bank by a powerful wave.

It was as the little chick was shaking itself free of the water and preparing itself for another brave attempt in the growing waves that something in the grass caught my eye. It was white and brown and was moving against the bank in time to the water's movements. I quietly craned my neck to see what it was. An egg had not hatched. The mother duck had apparently pushed the egg from her nest when she realized her eleventh chick would not come. The egg was covered in mud and bobbed in the water as the waves pushed it against the grassy, muddy bank.

A lump arose in my throat and my eyes began to burn with unexpected tears. I watched the egg bobbing and bouncing, resisting the water's attempt to break it.

My thoughts turned instantly to Jack.

I wondered how he had managed living his life after his only son was taken from him. He was only six. I knew how difficult losing Brianna was on my brother-in-law Shorty and my sister Barbara, and they had two other children to help buoy them in the tumultuous torrents that followed.

I could not imagine how the mother duck must have felt—if ducks had feelings—pushing the dead egg from her nest or how Jack must have felt watching his son's casket being lowered into the ground. I remember Shorty crumbling against my sister at the graveside, the ceremony cut short as people hurried away to allow the parents a very private moment with their dead daughter.

I thought about all the parents of the children who had been abused or murdered over the years. And about those who still had not found their lost lambs, their children who'd disappeared.

How appropriate that I had just witnessed ten little chicks on their first swim. In the past ten days, I had identified ten little kids who'd been brutalized, murdered in active and cold cases. Vanessa Greenwood, Shelly Jones' boys, Tia Mulberrry, Kesha Ryan, Carlita Menendez, Rhonda Kuehl, infant Timmy Riley, Rebecca Douglass, and my Brianna Keller.

All the work I'd put into researching those cases would hopefully help me solve Rebecca's case, somehow tie in a connection, and put Brianna to rest once and for all. More so, by focusing my attention on those ten angelic faces, I hoped I might release their tiny spirits from the stubborn shackles their violent deaths had placed on them, holding them to this earth. I wanted each of them to be free, to laugh and to play in heaven. I suppose Sister Delilah had a great impact on me after all, wishing my thoughts and prayers might help these innocent souls move out of purgatory into a better place.

I wondered how Jack could stomach his work every day, researching and analyzing information about the most loathsome of criminals, some of whom had robbed children of their lives, their innocence, and their futures by their wretched acts.

And I cherished the sword of Solomon.

I understood why Mitch Dodson wanted that so much now, why he held that credo higher than anything else in his life. Of course he'd want the sword of Solomon. Who wouldn't?

The hot tears streamed down my chilled cheeks and were thankfully lost in the strong winds. I wondered how someone could strangle that sweet little reality show star, six-year-old Rebecca Douglass, to death. And I was convinced that Wayne W. Wilson would show up tonight with the intention of framing—or possibly killing—Debra Douglass.

Because of me. I'd set the ball in motion for him to be nervous, for him to know we were onto him. Hoping he'd understand that with us bearing down on him, leaving him little time to react, that he'd make a mistake.

We'd instructed Debra Douglass to text her intentions of staying home alone tonight.

To Willie.

And to tell him that I'd be showing up at nine o'clock to question her—confront her—about proof I'd found connecting her to Rebecca's death. Alone. No doubt Willie would not let that happen. If Wilson thought he could pin all of this on Debra and be blameless in Rebecca's death, he would be here tonight to find out what I had to say. Without a doubt.

But Debra Douglass would not be here tonight.

Instead, Jenna Tate was made up to look like Debra Douglass. I admitted that even I was convinced by the remarkable transformation and uncanny resemblance Jenna had to Debra. And I hoped that if Willie showed up, he wouldn't get too close to Jenna before we uncovered all that we'd hoped, or else her life might be endangered more than it already was.

The serial killer would show up, would listen to what proof I'd have, just to make sure he was killing the right murderer, Streeter was sure of it. So was I. No one knew our plan but the four of us—me, Streeter, Fiero, and Tate—and we were expecting a murderer to show up. Theresa had alerted law enforcement personnel to stand by, told them about the general proximity, and to hold off unless Fiero herself called them in to assist.

They had no clue it was Debra Douglass's house we were surrounding.

As I wiped away the tears, emboldened by my action, I saw that the tenth chick had charged the wave with determination and had finally swum over it successfully. Quacking loudly and wildly, the chick called to his mother, attacking the numerous waves that separated them and narrowing the distance. The mother duck quacked reassuringly back to her littlest chick, who was fast approaching his family. I smiled. Just as the littlest chick successfully maneuvered his way through the rough waters, falling in line behind his siblings, the rumble of the clouds above sounded and the rain began to sprinkle. The mother duck led her chicks in a wide circle and made her way back through the cold, black waters to shore, allowing the waves to carry them the distance. Leaving behind the unhatched egg. The eleventh chick.

The eleventh child. Benji Linwood.

I wiped my cheeks dry with my sleeve and cleared my throat just in time to hear Streeter say, "Get ready, Liv. She's here."

CHAPTER 42

THE CAR THAT MADE its way quickly up the driveway had lights low to the ground and spread wide apart. Streeter whispered, "That's Debra's Mustang. Get into position."

As Jenna Tate drove Debra's car into the driveway and parked in the garage, I hoped our plan worked, that she was luring the murderer into position. Whoever the killer of killers was had been led to believe by my email that Debra Douglass's bodyguard was the likely murderer of Rebecca. And that the bodyguard could most likely be found in the company of Debra. I used the cover of darkness and the sound of the garage door opening to creep from my position by the lake behind Debra's house back to where I parked.

I moved in a crouch from lakeside to the hedges rimming Debra's lot. I could see Streeter's form nearer the front of the house by the driveway, ducked into the base of the hedges lining the right side of the house—my left as I faced the back door—and knew that Theresa was set up opposite him on the left side of the house—to my right—in a small alley. I moved quickly to my left, ducking behind hedges and climbing the fences of neighboring yards, until I found my vehicle tucked along a privacy fence four blocks from Debra's house. I slid in behind the wheel of my SUV and quietly pulled the door shut, thankful I had thought to unscrew the over-head dome lightbulb earlier.

I used a penlight to check my watch, dusk turning to dark. Five min-utes after nine.

Streeter's breathing in my earpiece had hastened and I heard my own heart beat against my lungs.

As I stripped off my sweater and slipped into my suit coat, Theresa Fiero's hushed shout sounded in my earpiece: "Streeter, we need to move in. I see someone along this side of the house. Coming up the alley a block away across the street. Coming right towards me."

Streeter replied in a loud, raspy whisper, "Hold your position. Mute your radios until he's out of range from you. Earpieces only. As low as pos-sible. Be careful. That's our guy. And I think he'll stop by the door to hear what Liv has to say to Debra. If not, if you're in any danger whatsoever, shoot first and ask questions later."

"Got it," Fiero said.

I asked, "Can you tell if it's Wilson?"

"Can't. He's dressed in black, wearing a facemask. Tall though. Might be Wilson. Definitely a man."

Finally, I thought. We have him.

I added, "Theresa, please don't kill him if you don't have to. I need to find out what he knows about my niece. Please."

"I know. Streeter told me."

Streeter said, "Tate, you ready?"

"Not yet. Just making adjustments to the wig. Okay, ready."

"Everyone off the air. Liv, wait for my signal to move in."

I lifted my shaky hands to the steering wheel and waited. The silence was deafening. Through my open window, the summer crickets sounded their melody in unison as the night skies filled with bright stars. The min-utes dragged. I practiced the script in my head of what I'd be saying to Debra Douglass, reminding myself to speak loudly enough for the tall man in black to hear.

"Now," Streeter whispered.

I turned the ignition and slowly pulled out of the alley. Weaving through the streets, I passed a car parked nearby that reminded me of the one that had followed me the other night, near the fast-food restaurant. The one that took a sharp right when I applied my brakes. And my heart began to race. A 1980 two-door Thunderbird. Bologna-colored. The same car Stewart Casey described to me.

Had the killer been following me?

I tried to control my breathing, relax. I thought of the ten strong chicks. After two turns, I was on Debra Douglass's street and pulling into her driveway. I studied her house. A concrete sidewalk led from the drive-way to the porch. The front door was centered on the front porch, above four wide steps leading up from the sidewalk, and a rickety rail rimmed the wooden deck. Two other sets of stairs had been built on either side of the porch, each leading to the side yards.

I studied all exit and entrance options for my coworkers hidden in the hedges and saw the lights glowing inside Debra's home, knowing what an expert marksman Jenna Tate was. I drew a breath, shut off my car. Nine fifteen. Just as I opened my door, a car came screeching around the corner and pulled along the curb in front of Debra's house.

Streeter's whisper through my earpiece was urgent, "Hold. Hold."

I had stepped out of my car and now waited for the man who had just arrived to reveal himself, to step out of his own car and into the streetlights so I'd know who he was. The sight of him froze my blood. He was eight feet from me but there was no mistaking who it was.

Slamming the door to cover my voice, I spoke into the microphone on my collar. "Wilson."

"Shit," I heard Fiero say.

We were all thinking it. Who the hell was the tall man near Fiero in the hedges by the front door if Wilson was here with me in the driveway?

"Who are you?" the man called.

"None of your business," I answered, turning my back to the man and walking toward Debra's door.

"Oh but it is my business," Wilson said, rushing toward me and putting his hand on my shoulder.

I jerked away from him and turned quickly, dropping into a ready stance for fighting. Wilson started laughing.

"You won't think it's so funny once I mace you and call 911," I said, knowing that pulling my Glock on him would ruin the entire operation. So I had opted for looking more like a suburban housewife, preparing myself against a would-be attacker. And I hoped Streeter, Jenna, and Theresa would understand I was okay and hold their fire.

"Calm down," Wilson said. "I didn't mean to startle you. I was hired by the owner of this house to protect her, so I'm going to ask you again to tell me who you are or I'll be happy to call the police for you."

I relaxed, letting my arms fall to my side, wondering how to keep Wilson from coming inside, from noticing that Debra wasn't really Debra.

"So you're Willie? I've heard a lot about you." I shoved my hand in his direction in a friendly gesture. He pulled his hand from his pocket and shook it. "It's about time we met. I'm one of Debra's friends. She talks a lot about you. Only, few of us believed you actually existed. No offense."

"None taken," he said. He moved past me toward the front door, retrieving a key from his pocket.

"You have a key? To Debra's house?" More for Streeter's sake than for conversation.

I heard Streeter's voice sound off in my ear. "Tate, get out of there. Back door. Liv, stall him. Then get out of here."

"So Willie, how long have you been Debra's bodyguard?"

Wilson didn't slow. He was at the front door and working his key into the lock.

I grabbed his shoulder like he had mine and tugged him in my direction, his face under the lights of the front porch. "Say, you are handsome. Debra is smitten with you. Did you know that?"

His eyes were hard and his expression angry. But he worked the words carefully from his lips: "And I am smitten with her. Now do you mind?"

He turned back to the door and I grabbed his shoulder again. "Oh come on, let me surprise Debra. Let me at least ring the doorbell, won't you? I came all this way. Don't be such a party pooper. It won't be as much fun if I just walk right in with you, Willie."

He hesitated, shrugged, and stepped aside. I pressed the bell, hearing a muffled ring from inside. I waited, flashed Wilson a smile, rang the bell again.

Streeter whispered, "Leave. Get out of there, Liv."

"Well, it looks like she's not home. Or she's in the shower. And I do not want to walk in with you if she wasn't expecting me. Awkward," I said, in a singsong tone. I stepped off the porch, down the sidewalk, and to my car. "Nice meeting you, Willie. Later!"

I slammed my door and watched as Wilson let himself in the house. "Now what?"

"To the alley and come back here on my side. Tate, you hold the back door. Fiero, hold. Is the man in black still there in the hedge?" Streeter's whisper was almost inaudible.

I heard a click of a mic. Fiero. The tall man dressed in black must be standing too close for her to answer.

"Close to you. I see him," Streeter's voice said. "Hold. He just stepped onto the porch. Left side. He's flattened against the wall of the house in the shadows. He has a gun. Mark him, Fiero."

Another click. Fiero was on it.

I parked my SUV on another street a block away and was creeping toward Streeter in the shadows when I heard a car approaching.

Lights swept across the front lawn as the car rounded the corner and pulled into Debra's driveway. I didn't recognize it, but I did recognize the tiny woman who immediately got out of it and began marching toward the front door.

Colonel Bergen. My sister Barbara.

CHAPTER 43

"WHO THE HELL IS that?" I heard Streeter whisper.

"My sister Barbara. Brianna's mom," I said.

"Oh no," he whispered.

"I'm going back to my car," I said.

"No! Get your ass over here. Now!" Streeter barked.

I slid through the neighbors' yards and over the fence to where I knew Streeter was crouched, the shadows shielding any view of me.

"Where?" I mouthed, wondering where the tall man with the gun had disappeared to.

Streeter pointed to the porch.

The man stood tall against the house, near the door to the left. Silently watching from his shadows. Was he waiting for Wilson or Debra? Or both?

My sister clearly hadn't seen him standing there. Apparently, Wilson hadn't noticed him either, his attentions clearly focused on Barbara. The thought of a killer being so close to Barbara made my blood turn to ice. I sprang from my crouch, thinking it would take me no more than three long strides to reach the porch steps to the right of the front door, opposite the man with the gun. Until Streeter grabbed me, pulling me back behind the hedge.

"Dodson must have told my sister that Wilson was hanging out with Debra. Where Debra lived," I said.

Helplessly, I watched as Barbara rang the doorbell just as I had done, standing clear of the door. The tall shadow was outside the web cast from the porch light, flattening himself against the wall.

Wilson opened the door, peered out at my sister.

"Are you Wayne Wilson?" she said.

"Who wants to know?" The light shone on both of their faces. And I could tell Wilson was confused, my sister pissed.

"You don't remember me, do you?" my sister said.

Wilson opened the door wider, took a step out onto the porch, squinting as he studied Barbara's features.

"Maybe if I was wearing my army uniform. Would that help?" she said. "Seven years ago. You asked me for directions. Outside my house. The day you followed my daughter home from school."

I drew in a sharp breath, almost giving away my position. She'd never told me that.

Doubt shadowed Wilson's face. "I have no idea what you're talking about."

"Yes, you do," my sister said. "And it wasn't until I saw your face just now that I recognized who you were. I knocked on your car window. You were parked across the street. Looking at my house. You said you were lost. Looking for an address that didn't exist. In Hawthorne, Nevada."

At first, Wilson swayed, took a step backward. Recognition registered on his face. I assumed he realized now who she was. He took a step toward her and froze, staring at the pistol in my sister's hands. "You lied, didn't you? You followed my little girl home that day when she walked home from school. You were casing our house."

"Lady, I don't know what you're talking about," Wilson said, his hands held in surrender.

"You killed my little girl," she said, holding the gun on Wilson, her hands steady. "And if you don't tell me in the next thirty seconds exactly what happened to my daughter, I will put a bullet between your eyes without another thought."

We could all hear the click as Barbara pulled the hammer back into position.

"Tell me, or you die."

I had no doubt she meant every word.

"Streeter," Theresa whispered.

Streeter hurriedly whispered, "Hold, hold."

I started to move again, to call out to my sister and tell her to stop, until Streeter grabbed my arm and yanked hard.

My sister fired once at the man's feet. We instantly readied our weapons. Instinct. Wilson dropped, his butt hitting hard on the porch. His yelp startled me, as did the way he curled into a ball, grabbing his bloody foot. The shadowy figure flinched but didn't make a move on my sister. She still didn't seem to notice him standing there.

I heard three quick clicks in my earpiece.

"Fiero, it's me," Jenna's voice sounded.

"Shit, I almost shot you," Theresa whispered.

I heard Streeter say, "I thought I told you to hold in the back."

Tate clicked her mic once.

"I. Said. Talk," Barbara growled at Wilson.

My sister was quite convincing when she wanted to be.

Wilson whimpered and swore. Barbara cocked her gun again and aimed at his crotch.

"No! Stop! It was an accident," Wilson said. "I wasn't going to hurt her. I was trying to be nice to her. Even gave her a toy, to make her stop whining."

"A bunny?"

"Yeah, just some kid's toy I had. But instead, she started screaming, yanked open the door, and jumped. How was I supposed to know the kid was crazy?"

Barbara let off another quick-fired round into Wilson's hand.

Wilson screeched.

"Brianna wasn't crazy."

Sirens sounded in the distance. A neighbor calling in the commotion?

"Hold," Streeter's insistent voice sounded in my earpiece.

Barbara looked over her shoulder when she heard the sirens and was as startled as the rest of us when the shadowy figure on the porch stepped forward and said, "Get out of here, Barbara."

How did the man know my sister's name? That couldn't be Shorty. Too tall. My sister jerked her gun toward the tall man in the shadows. Startled, she held her aim steady, regained her breathing.

"Before the police come. Go," the man said.

His voice was low, steady. Convincing. And somehow familiar to me. I realized now that Wayne Wilson was exactly who Doc Duncan feared he was. Wilson, the Cowlitz County deputy sheriff, had been the killer—the sexual molester and murderer—of Rhonda Kuehl from twenty years ago. He made a passionate plea for the community to level their sights on Gary James for three reasons: because James was there that night as a witness, because he was believable as a suspect given his past and his resemblance to Wilson, and because if he was convicted, Wilson was freed.

Doc was right.

I knew it to be true, but now the realization that Wilson not only killed Rhonda, but Brianna, too, was slamming into me with such force that I wanted to bolt toward the door and throttle the man with my bare hands. Barbara had just coerced a confession out of him. And he was probably responsible for little Rebecca Douglass's murder, sidling up to Debra as her bodyguard after the killing to frame her for the murder, just like he had Gary James.

I held my breath, willing my sister to do the right thing and leave, afraid she would do as I wanted and shoot the bastard right where he sat on the bloody porch.

She surprised me. The shadowy man had convinced her. She lowered the gun slowly as she took two steps back, turned, and walked down the wooden porch stairs and across the sidewalk to her rental car in the driveway.

From his slumped position near the doorway on the porch, Wilson retrieved his pistol from the back of his jeans and leveled it at my sister's back. I leapt to my feet and ran, shouting, "Barbara, drop!"

At the exact moment, the man in black to the left of the front door shot the gun out of Wilson's hand, two shots firing instantly. I saw where Barbara had dropped in the driveway and ran to her, throwing myself over her body, not knowing what was happening on the porch.

Nor caring.

I lay near Barbara, who had flattened herself in the driveway and was creeping toward her car. I pulled her around the car in the dark to put as much metal between Wilson and us as possible.

My sister hugged me and whispered, "Boots? What are you doing here?"

"Are you hit?"

"No," she said.

"Then stay down," I said, lifting a finger to my lips to make her stay quiet.

I peered around the front of the car and saw the man in black with the barrel of his gun pressed against the side of Wilson's head.

"Stand still," the man hissed. "Or die."

"Hey, man," Wilson said, "what are you trying to do?"

"Barbara? Are you okay?" tall man called from the porch.

I nudged my sister to answer.

"Yes, I'm fine," Barbara answered.

"Then get inside your car and drive away. Hurry. Before the police arrive."

My sister looked at me. In the glow of the street lamp, I nodded.

"Okay," she hollered.

I whispered. "Just park a block away and wait for me."

She nodded, stood up, and climbed in behind the wheel of the rental car. I used the opportunity to commando crawl across the driveway and duck behind a tree on the front lawn. I was relieved to watch Barbara drive off.

"Is Douglass inside?" tall man said.

His voice was odd, clipped. The way he spoke in husky, whispered demands wasn't helping me figure out why it sounded somehow familiar to me. Then I thought of Stewart Casey. The bologna-colored car he'd seen, that I'd seen, that was parked a few blocks from here. This is the man who had been stalking me. Why? Was I closing in too fast to the truth about him as the vigilante? Was he preparing to kill me if I'd come too close to the truth? I shuddered at the thought, glad to have Streeter, Jenna, and Theresa here with me tonight as witnesses. And as backup.

I heard Streeter whisper through my earpiece, "He didn't hear you, Liv. So hold. Everyone. Hold."

I realized the shadowy man must not have seen me, probably too preoccupied with Barbara and Wilson. But surely he must have heard me shout. Then I realized the gunshots had sounded when all of that was happening. Neither the man nor Wilson knew I was there.

The man in black leveled his gun toward Wilson. "Now answer me. Is Douglass inside?"

Wilson said nothing. With a swift kick from the man, the pistol Wilson used to shoot at my sister skittered farther from his bloody reach. Even more quickly, the man handcuffed Wilson to the porch railing with what looked like flex-cuffs; I couldn't tell for sure. Reaching inside the door, the man in black turned off the porch light, shut the front door, grabbed Wilson's pistol, and leveled it at the bodyguard's chest.

"Just in case she's inside," the shadow man said. "I have no issues with Debra Douglass. You on the other hand . . ."

"What do you want?" Wilson barked.

The police sirens sounded like they were drawing nearer, but they were still far off, and I couldn't be so sure they were intended for this house. Plus I knew Fiero had warned them to stay back until she called them in. They were probably surrounding the lakeshore neighborhood from a distance, just in case.

But the shadow man wouldn't know that.

"I don't have much time. So what I want is for you to answer some questions for me, Wayne," the man demanded. "Quickly. Let's start with Rebecca Douglass. When did you become fixated on her?"

"What are you—"

The shadow man pistol-whipped Wilson's temple. He collapsed to the porch, his bloody hands still handcuffed to the upper railing.

Streeter's voice was insistent. "Hold, everybody. Hold!"

"Answer and you live. Lie and you die. Got it?" the shadow man asked.

Wilson groaned.

"Now I know what you did to Brianna Keller. I should have let her mother kill you a few minutes ago. She's earned the right. But let's start with what happened with Rebecca."

Wilson didn't say anything. The man stomped on the bloody foot that Barbara had shot. Wilson sputtered and coughed, agony robbing him of his breath. Eventually, Wilson answered, "Nothing, I swear. We had a . . . relationship. She trusted me."

"Theodore Douglass hired you at his company on the security team last fall. And you cozied up to his daughter. Too cozy. So he fired you."

"Douglass asked me to keep an eye on his wife and daughter as the TV crews filmed for the reality show. And while they worked the pageants over the holidays. I got to know Rebecca. She liked me. I was her protector."

"You bastard," the tall man wearing black said. "You messed with her, didn't you?"

Whomp! The tall man kicked Wilson in the gut.

Wilson sobbed, "I loved that little girl!"

"Then why did you kill her that night? Before you ever got her out of the house?"

"It was an accident. Debra was stoned. Everyone was asleep. I just went upstairs to spend a little time with Rebecca. She started screaming. I covered her mouth and . . ."

I drew in such a sharp breath, stunned by his confession.

"I didn't mean to kill her. I swear!"

CHAPTER 44

I WAS GRATEFUL THAT the shadow man hadn't heard me as he had reached down and dragged Wilson to his feet. I drew in a quiet breath to calm myself.

I just couldn't believe my ears. Couldn't believe how correct Doc Duncan had been all these years. Wayne W. Wilson wasn't the killer of murderers, wasn't the vigilante. The man in black was the vigilante, whoever he was.

Wilson killed Rhonda Kuehl. Killed Brianna. Killed Rebecca, too. I was right. Wayne W. Wilson, Debra Douglass's secret houseguest that Valentine's Day, killed Rebecca Douglass. Debra's bodyguard—Willie, a.k.a. Wayne W. Wilson—had been wearing Theo's robe, the fibers ending up on the duct tape he'd placed on her mouth. Wilson had told Debra he saw Cathy Douglass kill Rebecca, probably convinced Debra to write the note to make sure the law focused on her stepmother, but Debra was likely oblivious to the fact that her boyfriend was the one responsible for killing her half sister. For Rebecca's death. Debra was too stoned.

"And when Theo fired your ass on New Year's Day, when he found out you were getting too close to his baby, you wanted payback."

"I wanted to be with Rebecca." Wilson's words were so soft, muffled. I'm not sure what he actually said.

"And you wormed your way into Debra's world as her bodyguard so you could direct the accusing finger her way, didn't you?"

"Not at first. I just wanted to hear stories of Rebecca, be near her. Through Debra." Wilson's tone was turning angrier. "But she was so mean. Was jealous of the little angel. My angel."

"Not your angel, you piece of dirt. How many, Wayne? I know about the Malley girls, you sick freak." The shadow man leveled a quick kick to Wilson's kidney, Wilson moaning in the moonlight.

Who were the Malley girls, I wondered? How many murdered children had I missed?

Wilson drug himself up to standing again, to avoid the vigilante's kicks. He hung his head over the lawn as he leaned his weight on the wood railing of the porch. I wondered if he might be about to throw up.

"They were only five years old. Five. How long did you keep them alive, Wayne? How many times did you rape them?" The man stomped on Wilson's bloody foot again. He screamed and dropped down on his butt again. I didn't feel sorry for him. Not one bit. "And Bonnie Lowell? She was seven. How long did you keep her alive as your sex slave, you sick bastard?"

Whomp! Whomp!

"Stop . . . please . . ."

Who was Bonnie Lowell? Fiero's voice pierced the unreal sounds of this dark night. "Streeter?"

"Not yet. Hold. Trust me. Just listen," Streeter said.

"How many others did you kidnap and rape? How many, Wayne? When did it start?"

Wilson spat. I hoped it was blood.

"Gary James didn't kill Rhonda Kuehl, did he?" the shadow man said. "Did he? You let everyone believe that Gary James was responsible, didn't you? Even Doc. But I found out. Too late to warn Gary. You got an innocent man killed. Tried to get an innocent woman killed here tonight."

I knew the voice. Knew the man. My mind spun itself into a whirlwind.

Wilson scoffed. "Innocent, my ass. James preferred boys."

This made the shadow man falter.

"Ha, you didn't know, did you? Doc never told you, did he? That Gary James diddled the boys in town. My first case on the force. Didn't Su tell you? I met with her, talked to her about Gary's relationship with your boy."

"Su? As in Panini?" I whispered into the microphone.

Streeter whispered back. "Su was his wife's name. Died in an accident."

"You know who he is?" I squeaked. The word Sukanta came to mind again. East Indian name. I was thinking Italian, with Panini. This really was the serial killer, my vigilante. The man who'd been righting so many wrongs over the past few years. Panini had truly been responsible for killing Lance Bovier, for killing Daryl Cleveland.

My vigilante said, "You told her that Gary James killed Rhonda Kuehl. You lied."

"I did. But not about James and your son." Wilson pushed himself off the porch and draped himself against the rail. "I lied so you would kill him. I knew you were the one going around the country taking out all those slimy killers of children who'd slipped through the long arms of the law. It had to be one of us BOLOs. And you were always the one taking the group pictures, never in them. I got to thinking why you'd avoid cameras like that."

The shadow man took another step back into the dark areas of the porch, away from Wilson. His talking had calmed the vigilante down. He must have realized that, because he kept talking.

"I let you have Gary James. Thought he deserved what he got."

"An innocent man was murdered. He didn't kill Rhonda," the man said, his voice low.

"Aren't you listening? He killed your son. Don't you get it? Didn't Doc tell you? Photos I'd taken from James's home. He had several. Of many boys. Your son's photo was in there. I saw it. Gave it to your wife. The night she drove her car off the road. Weren't those photos ever recovered?"

I saw my vigilante teeter and lean against the house, Wilson watching and twisting his hands to find a way to free himself while his captor staggered from the news. He hadn't known any of this. Hadn't known about the photos. Hadn't known about Gary James killing his son.

Which meant he probably hadn't killed Gary James.

Not the vigilante? Was I wrong? Or was it that I wanted to be wrong? Did I love this tall man that much? Had he been following me all week to protect me from Wilson?

"James deserved to die. For getting away with your son's murder. For getting away with so many boys' murders. Why do you think James stayed quiet about seeing me with Rhonda all these years? We had a deal. I wouldn't tell anyone what I saw James do if he didn't tell anyone what he saw me do." Wilson rose to his feet, pulling himself up by his bloody hands. He spat again over the rail and stood erect, twisting awkwardly to see the vigilante. "And I thought you deserved the thrill of ending his life. So you're welcome."

The shadow man regained his composure and walked quickly over to Wilson, swinging his fist into the bodyguard's gut. Whomp!

The shadow man's punch caused Wilson to fold at the waist.

Fiero clicked in on the mic three quick times. Streeter whispered, "I said hold. We're getting more and more information the longer we let him talk. He's one of us. Wilson will clam up if we move in on him now."

Streeter didn't mean Wayne Wilson was one of us. He meant the vigilante was one of us. And Wilson would most certainly clam up if he knew we were all here, listening. But I had to agree with Theresa on this one. If we didn't move in soon, the shadow man might beat Wilson to death.

"I figured your whole story out because of this bunny, you piece of dirt," the tall man said, pulling the squished-face bunny from his pocket and shoving it into Wayne Wilson's face.

The thump of that bunny in the desert sand near Las Vegas sounded in my head. It was this man who had taken the bunny from Brianna's cold case files. He was not only researching his son's death. He was investigating Brianna's, too. And he knew the bunny was a key to finding Wilson, just as I had believed.

I'd been right about the bunny all along. It was not Brianna's. It had belonged to another girl before Brianna.

"This bunny belonged to Rhonda Kuehl," the tall man said. "I asked her mother. She said she never had any problems with Gary James coming around the house. But she didn't fancy you sniffing around, showing so much attention to her daughter. Whenever I mentioned your name, all she'd say is that you deserved the swift sword of Solomon."

That's where the saying came from. All those years ago. But the man on the porch was most certainly not Mitch Dodson.

"Rhonda loved me. Really loved me," Wilson wailed. "She was my first. We talked about getting married when she was old enough."

Sick bastard, I thought.

"She was thirteen," the shadow man said. "She didn't even know what love was."

"You sound like her mother."

"Her mother told me you gave Rhonda this bunny. Didn't you?"

Wilson turned away from the bunny. "I loved her."

"To death."

"You don't understand," Wilson mumbled.

"No, I don't."

We all watched in horror as the masked man dropped the bunny to the porch and clutched his pistol in both hands.

And aimed the gun at Wayne W. Wilson's forehead.

CHAPTER 45

WITH THE RED DOT dancing on his forehead, Wilson cowered against the porch rails, begging, "Don't shoot! Please, show some mercy, Linwood."

The name hit me like a thunderbolt.

Even though I'd figured out it was Jack, I did not want to consciously recognize him as a killer. The voice had sounded familiar, but I had never heard Jack angry before, so filled with emotion and hatred as he was tonight. I didn't recognize him at all. Yet, loved him all the same.

"Jack?" I said, pushing myself from the ground.

Barbara rushed at me from the neighbor's yard. "Boots, no!"

"Liv?" Jack said, staring in my direction for a moment. Then, he swung his gaze back to Wilson, locking his elbows and wrist into full aim, and said, "Liv, stay back. You don't want this man's blood on your hands tonight."

Streeter jumped to his feet from his hiding place behind the bushes and ran to the right of the house, storming up the wooden steps from the side yard and yelled, "Freeze! Drop it. You're completely surrounded."

I ran from behind the tree and rushed toward the porch, my Glock leveled at Wilson, not Jack. From the corner of my eye, I saw Jack remove his mask, offering me a hint of a grin when he noticed my aim. I stopped short a few paces from the bottom of the wooden steps, a short few yards from Jack, who was facing Wilson on the porch. Wilson cowered against the rails between us, his hands locked into a position where he should have been facing me, but he'd twisted to watch his executor, Jack.

And I suddenly realized if Jack missed his aim at Wilson by inches, he'd shoot me instead.

I saw Jenna Tate come running from around the other side yard a step behind Theresa Fiero. They stormed the porch from the left, all of them pointing their guns at the tall man in black. At Jack. Except for me.

Jack was clearly aware of all of us lawmen rushing him, surrounding him, yet never paid much attention to any of us. Except maybe me, for a split second. With nearly all service weapons aiming at him, Jack didn't drop his gun, which I didn't quite understand. I wondered why everyone else still thought Jack had something to do with any of this, was the vigilante, when clearly he was just doing his job. Stopping Wilson from shooting Barbara in the back. Investigating his son's death. And Brianna's. He said he'd tried to warn Gary James, which meant he wasn't the killer.

That had to be what this was all about: Jack doing a helluva a job as an investigator.

Yet Streeter Pierce, Jenna Tate, and Theresa Fiero had their weapons trained on Jack.

And Jack never took his eyes off the man slumped on the porch, the bunny at his feet.

"Don't shoot me! Please!" Wilson pleaded. His sobs were not clear. "I gave you Gary James. Isn't that enough for you to spare my life?"

Doc said he suspected Gary James of molesting several boys, killing at least one—Benji Linwood—yet they never had enough proof to convict him.

"Stay back, Streeter," Jack said, his voice hard and angry, a tone I wasn't accustomed to hearing.

"You don't have to do this," Streeter said.

"Yes, I do. I don't want to hurt anyone. Just Wilson."

"No one needs to get hurt," Streeter said. "It's over."

"Not yet. I'm going to blow this scum's brains all over the porch if you come anywhere near me or if he doesn't tell me the truth," Jack said. "Now that sounds fair, doesn't it?"

"Put the gun down." Streeter's voice was calm. Oddly, he almost sounded scripted, not the least bit unnerved by the revelations of Jack Linwood. Why not? Is this what Christian Doonsberg had told Streeter at the airport? Had Streeter had time to process the information long enough not to be ruffled by the events? Is this what he wasn't telling me earlier?

Jack ignored Streeter, focused on Wilson. "How many others were there?"

"Please! Please!" Wilson begged.

"I won't ask again. The two Malley girls. Bonnie Lowell. Rhonda Kuehl. Rebecca Douglass. Brianna Keller. And how many others?"

Jack was accusing Wilson of abducting and killing six girls? How could that be? Wilson had been a deputy sheriff, was the law, at least at one time.

"How. Many. More," Jack growled.

"Four, okay? Four others."

"All dead?"

"Yes, they're all dead," Wilson whined.

"Names."

He listed them with no effort. Even gave the towns the girls were from. Four more unsolved crimes. Ten dead children. I understood now why Streeter was so calm. He knew Jack wasn't going to kill Wilson. He knew that Jack was coercing a confession out of Wilson by pretending to be maniacal, willing to execute him unless he told the truth. Wilson would have never confessed without that threat.

Go, Jack! I was glad I'd decided to train my gun on Wilson, not Jack, when I rushed the porch.

"Now Streeter, listen to me carefully," Jack said, his two-handed grip steadying the pistol on Wilson's forehead. "Two killers here tonight. You understand?"

"I do."

I didn't. I thought we only had Wilson as a killer. Had I been fooled by Jack?

"You have the list of the girls who were abducted and killed over the years by this piece of dirt. But you need the second list."

Streeter said evenly. "I understand."

Jack listed off names. Most I didn't recognize. Some I did. "You have

Wilson now, so go easy on the Douglass family. Even Debra. This scum convinced her to write the ransom note by lying about seeing her step-mother kill Rebecca when all along he killed her. Am I right?"

"Yes, yes," Wilson sobbed. "She was too doped up to know any differently."

I felt a weight rise from my chest. I glanced over at Theresa Fiero, who also drew in a sigh of relief. And I noticed Jenna step closer on the porch. To Jack.

"Isn't someone going to save me from this maniac?" Wilson screeched, looking wildly from face to face, seeking help from each lawman on the porch.

No one answered.

Jack said, "All of the Douglass family members are innocent in all this. And as for the person killing all these scumbags who got away with mur-dering kids? Christian Doonsberg had nothing to do with any of this. Neither did the kid who works for Doonsberg. What's his name . . ."

"Andy Shriver," I said, holding aim at the back of Wilson's head. His hands were still shackled to the porch rail over his left shoulder, but Wil-son was fixated on the business end of Jack's pistol, mesmerized by its power over him.

"Right, that's it. Andy was tricked into doing the dirty work on Menendez. He took off, is on the run, afraid he'll be pinned with Menen-dez's murder. But go easy on him. He wasn't told what was in the vial he injected into Ramir's arm that day. And don't blame Morris Kuchenberger. He was tricked into giving up the information about Daryl Cleveland. Are you following all of this, Streeter?"

"I am," Streeter said. "I'd figured most of this out already based on what Liv uncovered in the past couple of weeks."

I wasn't following.

"Are you going to let this madman kill me? Shoot him already! Shoot him!" Wilson screamed at Streeter.

"The only one who's going to get shot tonight is you, Wilson," Jack said.

I could already tell his demeanor was changing. A sweet calmness was settling into his tone. But I didn't understand what Jack was saying. Or

Streeter. Was Jack confessing? Was he the vigilante and wanted to make sure no one went down with him for any of the murders he'd committed?

"Carl Halbrook is really Clyde Hall. The PI that Mrs. Greenwood hired figured it out, found the cash, and used some of it to bail out Shelly Jones last Friday. So tell Nick Sewell at the KCPD to stop looking for what's left of the ransom money. The rest of it was spent to get at Margaret Thurgood, who was going to be acquitted."

"How do you know?" Streeter asked.

"I was there."

I heard one of the women to my left draw in a breath, make a startled noise. I saw Jenna Tate shift her position on the porch from the corner of my eye, just before I saw Streeter shift his aim. But his new aim wasn't on Wilson. It had shifted to Streeter's left a bit. Toward the women.

I held my aim on Wilson, confused.

Jack continued, unaware that the edginess had intensified. "I sat through the trial last week. She shook that baby to death because he was crying. And she couldn't hear her soap opera. But that's not what came out in trial. And it was her word against a silenced baby's. The jury would have acquitted Margaret Thurgood if someone else hadn't gotten to her first. On Tuesday night. And Lance Bovier? I wrote that letter. Su had nothing to do with it. She never knew any of this, that I was deep into investigating our son Benji's death. She never knew I had joined the FBI for better access to systems and equipment to help in my fishing expeditions. I'm sorry about that, Streeter. That I used the FBI for personal gain."

"No one can fault you for that, Linwood," Streeter said. "Except maybe the one who turned a blind eye to your past when she interviewed you."

A final click fell into place on a heavy combination lock I'd been working with all my strength. It explained why Streeter refused to tell me what Christian had told him. It's why he had asked me to consider the timeline. Everything happened over holidays and in May, during Jack's vacation or on his annual fishing trips.

I hadn't seen it before. I hadn't wanted to.

"Streeter, you remember where you were when Lance Bovier was killed in Atlantic City?" Jack asked.

My mind was still stuck on the puzzle pieces slamming into place.

That's why Jack was so secretive at Christmas when I saw him at DIA while I was working the case with Beulah. Jack had begged me not to tell Streeter he'd been in Kansas City visiting an old friend from college. He'd been investigating the Greenwood cold case, trying to figure out what happened to Clyde Hall. And then killed him the weekend before last, when he said his college buddy needed help moving. Had he buried Clyde in the backyard beside Vanessa Greenwood?

After a long moment, Streeter said, "I remember exactly. I was at Quantico with you. I understand now. But why? What was the motive?"

And that's how Mitch Dodson knew so much about the murders. He was reading Jack's emails, which were filled with information and facts about the various cases. And he was passing on all the information to BOLO. Through the S.O.S. website.

My world tilted so far off its axis I could barely walk. I heard the hammer of a gun cock.

"Jack?" I cried.

He hesitated, turned toward me, startled that I had taken steps toward him, my pistol growing heavy, my arm dropping to my side.

Jack's words were tender. He was no longer speaking to Streeter. He was talking to me. "When Vanessa Greenwood was abducted from the classroom of St. Margaret's, one little girl tried to stop her. Even at a young age, the schoolgirl sensed the danger Vanessa was in and begged the teacher to let her go with Vanessa. I suppose that little girl never forgave herself or the authorities for letting her friend slip so easily from life's fingers," Jack said, lowering his pistol slowly as he spoke.

I knew what he was saying now. Knew what he was trying to tell me.

"A little girl who had few friends, having moved far from her home in Mobile, Alabama," Streeter said, leveling his gun on Jenna Tate.

"And who also made a career with the FBI to access the systems and equipment to gather data," Jack said, glancing over his right shoulder at Tate.

I noticed that Fiero had swung her aim toward Tate as well.

"Taking a position in recruitment that allowed her travel all over the country at a moment's notice," Streeter said. "And to recruit an army of investigators who might someday need to turn a blind eye to her kind of justice."

"As well as moonlighting as a private investigator for people like Greenwood so she could cozy up to even more data," Jack said, exhaustion evident in his slack shoulders, his defeated tone.

To Jenna, I said, "You are the one who created the S.O.S. website, who used BOLO to your advantage, recruiting those of us who are damaged from our past, motivated to bend the law."

I nearly let the pistol loose from my fingertips, expecting to hear it clatter to the concrete sidewalk, the revelations so profoundly stunning to me. Jenna Tate was the vigilante. She likely used her manipulative skills to convince Andy to inject Menendez with the HIV yet had murdered all those child killers who had gotten away with their crimes herself.

Jack asked Tate, "I didn't kill Gary James. Did you?"

Jenna stood still, midway between the end of the dark porch and the front door, her pistol still trained on Jack. From the corner of my eye, I saw Wilson lift his foot to his shackled hands, his fingers fishing for a hidden pistol in an ankle holster.

I leveled my gun and ran toward him, screaming at Jack to get down. I saw Streeter from the corner of my eye rush across the porch at the same time.

Jack dropped his gun, not wanting to shoot me, not understanding that I was charging Wilson, not him. I didn't want Wilson to shoot Jack. I knew Jack wouldn't shoot me. But I had to get to Jack before Wilson got to his gun.

Jack didn't seem to hear me. Maybe because he was surprised to see me. Maybe because everything was happening so fast. For me, time had slowed to a near stop. Like God had reached down into the world and pressed the pause button.

Jack's words were clear. Meant only for me to hear.

"Sword of Solomon," Jack Linwood said, offering me a sad smile.

I was stunned.

I fired my gun just as I saw Wilson fire his. The double pop exploded milliseconds before I heard a third crack of gun to my left, saw a flash of muzzle fire in front of Jack and another from the left side of the porch. At the same moment, I dove past Wilson and hooked Jack with my left arm, clotheslining him at his chest to knock him off his feet. I tumbled over him and down beside him on the porch, against the house.

In the firestorm that followed, all I could hear were my own words replaying in my mind.

Screaming Jack's name over and over and over. To get down. To watch out.

I pulled the trigger, but I never saw what I hit. I'd been aiming for Wilson.

The smell of blood and gunpowder filled my nostrils and my mind's eye tried to take in the war zone around me—Wilson's missing face, Tate's blonde wig lying in a rapidly spreading pool of blood, Fiero and Streeter shouting as more agents and police stormed the porch—but I was too focused on one person to grasp anything else.

All I could see was Jack's body crumple in a heap like a marionette with its strings instantly cut as bullets fired from all around us just before my shoulder and arms reached him in a tackle.

I had gone down with him, on top of him, to protect him, and I felt helpless as the life seeped out of him like air from a punctured inner tube.

My ears were ringing. I laid my ear against his lips, my lips against his ear, begging him to stay with me.

He managed a few words that I could hear through the commotion. "I never killed anyone . . . So sorry to leave . . . Love you."

I don't know how long I cradled Jack's head in my lap as his blood soaked through my shirt and suit pants, his dead black eyes staring up at me. But I know that neither Barbara nor Streeter tried to console me—both knowing personally how it would do me no good—and instead gave me all the time I needed with Jack until the emergency teams took him from me.

I stayed fixed on Debra Douglass's porch until the early morning hours, sitting in what was left of Jack's life, clutching that blood-soaked bunny until the cleaning crew arrived and made me leave the porch.

Streeter was there for me, draping me in a clean blanket and leading me to Barbara's rental car. He followed us to my apartment and helped Barbara clean me up. Neither one of them ever even tried to take that blood-soaked bunny from my grip. I stood in my shower, fully clothed, watching the last of Jack's life slip down the drain. Pink and beautiful as it was.

I don't recall how they got me to change into dry, clean clothes without letting loose of that damp bunny, nor do I remember taking any little white pill that Barbara told me about later. But I do remember Streeter tucking me into bed, kissing my forehead, and telling me to sleep.

"Remember this. You loved a hero," he whispered in my ear. "And so do I."

He left my room, shutting the door behind him.

And I slept as if it was the sleep of the dead.

Maybe it was.

THE END

ACKNOWLEDGMENTS

MY FANS ARE AMAZING! You are absolutely wonderful for sending me ideas, critiques, and accolades. The fact that you'd take the time from your very busy schedules to contact me is humbling, and your kind words of encouragement are so rewarding. Not only have you welcomed me into your reading world, but many of you have welcomed me into your homes for book clubs. Since my first book tour for *In the Belly of Jonah* when those of you in book clubs taught me how to improve Liv Bergen's world, I have asked book clubs to beta read my manuscripts before submitting them to my publisher. Thank you for your honesty and improvements and for knowing Liv Bergen better than I do.

A huge thanks to all of you from book clubs across the country who volunteered to be my beta readers on this book. To the winners of this contest—Killer Coffee Club from Ithaca, NY, and the Church Ladies Book Club from Rapid City, SD—thank you for putting in so much time and effort to making my book so much better for the fans.

Killer Coffee Club—Nikki Bonanni, Roberta Dannenfelser, Mary Martin, Marilyn Ackley, Bonnie Wojnowski, Barbara Pease, and Pat Costentini.

Church Ladies Book Club—Kathy Cordes, Becky Berreth, Laurie

Hallstrom, Linda Batman, Linda Stepanek, Suzie Lambert, Shelly Garman, Darcie Lanam, and Dottie Borowski.

Also, a special thanks to Sandra Salinas and her book club in Florida (stay strong, Geneva). Snadra won the fan contest for naming this book and provided the inspiration for the theme throughout. Her submission— "Sword of Solomon"—was the title that fans voted for the most, and my publishing and publicity team were able to use that concept to create "Solomon's Whisper" (thank you, Samantha with JKSCommunications).

To Aaron Hierholzer, my editor with Greenleaf Book Group, I thank you for making this very complicated storyline (with more characters than I should have listened to) an easier and cleaner read for my fans. And to the lovely Jordan Smith, too, who helped with final polish, as I needed the extra touch. And as always to Jenny Simonson, my first reader and critic, I am humbled by your continuing efforts to teach me.

Note to Book Clubs:

If your book club is interested in being beta readers for future Liv Bergen Mysteries, please email Sandra at <u>Sandra@SandraBrannan.com</u>.

AUTHOR Q&A

1. Your family has worked in mining for generations, and you've continued that tradition. What prompted you to expand your career into writing mysteries?

I was always going to work in the family business as a quarrier. I love mining and always have. Maybe it's because I come from a long line of responsible, respectful quarriers who are entrenched in their communities and beloved by so many neighbors. In high school, I focused my studies on the sciences and math so I could earn an engineering degree. But one high school teacher thought I should consider a different path. Although I tolerated my English classes, I never dreamed a teacher would think highly enough of my writing to award me a creative writing scholarship when I graduated. I used the money to pursue that engineering degree and carried that guilt ever since.

As an adult, I wrote at nights after my kids went to bed and all my chores were done for many years and was rewarded when that same ninety-something ninth-grade English teacher showed up at my first book release and said, "I learned ya good, didn't I?" Yes, you did, Mr. Harry Putnam. And I will always be proud of being a student of this WWII vet, who made English fun and saw my potential long before I did.

2. **The final pages of this book are quite explosive. Is there a follow-up in the works? Will we get to see how the events of this book affect Liv's life in the future?**

You can bet there's a follow-up in the works. Liv never slows down. As long as my publisher will have me, I will continue to produce a Liv Bergen book. The very tangled, mind-bending ending to *Solomon's Whisper* was both necessary and tragic, which means Liv needs another time out with much rest and rehabilitation required. Of course, another sibling will take her under their wing, this time Sister Catherine (the Catholic nun and older sister fans met briefly in *Lot's Return to Sodom* who pauses between every decade of the rosary to snack). Since there is so much history to be told about Deadwood, South Dakota, I plan on setting the book primarily there and sharing a local tale that twists this next book into a Liv Bergen adventure.

3. **Your writing thus far has been firmly in the mystery genre. Are there other writers in this field, whether classic or contemporary, who inspire your work?**

I love reading YA, especially winners of the Newbery Medal. I also love reading the classics on occasion. But mostly, I love, love, love reading mysteries and thrillers. Lee Child, James Patterson, Jeffery Deaver, Tom Clancy, C. J. Box, Harlan Coben, Vince Flynn, Robert Crais, Sue Grafton, Patricia Cornwell . . . *breathe*. I never tire of Agatha Christie and John D. MacDonald. I love reading scary books, from R. L. Stine's Goosebumps series to Stephen King, just to keep the scare alive. The only aspect of becoming an author I don't like is that I find myself with far less time to read, which is unfortunate. These days I mostly read books by newly established authors to give endorsements.

4. *Solomon's Whisper* gives readers a glimpse inside the FBI, through the eyes of the relatively inexperienced Liv. Since you've never been a special agent yourself, how did you write these scenes? Did you do any kind of research?

When I was a teen, my best friend was my softball coach, Mick. Odd that we'd be such good friends, but I suppose it was because I was so darned interested in his profession. He was an FBI agent with the Rapid City bureau and worked a lot of the reservation issues and the Sturgis Motorcycle Rally. *Lot's Return to Sodom* was his story, an inside look at the troubles law enforcement has each year during the famous gathering of a half million motorcycle enthusiasts in the tiny town of Sturgis, South Dakota (population five thousand). I wrote that book as a tribute to my friend Mick and all the heroes who have to keep us safe each year from the "one-percenters"—the self-proclaimed 1 percent of motorcyclists who are *not* law-abiding citizens, and who are second only to terrorists as the most dangerous network of criminals in this country. On the day of my second book's release, this FBI mentor of mine actually autographed a few books as Streeter Pierce. Shortly after that, Mick slipped the surly bonds of this earth, so I no longer have him to consult. Fans may notice more mistakes on FBI procedure now that he no longer proofs my work, but I hope not! (And in case you're wondering, Mick did not have Streeter's shock of white hair, but he was at once forgettable and indescribably handsome, with a just-gargled-with-barbed-wire voice.)

5. Your books have dealt with a conflict between ends and means before, but this book really homes in on the lengths some go to for a good cause. What sparked that idea in your head and made you decide to feature a vigilante?

I've found that I have tendencies similar to those you see in some of the characters in *Solomon's Whisper*. I want to cheer on the dark side of vengeance sometimes, even though I know that's not what God has planned for me. At times I am overwhelmed by reading the news about too many bad people getting away with doing evil things to good people. Especially children. The conflict arouses my creative tension when I write. So I quietly revel in books like Reavis Z. Wortham's *The Right Side of Wrong*, cheering on my heroes Tom Bell and Ned Parker for doing what seems like the right thing, even when I know it goes against my moral compass.

6. **When you're working on a new book, what's the writing process like? Do you have any special routines or techniques?**

I have to know the story start to finish before I sit down at a computer. And I use basic outlines, but I don't force them. Each night as I fall asleep, I watch the storyline I'm developing as if it's a movie in my head, and when I get where the characters are taking me, I sit down and pound on my keyboard until I'm finished. Sounds a bit scattered, but I like the combination of outlining and organic writing that this process affords me.

   If I'm not interested from beginning to end in the storyline that's developing, I can't invest in it; I toss it aside in my mind and start a new movie in my head. Sleep is some of my best writing time. And yes, I definitely see the characters in my head as they work through their troubles, but no, I can't describe them other than to say Liv sorta kinda looks like Jessica Biel, Jack Linwood is a grown-up Mowgli (my childhood crush, of course), and Streeter Pierce is—as I mentioned before—at once forgettable and indescribably handsome. Fans tell me all the time who should be cast to play these characters, but that's the best I can do.

7. This book, like the others in the series, features a Biblical story as a central metaphor. Why have you been drawn to Old Testament figures as a component of your fiction? Was this always planned as a characteristic for the series, or did it just sort of happen?

I was raised Catholic and attended a private school with several nuns for teachers from kindergarten through the eighth grade. In third grade, I had a teacher who shared with us some Bible stories that scared me to death. I have to admit, it did get me interested enough to read the Bible through middle school and high school, and I can say with certainty that some of the scariest stories I've ever read came from the Bible. Frightening. So, at the risk of getting confused with Christian fiction, I decided to use the powerful fright of all those stories as the underpinnings of my modern fiction.

For example, my first book, *In the Belly of Jonah*, was a twisted version of the tale of Jonah, who was trapped in the belly of a whale for three days. A smelly, dirty, dark and slimy three days. Likewise, for three days Liv Bergen found herself trapped in the sadistic world of Jonah, a murderer who cut out the belly of Liv's employee and left her propped on the shore of a reservoir. Each story has some warped twist on the original Bible story. Fans don't have to know the stories to enjoy the books, but those who do know the references I'm making will understand how I used the twisted tale to my benefit. I think it adds a level of complexity for some readers.

I've had Catholic priests—some who were around in my old school days—contact me to tell me how much they love my stories. One monsignor in particular is an avid reader because he recognizes a real-life story or two I reference when writing about Liv in grade school. That's fun for me!

8. Some of the cases in the book seem to mirror real-world cases—for example, the Rebecca Douglass case has similarities to the JonBenét Ramsey case. Do headlines and true crime serve as a significant source of ideas for your fiction?

Several times, book club readers have described to me what it's like to have a family member who's the victim of an unsolved murder. Those true-life stories do haunt me. I understand how horrible it is to lose a loved one, especially a child, but I can't imagine not knowing what happened to that loved one, not knowing who murdered them or why.

I lived in Fort Collins during the JonBenét Ramsey murder, which happened in nearby Boulder. Although my stories have nothing to do with that case or any real case, the tragedy surrounding the family certainly haunted me. How horrible would it be to lose a child and then be accused of her death? Or worse, to have someone in your family accused of that child's death? I can't imagine a worse pain than that as a parent. So of course that source of suspicion and the hurtfulness of accusations and supposition became cornerstones for characters in my book, yet I would never do that family a disservice by saying I've captured what they had to endure.

In the end, I always want to know the answers. Sometimes I solve cases in my head or on the page just to let my mind rest, even if the murderers and cases are complete fiction.

9. You're on a desert island and can only bring along three books. What are they?

Can I bring two books and genie-filled lantern so I can wish for more books? No? Okay, fine . . . Well, I couldn't live without my Bible. I know a lot of folks might think that's trite (or a bit strange coming from an author who writes such dark, gritty mysteries), but I do depend on that book daily for my morning prayers. And those who know me would guess the second book I'd take: I most definitely would have a Peterson

Field Guide on edible plants or native wildlife, because I'm an avid outdoorsman who loves to eat, but I know nothing about desert nor island living. And the third book? Gosh, that's a tough decision between a book that would make me laugh, a yellow tablet on which to write my own stories, or a book about how to build a boat so I could get off that island!

10. **You've mentioned that fans frequently get in touch with you, offering ideas and even critiques. Has fan input on early books affected your writing in later books? Can you give an example of that?**

I definitely want to thank fans who've contacted me about Liv Bergen. I internalize their comments—good and bad—and let Liv deal with them. Each time, I think we both grow from the comments and critiques. Having worked in the mining industry all my life, I am well versed in taking criticism, and I find that the intent behind the words is the key to turning a critique into a positive springboard for improvement.

I have to say, all my fans have wonderfully kind intent and a whole lot of great ideas on how to improve my writing—even if it's a simple detail I got wrong. For example, early on a man contacted me to say that I had Streeter Pierce aged forty in the first book and thirty-nine in the second. I responded by telling this fan that vampire books were so popular these days that I thought I'd have Streeter age in reverse. But seriously, I do watch details like that a lot more carefully now, thanks to fans.

11. **Describe the process of naming this book "*Solomon's Whisper.*" It was originally called "Sword of Solomon" based on a fan submission. Can you let us in on the thought process behind that change?**

My fans are integral in the editing process of the Liv Bergen books. Each time I'm writing a book, I let a book club be my "beta readers" to make sure I'm staying true to Liv from my fans' standpoint. For this book, I had forty-eight club requests to review it, so I decided to let some of the fans who weren't in book clubs name the book, then let my social network vote on the titles submitted. "Sword of Solomon," suggested by Florida fan Sandra Salinas, came out as the winner, and I submitted the book with that title.

My awesome team of publishers and publicists tweaked the name to be more ominous, and we ended up with "Solomon's Whisper." Creepy, for sure. And of course I'm so excited because the title works quite well with the storyline. This is the first title I didn't come up with myself, and of course, I think it's the best one so far. Leave it to a fan!

12. **How much more of Liv's world do you think you have in you? Do you plan to branch out and do unrelated books or series? If so, do you think you'd ever return to Liv and her fellow characters later in your career?**

Funny story here. I think my publisher is politely telling me the sands in the hourglass are running out and I better get to the end of Liv's stories. Why? Because each of my Liv Bergen book covers, from the second book on, feature a geometric element, and the number of lines decreases each time. With *Solomon's Whisper*, we're down to four lines, so I'd say we still have some time!

But, seriously, I have many more stories that Liv would like to tell and for now I'm listening as long as fans want to hear her voice. I've been working on a separate thriller series—I'm well into my third book—but only time will tell if that's a keeper. Liv had to tell me ten of her stories before that series ever sold, so who knows how long I'll have to listen to this new woman's voice?

So far, I'm not having any trouble keeping their voices apart in my head, since both women are quite interesting to me.

READER'S GUIDE
DISCUSSION QUESTIONS

1. In *Solomon's Whisper*, there are numerous overlapping cases covered, spread over decades and across the country. How early on did you spot the connection between them, and did that help you process all the different storylines?

2. When Liv first reads Su Panini's letter, she seems highly sympathetic to the position taken by the columnist, as she thinks about how Brianna's family never received the closure justice can bring. By the end of the book, Liv has helped take down the vigilante. How much of that initial sympathy for the Panini position do you think remains by the final scene? Has Liv altered her view, or is she still highly conflicted?

3. What do you see in Liv's future, given the shocking outcome of the novel's events? Do you see this significantly changing her relationship with Streeter?

4. In the end, the murderer-of-murderers turns out to be someone Liv hadn't expected. Thinking back, where there clues to the identity of this person? Does this person's personality line up with their actions?

5. The story of Solomon is clearly central, at least thematically, to this book. At one point, Liv recalls the story and wonders whether "that's really what the king intended or if he had simply grown tired of the two mothers' squabble over the child." Do you see the vigilantism the Brotherhood of Law Operatives sympathizes with as more of a principled alternative method to achieve justice, or as a lazy option these public servants take when the justice system throws up too many obstacles?

6. Stewart "Camera" Casey, though not directly connected with any of the murder cases, plays a somewhat central role in the book, with some chapters devoted in large part to his perspective. What function do you think his character served?

7. The complexities of vigilante justice are thoroughly explored in the events of this book, revealing gray areas even in the process of holding murderers of children accountable for their crimes. Did the varying nature of the murders cause different reactions in you when you thought about that murderer being killed him- or herself? For example, was the au pair who shook the toddler to death equally as deserving of vengeance as the individuals who stalked, abused, and murdered children? Is the age of the perpetrator, explored to some degree in the Lance Bovier case, a factor in the person's culpability?

8. In chapter 38, Christian tells Streeter something on the phone that Liv, who's with Streeter in that scene, doesn't

overhear. Given how the action of the novel plays out, what exactly do you think Christian told him? Why did Streeter not choose to share the information with Liv?

9. In the final scene of the book, Liv learns that she and several of her colleagues were recruited because of their painful pasts, because this might make them more apt to bend the law. How do you think this works in real life? Might a police officer or FBI agent be compromised if they have a painful injustice in their past? Could this ever be a positive motivation, driving the person to work harder for justice without breaking the law?

10. Just before the climactic final scene of the book, Brannan pauses the plot for a moment as Liv ruminates on a set of chicks trying to navigate the choppy waters of the lake. Was this scene effective in your opinion? Was it a roadblock before the action, or did it help magnify themes and give a needed glimpse into Liv's thoughts?

www.ingramcontent.com/pod-product-compliance
Lightning Source LLC
Chambersburg PA
CBHW020258120726
47904CB00001B/257